Thinly disguised autobiography

James Delingpole is rock critic for the *Telegraph*
and TV critic for the *Spectator*. This is his third novel.
He lives in London with his wife and children.

Also by James Delingpole in Picador

FIN

James Delingpole

Thinly disguised autobiography

PICADOR

First published 2003 by Picador

This edition published 2004 by Picador
an imprint of Pan Macmillan Ltd
Pan Macmillan, 20 New Wharf Road, London N1 9RR
Basingstoke and Oxford
Associated companies throughout the world
www.panmacmillan.com

ISBN 0 330 49335 3

A CIP catalogue record for this book is available from
the British Library.

Typeset by Intype London Ltd
Printed and bound in Great Britain by
Mackays of Chatham plc, Chatham, Kent

All Pan Macmillan titles are available from
www.panmacmillan.com
or from Bookpost by telephoning 01624 677237

For Wilton, Tim and Alain

Acknowledgements

'Lenten Thoughts of a High Anglican' and 'The Varsity Students' Rag' by John Betjeman. All rights reserved. Reproduced by permission of David Higham Associates.

'Jump' – *Derek and Clive Live* by Peter Cook and Dudley Moore. All rights reserved. Reproduced by permission of David Higham Associates.

'Telling stories is telling lies.'

B. S. Johnson, *Aren't You Rather Young to be Writing Your Memoirs?*

Hide in your shell

My first joint tastes of sausages: the sweet, ultra-fine ground, condemned pork 'n' beef, 100 per cent pure hoof 'n' testicle variety that mums buy from freezer stores for children's parties. The sort that make you want to heave.

Which I do. In the basin that Norton has just pissed in. (A filthy habit which I'll soon learn to adopt myself, the nearest bogs being two annoying flights of stairs down below.)

'Trust the drug,' he says, not long before it happens.

'Feel sick.'

'Another toke,' he says. 'That'll make you feel better.'

And I know it won't. The vertical hold has gone on my vision; my stomach's in free fall; and what's left of my mind is already rehearsing the three-second dash from the bed to the beckoning porcelain. In very slow motion.

But I can't just say 'No', can I? This is, after all, a Significant Moment. Right up there with first illicit drink (the Dirty Duck, school trip to Stratford, 1981), first snog (Wendy, Crete, 1980), first solo drive (Bromsgrove, 1982) and first actual, genuine fuck (?) (!!).

And obviously, you don't want your first drug experience to be a bad one. Any more than you want your first actual, genuine fuck to be an 'Is it in yet?' – Squelch – 'Was that it?' one. So you persevere with that foul, sausage-tasting stub. You inhale more deeply than before; you smile a smile as queasy as the clarinet intro to Supertramp's 'Even In The Quietest Moments', which, being as you're not cool enough to know better, you've got playing in the background; and you say to yourself: 'I'm enjoying this! I'm enjoying this! I'm enjoying— noI'mnotI'mnotI'mnotinfactIthinkI'mgoingto—'

'Better?' asks Norton.

I would nod but my head's between my legs and too heavy and anyway it would be a lie. I don't feel better I just feel differently horrible: a mix of post-sick blues (sour nostrils, acrid throat) and terminal disappointment. This drug thing, I've decided, it's just not what They promised us.

Norton takes this as his cue to roll another one. To 'skin up', as we drug professionals say.

Which is one of the few things, it strikes me, that this wretched experience has to recommend itself: the terminology; the ritual; the anticipation.

Norton nursing the Rizlas into shape (one on the bottom, two on top, I note studiously).

Norton unfurling the foil to reveal a pea-sized red-brown lump. (Wow! Can I see? Can I see? Is it good stuff?)

Norton singeing the lump – oily smoke; that chipolata smell – and Oxo-crumbling a trail along the paper trough.

Norton running his tongue the length of his Rothmans so that – the man's an artist! truly, an artist! – the tobacco spills forth neatly in a pristine tube.

'Can you do me a roach?' he says.

'A what?' I say.

'Just pass me that stiffie,' he says.

He's talking about my treasured invitation to Freshers' Drinks at the Union, where I am going to meet my Sebastian, make my name and end up with the most beautiful, clever undergraduette of her generation, before I settle into my massive estate in the country and write the Great English Novel about my salad days with the Brightest Young Things since the days of Brian Howard and Evelyn Waugh.

Norton takes the white card. I watch, half appalled, half thrilled, as he rips off a corner and rolls it into a tube.

Not long now. Just a few more adjustments – God this is clever! Who would ever have guessed that Clipper lighters came with a detachable tobacco prodder? – and we'll be there. Any second I'm going to be actually, genuinely, totally high!

And then suddenly you are high. And you don't like it. And you realize that the foreplay is really all there is to this drug-taking thang. The rest is pure anticlimax.

Unless, perhaps, there's some important extra dimension that you don't know about yet. Better have a toke – note use of cool terminology – on that second spliff – ditto – just to make sure.

And yes, the nausea's subsided a bit. Now I just feel—

I feel—

Um.

'God, isn't the production on this album fucking brilliant?' I say.

'Mmm,' says Norton.

'No, but really though. Isn't it just totally fantastic? I mean, obviously it's not as good as *Crime of the Century* but still. I can play this bit on the piano, you know. Fool's Overture.'

'Cool.'

'You're just saying that to agree with me.'

'I'm going with the flow.'

'Hippie,' I say.

'Rich. From a Supertramp fan,' he says.

'Supertramp isn't hippy music. Is it?'

3

'It's not Joy Division.'

'God, you don't like Joy Division, do you? That spackhead at school – you know, year above, skin like a frog – liked Joy Division. Do you want to be like him?'

'Drabble. He was cooler than we knew.'

'All right. So what do you want me to play?'

'Supertramp's fine,' he says.

'Jethro Tull? Focus? Bowie?'

'Got any Smiths?'

'Not yet.'

Norton laughs.

'What?' I say.

'It's such a you thing to say.'

'Meaning?'

'Cool, Josh, cool. You're getting paranoid.'

'I'm not getting paranoid.'

Oh but I am. I am. My record collection's shit. I can't hold my dope. And now my best friend's accusing me of some terrible character flaw that I'm not even aware of.

'I meant it in a nice way,' Norton says. 'You know. This thing you have of wanting – everything.'

'Yeah. So what's wrong with that?'

'There's nothing wrong with that. I just said. It's just – those shoes . . .'

I glance down at my shoes. My chunky brown Alan McAfee brogues which I bought just before coming up, having read in the *Sloane Ranger's Handbook* that they were de rigueur for the smart young Oxford undergrad. Shoes which, under the combined assault of reefer paranoia and Norton's quizzical stare, I now perceive look remarkably similar to those sported by the hero of Roger Hargreaves's *Mr Silly*.

'. . . and the cords,' he says

Not from Hackett – and this shows what scrupulous attention I'm paying to historical detail here because Hackett hadn't been invented then – but from a shop in the Burlington Arcade.

'. . . and the shirt . . .' he says.

Viyella. M&S.

'. . . I mean. You know. You never wore that sort of thing at school,' he says.

'For the rather obvious reason, I'd have thought, that at school we had to wear a uniform.'

Norton gives me a cut-through-the-crap stare.

'Josh. You're from Birmingham.'

'I live, as well you know because you've been there often enough, *outside* Birmingham. In an Old Rectory. With a big garden. Surrounded by fields. With horses and foxes in them. And excuse me. While we're on the subject of unconvincing new images, the last time I saw you, you were blond.'

'So you admit your new image is unconvincing,' he says.

'A sight more convincing than if I'd turned into some wanky student lefty trying to undermine the system by dying my hair black and voting to rename the college bar the Mandela Room.'

'It already has been in my college.'

'Well, it hasn't in Christ Church and it's not going to be. It's the reason I came here rather than your scuzzy bicycle shed. Class. Tradition. Style. The things you're meant to come to Oxford for.'

'Not the dope or the sex or the education?'

'Oh well, yeah, the first two.'

'But that's exactly what I mean. It's the thing that's so you. You want to smoke dope and you want to wear tweed.

5

You want to prance round like a hooray and you want to get laid.'

'Hoorays get laid too, you know. What do you think seccies are for? Not that I am a hooray—'

'So what are you, then?'

'I'm me. Like you said. Me. Me. Me. I want to like Supertramp and I want to like the Smiths. I want to be cool and I want to be smart. I want to take drugs and I want to drink Krug with the Assassins and the Buller and the Loder and all the other dining societies that I definitely want to join. I want – fuck. Is this stuff like alcohol? Do you get, you know, one of those guilt nightmare hangovers where you think of all the things you said the night before and think, "Jesus, I'm such an arsehole", because if you do I'd better shut up now. Because I'm only telling you this because you're my friend, you know. I'd never say this to anyone else. Well, I don't think I would. I mean, I know I've got a bit of a problem with this. Not that it is a problem really because actually I think it's quite charming – the way I reveal so much about myself, even to people I've only just met. But I do sometimes wish I didn't do that. It would make me a lot cooler for a start. Because that's what cool is, isn't it? Not giving too much away. Never revealing your emotions. Like you. 'Cos like – wow, that's what this drug does, it makes you say things like "like". I'll be saying "man" next. Man. Hehehe – but no, you know how when you're at a party and you meet someone who's all warm and open and friendly. You think "nice guy" but at the same time you think, "Well, I don't need to go any further with this because I know what he's like." Whereas, when you meet somebody who's a bit stand-offish and reserved you think, "Wow! This chap's so deep. So fascinating. And he's obviously not interested in me," which makes him even more interesting because then you get really determined to prove what an incredibly interesting person you are and make him like you so you work much harder with a person like you than you would with a person like me and you end up making more friends. Don't you think?'

'Um. What was the question?' says Norton.

'Christ knows. Better give me some more of that joint and I'll see if I can remember.'

So we both smoke some more of the joint and we lie on the bed and roll around and giggle a lot and bond and feel very glad that we're friends even though something tells me, and probably Norton too, that we're heading in different directions and that we might not be seeing as much of each other as we did at school.

And while we're doing that, I might as well shove in a bit of visual detail for those of you who like that sort of thing.

Norton: blond curly hair dyed black, as I said. High fore-head, thin mouth, spiky nose, thinks he looks like that poster of James Dean and he does a bit, in the right light, but not very. Blue trousers spattered with paint, nasty floral shirt, black suede winkle-pickers all bought from a second-hand shop because a) that's what trendy painters do and b) he hasn't got much money.

My rooms. Correction, room. Because even at Christ Church, unless you're a scholar, you get a pretty crap deal in the first year. It's a poky little number at the top of the Meadow Buildings whose only saving grace is the rather splendid view towards the Cherwell across Christ Church Meadow. Which was where, I think, Anthony Blanche declaimed *The Waste Land* in the TV version of *Brideshead Revisited*. But anyway, apart from that my room is deeply uninteresting: bed, desk, basin, wastepaper basket that gets emptied every morning by my scout, Janet.

Norton and I, meanwhile, have stopped giggling and rolling around on the bed (not in a God-we've-just-discovered-we're-homosexual sort of way because that would only ever happen in a novel and this stuff's all true, pretty much) and I'm wondering whether to treat him to the Big Life statement which has been bubbling through my subconscious ever since he picked me up on that image-change business.

'You know what Leonardo da Vinci said?' I say.

'No.'

'Remind me how you got into the Ruskin.'

'So what did he say?'

'He said that the majority of humankind were just fillers of latrines. And he's right, you know. Most of the people on this planet, they just get born, they breed, they live, they die. They shit an awful lot. And that's it.'

'Wise words from the master.'

'Yes, but doesn't that scare you? The possibility that you might end up as just another latrine filler? You know, OK degree, nice job, nice house, nice wife, nice kids—'

'Sounds, um, nice.'

'You don't mean that. You want to be an artist. And being an artist isn't about nice. You want struggle, you want recognition, you want fame, you want money. Loads and loads of it.'

'That would be nicer.'

'But imagine if it never happened. Imagine, you know, the painting doesn't work out. I mean obviously, we're talking hypothetically here because I've no doubt with your talent you're going to be absolutely mega-famous. But suppose it didn't. Suppose there came a point when you decided that all the ambitions you've got now were just the idle fantasies of youth; that the time had come to be more realistic about things; to accept that, after all, you were destined to be a nobody.'

'Oh well. If that's what destiny says, there's not much you can do.'

'Of course you can. Your destiny's what you decide it's going to be. If you don't realize that now, you're going to be totally fucked when that little voice in your head starts squealing: "It's time to grow up. You've got a mortgage now. Kids to educate. Little Tibbles the cat to keep in Whiskas." And all the rest of the middle-aged, middle-class mediocrity.'

'So skip the cat.'

'I'm serious, Norton. It would be so easy to buy into that. The middle-class dream. And I'm not saying I don't want all that myself. I do want a nice house, a nice wife and nice kids. But I want them on my terms,' I say.

'Which are?'

'Well, I tell you what they're not. In fact I'll tell you what my all-time worst fucking nightmare is and it goes like this. I'm in my beautiful house with my beautiful wife and my beautiful kids and I think: "I've served my purpose. That's what I was really here for all along. Forget ambition. My kids are the future now!" Because it happens, you know. I've seen it in my father. Which is why I'm so fucking desperate to make sure it doesn't happen to me.'

'Then it won't.'

'Too right it won't. And you may think it's silly, my wanting to be into the Smiths and into beagling; drugs and fine wine; sex and tweed. But that's one of the fundamental differences between you and me. You think that life is just a question of choosing which path you're going to take. Me, I want to take every single path there is. I want the whole fucking world, Norton. And I'm not going to stop until it's mine.'

I take a final drag of the minuscule stub. 'Not that I'm a sad, fucked-up, pathetically deluded megalomaniac or anything.'

Silly stunts prove you're
the goods

It's a mild winter evening towards the end of the Hilary term, 1984. And it hurts me to go on, it really does, but what can you do? This is me at the age of nineteen.

There are five, maybe six of us in all and we've just finished hall. Hall's what you call dinner at Oxford, presumably because you eat it in a massively grand, fuck-off dining hall. In Christ Church, the dining hall is especially massively grand and fuck-off. At one end, above High Table where the dons sit, there's a portrait of the college's official founder, Henry VIII, and of the person who really founded it, Cardinal Wolsey, and of the College Visitor – because this is how amazingly grand it is – the Queen. Along the sides there are more portraits of the thirteen prime ministers and the eleven viceroys of India who once attended the college. And at the back, where the entrance is, there are still more portraits of distinguished alumni, including one of W. H. Auden looking less crater-faced in oils than he does in photographs.

Plus – because by no means does Christ Church hall's fuck-offness stop there – there's a high, painted ceiling which dates from something like the sixteenth century. And if you look down a bit, you'll see the gargoyles which – like the decorative brass heads in the fireplace below – inspired Lewis Carroll when he wrote *Alice Through the Looking Glass.*

The room smells of furniture polish, stale cabbage and history. When I visit it now, I find it hard to believe that there was a time in my life when I was surrounded by so much magnificence. But at the time, you don't notice it. At first because you affect not to. Later because you're inured.

It is quite hard, though, pretending you're not impressed when you attend your very first hall on your very first day as an Oxford undergraduate. You're dressed up in jacket, tie and gown (long for scholars, short for everyone else); you stand – trembling a bit – while a scholar declaims the Christ Church grace '*Nos miseri homines . . .*' in Latin; you take your place on the bench and maybe risk a surreptitious glance at the pictures, the ceiling, the gargoyles, High Table . . .; and you think, 'I'm here, I'm actually here. At Christ Church, Oxford.'

No doubt the people sitting next to you are thinking exactly the same thing, though you wouldn't know it. Even the pale, spotty ones with light-grey suits and polyester ties and Northern accents – they can't have been to boarding school so this must be their first time away from home – seem more self-possessed, less fazed than you. As for the ones with well-cut tweeds and fruity voices that go 'waf waf waf' – they really do look from day one as if they own the place.

So you eavesdrop on the conversation of the nearest tweedy waf wafs – Eton, year-off adventures, mutual friends – and try to work out how you're going to inveigle your way in. You wait for a gap but there isn't one. You weren't at Eton, you didn't do the right thing on your year off – you went to Africa: what you should have done is bummed round India or jackarooed on a distant cousin's farm in Australia – and you don't have any mutual friends. And now, unawares, you're staring too hard, which you only realize when this grey-eyed girl who's sitting with them – Molly, did you hear one of the boys calling her? – says in a voice of terrifying assurance: 'Did you want something?' 'Oh. Yah. The salt,' you say in the most strangulatedly waf waf voice you can manage at such short notice. 'Could you pass me the salt?' And you sort of hope that hearing your accent, they'll recognize at once you're one of them and become your life-long friends and invite you back to their massive stately homes where you'll get terribly drunk on the fine wines from their capacious cellars and fall in love with their sisters and do reckless things in sporty cars and toboggan down the Cresta Run and snort cocaine from crested spoons and dabble with smack and commune with the devil in ancestral caverns. Instead, they just pass you the salt.

The food, by the way, is disgusting. Tough, tasteless, institutional.

You turn briefly towards the Northern chemists. Before realizing, no, you have even less in common with them than you do with the Etonians.

So how do you make friends at Oxford? Fuck knows. But a few months later, on a mild winter's evening in Hilary Term, I'm hanging with five or six of them just after hall.

We're mildly drunk on beer from the buttery and we're standing at the bottom of the stone staircase through whose balustrade I will one day urinate drunkenly – but not deliberately – on the head of a passing female tutor.

We're preparing to make a cavalry charge along the east side of Tom Quad.

'Steady now, chaps, steady,' says Rufus, our de facto leader.

We reign in our horses.

'The jangling of the bits,' says Edward.

No one, I suspect, knows what the jangling of the bits is, except maybe Rufus who's up here on an army scholarship and will eventually join a cavalry regiment. Still, the bits are an established part of our routine, so we jangle them.

'Walk on,' says Rufus.

We walk on in line abreast until we've reached the cathedral entrance. (That's another cool thing about Christ Church. No other college has its very own cathedral.)

'Twats,' says a passing rugger bugger.

'Sffft!' goes Rufus, unsheathing his imaginary sabre.

'Sffft!' we all go, unsheathing ours.

'And CH-AAA—'

'—AAA—'

'—ARR—'

'—RRRGGE'

Galloping the length of Tom Quad, sabres thrust forward, hacking at any Russian gunner/surly college porter/Evangelical Christian/Northern chemist who happens to stray across our path. Today Christ Church. Tomorrow the world.

Or, to quote our bible – *The Sloane Ranger's Handbook* – which we pretend to despise but observe zealously: 'Silly stunts prove you're the goods.' Also in this category, you'll find racing supermarket trolleys round Tom Quad; fishing for goldfish in Mercury, the pond in the middle; and covering the winged statue, from which Mercury derives its name, from head to toe in file reinforcements.

I suppose, if I wanted to make a point here, I could have Norton saunter past while we're in mid-charge and register, aghast, the creature his schoolmate has become. But it wouldn't be true. Norton's in Wadham. He'd have no business coming to the House, unless it were to see me. And this he hasn't done for quite some time.

Breathless, red-faced, jubilant we halt in Peckwater Quad. In front of the library which, in an upstairs room to which only members of the college are allowed the key, sits Cardinal Wolsey's hat.

Here we disperse: some to deal with essay crises; others to create them by drinking when we should be working. Rufus, Edward and I fall into the latter category. We're such an item that already we've acquired a nickname: the Dull Boy Three.

Why dull, I don't really know, because actually, we all find each other fascinating. Or rather, I find Rufus and Edward fascinating. I'll just have to take it on trust that they feel the same way about me, though it's hard to be sure: they're so dry and ironic.

Edward's the drier of the two. The sort of person who can carry off a silk dressing gown. Which he does. It's in the blood. One of his titled ancestors, riding next to Wellington at Waterloo, had his leg shot off. 'By Jove, sir, I have lost a leg,' he said. To which Wellington replied: 'By Jove, sir, so you have.'

Rufus, who looks a bit like the German cartoon hedgehog with the rosy cheeks, is the more ironic. If it's pissing down he'll say: 'Well, the good thing is, at least it isn't raining.' And if it's boiling he'll say: 'Well, at least it's not too hot.' And if you try to out-ironize him he'll say: 'Phew. Lucky you're not trying to be ironic.'

Me, I don't know what my special quality is. I can just about do ironic, but not as well as Rufus. But I definitely can't do dry because, like I said to Norton, I'm far too open. Garrulous. Honest. And these aren't virtues, I sometimes think, that the others necessarily welcome. Some days they'll tolerate my ingenuous, self-revelatory drivel. Laugh with me, not at me. Others, they'll exchange embarrassed glances. And if I push it too far – ponder aloud how best to break in my new Barbour, announce how keen I am to go out with the Christ Church beagles or tell them, surprised but very pleased, that I've been asked if I'd like to join the OU polo club even though I can barely ride – Rufus will bring me up short with a terse: 'Because you're not trying to social climb or anything.' At this point my face will fall and I'll feel so cut up and betrayed but me being me I won't shut up I'll try to brazen my way out of it with a 'Do you think it is social climbing?' or 'Still it would be quite fun, don't you think?' until I see from the way Edward's buried himself in the *Spectator* and Rufus is flicking through the *Sun* that the conversation is over.

So why do I put up with it? Because Christ Church – known as the House to its inmates, after its Latin name Aedes Christi ('the house of Christ') – is a very cliquey college and membership of all the other cliques is now closed. Because Edward went to Eton and is almost a toff and because Rufus went to Westminster and beneath the patrician facade is alluringly hip. He understands rap music. He can dance. And he's got a real (and very beautiful) girlfriend with one of those gorgeous names I didn't even know existed before I came up to Oxford. Allegra. Because, dammit, they're my friends and however bad those bad moments are the good ones are even better.

Like now, for example. We're in Edward's rooms overlooking Peck Quad and because he's a scholar he's got really good ones with high ceilings, oak panelling and alcoves in the windows at which you can sprawl, languidly, and watch the comings and goings in the quadrangle below.

Rufus has discovered a new term of abuse. Hodman. This, he thinks, is what you call anyone unfortunate enough not to be a member of the House. We look it up in Edward's *Shorter*

OED to check. It's more complicated than we suspected. To call someone a Hodman you have to be not just a member of Christ Church but also a King's Scholar from Westminster. Rufus, who qualifies, is delighted. Edward, who doesn't, couldn't give a fig because he went to Eton which is even better.

Me, I feel a right proper Hodman.

After the statutory leafing through the *Speccie* and the *Sun* and a glass of claret Edward has ordered up from the Christ Church cellar, Rufus proposes a visit to George's Wine Bar so that we can get very, very drunk.

We order our usual. Brandy Alexanders – crème de cacao, brandy and fresh cream. It's what Anthony Blanche drinks with Charles Ryder in *Brideshead Revisited*. So it's what we must drink too. Sade, inevitably, is playing in the background. Mally, the walrus-moustachioed barman who we think is our best friend but is really just a barman, encourages us to run up an enormous tab. And we do get very, very drunk.

I've got the 'orn

'Jump, you fucker, jump!
  Jump into this 'ere blanket wot we are 'olding
  And you will be all right.
  'E jumped
  'It the deck
  Broke 'is facking neck.
  There wa-as no-o blanket.'
  'Hang on!' says Brewer.
  'Laugh? We nearly shat—' I'm leading now. My voice, enriched by three pints of Christ Church best, soaring towards the stone-vaulted ceiling of the buttery. None of the others knows the words as well as me, so they all follow a half beat behind. All of them, that is, save Tom Brewer.
  'We 'ad not laughed so much since Grandma died—'
  'This is a *Tab* song,' spits Brewer.
  'Or Auntie Mabel caught 'er left tit in the mangle,' I continue, trying not to catch Brewer's eye. Trying not to be bothered by the very bothersome fact that I'm the only one left singing.
  'We are miserable sinners.
  Fi-i-i-ilthy fuckers.'
  And in the pause before the final line, I glance at the other members of The Grom, in search of a glimmer of a

smile, a flicker of solidarity. But they're all staring guiltily into their pint glasses.

'Aaa-soles,' I conclude, with feeling.

Because they are. The whole fucking lot of them. Quite what I'm doing with them, I cannot think.

Well actually, I can. I'm doing it because I want to belong. I want to belong to The Grom, the pointless, asinine, drinking society which meets after hall on Mondays to consume the regulation five pints of bitter in the Buttery, followed by the regulation death kebab and the regulation five tequila slammers in George's Wine Bar. And I want to belong to a circle of Christ Church men who don't sneer about me behind my back like Rufus and Edward.

Nor do they. They sneer at me to my face instead.

'Right,' says Brewer coldly. 'Next drinks are on you.'

'But I got the first round,' I say.

'Penalty round,' says Brewer.

'Penalty for what?'

'Singing Tab songs,' he says. Tab is the Oxford insult for Cambridge people, as in CanTABridgian.

'What?'

'Peter Cook was a Cambridge man,' he says.

I sigh. The important thing is to keep a cool head. To get the others onside.

'Not by choice, I'm sure,' I say. 'And anyway where would we be without Jane Mansfield's lobsters? Or I've got the 'orn? Or the Knights who say "Ni"? Because if you're banning Derek and Clive, you may as well ban Python as well.'

'We did,' says Brewer.

'Did we?' asks Sutton. 'What about Terry Jones and Michael Palin?'

'And Eric Idle,' says Trevelyan-Jones.

'He was at Cambridge,' says Brewer.

'No he wasn't. He's funny,' says Trevelyan-Jones.

'We've been through all this,' says Brewer. 'What we decided was that since no one knew who went where or who wrote which bits, it would be a lot easier to impose a blanket ban.'

'Eric Idle definitely—' says T-J.

'What we also decided,' says Brewer, 'was that it didn't matter anyway because reciting Python sketches is what Northern chemists and Hodmen do and we're— Devereux, are you going to get these beers or not?'

While Brewer reminds The Grom what it is that sets them apart from Hodmen, Northern chemists and other lowlife, I add six more pints of beer to my shockingly large battels bill. I have to budget more carefully than the others. Even by the most conservative estimate, I'm already well into next term's allowance. Still, I sign the chit with a nonchalant flourish, and make sure there's a smile on my face and a swagger to my step when I return with the trayload of bitter.

'Heeere comes a-nother one,' I whine under my breath, as I hand out the pints. Trevelyan-Jones sniggers at the reference – until he catches Brewer's eye and decides to assume an expression of deep solemnity.

Too late. In the ensuing game of bunnies, T-J is punished for his disloyalty during Brewer's turn as general. On four occasions, when a dispassionate observer might have sworn that T-J's waggling bunny ears are correctly dispositioned, he is declared at fault and ordered to drink two fingers.

It's cruel and unfair and hugely gratifying. Normally, I'm the one who ends up as Brewer's chief scapegoat. So when my turn as general comes, I reward his kindness by making him my Chief Creep.

'Please, General Bunny, sir,' Brewer smarms. 'If I'm not very much mistaken – and I concede that only you, in your wisdom, are in any position to judge so grave a matter – but I believe, O mighty one—'

'That's quite enough snivelling, Chief Creep,' I say. 'Name the guilty party!'

'It was Fergusson, sir,' says Brewer. 'I distinctly saw him raise two ears when he should have put up one,' he says.

'Well done, Chief Creep! Truly you are the slimiest sycophant ever to crawl from my warren. Fergusson. Two fingers!' I say.

'Oh three, sir. Please make it three,' pleads Brewer.

'Very well, Chief Creep. Three fingers, Fergusson!' I command.

The regulation five pints consumed, The Grom weaves across Tom Quad – 'Get off the grass!' yells the porter known as George the Irish Bastard – towards the kebab van parked outside Tom Tower.

'One death kebab, hot chilli dressing, please.'

This isn't food. It's not even edible. It's just ballast to be wolfed down as quickly as possible to line the stomach prior to the next alcoholic onslaught.

Which begins ten minutes later. Brewer heads for the corner bar to sort out a tab. Mally the barman chalks it up on a blackboard as an incentive for other drinkers to spend similarly huge amounts. Someone else commandeers two tables. One of them's already occupied by a group of seccies from the Ox and Cow but that's OK. We know them vaguely.

I need a piss. I always need a piss. On my way back up the stairs, I bump into Rufus and Edward.

I smile at them drunkenly and slightly sheepishly. I've

done nothing to feel ashamed of but they make me feel as if I have.

'Nicetoseeyoulookingsowell,' is the first thing that comes into my head.

'The good thing is,' replies Rufus, 'that you're not steaming drunk.'

'No, I am actually,' I say.

Edward smirks and exchanges a look with Rufus.

'We were looking for you,' says Rufus.

'Oh, I'm sorry.' Why am I apologizing? 'What did you want?'

'Doesn't matter. We just had dinner at the Casse Croûte.'

'No? Bugger. Bugger. Bugger. Why didn't you say?' I say.

'You weren't there,' says Rufus.

'No but— Oh well. We're together now. I'm here with The Grom. Why don't you join us? I'm sure they won't mind.'

'We might,' says Rufus. And I can't work out whether he means he and Edward might join us. Or whether he means that they might mind even if The Grom doesn't.

When I get back to the table there's a tequila slammer waiting for me but no chair. Everyone else has downed their drinks in one, noisily and ostentatiously. No one's interested when I do mine.

I go to get a chair. There's none free. So I have to share one with T-J, at the rejects' end of the table, away from Brewer and the prettiest secretaries. Another round of tequila slammers has been drunk in my absence. I drink mine dutifully. The fizz shoots up my nose and I feel slightly sick. In the background Black is singing that there's no need to cry. It's a wonderful, wonderful life.

Things have grown a bit blurry and impressionistic now, as they do after five pints of beer and two tequila slammers.

I dimly register that Rufus and Edward have accepted Brewer's invitation to join him at his end of the table. I hear snatches of conversation. Brewer's holding forth about 'players and non-players', about people who can't hold their drink and don't know the form.

'Quite,' I'm thinking. 'Losers.' And I'd love to be over there with them so that I can join in their diatribe against people who can't hold their drink and don't know the form. But as I strain forward for a better listen, I nudge someone's glass and its contents trickle into the lap of a secretary sitting next to me.

'Shit. Awfully sorry,' I say extracting a grubby handkerchief from my cord pockets.

The girl insists she's fine, she'll mop it up herself.

So I get her another drink, it's the least I can do.

Brewer tells me that it's my turn to fetch the slammers.

'You might have said, I've just been to the bar.'

Brewer mutters something to Rufus and Edward, who look at me and nod slowly.

But it's OK. Now that I'm getting the tequilas in, I can be absolutely sure that I won't miss out on the next down-in-one round.

Together we cover our glasses with beer mats and bash them hard on the table twice. On the third beat – in one smooth motion – we raise the glasses to our lips, tip them back with a sharp flick of the wrist and pour the frothing contents down our throats. We execute the operation with military precision. I feel part of the unit once more.

'Is that nice?' asks the girl whose drink I spilled.

'Sort of,' I say. 'Want a try?'

'Better not,' she says. 'I'm drunk enough already.'

Suddenly I'm interested.

'Cigarette?' I offer her my pack of Consulates.

'Menthol,' she says. 'Don't they make you sterile?'

Everyone says that and I always give the same reply.

'Got to do something to keep my potency down.'

She giggles.

Which, if I were sober, I would probably consider quite a tragic response.

Is she pretty? Hard to tell, the way her face keeps swimming in and out of focus.

I don't know what to say next. Even if I did I wouldn't say it because that would be a breach of Grom etiquette. It's a boys' night out. Girls are there to look decorative and impressed but rarely, if ever, to be addressed.

Besides, Brewer is making an important announcement whose details I can't quite grasp because the girl has started asking me questions about what college I'm at and what I'm reading. Something to do with membership, I think.

'English,' I say to the girl. 'What's he saying, T-J?'

'We're having a Night of the Long Knives.'

'Sounds fun. Who are we killing?' I say.

'You, mainly. I think.'

I check to see whether he's joking. He looks serious. But then he can be deadpan sometimes, can T-J.

'Oh, right.' I laugh weakly. 'Like in that Bond film.'

'Eh?' he says.

'You know. *Live and Let Die.* Where the man's watching that funeral in New Orleans and he asks someone "Who's funeral is it?" and the man next to him says "Yours" and kills him.'

'Probably,' murmurs T-J, looking towards Brewer.

'I know the bit you mean,' says the girl.

'Good.' I too am trying to hear what Brewer's saying. Perhaps it will allay my growing sense of unease.

'The bit where he jumps over the crocodiles, that's my favourite,' she says.

'They're alligators,' I say. 'You don't get crocodiles in America.'

'Alligators, then,' she says.

'Actually, I've just remembered. You do get crocodiles in America. In the Everglades. What's your name?' I say.

As soon as she tells me I forget it.

I tell her mine.

'I know,' she says.

'That's clever. How do you know?'

'You told me before.'

'Damn. I thought my reputation might have preceded me.'

'Reputation for what?'

'Um. Being a cool, interesting—' I'm about to add 'sexy' and 'good-looking' but that would be crass – 'er – person.'

The girl appraises me with a knowing, woman-of-the-world look I find disturbing.

'So you're cool and interesting, are you?' she says.

I look across to T-J for support, a laddish put-down, anything to stop it all getting so heavy and serious. But T-J's distracted by a girl on his lap. And now I'm distracted by something horrible I've noticed. Everyone in The Grom has got another tequila slammer in front of them. All of them except me.

It could, of course, be an oversight. In fact, I'm sure it's an oversight. They couldn't possibly be that cruel. Could they?

My eyes flit from face to face to face. No one acknowledges my pleading looks. It's not a deliberate snub, obviously. They've just got their minds on other things.

Like the next down-in-one-session.

'One . . . two . . ?'

Maybe I should say something.

' . . . three . . ?'

But suppose it is a deliberate snub. Do I really want to give them the satisfaction of letting them know I've noticed? That I'm hurt?

'Are you OK?' says the girl.

'Yes. Fine. I think, maybe, I'll just go outside to get some air.'

'Would you like me to come with you?'

'No. Yes. Whatever. If you like. Thanks.'

I want to slip out discreetly. But my chair screeches as I slide it back, glasses rattle as I hold myself steady on the wobbling table and anyway, the girl wants to say goodbye to her friends, which means I have to linger nearby looking stupid. The Grom are torn between pretending nothing's happening and sneaking a look at sad, pissed, loser fuck.

'Not leaving us?' calls Brewer.

I should ignore him. I know I should. But I lack his facility for vileness.

''Fraid so,' I say 'Feeling a bit – you know.'

I can't believe it, I really can't. I'm actually making out that it's somehow my fault. I'm helping to make them feel better about what they've done. I'm smiling at them and waving at them and saying: 'Catch you later.'

As fucking if.

This is the first time I've ever left George's Wine Bar with a girl in tow and I should be glad but I'm not. All I can think about as we push our way through the crush of drinkers standing in the downstairs bar is how much better off everyone is than me. I recognize one or two of them from college. If I'd chosen them as my friends instead of the evil bastards upstairs, I'd be with them now, gossiping, laughing at in-jokes, basking in our cosy togetherness. And if ever I felt down like I am now, I'd have a shoulder or two to cry on. I'll bet they wouldn't mind. Bet, in another world, we would have really got on.

If I knew this girl a bit better maybe I could cry on her shoulder. That's what I feel like doing. Having a really good, hogwhimpering blub. But I don't know her and anyway, she's a girl. You don't want to show weakness to girls. They hate it. They only like it when men are bastards.

'Feeling better?' asks the girl.

'A bit, yeah,' I say.

No, I'm not. I want to be sick. Just the strain of talking makes me want to heave.

'Do you want to come back to my rooms for a drink?' I just manage to gasp.

'Coffee maybe,' she says.

'OK.'

We walk to Tom Gate in silence. For once, I haven't forgotten my late key. The heavy, studded oak door clicks shut behind us.

'Got her!' says a tiny voice in my head. I tell it to shut up.

As we walk across Tom Quad, the girl looks round in awe at Mercury, the cathedral, the illuminated yellow stone, the majestic skyline. 'She's impressed,' says the tiny voice. 'So?' says the dominant part of my brain.

Because it's sod's law, isn't it? Here I am, enacting the very scenario I've been fantasizing about since coming up to Oxford – wasn't it the House's matchless bird-pulling potential which drew me to Christ Church in the first place? – only I'm too drunk, too sick and too depressed to enjoy it.

We walk through the sepulchral cloisters which lead to the Meadows Buildings.

'They dug up a skeleton there the other day,' I say. I'm only trying to be polite but the girl misinterprets it.

'Urrgh,' she says, seizing my arm and pressing herself against me. 'I hate skeletons.'

I put an arm round her waist. Again, so as not to be rude.

'Excuse the pit,' I say, ushering her into my room. The bed's unmade, my desk's strewn with paperwork, books, fag butts and cups of mouldering coffee dregs. It's stiflingly hot too. The heating's on too high and stupidly – here's yet another reason to hate myself – I've left the window closed. As I try to wrestle it open, a wave of nausea hits me and it's not going to go away. There's not even time to make a discreet exit towards the loo on the floor below.

But at least I make it to the sink in time. Since that first night with Norton, I've been putting in quite a bit of practice.

'I'm sorry,' I say into the basin, shaking my head slowly. 'I'm so sorry.'

I turn on the tap and rinse the acrid spew, forcing with my fingertips the gobbets of half-digested kebab through the plughole. I'm so ashamed I daren't look round. I scrub my teeth until the gums bleed and any lingering aftertaste has been erased by mint. Then I study myself in the mirror: death-pale skin, bloodshot eyes. Really, darling, I'm not worth it.

But she's still there, poor deluded thing. She's still there. Perched on the edge of the bed, flicking through my record sleeves.

'Sorry,' I say again.

'It wasn't unexpected,' she replies, sweetly. She has a nice smile.

'Found anything you like?'

'You choose,' she says. 'Shall I make the coffee?'

I put on *Trick of the Tail*, while she fills the kettle and washes the cups. Not just two, but all of them. I like this girl. Like her as person, that is. The sex bit I'm still not sure about.

Her back's turned to me, so I can't inspect her properly. Mousey hair. Regulation issue Norwegian sweater, plain skirt, sensible shoes.

Oh God. Beer fart brewing. Do I let it out and risk stinking out the room? Or do I – well, there really isn't another option. It's coming but if I can just ease it out gently, before she gets near me, maybe—

Shit.

Literally.

And I know, I know – this is really more information than you needed. You don't want to hear about vomit and follow-throughs. You want burgeoning romance. But do you think I want vomit and follow-throughs? Do you think I haven't suffered enough already this evening? Do you think I wouldn't mortgage my soul just to make it all go away? I tell you these things because they're true. They're what happens when you're nineteen and drunk and yet to gain full mastery of your bodily functions.

'Excuse me,' I say, crabbing towards the door. 'Just popping to the loo. It's outside, you see. And I'd better take a towel with me. So I can wash my hands.'

With hindsight, the long explanation strikes me as having been unneccessary. 'Excuse me' would have done perfectly well. It's like when you're at a dinner party at someone else's house and you're dying for a crap. And it's not something you'd ever normally do, go for crap in someone else's house. Still less in the middle of a dinner party. So you try to do it as quickly as possible in the hope that maybe everyone will assume you've been for a long pee. A very, very long pee because, of course, the harder you try to crap quickly the less relaxed you are and the longer it takes. Which means that when you get back, everyone knows what you've been up to. Which makes you feel compelled to make some airy remark like 'Lovely prints you've got upstairs' or 'Great choice of loo books', just to indicate to everyone that you haven't been doing anything so gross as having a poo. Which, of course, only serves to underline the fact that having a poo is exactly what you have been doing. Whereas if you'd just sidled back in, sat down and rejoined the conversation, no one would have noticed.

So what I've really been saying to the girl, I can't help thinking – as I hurry down to the basement where the showers are, give my bottom a good clean (and while we're at it, my tackle), taking care not to get my hair wet because that would be a dead giveaway, inspecting my underpants, deciding they're too far gone and chucking them in the bin, drying and dressing myself and scurrying back upstairs – is 'Excuse me. I've just shat myself and I need to clean up.'

If the girl has noticed, though, she's too polite to say so. In my absence she has turned off the main light, put on the bedside lamp and made my bed. She's sitting at the top end, legs crossed, pillow propped between her and the wall, hands cupped round her mug of Nescafé Blend 37. My mug is waiting for me on the desk.

'I wasn't sure how you take it,' she says.

'White no sugar,' I say, adding some milk.

'Sweet enough already?'

I wince. 'Ha ha. Yeah.' I perch on the far end of the bed and stare into my cup.

'You're too hard on yourself,' says the girl. 'Come over here. It's more comfortable.'

'Is it?'

There's something grimly inevitable about all this.

The girl snuggles up next to me.

'That's better,' she says. She squeezes my side and pulls me closer. 'You're nice. Different from the others.'

It's her proprietorial attitude that I find disturbing. That and the fact that she's got me completely wrong. I'm exactly like any other bloke: up for sex; most definitely not up for a relationship.

'Thanks,' I say. 'But I'm not really, you know.'

'You're doing it again. Stop being so hard on yourself.'

'All right, I'm very nice and different from all the others.'

'I never said very,' she says, leaning forward and looking straight into my eyes.

Our lips meet briefly. I pull away.

'Um. Hadn't we better put these down first?' I say.

As I take the coffee cups and put them on to the desk, I'm uncomfortably aware that I'm still not aroused. It could be the drink, it could be her looks, it could be my inexperience, it could be her scarily forward manner or it could be my fear of the awkward question she might ask when she discovers I'm not wearing any underpants. Take your pick. The combination's devastating.

We kiss. My mouth's dry but I won't excuse myself again to get some water. I want to get this over with. Maybe, if I probe more deeply, more passionately, something will happen. Maybe if I can just get hold of a breast—

I slip a hand beneath her sweater and steer it upwards –

not too quickly, lest she notices what I'm doing – towards her chest. So far, so good. The assault on Hill One has been completed without any serious resistance. Well, almost. There's still that tricky business of the bra to negotiate.

I play with her bra, as if I'm too much of a gentleman to venture within without an invitation. Really, though, I'm just probing her defences. How do you get inside this thing?

The route from below is evidently a non-starter. There's a tight band hugging the base of her breasts, which traps your fingers. And the top route's no good either. Though the material there is much flimsier, it means bending your wrist round at an impossible angle in order to get a grope.

If this goes on much longer she might get the impression that I'm an amateur. To distract her, I start sloshing my tongue around her mouth more vigorously still. Grunting, she pulls away. She looks at me briefly, as if trying to decide whether it's worth carrying on.

'Here,' she pulls off her sweater, unbuttons her blouse and replaces my hand. Then she unclips her bra. It flaps loose. I make straight for the nipple. It seems to be growing harder so I try helping it along with a firm tweak.

'Ow!'

'Sorry.'

'You're a virgin, aren't you?' She doesn't actually say it but I'm sure she's about to. So I launch a diversionary attack with my mouth, slopping at her breast like a hungry puppy.

Now she's fumbling for my flies, which is not good. Any second now, she'll discover the total absence of erectile tissue. I twist my body away from her, feigning a frenzy of passion and lick her stomach and her belly button, one hand on a breast, the other unhooking the catch on her skirt and slipping beneath the waist band of her panties.

Now what?

I've done the top bit before but the bottom bit is terra incognita. It shouldn't be, of course, at the age of nineteen. But when you've spent the last decade cloistered in a boys-only private school, you're lucky ever to have reached second base let alone third.

And it has to be said that this territory I'm investigating now isn't at all what I expected. Women's pubes, it turns out, aren't all soft and downy like the feathers on a baby chick. They're dark, curly and coarse, like a man's only shorter. And they go on for ever. You keep expecting to find one of those gaping cracks like you see in split-beaver shots in porn mags. And instead, all you get is more pubic mound.

I brush my hand up and down and from side to side, checking to make sure I haven't missed some sort of secret entrance. But no. It would appear that a woman's vagina is not situated in the logical place, where a man's willy would be. It's further down. Dangerously close to the bottom region.

Oh God. What if I overshoot and end up sticking a finger up her bum? What if she works out that these exploratory fumblings are not designed to reduce her to a jelly of quivering anticipation; that they're the result of being lost?

Too late. She already has. She's guiding my hand down and down until—

Eureka!

This is more like it. All slippery and cavernous. Just like they promised us in the 'Readers' True Experience' sections.

Somewhere round these parts, I've heard, lurks that mythical beast, the clitoris. But I'm buggered if I'm going to try looking for it now. How would I recognize it even if I accidentally found it? I'm in, that's the main thing. If I just keep poking my finger in and out, I'm bound to make some sort of connection.

So I do for what seems an age. My hand's aching like mad but I daren't stop because she'll only ask me to do that thing I'm completely incapable of doing at the moment.

'I want you inside me,' she says.

I WANT YOU INSIDE ME. Is there any more beautiful sentence in the English language? Are there any words more nicely calculated to bring a man from limp to erect in the time it takes to utter them?

Well, clearly there must be. Because the phrase that I've so often dreamt of hearing in the six or seven years since I properly acquired sexual consciousness completely fails to work its magic. Indeed, if anything, it does quite the opposite.

'Better not. I've got no protection.' An arrant lie. I've got dozens of them – coloured ones, ribbed ones, Fetherlite for extra sensitivity – stockpiled in my drawer.

'It's OK, I'm safe,' she says.

Oh God, this is terrible. The urgency in her voice. The yearning need.

'In my bag, then,' she says. 'There's one in my bag.'

Here, at least, is a temporary excuse. The detumescent rummaging amid the powder compact and spare knickers. The 'Oh now look what's happened, so off-putting these bloody rubbers.'

But it isn't going to wash for much longer. Not now she's attempting to tease my willy into life, stroking, then licking, then enveloping it completely in her mouth only to find that it's diminishing still further. Finally, I'm forced to interject: 'I think we'd better leave it just now.'

And it's when I see the hurt, the wounded pride, the pitiful conviction that if only she can give it just a little more

I'll be there for her, that I realize there's only one way out. I'm going to have to make the ultimate sacrifice.

'Let me,' I say and, with a deep breath, I plunge my head down between her legs.

'Ohhh!' she sighs, as I burrow amid the shredded wheat of matted curls – trying to ignore that sweet, sour, stale female tang and the stray hairs lodging between my teeth – licking and plunging until my tongue aches. How much longer, O Lord?

What's so frustrating is that just when her breathing turns so heavy that you think she's going to come any second and you start licking extra hard so as to tip her over the edge, she suddenly starts breathing normally and you have to start all over again. After I've come up for air for the umpteenth time, she says: 'You don't have to go on, if you don't want to.'

And I know I'm meant to say: 'I *do* want to.' But, by this stage, I've developed a severe case of tongue-muscle strain and lock jaw.

'OK, then,' I say.

She dresses quickly and thanks me for the 'coffee'. We don't say much as I escort her back to the main gate. I say something about the enormous hangover I can expect tomorrow morning, well this morning actually because it's gone 1 a.m. She mentions that her first class starts at 9.30 and I say: 'Gosh, that's early.' And she agrees that it is.

I unlock the gate.

There's a nasty pause in which she seems to be debating whether or not to give me her phone number. Instead, she pecks me on the side of my mouth.

'See you, then,' I say.

'See you.'

I watch her for a few seconds. She doesn't look back.

Only once I'm back in my room does the enormity of what's happened sink in. Not half an hour ago, on this very bed, a woman was begging me to make love to her and I failed to oblige. I could have asked her to stay the night and tried again in the morning; I could have got her name and number and followed up the next day. But I didn't. I had my chance – several chances – and I blew it. I blew them all.

And I'm drunk. And I've got no friends. And I've been knifed by The Grom. And I can't sleep because I'm drunk, I've got no friends, I've been knifed by The Grom, I turned down the first and only opportunity I'll ever have to lose my virginity and the bed's spinning. Spinning so wildly that I'm going to have to get up and induce a tactical grom.

Finger down the throat. Spew. Clean up. Clean teeth. Back into bed.

The spinning's more or less stopped. But I'm still a failure and a virgin with no friends.

A wank. Maybe that'll help me sleep. So I tug at my treacherous prick which, of course, has no problems developing an erection now that there's no girl available to enjoy it. And I backtrack through the evening, only in a new revised version where I succeed in getting it up when the girl asks me and where I bring her to screaming orgasm within seconds of entering her.

And still I can't come. I backtrack again and again, struggling to relive the night's erotic highlights: the moment where she snuggled close when I mentioned the skeleton; the first kiss; I WANT YOU INSIDE ME; putting my tongue inside an actual girl's actual cunt. But whenever I get remotely close to achieving orgasm, the dark distracting thoughts intervene. Brewer saying: 'Not leaving us?' and me actually apologizing to him, the bastard bastard cunt. Rufus and Edward mocking me on the stairs. The girl not looking back.

My cock is raw by the time, with a grudging trickle, I finally get my release.

There's an uncomfortable tingling through its centre, as if someone has driven a hot needle through the shaft. When I piss in the basin, it only gets worse. I lie there, very awake, not thinking any more about the fact that I'm a failure and a virgin with no friends and no future. All I can think about now is the throb throb throb of my sore throbbing cock.

Just as I'm drifting off, I'm startled awake by the thought that the soiled underpants in the dustbin downstairs still have my name tag sewn on them. I get up to retrieve them, scrub them under the tap and slip them into my laundry bag.

Black Oxfords, grey loafers

'Dear Mr Devereux,

As Lyon King of Arms Pursuivant, it is my sad duty to inform you of the death of your third cousin twice removed, his Grace the Duke of Wessex. I understand that until today, you may have been unaware of this family connection. But I hope that you will not find it too much of a shock to learn that since his Grace died without issue, your father, as his closest male relative, will consequently inherit both the title and his estates whose value is not unadjacent to £100 million.

As the 26th Duke's eldest son you are, of course, entitled from henceforth – until assuming the Dukedom yourself – to style yourself the Marquess of Frome.

I remain sir, your obedient servant,

etc, etc.'

This is the letter I keep hoping I'm going to find when I check my pigeon hole in the porters' lodge. So far I have been disappointed. If the pigeon hole isn't empty, it will usually just contain something pointless like a note from my tutor or a photocopied reminder of the latest meeting of one of the numerous societies I joined at the Freshers' Fair and then completely forgot about. Or, on a good day, a stiff, embossed invitation to some swanky drinks party hosted by one of the People Who Matter, which I can stick up on my mantelpiece so as to prove that I'm a Person Who Matters too.

The letter however, remains stubbornly in the realm of fantasy. And my father remains equally stubbornly Mr Hugh Devereux, prosperous but by no means worth £100 million, West Midlands businessman.

Which is an awful shame, since if he were a duke – or, let's not be fussy, an earl, a lord or even a lowly baronet – I'd find it so much easier to show him off to all my new friends. As it is, well, there's no point in trying to explain the problem to him. He didn't go to Oxford. He wouldn't understand.

'Yow sure yow don't want to bring one of yer mates out to lunch with yer, arkid?' he asks me in a deafening voice which carries from Tom Gate across Tom Quad into Peckwater and through the windows of every single smart person who knows me.

I exaggerate. He isn't really talking loudly. And he certainly doesn't speak with a strong Brummie accent. In the Midlands, his voice would be considered posh, which is probably why I never noticed it before. After two terms at Oxford, though, I want the flagstones to swallow me every time he opens his mouth.

'Ow's about your mate Norton, f'rexample. Be noice to see 'im again, wouldn't it, Julia?' he says.

'Yes, darling,' replies Julia, poshly. And for the first time in my life I actually see the point of my stepmother. Maybe, I think, maybe I can pretend that she's my mother and this embarrassing Brummie bloke with her, he's my stepfather.

'Norton's too busy,' I lie. 'And the table's booked for one sharp. We'd better be going.'

Under the circumstances, I now realize, it was a bit of a

mistake to choose the Elizabeth. Yes, it is one of the smarter Oxford restaurants, ideally visited when someone else is paying. But that's precisely why so many Christ Church under-graduates go there when their parents are lunching them. If only I'd booked somewhere a bit further out of town. Nearer Birmingham, say. Or the Outer Hebrides.

The Elizabeth is fusty, low-ceilinged and very traditional French. The sort of place you eat pink rack of lamb. Fortu-nately there aren't too many people here I recognize. And those that are seem as keen to avoid introducing me to their parents as I am them to mine. Still, the tables are within easy earshot of one another, so one can't be too careful.

My precautions include: talking in a soft voice to ensure my father does likewise; seizing the wine list and ordering a bottle of claret ('Claret you're drinking now, is it?' *Shut up. Shut up, Pa!*) before my father has the chance to ask if there's any Anjou Rosé; dominating the conversation, so that my father can barely get a word in; addressing any questions I have about life at home to my better-spoken stepmother.

As a result, lunch is a strained, joyless affair. Instead of bantering with my old man, exchanging the usual family jokes, debating current affairs, I'm looking at the other tables and thinking 'Why can't my parents be tweedy, plummy and reserved like their parents?' and wondering whether it's as agonizingly obvious as it is to me that my father's suit comes from M&S, that his shirt is made of polycottton and doesn't have double cuffs, that his tie is neither polka dot nor regi-mental, and that his shoes – Oh God, the shoes! – aren't highly polished, black handmade Oxfords with thin laces but the type of vulgar grey loafers with a tacky metal emblem on them that only West Midlands businessmen wear.

And my father must be aware of this because God knows

he's known me long enough, he knows what I'm really like and he could so easily pick me up on this and say: 'What's got into you, Josh? You're acting like a prat.' But he won't because I'm his beloved elder son and he's so proud that I got into Oxford, which is what he might have done himself – he's bright enough – if only his ambition hadn't been thwarted by having to join the family business once he'd finished his national service in Hong Kong. So instead of raining on my parade, he puts up with this waf waf waf, I'm-so-frightfully-grand bollocks I'm spouting and he tries to play up to it. He tries to be the father I want him to be by adopting the accent he thinks (mistakenly) approximates to the one I'm using and raising his voice so that it can be heard by the undergraduates on the other tables. Which, of course, makes me cringe even more because I can hear it's not quite right and so, no doubt, can they. But my father can't stop because he's unaware he's getting it wrong, because he's embarrassed and, like me, when he's embarrassed he'll always try to brazen his way out and because the wine – we're drinking far too much to drown our discomfort – has taken hold and the drunker he gets the louder he gets until, oh Christ, let's skip pudding, let's get out of here.

The only person who's enjoying herself is my stepmother. How wonderful that I'm giving her all the attention I normally reserve for my father. How nice to see that all the values she's struggled for so long to instill in me – fake politesse, acute snobbery – have finally struck home. And how frightfully impressed her friends at Edgbaston tennis club will be when she regales them with tales of her day out with 'my stepson, the Oxford undergraduate'.

After lunch, I take them both on a swift – very swift: we don't want to bump into anyone – tour of the college. I show them Cardinal Wolsey's hat; the gargoyles and portraits in hall; my room; and the Master's Garden.

'Oh, it looks lovely. Can we go inside?' asks Julia.

But I can see some of my friends playing croquet, so I usher them towards the meadows instead.

It's a glorious spring day and Oxford is doing all the things that it is meant to do. Bells chime; spires dream; undergraduates ride by on bicycles with baskets on the front; bees buzz, wildflowers bloom, and cows low in Christ Church meadow.

We saunter down the broad, dappled pathway which leads to the river. ('*Char*-well', I correct my father's mispronunciation). I remove the jacket of my tweed suit, exposing my red felt button-attached braces. Liberated by the warmth and open air, I feel more free to be myself. Which doesn't mean that I stop talking in my languid, strangled accent; nor yet that I say: 'OK, guys. I admit. It's all a huge pose.' But it does mean that when I describe my adventures, I can do so with a certain wonder and amusement, rather than with affected nonchalance.

'And when we bump into one another in the quad, we say, "Nicetoseeyoulookingsowell."'

'Nice to see you looking so well?'

'Nicetoseeyoulookingsowell. Slurred. We're thinking of forming this dining club called the Slurred Speech Society.'

'What does it mean?'

'Just that we all talk in the same way. Like, if you like something, you say its "abslymaarvlous". Instead of absolutely marvellous. That sort of thing.'

'But why?'

'I don't know. It's just a Christ Church thing.'

We walk along the towpath, towards Christ Church boat-shed, and I explain the nuances of oarsmanship. Feathering, burning, catching crabs.

'You want to watch those. When I was in this brothel in the Far East—' says my father.

'Oh you're so vulgar, Hugh,' protests my stepmother. 'Isn't he, Josh?'

Normally I can never get enough of the old man's national-service 'brothel in the Far East' stories. I like the idea that he once had an exotic life; and I like even better the way they always end up with him failing to get his end away. It puts my own sexual non-adventures into some kind of perspective.

Today, though, all I can think of is how nice it would be to have a father who didn't make crude puns when you were telling him something interesting and important about rowing; and about how embarrassing it is that he did his national service with the RAF and not with a Guards regiment; and about how eerily sympathetic I've grown towards my stepmother these days.

I give her a complicitous grimace.

'A'solutely,' I say.

Just one Canaletto

Then one day my dream comes true. Not the handwritten note telling me I've become an earl but something almost as good and much more realistic: the one telling me that I'm the sort of person who gets invited to long weekends in huge country houses with massive estates and servants who unpack your suitcases and press your trousers and iron your shirts and hang them up in vast Chippendale wardrobes before the gong sounds and you head upstairs to change for your statutory black-tie dinner.

Well, I'm not totally sure about the servant and black tie bit. But I'm certain about the rest because I've seen the pictures in *Tatler*. Molly Etherege's old man's pile is enormous. Bigger probably than almost anyone else's in college, save maybe Gottfried Von Bismarck's, whose family owns half of Bavaria. When Gottfried goes into restaurants everyone stands up out of respect, so the rumour goes.

But why exactly has she invited me? That's the worrying thing I can't quite figure out.

It can't be because she likes me: she barely knows me.

It can't be because she's short of friends because she knows absolutely everybody.

It can't be because she wants a playmate for my fellow

guests Rufus and Edward: she must have heard by now that
the Dull Boy Three are no longer a trio.

And it can't be because she needs a lift and she's heard
I've got this flashy red sports car which can comfortably seat
three passengers and will get her there in half the time it
would by train.

Surely?

The car that I have on semi-permanent loan from my
father's company is a bright red, 2.0-litre Opel Manta hatch-
back with fat racing tyres and a top speed of over 130 m.p.h.
Lest you despise me too much I'd like to point out that a)
during my brief period of ownership my swift wideboy motor
enables me to pull precisely zero attractive females; b) zero
unattractive females, come to that; and that c) within a year,
I'll have it recalled and replaced by a battered shit-brown Ford
Escort because my father's engineering business is having
trouble weathering the recession and shiny red Opel Mantas
for the MD's son are a luxury it can ill afford.

Still, it's fun while it lasts. And never more so than on the
blissful, sunny Friday morning when we set off for Wales. It
may be that the others think I'm a counterjumping prat who's
only there on sufferance because no one else has a car. But
so long as this journey lasts, I hold the aces.

I get to decide:

1. How fast we travel.

2. When we stop for petrol, pisses and junk food.

3. What music we listen to (my cherished compilation
tape featuring excerpts from Jethro Tull's *Benefit*; Supertramp's
Crime of the Century and Genesis's *A Trick of the Tail*).

4. Where we stop for lunch (my mother's, for reasons I'll
shortly explain) and, most satisfyingly:

5. Whether or not Edward, Rufus and Molly get to die in a hideous road accident (see 1).

All of which puts me in a good mood.

'So,' I say loudly to Molly, who has bagged the passenger seat. 'Are we going to kill lots of pheasants and foxes and deer and stuff?'

'Oh, dozens, I'm sure. There's a meet at home tomorrow if you like that sort of thing.'

'Cool.' I glance in the mirror to check Edward and Rufus are listening. 'I've always wanted to do that thing when you bag – how does it go? – a fox, a salmon and a trout in the same day.'

'A salmon, a brace of grouse and a stag,' corrects Edward, wearily.

'A Macnab,' adds Rufus. 'Which you only get in Scotland. Hence the Mc.'

'Oh, but I'm sure there's a Welsh version, isn't there, Molly? An Ap Nab, maybe.'

Molly laughs, whether sincerely or – like Rufus and Edward – mockingly, I'm not sure.

'Have you done much shooting before?' says Molly.

'Loads.'

'Since when?' scoffs Rufus.

'Air rifle when I was a child. .22s and .303s at school. Came second top of my squad in CCF, I'll have you know.'

'I think Molly meant proper shooting,' says Edward.

'Shotguns? I expect they're a piece of piss after a Lee Enfield. From what I hear, you don't have to even aim.'

'That's right,' says Rufus. 'You just point and the birds fall right out of the sky.'

'Excellent,' I say. 'I'm on for that. How about you chaps?'

'Pigeons and crows,' says Edward. 'I don't think so.'

'Who said anything about pigeons and crows? I'm after pheasants and grouse and those ones with the long curly beaks.'

In the back Edward has started explaining that you can't just go off on somebody's estate blasting at pheasants, and that anyway it's the close season.

'Toucans?' asks Molly.

'The toucan, that's the one,' I say. 'King of all the game birds.'

*

One reason I've decided to stop for lunch at my mother's house is to show Rufus and Edward and Molly that I'm not quite as common as they think. My mother, you see, had elocution lessons at school.

She also, unfortunately, lives in a very ordinary-looking house surrounded by dozens of other very ordinary-looking houses on a lower-middle-class estate on the outskirts of Bromsgrove, a boring town in urban Worcestershire whose only claim to fame is that the poet A. E. Housman was born there. Before buggering off as quick as he could to Shropshire.

Until now this hasn't bothered me. I mean obviously if I'd had any say in the matter I might have chosen somewhere a bit more interesting to grow up. London, perhaps. Or the darkest, remotest sticks where you could go off on long bike rides, swim in rivers, explore fields, shag dairy maids and stuff. In Bromsgrove, all there is to do is wander listlessly up and down the pedestrianized shopping street, lurk near the foetid stream at the bottom of Bromsgrove School playing fields and throw stones at rats, or sit at home watching *Texas Chain Saw Massacre* over and over again on the video. That's how Dick and I spent our adolescence. It seemed normal.

But now I've got my smart Oxford friends with me, I see it all through new eyes. I see clichéd suburban red-brick houses with anally retentive front lawns and nasty little rockeries; I see polished Ford XR3is in every driveway; I see creosoted wooden fences and leylandii hedges; I see common mothers in common clothes wheeling common urchins in common push chairs and stopping to chat in common accents with other common mothers with common urchins; I see Rufus and Edward in my rear-view mirror, mouths agape. I see that I have made a big mistake and that it's too late to pull out now.

We park in Mother's driveway. Behind her polished Ford XR3i. I press the doorbell. 'Bing bong' it goes in a horrible suburban way. I want to explain to everyone: 'Look, my mother didn't choose that doorbell. It came with the house.'

'It's my Boy-Boy!' says Mother, pulling me towards her and covering me with kisses. I yank myself free, with much affectation of nausea and disgust. It's a little routine we've developed.

Mother looks at Rufus, Edward and Molly, as if noticing them for the first time.

'I'll bet you don't treat your mummies this way,' she says.

They laugh nervously.

Mother is wearing creased slacks and a bright, embroidered Escada jumper. Midlands posh.

'I hope you like Marks and Spencer's chicken Kiev,' she says. 'It's my Boy-Boy's favourite.'

'Was, Mother. Was.'

Mother looks at her audience with hammy outrage. 'See how grateful he is? It's that dreadful university I blame. Nothing we do is good enough any more. Is it, darling?'

'No, Mother.'

'Now, darling, you must help your friends to a drink and take them through to the lounge. I wouldn't want them to think you hadn't been brought up properly.'

Rufus and Edward have canned lager ('I know you like bottled, darling, but they didn't have any in Marks') while Molly and I have orange squash. I can taste the aluminium in the Midlands tap water, something I'd never noticed before.

We sit in the low-ceilinged, thin-walled 'lounge' on a big, modern, three-piece suite decorated with ochre and yellow floral patterns. I am lost for conversation. This isn't the sort of room where you can wander round admiring the old paintings and ancient heirlooms. Just tasteful Russell Flint reproductions of décolletées peasant girls, pastel prints of hedgehogs and robins; a corner unit housing Mother's extensive collection of Lladro china (the Otter, the Clown, the Girl with a Furled Umbrella . . .); a fake log fire; the TV; the hi-fi.

While the others stare blankly through the slide-doors towards the patio, sipping drinks, mechanically smoking cigarettes, I rifle through mother's LP collection. Billy Joel, Shirley Bassey, Johnny Matthis, Lionel Richie, *Night Moods* ('18 evergreen classics of love and romance').

I'm saved by the Beatles' *Blue Album*, which I must have forgotten to nick.

So we talk stiltedly about our favourite Beatles songs, until mother calls us through to the dining room for our Marks and Spencer chicken Kiev with M&S potato croquettes, M&S frozen sweetcorn and M&S frozen petits pois.

Mother doesn't eat with us. She pecks at a salad in the kitchen, making the occasional motherish comment through the hatch. Like:

'Ooh, I can't wait till you've all finished. It'll be time for my big treat. Josh is going to let me squeeze his spots, aren't you, darling. Do you let your mother squeeze your spots, Rufus?'

and: 'Josh tells me you went to Eton, Edward. That must have been lovely. Josh's father and I thought about sending him to Eton. He's never forgiven us for changing our minds, have you, darling?'

and: 'You must promise me, Molly, that you're going to look after my boy. He says you're going to take him hunting and shooting and we don't do much of that round here,' she drops into her best Brummie accent. 'Do we, ar kid?'

and: 'Now for pudding I can give you Angel Delight; jelly and blancmange; choc ice or fresh fruit. What would you all like?'

'Er actually, Ma, I really think we should all be going. Don't you think, everybody?'

'But, darling, I made you a blancmange specially.'

'I know, Ma, I'm sorry but you wouldn't want us to get caught in the rush-hour traffic and—'

'And your spots? What about your spots?'

'Of course if it were up to me, Ma. But the thing is, Molly's keen to get to her parents and—'

'Blancmange and jelly would be lovely, Mrs Devereux,' says Molly. 'Thank you!'

*

The second part of the journey passes much more slowly than the first. I stupidly decide to take the cross-country route and keep getting stuck behind lorries and bangers driven by old men with flat caps. After the first couple of hair's breadth passes the others start panicking, and something about that Mother lunch has killed all my confidence. So I'm forced to trundle along at 30 m.p.h., simmering over my passengers' cowardice while they simmer over my alleged poor driving skills and over my stupidity in not having taken the sensible route via the Severn Bridge.

When I'm not fuming about the traffic or my passengers' ingratitude, I'm worrying about lunch. Why did Rufus leave all his potato croquettes on the side of his plate? Am I the only person in the world whose mother squeezes his blackheads? How non-U is it to eat jelly and blancmange for pudding? Was Molly being sarcastic when she asked for a second helping?

It's getting quite dark by the time Molly asks me to slow down, we've almost reached her turn-off. And round the next bend, there it is. An elegant, well-proportioned, Georgian house at least three times the size of mother's red box.

'Bit smaller than I expected,' I say to Molly.

'Possibly because it's only the gatehouse,' sniffs Rufus.

'Just as well I was joking, then.'

And I was. I think. I'm no longer sure. I'm getting paranoid. Maybe I really am the bumpkin, the social climber, the fake, the character from an H. M. Bateman cartoon that Rufus and Edward think I am. Clearly I shall have to tread carefully: no more *faux*-ignorant remarks, no more ironic statements which might be misconstrued by the Class Police. From now on, I must act as if nothing could be more normal for me than a weekend on an enormous estate surrounded by miles and miles of stately red-brick walls in a huge house with landscaped gardens, stable blocks, tied cottages, barns, watermeadows, a lake, a forest and a mountain. Yes. Molly owns a whole Welsh mountain.

So we pull up on the inevitable gravel drive in front of the inevitable portico-ed front door and I'm thinking, 'Right, what now?' Do we wait for the servants to open the doors;

unpack our suitcases? Is there going to be some sort of liveried staff line-up to greet the homecoming daughter?

I pretend to rummage in the pocket of the car door so I can see what the others do.

The done thing, it seems, is to open one's doors oneself. To remove one's cases from the boot. And to carry them, in person, upstairs.

'Travelling light?' says Molly, as we pass through a dark and noticeably servant-free hallway towards a broad wooden staircase.

Indeed, I appear to have brought more luggage than all the others put together. With enormous difficulty I hump it up the three flights of stairs to my allotted room. Still, my frequent rest breaks do give me the chance – once I've checked I'm not being observed – to gawp at the paintings on the walls. Some of them are ancestral portraits dating right back to Lely; at least half the others are by artists I'd never expect to see outside a gallery: Rubens, Poussin, a couple of Canalettos.

I wheel round nervously to find Molly looking down at me.

'I like your . . .' (I'm about to say Canalettos but check myself just in time. What if the correct term is 'Canaletti'?) '. . . house.'

'Good. So do I. You're on the next floor, turn left, third bedroom on the right. Towels in the bathroom, spare blankets in the cupboard. OK for dinner in an hour?'

'Yes. Um—' She's hurrying off. 'Molly?'

'Mm?'

I keep my voice low. 'What do you want us to wear for dinner?'

Molly shrugs. 'Anything you like.'

'Anything?'

'Oh, we're not very formal in this house. I'm sure no one will mind if you wear black tie rather than white.'

Thank God, I think, as I place the contents of my suitcase on the bed: one dinner suit; one formal suit; one tweed suit; three shirts (one dress, one stripey, one Viyella); four ties; two jumpers; one spare pair of cords; one pair of riding breeches; one tracksuit; one T-shirt; one Barbour; three pairs of underpants, three pairs of socks; one pair of black Oxfords, one pair of brown brogues; one pack of condoms . . .

Thank God, thank God, thank God I came prepared!

I celebrate my narrow escape from social death by having a leisurely soak in the ridiculous country-house-sized bath I've spotted in the adjoining room.

It has dog's feet the size of a Great Dane's and tap heads the size of propellers on an ocean liner. And instead of a plug, some sort of clanky Heath Robinson rod inside a metal tube. And a streak of black where the enamel has been worn by generation after generation of gushing water. It takes ages to fill, clanking and shuddering like a steam engine. The water's all brown and smells of rust. But it's hot and copious and I love the way the room fills with steam. Why didn't I grow up in a house where the baths were this cool?

I'm lying on the bed, draped in a big white towel, rather getting used to this country living lark, toying idly with my tackle and wondering whether there's time for a wank – maybe over Molly, she'll do, being the young female I've seen most recently and being, now I think about it, not at all unattractive with those piercing grey eyes and that haughty, upper-class manner – when there's a rap on the door.

'You coming?' says Molly.

'Shit!' I hiss, scrambling off the bed. 'Just give me five minutes.'

'Meet you down there, then.'

'Where?'

'In the kitchen. You'll find it. It's . . .'

I'm too busy wrestling with my shirt studs and cufflinks to catch her directions. The cufflinks are particularly troublesome. They're the cheapo, knotted silk variety and their bobbly ends are too big to squeeze into the slits in the cuffs. Why couldn't I have been given a pair of gold, monogrammed oval ones for my eighteenth birthday, like any normal person?

Then there's the problem with the bow tie. Should I wear a coloured one to undercut the formality? Or a black one, because it looks smarter and I'm not at an undergraduate ball, I'm out in the reactionary sticks where people might consider anything too fancy a terrible breach of etiquette. I go for black which, being made of stiff barathea rather than malleable silk, is much harder to tie. And obviously, I want to get it right. I don't want to look like someone who only learned to tie bow ties when he went up to university. I want to look like I've been doing it virtually since the cradle, like it comes really easily. But making it look as if it comes easily takes an awful lot of time.

Many more minutes later than the five I promised Molly, I hurry downstairs and wander through dark hallways, opening and closing the doors of empty rooms, listening for voices. After about the eighth attempt, I strike it lucky, entering a brightly lit passageway. It's much more lived-in than the rest of the house: worn stone floors, grubby walls painted with institutional gloss and hung with old school photographs and hunting prints. At the end of it is a half-open door, through which I can hear the murmur of voices.

I'm striding briskly forward, assuming a sheepish smile, ready with my apologies, when I see something which stops me dead in my tracks. I see Edward and Molly sitting at the table, their backs turned to me. And opposite them, a pretty teenaged girl and a boy of about nineteen with spiky features and shoulder-length hair.

I would turn round and run, hide, drown myself in the ornamental lake, but I've already been spotted. The teenager's eyes meet mine. He smirks evilly. And a crusty middle-aged female voice calls out: 'Josh? Is that you? We're in here.'

'Um, er. I think I've forgotten something,' I call back, retreating slowly.

'If you leave it any longer you'll miss your soup,' says the voice. 'Marcus', – what is the matter with you?'

The teenager is pissing himself with laughter.

'Come on, Josh,' says Molly, turning round. 'We're – oh.' She looks at me solemnly for a moment, than she starts laughing too. So, when I edge gingerly in – feeling like the man in the urban myth who's just shat himself in a thin white suit – does everyone else. Rufus. Edward. The little sister. The beautiful mother. The severe-looking man at the head of the table.

Not one of them is wearing evening dress.

The comfort of strangers

Still somewhere in my cupboards is an old tweed suit. The trousers are too long and even when you wear them with braces, you have to pull them half way up your arse before the cuffs stop dragging through the dirt.

But the jacket's nice. Four buttons, high-ish, narrow lapels, raked pockets – the sort of cut they used to do in that Edwardian retro period in the high Sixties, which is when the suit was made for my father by a tailor in Birmingham called Hackett & Yearsley. It says so on the inside pocket and I remember being terribly proud when I first discovered this. I thought, 'Well, he can't be that common.'

As I say, it's a nice jacket but it used to be nicer. The shape got ruined when I wore it in the middle of a rain storm in Venice during the spring vacation of my second year at Oxford. I didn't need to get it wet. I could have sheltered in a café or something, but the thing was – well, it all had to do with my desperate and urgent need for sex. So that's where we're going now, you, me, my brother Dick and a few others we'll meet in a minute: to Venice in the spring of 1986.

More specifically, we're in the dormitory-like bedroom of the cheapest hotel of the least fashionable Venetian quarter imaginable, this being an educational trip organized by my old school's art department. Since my brother's there and I'm friendly with the art teachers, I've tagged along for the ride.

It's about seven thirty in the morning and though no one has got up yet, we've all begun to stir, what with that chill Adriatic light filtering through the cheap curtains, the renewed throbbing of our accumulated hangovers and the muted sound, somewhere in the room, of bedsprings creaking rhythmically.

As with so many disturbing noises, the harder you try not to think about it or filter it out, the more noticeable it becomes. If Concorde flew over as a dozen pneumatic drills started digging in the square while the side of the hotel collapsed in a huge earthquake, I'm sure that the main thing my ears would notice is that 'eeek eek eek eeek'. They're straining so hard it almost hurts. They're straining so hard they can hear everyone else's ears straining.

A mortified cry: 'Thompson!'

The creaking stops.

'Thompson, are you wanking?' persists Dick. He has a ruthless streak, my brother, which I like very much. Except when I'm on the receiving end.

'No.'

'Then how come the creaking stopped when I called your name?'

'It could have been someone else,' Thompson mutters.

'Anyone else in this room called Thompson,' says Dick, sarcastically.

'I am,' calls Nick, two beds along. Nick is one of my old mates from the year below me in my school house. He has long, suspiciously permed-looking hair to whose maintenance he devotes at least half his day. The other half he devotes to cultivating his musculature – 'my bod-ay', as he feyly calls it.

'And me,' says Dave, in the bed next to mine. Dave is the school's regulation-issue, more-of-a-boy-than-a-teacher, assistant art master. He has a baby face, a curly-ended handlebar moustache and a smoker's cough bordering on emphysema.

'I'm Thompson. And so's my wife,' I say.

Dick laughs at the Python ref, as I knew he would.

'I wasn't wanking,' says Thompson, sounding on the verge of tears. Before anyone can open the curtains and reveal him in his full, fat, blushing, caught-red-handed, post-wankal shame, he slithers from his bed and flees next door to the bathroom.

'Poor Thompson,' muses Dave, which is truer than he knows. Thompson will grow up to be a strapping, sportif London biker. Then one day, while cruising down the Embankment on his 'Blade, some tosser in a cab will pull a sudden U-y on him. Thompson will never walk again.

But we don't know this in Venice. In Venice we have no mercy.

'Poor Thompson nothing,' says Dick. 'You can't wank in a crowded bedroom when everyone's awake, it's disgusting.'

Dave, still lying sideways on his pillow, looks across at me. 'Such a fascist, your brother.'

'I can't see what's fascistic about doing everybody a public service,' says Dick. 'Because don't pretend you weren't lying there thinking the same thing. Thinking, "Oh my God, Thompson's got his sweaty hands on his stubby little cock and any second now he's going to shoot his slimy—" '

'Please, no more detail,' says Nick.

'God, he's probably doing it now, you know,' I say. 'He's using the basin as a cum receptacle and when you go and wash your face, Nick—'

'Thompson!' bellows Nick. 'THOMPSON, if I CATCH you WANKING in that bathroom – oh, hello, Mr Brown, sir. Morning. How nice to see you.'

I assume he's joking but, no, the school Head of Art, Mr Brown, really is standing in the doorway – looking slightly flushed.

'Good morning to you too, Kirkham, brothers Devereux, Dave,' says Mr Brown who, hilariously, always dresses in brown. 'I just thought I ought to remind you that we're meeting outside the Accademia at nine thirty.'

'Fuck, do you think he heard?' says Nick.

'Oh no, definitely not, because you weren't screaming at the top of your voice or anything,' says Dick.

'I'm sure it's a term Mr Brown is perfectly comfortable with,' I say.

'I hope you're not suggesting that our esteemed Head of Art is a closet masturbator,' says Dave.

'I wasn't,' I say. 'But now you mention it I expect that like any normal healthy male on this trip, Mr Brown is no stranger to the Room on the Second Floor,' I say.

'What room on the second floor?' asks Dick.

Dave looks at me archly. 'If he doesn't know perhaps we shouldn't tell him.'

'Well quite, the queues are long enough as it is,' I say.

'Fine, then I shan't tell you about Gavin Chapple's sister,' says Dick.

'Who's Gavin Chapple?' I say.

'Who's his sister, more to the point?' says Nick.

'OK, so this Room on the Second Floor, it's just a posh toilet, basically,' I say, 'but it's got a really quite nice view of the piazza outside the hotel but not so big a window that anyone outside can see what you're up to.'

Dick looks puzzled.

'And a very solid lock,' says Nick.

Dick looks less puzzled.

'And lashings and lashings of extra-soft bog paper,' says Dave.

Dick looks at me, appalled.

'What?' I say.

'I just thought, you know, maybe that sort of thing was something people stopped doing once they'd left school,' says Dick.

'Really?' I say.

'Why would they want to do that?' asks Dave.

'I thought you'd be too busy having sex with girls,' says Dick.

'Have you seen us having sex with girls recently?' asks Dave.

'I think my brother here, being inexperienced in these matters, has a slightly unrealistic idea of how difficult it is persuading girls to have sex with you,' I say to Dave.

'The little fellow, on the other hand. It's never his time of the month, he's never got a headache, and he always puts out on the first date. And that, dearest Dick, is the essential difference between an egg and a wank,' says Dave.

'What is?' says Dick.

'You can beat an egg.'

*

Which isn't strictly true. If it were, I wouldn't be going up to this boring, spotty, generally worthless and foetid adolescent I've never met after our group tour of the Accademia and saying, like I've known him all my life: 'Hey, Gavin. What are you doing at lunchtime? Fancy joining us for a drink?'

Gavin Chapple looks stunned, his face registering the sort of uncomprehending awe the Aztecs might have worn just after being addressed by their first conquistador. I mean, even the lowliest of our gang is a whole school year above him. One of us is at Oxford and another's a cool master that everyone wants to hang out with, for God's sake.

'Uh, yeah. Sure,' he says, eyes flicking warily from mine to Dick's to Nick's to Dave's, wondering when we're all going to start laughing and admit the invitation was just a piss-take. But the smiles we give him are benign and encouraging.

'Oh, God, no, hang on. I've just remembered,' Gavin says. 'I'm supposed to be meeting my sister for lunch.'

'Oh. Does she live here then?' I say.

'No, she's on a school trip same as us. In the sixth form at Ellesmere.'

'Ellesmere. Right,' I say, hoping the leer in the 'right' isn't too obvious.

'Hey,' he says. 'Maybe you could join us.'

'Are you sure?'

'Oh it's not a problem. There's loads of us meeting up.'

'OK, then. Cool.'

As soon as we've got the details, Dave, Nick, Dick, this weird boy called Alex and I escape to the nearest vaguely affordable bar for a pre-prandial sharpener. The nearest affordable bar being a long way from the Accademia, this takes far more time than is right or civilized.

'*Quattro grande birra, per favore,*' says Dave, exploring the full extent of his Italian. Then again, it's all the Italian he has ever needed.

'And me, please,' asks Alex, somewhat impertinently, I think, for a junior.

'*Cinque*,' Dave corrects himself.

We all roll cigarettes apart from Nick, who takes his body beautiful routine far too seriously. Dave, in his role of corrupter of youth, shows Dick and Alex how it's done.

'Fuck, I suddenly feel bad about Chapple. Do you think we should have invited him?' I say.

'Any more babies and we'd be a kindergarten,' says Nick.

Everyone looks at Alex. Alex's cheeks colour slightly.

'He didn't mean you, Alex,' I say.

'I did. But only in a nice way,' says Nick.

Alex doesn't say anything. He hardly ever does, from what I can gather. But that's one of the reasons we tolerate his company – that and his pleasing strangeness. This morning, just after the Accademia tour, we watched him kick an elderly pigeon to death. There were bits of guts stuck to his shoe.

'So you don't think I should feel bad?' I say.

'Why should you feel bad?' says Nick.

'Well, he is offering us up his sister as a virgin sacrifice.'

'Virgin? Ellesmere?' says Dave.

'Oh, do please tell me that Ellesmere girls are especially loose and up for it,' I say.

'Why else would any girl join the sixth form of a public school swarming with sex-starved boys?' says Dave.

'God, you're right!'

'There's another reason for hating our parents,' says Dick. 'If they'd sent us to Ellesmere we wouldn't still be virgins.'

'Speak for yourself,' I say, perhaps a touch too hastily.

'You still left it pretty late.'

I notice that Alex is following this conversation with rapt interest. Unless I can nip this one in the bud, my reputation as a raffish man of the world might be jeopardized. 'Yeah, well, you'll probably be the same,' I say.

'Bloody hope not,' says Dick.

'So who did pluck your cherry? Was she a titled lovely or a pigfaced slapper?' Dave asks me.

'Do you mind?' I glance at Alex. '*Pas devant les enfants.*'

'One more round?' asks Nick.

'Better not. We've got to be there in twenty minutes,' I say.

'Better stay off the beer, then,' says Dave, wisely. 'Er, *padrone. Per favore. Cinque grande grappa.*'

*

Her name is Camille, I think. Or possibly Simone. It's one of those vaguely but not too French ones, anyway, and yes I know it's a disgrace that I can't remember the name of the girl to whom I lose my virginity, but I don't think it's altogether surprising given the circumstances.

The circumstances are a) I don't spend an awful lot of time getting to know her b) I'm quite drunk. She is too, I seem to recall. She must be, poor girl, to fall for the callow, ridiculous and embarrassing figure I am at this stage in my life.

For, in case you have forgotten, this is me at the height of my Sloane period. When I'm trying to impress I talk in a fake upper-class accent, I pronounce 'really' 'rarely' and I sometimes even remember to say 'yah' instead of 'yeah', though not too much in front of Dave, Dick and Nick, obviously, because they know how I used to talk and they might take the piss.

True to the rules set out in the *Sloane Ranger's Handbook* I dress like a country squire thirty years my senior: tweed suit, Viyella shirt, chunky brown brogues, amusing red socks and paisley tie or – if I want to cut a more youthful dash – red neckerchief. Plus, on my head, I've got this brown trilby which I bought a few months earlier from Locks in St James to help me fit in at point-to-points. Naturally Dick had to get one too. His clothes are a slightly more street version of mine – pale brown cords, brogues, stripey shirt, waxed Barbour jacket – the Sloaneness of the whole gently subverted by one of those Benetton sweaters with a big B on it.

With hindsight we both look like prats. But I'm not sure that it's fair to judge your younger self with the benefit of hindsight. It's like blaming the Spartans for being too hard on their kids. The early Eighties, you have to remember, are another country. Different values, different clothes, different everything.

It's like when I look at photos from that era of me and my friends. My instinct is to cringe, to tear the pictures into tiny shreds, so that never again will I have to be reminded of the terrible haircuts, the ridiculous outfits, the puke-making gaucheness. How could I ever have allowed myself to have looked so absurdly, obscenely, twattishly Early Eighties?

But then I recall that it wasn't just me. Everyone was like that. You see the thing about living in the Early Eighties was that you never realized you were living in the *Early Eighties.* At the time, you thought of it not as the past but as something so present it was almost the future.

Anyway, I was telling you about Camille/Simone/Whoever, who is about to prove my theory correct by not looking at me and going: 'Urrrgh! What a total dickhead!', but instead going: 'Hmm. He looks all right. I think I'll sleep with him.' I know this because one rainstorm, several brandies, umpteen fags and three hours after our meeting that's exactly what she does.

The café where we meet is way too expensive because it's

not far from the Piazza San Marco, which means that neither
my party nor the Ellesmere party comprising Gavin's dis-
appointingly plain sister and about five or six other girls can
afford to buy anything more exotic than a single espresso,
eked out by sipping the free glass of water that comes with it
very, very slowly indeed. A waiter with a starchy white apron
hovers agitatedly nearby. We are lowering the tone.

Because there aren't enough chairs to go round, the boys
all stand slouchily near the girls apart from Dave, who heads
indoors for a chair and a quiet grappa because being a teacher
he can hardly afford to be seen chatting up nubile teenagers
from a rival school. This means that by default, I become
our group's elder statesman. When the girls learn that I am
not at school any more but am a fully-fledged Oxford undergraduate, they are very impressed.

All of them, that is, apart from Camille/Simone/Whoever,
let's stick to Camille, shall we? Not only is she clever enough
to be sitting her Oxbridge exams herself later this year, but
also she has a brother at Magdalen. He's in the year above
me, he's grand and madly social enough to have been elected
a member of the Buller and she's been to stay with him loads
of times, so she's hardly going to be fazed by my fake posh
accent, my fancy dress or my thrilling tales of undergraduate
japery, is she?

Though she's not the best-looking of the group, I do seem
to remember her being by far the most attractive. Obviously,
if we went into a police station now and I had to put together
a photofit, I doubt it would result in an arrest. But there are
details that stick in the brain: the scent of stale tobacco and
public-schoolgirl perfume – Chloë, I think – but really your
guess is as good as mine, just give her the sort of features
you'd like her to have had, according to whether you're a girl

and you're imagining you are her or whether you're a boy and you're imagining you fucked her.

My chat-up technique at this stage of my romantic career is not sophisticated. It consists of getting the girl as drunk as possible as quickly as possible in the hope that her standards will drop sufficiently for me to be able to do with her what she might otherwise not have done. So half an hour after our encounter, with the conversation beginning to flag and the aproned waiter starting to grow a cancer, I suggest to Camille that there's a bar I know where the drinks are cheaper and why don't we head off there instead?

This bar, though it does actually exist, is impossible to find – as so many places are in Venice when you've only been to them once before, and where the bridges, canals, old buildings and piazzas are all virtually identical, gulling you into thinking they're familiar even when you're seeing them for the first time.

'Can't we just stop here?' begs Camille after a while.

'It's not far now,' I say, quickening my pace, because superstitiously I've got it into my head that if we find this grail among bars it will mean I'll definitely get her into bed.

'I'm sure we've been here before,' says Camille, as the first drops of fat, heavy rain start to spot our shoulders.

'Yah, it's like that, Venice. Have you read *The Comfort of Strangers*?'

'No, should I?'

'Yah, it's rarely good. Ian McEwan. Rarely creepy. Kills stone dead any idea you might have about Venice being romantic.'

'Not that I was under that misapprehension.'

I slow my pace and look at her, crestfallen.

'Look, I might feel differently if you'll let me get out of this bloody rain,' she says.

'OK, just one more try and then we will, I promise.' Unfortunately, this if-I-don't-make-it-to-that-bar thing just won't go away.

But the last try is no more successful than the previous ones. The rain gets so precipitous we're forced to shelter in our doorway, with nothing but a shared fag for consolation. ('Drenched in Venice. Come on, you must admit it's a teeny bit romantic?' I say. 'Must I?' she replies.) And when we do decide to make a run for the nearest bar, wherever it might be, it turns out not to exist for miles and miles, which means that by the time we get there we're both sodden to the bone.

'Grappa?' I say.

'Make it a treble,' she says.

*

We end up doing it in the dormitory-like room of her studenty hotel and even by the standards of first-time fucks in general, it's dismally bathetic. For one thing, though there's someone on the bedroom door keeping cave, I can't stop worrying that one of her schoolteachers is going to burst in. For another, just a few beds away from ours is another couple. Their rival grunts and squelches are distracting. But what's worse, far worse, is that one of them's my brother. And unless I move swiftly, there's a serious danger he's going to end up losing his virginity before me.

Which would be outrageously unjust given that it's only thanks to me that he's there in the first place. How it happened is that on the way back to Camille's hotel we bumped into her gang and one of the girls let slip that she'd really fancied my brother. In fact, she gathered from one of Dick's friends that he was virgin, which she couldn't quite believe, a boy as good looking as him, but if this were the case and he wanted some help, well—

'Any idea where he'll be now?' Camille asks.

'Back at the hotel, I should think. Getting ready for supper.'

'Is it too far to go and get him?' says Camille.

'We-ell—'

Dick's little friend looks at me pleadingly.

'I'll still be here when you get back,' says Camille.

And here we are now in the same room, he with his girl, I with mine. Which of us will get there first?

My main advantage, of course, is that I'm the only one who knows it's a race. But I'm not sure how much of an advantage this is. What if the awareness makes me so tense that I fail to get a hard-on? What if, in my eagerness, I come in my pants? What if she finds my advances so unsubtle that she starts screaming: 'Rape!'?

While part of my brain occupies itself with these worrying possibilities, another part attempts to decode the noises from the other side of the room. A muted slurp here. The rustle of sheets there. Are they preliminary snog noises? Breast-feeling noises? Third-base noises? Or are they—? No. Surely not. The creaking isn't rhythmic enough.

'Are you OK?' whispers Camille, temporarily pulling herself free of my tongue.

'Mm yah.'

'Only you will let me know if I'm doing it wrong,' she says, and it's then that I realize what's she on about. So preoccupied have I been with what might or might not be happening in the next bed that I have failed to notice that she has been rubbing her hand against my willy. My not remotely erect willy.

'Just worrying about whether you were safe.'

'It's OK,' she says, pressing the contents of her other palm against mine to show that she already has a condom at the ready.

I work my way down her neck towards her breasts. Important, I think, that she shouldn't feel too cheated on the foreplay front.

But time is running out and now another horrible thought has struck me. These rhythmically creaking bedsprings I've been listening out for: they might not be such a definitive indicator after all. Suppose, for example, Dick just enters this girl, slops about a bit without ever managing to work up a proper rhythm, comes, and slips out again. You wouldn't hear any creaking bedsprings then, would you?

Below, I can feel my erection diminishing once more.

I try to concentrate on the fact that Camille has a very lovely pair of breasts, some of which are in my mouth, and that I have half my hand up her crack, which is jolly rude.

Perhaps to seize the moment, perhaps simply to get the whole wretched business over with, Camille begins unrolling the condom over my penis.

I think: 'Wow! There's a girl rolling a condom down my willy. That's never happened before.'

Shortly afterwards, Camille loses patience and guides me in personally.

I think: 'I've done it. I'm no longer a virgin! I am no longer a fucking snively virginal girlie stupid virgin!'

Then I think: 'Or am I?' For it suddenly occurs as I pump away that maybe you don't cease to be a virgin until you've come.

(Oops. No more worries on that score.)

Or that maybe you don't cease to be a virgin until your partner comes.

(In which case, I still am one.)

After my swift and apologetic exit I try to give Camille a bit of reciprocal pleasure.

'It's OK,' she says, pulling my hand away.

'Thanks,' I whisper, giving her a final long kiss on her mouth. 'That was great.'

She doesn't say it back. And though, later, I do try to arrange to see her again, it turns out that she has too much stuff going on – galleries to tour, churches to visit, day trips to Verona and so on. Otherwise she'd love to, obviously.

*

We've scarcely the breath to talk on the way back to the hotel, Dick and I, because we're hurrying so fast to catch the end of supper. If we don't make it we might get into trouble. Dick might, anyway, being still a schoolboy under the masters' care.

'You did it?' I gasp.

'Yeah. You?'

'Yeah.'

We hurry on, spurred forth by smugness. There's only one thing that worries me. I wait until exhaustion sets in and we've slowed down slightly.

'So were you straight in there or did you, um, go for the tongues and breasts option first?'

'Um. You sort of take it as it comes, don't you, really?'

'Yeah. Yeah, you do. Only I was wondering. Did you notice when Camille and I were talking?'

'Hardly. I was a bit preoccupied.'

'But you do remember hearing us talk?'

'Vaguely. I think.'

'And had you started actually shagging your girl by that stage. Or did it come later?'

'God, you do ask some weird questions,' says Dick.

I'm afraid the fellows in
Putney . . .

The problem with Oxford is that it isn't like it's supposed to be. Your dons aren't amiably batty and they don't serve you sherry or try to recruit you to MI5. Your college porters don't think you're an amusing young scamp. Your scouts aren't really trusty old retainers who clean your room and dispense advice, they're just there to empty your bin and spy on you. Your rooms are hardly ever wood-panelled and vast, they're mostly poky fish tanks tucked into some scary, alien side quad your college had built in the Sixties. Your fellow undergraduates aren't scholarly or civilized, they're just like any other fucked-up teenagers fresh out of school, only more pretentious, socially confused, aggressively ambitious and with the added disadvantage of being alternately puffed up and crushed by the grandeur of their surroundings.

All this, by the middle of the summer term of my second year, I have gleaned. But that still doesn't mean that, now and then, you don't get one of those rare and magical days where Oxford does all the things that it's meant to do: days involving slender-limbed beauties in straw hats, dappled meadows, picnics by the Cherwell, punting, Pimm's, undergraduate camaraderie, decadence, debauchery; days which make you wonder whether it wasn't such a huge mistake coming to this toilet of despair after all.

Today looks all set to become one such day. Even at the revoltingly early hour of 8.30 a.m., there's enough warm light penetrating my garret on the top floor of Peckwater Quad to make it worth opening the window. The essay crisis I'm in the midst of is proving surprisingly manageable. And the hangover I acquired last night isn't nearly as debilitating as I'd feared. Indeed, it seems to be one of those useful hangovers: the friendly, alpha-state variety which enable you to filter out all the quotidian crap and think with the effortless purity of the divine being you wish you were all the time.

Thus, when I wade through the relevant section of my tutor's *Companion to English Literature*, I actually understand what he means by Marlowe's 'arena of fantasy' and am able to paraphrase the text closely enough for him to recognize that my essay is right and true, but not so closely that he can dismiss it as gross plagiarism. And still I'm left with enough brain cells spare to throw in a few jokes of my own. For once my tutor might almost think that I am not a total waste of intellectual energy.

His name is Mr Kurtz, a ridiculously apposite name for an English don, but it can't be helped: that is what he is called. Waiting outside his rooms is like waiting outside a headmaster's study, only more nerve-wracking. Especially, when you arrive to discover that today's tutorial partner isn't Benedict, the oarsman who makes everything you say look clever by comparison. It's Molly bloody Etherege.

Molly probably looks forward to these sessions, the cow, which would explain why she's there five minutes early, flaunting her scholar's gown, clutching an essay that, even allowing for her large, rounded, girlie handwriting must be at least three times as long as mine. I don't normally hate Molly. In fact I'd say that, despite that disastrous weekend in Wales and the fact that she's still going out with my former-but-most-definitely-no-longer chum Edward, she is probably one of my closest college friends. But, as I remember from the last time we shared a tute, put her in a competitive environment and she turns into this creature of purest evil. No longer are you her mate; you're there, at best, as a foil for her brilliance; at worst, as a rival to be mercilessly crushed.

'Please be kind to me,' I beg her in a pathetic, mewling whimper, which I pretend is a joke but actually I mean it.

'God, don't be silly, you're bound to know far more about this than I do,' she says. 'Do you know I haven't even read *Hero and Leander*? Or *The Massacre at Paris*?'

I'm about to tell her that I haven't even heard of *The Massacre at Paris*, when the door is opened slightly and through the crack a pair of big brown eyes examines us with half-amused contempt. If you were going to cast Mr Kurtz in a film, the obvious candidate would be Kevin Spacey. Not, of course, that we realize this at the time, because *Seven*, *The Usual Suspects*, *LA Confidential* and *American Beauty* haven't been made yet and Spacey is still probably some obscure thesp, playing spear-carriers in Off Off Broadway theatres or whatever it was he did before he got so famous.

'Usually it's a good idea to knock. Then you'll know whether or not I'm in,' says Mr Kurtz in his faintly quizzical, hypnotic, Pacific rim drawl which generations of undergraduates have tried and failed to imitate, once even setting it to music and turning it into a rap tape. It reminds me a bit of Kaa the *Jungle Book* snake, the way it lulls you into unsettled ease. 'You'd better come in.'

But by the time we've done so and perched awkwardly on

the Sixties-looking chrome and black leather banquette which is probably very collectable but isn't much fun to sit on, he has already disappeared through the door in his bookcase into the mysterious inner sanctum where no undergraduate has ever been.

During his absence Molly shuffles and reshuffles her notes, while I gaze wonderingly at his huge piles of books and his collection of opera LPs and the framed black and white photos of lilies and naked men. I gather they're by someone I should have heard of called Robert Mapplethorpe, which impresses me greatly with hindsight but not at the time. They just make me think: 'Do the nudey bloke pix definitely mean he's gay, then, or what?'

Because none of us really knows. Not about his sexuality nor any other aspect of his private life or history. We've heard the rumours: that he was the brightest English scholar of his generation, elected a fellow of All Souls when only twenty; that he earns so much money from his journalism that he has an apartment in New York and a house in Spain or is it Portugal?; that he despises undergraduates and only goes on teaching them because his spacious set on Tom Quad and his Christ Church dining rights are too pleasing a perk to lose. But there's hardly anything we know about him for certain because frankly we'd rather not discover, because it all contributes to the mystique which enables us to fear and worship him like the demi-god he surely is.

Mr Kurtz lingers a little longer in his mystery chamber, probably for no other reasons than to build up pre-tutorial anxiety and encourage speculation. Then he saunters in, with his cropped hair, leather trousers and an air of such insouciance as if he's forgotten he's supposed to be teaching us at all.

Being impressionable undergraduates, we think this is

desperately cool. When he hands out the lecture lists at the beginning of term, and says, 'I'm supposed to give you these. But why go to lectures when you can read the critics? And why read the critics when you can read the texts?', way to go, Mr Kurtz, we think.

But now Mr Kurtz has begun pacing the room very slowly, still not looking at us, still giving no indication that he knows there's a tutorial going on or that he expects us to say anything and I'm reminded, not for the first time, of the main and bowel-churningly ghastly downside of Mr Kurtz's patented and otherwise splendid no-lectures, no-critical-textbooks system. It means you to have read the text.

Not just 'read' as in 'pass your eyes over and get a rough idea that Tamburlaine was a pretty tragic kind of guy'. But read as in 'absorb so deeply that you can quote whole chunks verbatim and express really strong opinions on what it's all about'. Like Molly's about to do any second, I can see her consulting her notes one last time, not that she needs to, it's all in her head, evil scheming bitch that she is, and if she does speak before I do that's me fucked completely because whatever she says will be so supersubtle and ingenious I'll never stand a chance of being able to think of something clever enough to take the argument a step further, which will make Mr Kurtz think that I haven't put any work or thought into this, which would be so unfair because I have I have, I'm just not quite as big an egghead as Molly the Mekon, that's all.

I'm right too because what she goes on to argue for most of the next hour is indeed quite puke-makingly smart. 'Don't you think that in some ways Faustus's predicament in the play is Marlowe's expression of his understanding of the predicament of the theatre itself—' she begins, in a low, soft, lilting voice so similar to Mr Kurtz's from the faintly quizzical tone to the dying cadences that you think, 'God, this is too embarrassing, he's going to pull her up any second. Surely he's going to notice? How can he not notice an impersonation as flagrant as this?'

Mr Kurtz, however, is far too entranced by his star student's brilliance to worry about minor details like blatant mimickry. 'I mean with the tawdriness, artifice and bathos of Faustus's desperate conjuring isn't Marlowe almost mocking the whole nature of the dramatic experience?' Molly continues as Mr Kurtz's breathing grows so heavy I fear he's going to come in his trousers.

I glance surreptiously at my watch and think: 'Ten minutes gone. Fuck, is that all? No way is she going to sustain this bollocks for another fifty minutes.' It occurs to me that far bigger a tragedy than anything Marlowe wrote is the fact that Mr Kurtz isn't one of those tutors who lets you spend the first half of the session reading out your essay in a faltering monotone, allowing your tutorial partners to have a quiet snooze until its their turn to read their similarly turgid essays; because if he were, we'd almost be done by now. In the midst of this reverie I am suddenly aware that Molly has stopped speaking and that Mr Kurtz is staring at me as if he expects me to contribute.

'Mm, yes, in a way,' I say. 'Only, um—'

At which point Molly, bless her darling wondrous brain, starts speaking again. It's not an act of mercy; it's more the sublime arrogance of someone who doesn't give a toss what I was about to say because her argument's bound to be miles more interesting. Still it's the action that counts not the intention. 'Molly,' I think. 'Carry on like this and I will love you for ever.'

Amazingly she does. Barely ten minutes to go before the tutorial is due to end and Molly is still holding forth, this time developing her novel thesis that what Marlowe really is is a sort of 'Nazi pornographer', at which point Mr Kurtz bends down on one knee and says: 'No longer am I gay, for you have converted me. Make me yours, O Great One!'

Then suddenly, joy of joys it's over; Mr Kurtz has summarized what he thinks Molly was saying, next week's essay has been set and I'm free not to think about work for, oh, at least another five and a half days. And I don't even have to worry that Mr Kurtz thinks I'm an imbecile because the thing I haven't told you yet is that right at the beginning of the tutorial, in the nick of time, I managed to say my one and only clever thing before Molly did.

'I suppose the thing that Faustus and Tamburlaine have in common,' I say, in a lilting voice, with dying cadences and a soft, quizzical note, 'is that their achievements are more linguistic than physical or intellectual. They construct these vast, tottering edifices of words which come tumbling down the moment they lose faith in their ability to speak. And maybe that's what the plays are really about: they're a sort of fantastical arena in which the protagonists speak their dreams into reality.'

The sides of Mr Kurtz's lips turn up slightly into a near-approving, almost-smile.

'Yes,' he says, nodding hypnotically. 'Marlowe's arena of fantasy.'

*

Afterwards, we retreat for coffee and a post-tutorial analysis. As a scholar Molly has managed to nab some of the best digs in college, a ground-floor set large enough for two, whose

strategic position at the end of the walkway connecting
Tom Quad with Peck means that people are forever stopping
by for a chat and a mug of Molly's Java filter. Which is why
Molly now spends most of her days in the library.

It's why I feel so privileged to have been granted an
audience – especially when Rufus and Edward, attracted like
moths by the glow of the Chinese paper lampshade visible
through Molly's muslin curtains, turn up seconds later only
to be informed: 'Sorry, boys. We're talking work here. And
we don't want to bore you, do we, Josh?'

Molly pours me a coffee and bums one of my minty
cigarettes.

'I can't believe you said that,' she says, very amused.

'What?'

She puts on her Mr Kurtz voice. 'Marlowe's arena of
fantasy.'

'I didn't say "Marlowe's arena of fantasy". I said: "Sort of
fantastical arena".'

'They're quite similar.'

'Stop! You're making me paranoid. Do you think he
thought I was taking the piss?'

'Weren't you?'

'No! Only slightly. Oh God, Molly, this is awful. He thinks
I was taking the piss and now he's going to hate me.'

'I'm sure he won't.'

'Why won't he?'

'He likes you. He thinks you're funny.'

'How do you know?'

'Because you are funny.'

'Am I?'

'Yes.'

'How funny?'

'Very funny.'

'Very funny?'

'Very, very, very funny.'

'Wow. Very, very, *very* funny?'

'Hmm. Maybe not that funny.'

'Oh,' I say, suddenly downcast.

'That's funny, though.'

'What?'

'The way you care so much about what other people think of you.'

'Doesn't everyone?'

'Normally they don't make it quite so obvious.'

'Ah. But you said yourself, it makes me funny. So that must be a good thing. Mustn't it?'

'Might be.'

'What do you mean, might be? I thought that was the main thing girls look for in a boy – a good sense of humour.'

'One of the things.'

'All right, put it another way. If you were a girl – I mean girl as in girl rather than girl who's a friend – and you weren't going out with Edward—'

'Which I'm not.'

'What? Since when?'

'Since weeks ago.'

'Oh. Well, I won't ask the question I was going to ask, then.'

'Why not?'

'Bit of a tricky area, I would have thought.'

'It's not a problem. I'm over it. You saw – we're still friends.'

'If not for you, then for me.'

'I don't get you.'

I sigh. 'All I mean is that if I ask you hypothetically whether if you were a girl and you weren't my friend you'd go out with me, you might think, I don't know, that I wasn't asking you hypothetically at all.'

'And would I be hypothetically right?'

My cheeks are turning red, I can feel it, and my synapses are going haywire and it's so unfair, so totally uncalled for because this isn't where the conversation was leading at all. It's been hijacked and I've lost all control.

'About what?'

'Would I be right to think that you were trying to ask me out?'

'What. Me? You? Going out together?'

Molly's looking at me very coolly, very matter-of-factly. No clues there, I'm afraid.

And of course, I know the word I'm meant to say. The one I want to say.

But the word that comes out is:

'No!'

Closely followed by:

'God, no!'

And then a truly suicidal:

'I mean I couldn't think of anything more embarrassing. Could you?'

'Absolutely not!' says Molly.

We both sigh simultaneously. And then equally simultaneously we reach for my packet of Consulate. Our hands brush together briefly. We pull them quickly apart.

'After you,' she says.

'No, please. After you.'

We light our cigarettes, raise our coffee cups and together

we toast our resolutely platonic future in caffeine and burning tobacco.

*

Back in my room, I have a frenzied wank. In the accompanying fantasy, I rewrite the above scenario so that instead of answering 'No' I say 'Yes.' Molly says, 'Then let's not waste any more time. Take me! Now!' Gallantly, I oblige and it's all over in seconds. In my post-orgasmic tristesse, I feel faintly disgusted with myself for having thought such filthy thoughts about someone who was clearly only ever meant to be a good friend. I feel even more disgusted with myself when I hear a knock on the door (locked, fortunately) and a voice saying: 'It's me. You going to let me in or what?' My brother's.

As I scramble for some tissues, my bedsprings creaking, he adds cheerily, 'I hope you're not wanking.'

'Fuck off,' I say, in a tone which I hope conveys the utter monstrousness of such a suggestion. It's always a joy to be accused of wanking when you're not wanking. But when you are wanking, it's horrible. Especially if the person asking the question is a member of your family.

Just as my brother and I refuse to accept that our parents ever had sex, so we'd rather eat worms than contemplate the idea of each other having a furtive glop. I actually caught my brother doing it once. Or rather I thought I did. Even now, I'm haunted by that moist, rhythmic slapping.

It happened when he was about fourteen and I was sixteen, on a night when mother had a guest staying, forcing Dick to vacate his bedroom and sleep in the bed next to mine. I was just drifting off when I heard a sound that froze me to the marrow. 'Slop slop slop,' it went. 'Slop slop.' In the pause that followed, I tried persuading myself that I hadn't heard what

I thought I'd heard. But then it started again, more freely this time, as if the perpetrator of the dreadful crime had satisfied himself that no one was listening and now felt free to indulge himself at his leisure. 'Slop slop slop. Slop slop slop slop slop.'

Oh God, this was too awful. What should I do?

Lie there and pretend it wasn't happening? But it might go on for ages. I'd find it impossible to sleep and worse still, I'd have to listen aghast as that awful sound accelerated with increasing urgency, culminating in a squirm-inducing sigh of release and followed by a nauseating rustle of tissue paper.

Tell him to stop? But then he'd know that I knew. How could we look one another in the eye again?

Indicate subtly that I was still awake? Much the best solution: I yawned ostentatiously, stretched and rolled over.

'Slop slop. Slop slop.'

Oh, for goodness' sake. Did the boy have no shame? Was he – heaven forfend – actually enjoying the fact that I was listening? Or had he simply mistaken my yawn, stretch and roll for the movements of a light sleeper?

Perhaps I should make things clearer. I sat upright, picked up my pillows, plumped them noisily and vigorously. I lay down again and listened.

Silence.

Thank Christ for . . .

'Slop slop slop slop.'

'DICK!'

'What?'

'Can you fucking well stop!'

'Stop what?'

'You know what!'

'Oh. *That.*'

'Yes, that.'

'I thought it was you.'

'WHAT?'

'Slop slop slop.'

'Promise me that isn't you.'

'Promise me that isn't *you*.'

'Well what the fuck is it, then?'

I turned on the light.

At the foot of our beds, our mangy black and white cat Whimsey looked at us with wide yellow eyes. Then, with a slop, slop, slop, slop, slop, he carried on licking his balls.

*

Clutching a half-opened book to indicate that, of course, the only thing he interrupted was a bout of intense study, I let my brother in. He is looking tanned, thin, and ethnic, having just returned from six months' overland to Kathmandu.

'Here. Present.'

He hands me a duty-free bag containing a hash pipe handcarved in polished stone and a pair of stripey black and white drawstring trousers made of rough Indian cotton.

'Cool,' I say. 'Do you think I should wear them now?'

'Well, I'm not going out with you as you are,' says Dick, eyeing my yellow candy-striped trousers, open-necked blue shirt and dark blue silk cravat.

'You can talk, Mr Hurdy Gurdy Man.'

'What's a Hurdy Gurdy Man?'

'Dunno. But you look like one.'

He does too. He's wearing a badly stitched boxy jacket in very bright blue with matching trousers, patched with big square yellow and red pockets. It's called a Jak Pak, apparently.

'You're just jealous,' he says.

'Yeah right, because, if I'd been to India, I'd have a whole new karma and like—'

'Do you want to try it on?'

'NO!' I say. Then. 'Yeah. All right.'

What I'd do now if this were the film of my life story would be to examine my new groovy, ethnic, multi-coloured image in a full-length mirror, my expression slowly changing from horror and scorn through dawning realization to delight. 'At last,' I'd murmur. 'The real me!' Then I'd take my neatly folded Brideshead-style togs, screw them into a ball and hurl them into my wastepaper basket, crying: 'Good riddance, you social-climbing twat.'

In real life, though, dramatic transformations take a bit longer. And besides, I don't have a full-length mirror.

*

To impress my brother I have arranged an afternoon so abundant with Oxford clichés that it might almost be an episode of *Inspector Morse*. First we'll saunter through the meadows to watch the rowers before doubling back to the special private pull-yourself-across the river Christ Church ferry to the Christ Church cricket ground, not because we care about cricket but because the ferry's quite a fun toy. Then we'll have an elaborate picnic by the river and possibly a stroll round the Botanical Gardens before cycling to North Oxford where we'll hire a punt for a few hours, drink Pimm's and pole our way past Parson's Pleasure to see whether there are any naked dons to laugh at, before taking tea at Browns so that Dick can try and pull himself a waitress. He'll need to find something to do with himself this evening because, sadly, I have a prior engagement at a new dining society some friends of mine in Trinity have invented. It's called the Felchists.

'I think it has something to do with licking the cum you've just squirted up someone's arse,' I explain to Dick.

'Is that the initiation ceremony?'

'I do hope so,' I say, rubbing my stomach and licking my lips.

Dick makes as if to heave.

'You don't want me to see if I can wangle you an invite, then?' I say.

'I'm just bloody glad I'm going somewhere normal,' says Dick, who couldn't get into the Ruskin and is starting at Cheltenham Art College next autumn instead.

'Don't be silly, Dick, it's full of protein.'

'Stop, seriously. Stop,' says Dick, clutching his mouth.

'Talking of which, we must get some mayonnaise for this picnic.'

Before we can head off to the Covered Market, unfortunately, Marcus Etherege turns up. Since he started up at Brasenose at the beginning of the year, we've been seeing quite a bit of one another. More than I've been seeing of his big sister Molly, in fact. This may not be unconnected with the fact that he always seems to have the most excellent weed, a new batch of which he is now keen to road test on the Peck Quad roof.

'Any chance we can make it a bit later, only if we're going to have this picnic—' I say.

'Oh, it's all right by me,' says Dick, checking out Marcus's long hair and multi-coloured Guatemalan jacket. Marcus checks out Dick's Jak Pak. They're like dogs sniffing each other's bottoms.

'Your brother can be such a straight sometimes,' says Marcus.

'Not this evening, he won't be,' says Dick.

'Marcus is a Felchist too,' I say.

'Seriously?' says Dick.

'What's your brother been telling you?'

'Are we going to smoke this stuff or what?' I say, jostling them towards the window.

'About how you have to lick sperm out of people's bottoms.'

'In his dreams,' says Marcus. 'It's just a bourgeois drinking club for people couldn't get into the Buller or the Piers Gaveston, that's all.'

'How am I ever going to sell my little brother the Oxford myth with you around?'

On the roof, Marcus's new batch of weed proves every bit as dangerous as he'd hoped. We don't quite get as far as tiptoeing along the parapet, hurling ourselves into the quad below gibbering 'I can fly! I can fly!', having our young lives cut tragically short and earning a place in the tabloids as happens, by statute, to no fewer than three undergraduates every year. But we do get sufficiently wrecked for me to have to reconsider the afternoon's plans.

'Picnic,' says Dick.

'Where's least hassle?' says Marcus.

'There's Marks, I suppose, but if we're going to do things properly surely the Covered Market—?'

'Marks,' say Marcus and Dick.

The good thing about Marks and Spencer is that it's easily accessible from Christ Church. There's a back entrance in the street opposite Tom Tower, next to the Museum of Modern Art, and not far from the pub where the Gridiron Club is, which means you can nip in without having to jostle with the shell suit and pushchair brigade in the Cornmarket.

The bad thing about Marks is that its pricey, prepackaged

food selection isn't remotely conducive to elegant picnics. We leave five minutes later with nothing more exotic than ten packets of prawn mayonnaise sandwiches, ten different types of crisp-like snacks and two bottles of red wine which we've decided to drink instead of Pimm's because putting together the ice and the mint and the fruit is too much hassle, and anyway, we're hardly going to notice because we're fucked on Marcus's weed.

Still, I do feel slightly guilty about this. For all Dick has experienced so far, we might as well be at a red-brick. So to raise the tone, I propose that we scoff our grub in the Master's Garden, the stone-walled enclave of flowering borders, mani-cured lawns, medieval vistas and recumbent undergraduates, which comes as close as anywhere to embodying a tourist's idea of what Oxford is all about. In fact it's one of the things that makes going there such a pleasure, the way every few seconds another party of Japanese or American rubberneckers stops to peer enviously at you through the stretch of iron bars in the wall separating you from the world beyond. It makes you feel like the star attraction in a zoo.

Being as it's such a hot day the lawn is heaving with Christ Church undergrads, sunbathing, reading, revising, drinking, smoking, playing croquet. As we saunter past, quite a lot of them look up and say hello, some of them – and I hope Dick is impressed by this – young, pretty and female.

'Hey, groovy trousers,' one of them calls after me, and I suddenly become self-conscious. In my uffish state, I'd com-pletely forgotten that I'd slipped out of my Brideshead kit and into the stripey, baggy, Indian cotton ones which you tie at the bottom and make you look like a hippy.

'So,' I ask Dick as we settle on to the grass. 'Is this place cool or what?'

Dick looks round through his Rayban Wayfarers.

'It's amazing.'

'Yeah, and do you know the really cool thing? We won it in a game of cards with the dons at Merton.'

'What, recently?'

'No. Years – hundreds of years – ago, I imagine. Any idea, Marcus?'

'How should I know, it's not my college.'

'Marcus is just jealous because he's only at Brasenose.'

'God, I wouldn't want to be at this place. Reminds me far too much of school,' says Marcus airily. Suddenly, I wish I hadn't said anything.

'Where was that?' asks Dick.

'Eton,' says Marcus.

Dick opens his mouth and I know what he's going to say because he's a bit like me and doesn't have a very effective in-brain auto-censor. He's going to say: 'Oh. Where Josh wishes he'd been.' He notices my evil look just in time.

The afternoon floats past and we're helpless to stop it. Sometimes I catch myself looking at my watch and counting off the things we can no longer do – the Botanical Gardens, the punting expedition, tea at Browns – because it's getting too late. Mostly, I don't resist.

Quite a bit later, when we're thinking about going because our patch of lawn has been stolen by shadow and I'm starting to sneeze because hay fever's always worse in the evening, Molly turns up. She has changed into this flimsy floral dress and I can't help noticing that in the evening breeze her nipples are quite prominent. I notice Dick noticing the same thing.

'Corrupting my sweet little brother again?' she asks.

'What? It's your little brother who has been corrupting mine,' I say.

Molly studies Dick more closely.

'You're never Josh's brother.'

''Fraid so.'

'But you look nothing like him. And you're so much taller.'

'Only one and a half inches.'

'An inch and a half can make all the difference,' says Molly.

'And you call me a corrupting influence!' I say, as Dick reddens.

'Molly, Dick. Dick, Molly,' I add.

'Hi,' says Dick.

'Hi,' says Molly. She turns to me. 'He's a bit cooler than you too.'

'Yes, and he's ten times funnier. Maybe you should shag him.'

Dick covers his face with his hands.

'Sorry, Dick, are we embarrassing you?' says Molly.

'Nothing I'm not used to.'

'Want some of this wine?' I ask.

'Better not, I'm back to the libes in a bit. I'll scrounge a cigarette, though,' says Molly.

'What do you want? Minty?' I ask, reaching for my Consulate.

'Try one of these, if you like,' says Dick, offering a pink, conical paper pack of what look like very skinny cigars.

'What on earth are they?'

'Bidis,' says Dick. 'They taste of strawberries.'

'Saddhu's sweaty loin cloth, more like,' I say.

'Thanks, Dick, but I think I'll pass,' says Molly, taking one of my Consulates instead. Pathetic, I know, but I can't help considering this an enormous victory.

Not long afterwards, the croquet mallets become free for

the first time all afternoon and we prevail upon Molly to put off her swotting a bit longer so that she can make up a four. She plays with her brother. I play with mine. Despite my being handicapped by streaming eyes, constant sneezing and a liquid nose, we win.

'Didn't know you had croquet lawns Up North,' teases Molly, just after we've whacked our second ball to victory against the post.

'The Midlands aren't Up North. It's why they're called the Midlands,' says Dick.

'At last. Something you have in common. Touchiness,' says Molly.

'No,' says Dick. 'It's just we don't take shit from poncy Southerners.'

'Actually, she's Welsh,' I say, dabbing my red nose with a hanky.

'God, well you can hardly talk, can you?' says Dick to Molly. 'And for your information we always had a croquet lawn because we grew up in a big house with a big garden. Bigger than yours, probably.'

'Um, not quite, Dick. Her old man owns half of Wales.'

'Oh. Right,' says Dick.

'Gosh, you're so similar it's uncanny,' says Molly.

'Make up your bloody mind, woman,' I say.

'Can't help it,' says Molly. 'It's this being the weaker sex thing. Our brains are all over the place.'

'You can see why she got a scholarship, can't you, Dick?'

'Yeah, she knows her kind so well,' says Dick.

'For that you definitely owe us a drink in the Buttery,' says Marcus.

'For what?' says Dick.

'Racism. Sexism. And insulting my sister.'

'Marcus thinks he's left wing because he's been to Nicaragua,' I explain to Dick.

'Doesn't he owe us a drink for being crap at croquet?' says Dick.

'He does. But you have to be a member of college to buy drinks in the Buttery,' I say, adding to Marcus, 'anyway, don't you think we should be saving ourselves for this evening?'

'What are you boys up to?' asks Molly.

'They're off to this new club where you have to lick sperm from each other's bottoms.'

'Oh, nice! And you, Dick?'

'I'll probably make do with McDonald's,' he says. 'With extra mayonnaise.'

'Excuse me, that was my joke!' I try to protest, through yet another bout of intense sneezing. 'Fuck, the pollen's bad today.'

'If we don't have a drink right now, I'm off,' says Marcus.

'You can. I need to get to my hayfever pills.'

'But who's going to sign the battels?' he says.

'I will, if you like,' says Molly.

'I thought you were going back to the library,' I say.

'All work and no play,' says Molly.

'Huh, you never come and play with me,' I say.

She gives my cheek a gentle pinch. 'You never ask.'

*

When I tumble back through Tom Gate sometime after midnight, I am nearly as drunk as I have ever been. Not so drunk that I am in danger of vomiting – I did that earlier, twice, and I feel much better for it. But drunk enough to know that

I am as fascinating and entertaining a person as ever lived and that I owe it to the world to share this insight with as many people as I can find.

The problem is, everyone seems to be asleep. I doubt even Dick will be awake, now, but maybe if I can make enough accidental-on-purpose noise when I come in – he's sleeping on a camping mat on the floor of my study area – he'll stir sufficiently for me to be able to tell him my stories. And my, what stories do I have to tell.

None of them involves sperm, happily, though we did take turns to lick sorbet from each other's belly buttons, boys' and girls', which I think is pretty damned decadent. I also think Dick will appreciate the amusing rule we invented about men being banned from using the loo and having to pee out of the window instead, especially when some of the girls started having a go, and the junior dean, alerted by the noise, came in and caught them in flagrante.

But as I enter the passageway that leads from Tom Quad to Peckwater, I have a better idea. By some truly amazing miracle, Molly's light is still on. No doubt she's catching up with the work she failed to do earlier, and it's obvious that what the poor girl needs at this hour is someone to jolly her up. In fact, isn't that just what she was asking me to do earlier, when she pinched my cheek?

Of course, of course. It all makes sense. Molly is as smitten with me as I secretly have been all along with her. It's what she was hoping I would tell her this morning, after the tute. Only, stupidly, I got embarrassed and went and blew it, didn't I?

Well, this time I'm not going to blow it because, thank God, I've got the booze on my side. This time I'm going to tell her like it really is.

I've just passed through the entrance leading to her staircase, though, when I hear a voice I recognize. And I'm not sure why, but I find myself stepping into the shadows.

'First floor, second door on the left?' asks the voice. My brother's.

'Yes, and make sure it's not the first. It belongs to an American with no sense of humour,' says Molly.

I lurk in the darkness until my brother's footsteps have receded towards the toilet upstairs.

Should I use this moment to confront Molly? Should I knock on her door and pretend I was just passing by, leaving Dick to do his explaining on his return?

Even through the alcoholic blur, though, I can see that the sensible option is to cut my losses and go to bed. There's a chance that their behaviour is innocent, I suppose.

For a long time I lie awake, trying to keep the head-spin to a manageable level, listening out for the footfalls and creaking door which will alert me to Dick's return. But all I hear is the bell of Tom Tower striking one; then two; then three. After that, I can hold my eyes open no longer and I tumble into a queasy, troubled sleep.

It's cold enough outside

Worcestershire, where I come from, is a schizoid county. One side of it – the far side of it – is quite idyllically rural with gently undulating fields and darling copses and shady glades and gurgling streams and lush valleys and superabundant orchards and tweely pretty market towns with double-barrelled names. The other side of it – my side – likes to kid itself that it still has something in common with the idyllically rural side. But that was a long time ago. Now all my side of Worcestershire really is Birmingham's back garden, intersected by motorways, dual carriageways and ring roads, greyed over by new towns like Redditch and once-attractive-but-no-longer dormitory towns like Bromsgrove and Droitwich Spa.

The good thing about this is that when I want to impress people with my urban proletarian credentials, I can say I'm from Birmingham. And when I want to make out that I'm a provincial innocent or a country squire, I can say I'm from Worcestershire.

The bad thing is that I've never felt I really belonged in either. I'm just a middle-class nothing from the middle of middle England, half way between the town and the country, between rich and poor, between smart and common: as I'm reminded during the Christmas vacation when one of my relatives – my stepmother probably or possibly my rich uncle

– insists that it would be a good idea if I did some barwork at a pub near Chaddesley Corbett.

When I go for my first evening – I arrive an hour early so that I can be trained up for the job – I decide not to tell the bar manager Dave where I'm studying nor that my uncle is best mates with the publican.

'Done any bar work before, have you?' he says.

'Not much.'

'How much is not much?'

'None,' I say, reddening.

Dave looks at a squat, blonde girl about my age, who is refilling the shelves with bottles of Schweppes orange juice.

'You just can't get the staff these days,' he says, cheerfully.

'Talks noice, though, doesn't he? Customers moit loik a birra posh,' she says.

'For a change,' says Dave.

'Oi shurrup, you,' she says.

'I'm sure I'll learn on the job. I mean—' I'm about to add, 'it can't be that difficult' when it occurs to me that this might not be what professional bar workers need to be told. Instead, I say: '—I'm keen to learn.'

'That's what the last one said,' says Dave.

'Who was that, then?' says the girl.

'You remember, Trace. Posh bloke studying at one of them famous universities, Cambridge, I think, or maybe Oxford.'

'Oh ah,' says Trace.

'Didn't know one end of a bottle from a bottle; couldn't remember the ingredients for a lager top; every time he added up a round it came to something different. That's the trouble with these head-in-the-clouds university types. Far too clever to be doing the likes of what we do, eh, our Trace?'

'Ah I remember now. Useless he was, bloody useless.'

'But tell us a bit about yourself, Josh. You'll have just left school, I expect. Be looking to find some sort of gainful employment?'

- 'Um, well actually, I'm at college.'

'College, eh. Anywhere I'd have heard of?'

'Yeah, um. Probably. It's um—'

While I am struggling to find a way of telling them I'm at Oxford without telling them I'm at Oxford, Trace and Dave burst out laughing. They know already. Of course they do. Roger the publican will have told them.

'Don't mind Dave,' says Trace to me, when she has recovered her breath. 'He's got no respect for his betters.'

'Ah, you've got a point there, Trace. In a couple of years' time, Josh might be our boss.'

*

The first hour or so of my shift is quite staggeringly tedious, with little to do but stand behind the bar looking eager, trying not to be too upset by the fact that every customer who walks in gravitates straight towards Trace, talks to her like an old friend, and gives her an enormous tip. Most of the punters don't even glance at me. Those that do look away the second they've realized it's someone they don't know. And if Trace is serving some people in front of them, they don't come to me, they just wait until Trace has finished. Because she's got big tits and the right accent and I haven't.

After a time I try greeting those punters who catch my eye with an 'awroit', which is how you greet people in the Midlands, the correct reply being another 'awroit'. But perhaps two years at Oxford have corrupted my pronunciation because it only makes them scurry towards Trace even faster, stricken with the same sort of terror I've noticed in Chinese waiters whenever my father tries to engage them with his rusty national service Mandarin.

In the middle of my umpteenth unnecessary mission to the near-empty lounge area, wiping up invisible spots of beer, emptying customers' ashtrays before they've finished their first cigarette, I console myself that at least things can't possibly get worse.

Then they do. It's like watching one of those nature documentaries about frogs that lie dormant beneath the desert sand for years only to spring forth en masse at the first drop of rain. One second I see an arid wasteland of empty stools, pristine ashtrays and dry beer mats; the next a pullulating host of noisy, red-faced, tired, irritable, parched, shivering customers, seething and pushing and elbowing their way towards the bar. They come in wave after wave, and for every one you serve, ten more seem to spring up in their place. Trace no longer has time to flirt. Dave has stopped leaning proprietorially against the corner of the bar and begun to earn his living. Even Roger, the publican himself, is now deigning to pull the odd pint. But that still leaves dozens and dozens of thirsty customers left unserved – some of them so desperate that they come to me.

'A couple of lager tops, one Pernod and black and a snowball, ta, mate,' says a man in a rugger shirt.

'Right, OK, do you want ice with any of those?' I say, stalling for time because the rush of different ingredients has caused a log jam in my brain.

'Oice, girls?'

'I'm cold enough already,' shivers something with dark hair, heavy make-up and fake fur.

'Now oice, ta, mate.'

'Right.'

'What flavour crisps do you have?'

'Um—' I look below the bar. 'Ready Salted. Cheese and Onion. Salt and Vinegar. Or Hula Hoops.'

'Has he got any Smoky Bacon?' asks the other girl.

'Gorrany Smoky Bacon?' asks the man.

'Um – I'll just find out if you want to hang on a second—'

I try to attract Dave's attention but he looks straight through me and pushes past, an overflowing pint in each outstretched hand. I tap Trace on the arm. 'In a minute,' she says out of the corner of her mouth, then adds to the customer she's serving, 'six forty-five, six fifty, there's seven and that's ten, ta, that's very kind – I'll have a half a shandy for later, now what was it, Josh?'

But the man in the rugger shirt has already said he'll have Cheese and Onion instead, which is the one part of the order I remember, but not the first bit because he said it so long ago, now what was it again?

'Two lager tops, a Pernod and black and a snowball,' says the man, slightly exasperated.

I do the Pernod and black first because I know how to make it: Pernod and blackcurrant cordial, but no ice because the girl who wants it is cold enough already. If I were good, I would, of course, be simultaneously filling two pint glasses with lager but I know if I try they'll only overspill while I'm wrestling with the optic and trying to decide how much blackcurrant to put in the Pernod.

As soon as I've put my completed effort on the bar it's snatched greedily away by the girl in furs. Behind her, Rugger Shirt's mate looms.

'Message from Vikki,' he says to Rugger Shirt. 'She says would you mind asking the barman when her snowball's going to be ready, only it's Christmas in foive days and she's worried she might not be back in time to stuff the turkey.'

Rugger Shirt laughs.

'And could you ask him next time he does me drink, could I have a bit of Pernod to go with me pint of blackcurrant,' adds the girl in furs.

I try catching her eye and smiling to show, yes I heard, and I get the joke, she's very funny and she's quite right, but I'm only human just like her and it is my first night and I'm doing my best. She pretends I'm not there.

Instead, I end up making eye contact with a man waving a tenner behind Rugger Shirt. I give him a twinkly look that says: 'Customers, eh?' But all I see in return is distraction, impatience and a flicker of that calculation you have to make at supermarket checkout queues when you've accidentally chosen the till manned by the spotty youth trainee who doesn't know an artichoke from an aubergine: which is going to be quicker – hanging around, second in line, to be served by this gormless prat or dropping to the back of another, longer queue so your groceries can be processed by someone competent.

At least, while all this has been going on, I have been sufficiently coordinated to nearly fill the two lager glasses. All I need to do now is to top them up with – God, is it just lemonade, or are you supposed to chuck in a bit of lime cordial instead? I would ask the customer but I daren't in case he thinks I'm crap. And I daren't ask Dave, not after that story he told about the Oxbridge undergraduate who was so useless he didn't even know the recipe for a lager top which, come to think of it was probably what got me into this mess, I'm sure I would have remembered if he hadn't planted the idea in my head. And if I ask Trace, I'll bet she'll only tell Dave.

'Um, excuse me, mate,' Rugger Shirt is asking. 'Is that lime you're putting in me lager top?'

'Er yeah. Didn't you ask for—?'

'I asked for a lager top. Not lager and lime.'

'Uh, yes, of course,' I say, making to pour the lime-contaminated lager down the drain.

'No, mate, I'll have that,' says Rugger Shirt, reaching quickly towards it. 'At this rate it's the only drink I'll ever get.' He exchanges a knowing glance with the man waving the tenner. The man with the tenner rolls his eyes. He could have bailed out but he made the wrong decision. And now the only person he hates more than himself is me.

'I'm sorry,' I say to both of them. 'It's my first day, you see.'

'But we'd never have guessed,' says the man with the tenner.

'Is that your way of telling me you don't know how to make a snowball?' guesses Rugger Shirt.

When eventually Rugger Shirt pays for his round, I half expect him to give me a tip. But he doesn't – nor does the man with the tenner after him. I don't know why I should be so disappointed by this, but I am. Maybe I was hoping they would take pity on me.

Barwork, I come to realize, doesn't work like that. When someone comes to a bar to buy a drink, they don't want to know that the person serving them is a warm, intelligent, simpatico human being with a rich, fascinating personal history, a thin skin and a desperate craving for friendly personal interaction and a sympathetic appreciation that he's only doing this part time, it doesn't define his life or anything. What someone wants when they come to the bar is a drink.

I learn my lesson on the night I man the bar in the Function Room, where some local nut and bolt firm is having its Christmas party. A cheeky-chappy local DJ is spinning 'The Birdie Song' and 'Agadoo', the room is getting hotter, the lads more lairy, the girls more scantily clad, and the orders decreasingly intelligible. All this, Trace tells me beforehand, is a good thing. 'If yow down't get tipped tonoit, yow never will,' she says. ''Alf the time, they're sow pissed they don't even pick up their change.'

And I try to enter into the spirit of things. I put on my least unconvincing rictus, I sway vaguely in time to the cheesy hits of yesteryear, I try to suppress my wince every time someone quips 'It's cold enough outside' until I can bear it no longer and push the ice box to the front of the bar so they can sodding well help themselves.

What's tragic is that these were once my people. One set of grandparents is proper Black Country, the other from Birmingham. My family has been in business here for generations. My mother might well have taught some of these people PE or French at the local secondary modern. My uncle probably plays golf with them. My team – insofar as I have one – is the Wolves. Whenever I come back to the Midlands, it feels like home. I like the people, the accent, the sense of humour, the way the shop girls are so much friendlier—

But I no longer belong and they know I don't belong. My Midlands repartee isn't up to scratch, the girls with their heavy make-up, pearl-white underwear and sunbed ultra-tans are all too brassy and terrifying to flirt with, the men only interested in football and cars and anything else I know nothing about. I'm like a struggling Cockney comic on his first professional gig at a Northern working men's club.

It starts bearably enough: just the occasional sotto voce

rendition from the back of the queue of 'Whoi are we waiting?' and the odd mildly aggrieved query about why the round cost £4.70 this time when last time it was only £4.65 for exactly the same drinks and I try to explain that it all depends on whether you count the blackcurrant cordial as a shot in which case it's 5p or a full measure in which case it's 10p, but don't worry, if I charged you £4.65 last time, it's what I'll charge you this time, awroit?

But after an hour or so's relentless relentlessness *sans* fag, *sans* drink, *sans* the remotest sign of apprecation from anyone I serve, my veneer of barely-contained competence begins to crumble. I fail to register anyone's order until it's repeated at least three times, I get the proportions wrong on the mixers, and I always fumble the adding up, not to mention the counting out of people's change which, contrary to Trace's optimistic predictions, they're always extremely careful to collect. I've started to lose it. I'm growing afraid. And the punters can smell my fear. Some are merely pissed off that they can't get their next round as soon as they'd like; others have started to relish my suffering. Out of the corner of my eye, I notice pairs and trios of lads, nudging each other in the ribs.

'Go on. Ask him for a screwdriver,' I hear one of them say.

No doubt the sensible response would be to harden my heart, to stiffen my resolve, prove them all wrong. But I don't. I start feeling sorry for myself. I ham up my incompetence, I abandon all pretence that I'm a local who talks just like them, I explain time and again in my public school voice how sorry I am but I'm new to this job and I've a memory like a sieve and I never was much good at maths. I'm like the shattered, bloodied gladiator lying in the dust with the trident pressing against his neck, waving a floppy arm towards the baying crowd in a last frail plea for mercy. 'Don't hurt me, please. I know I've been crap. But I'm a nice guy really.'

Naturally, as one, the crowd all jerk their thumbs towards the floor.

'And this next one's for the barman,' announces the DJ, putting on the next record. It's by the Beatles.

'Help!'.

Selling out

'The thing I normally recommend to a young man in your position,' says the man at the other side of the desk, 'is a career in investment banking.'

And I know he only met me for the first time half an hour ago and I know I'd been hoping he might suggest something a bit groovier. Advertising, maybe. Film. Books. TV. Journalism. But he is a professional careers adviser. He must know what he's talking about.

Anyway, now that he has said it, I can see it makes perfect sense. I've told him my most important job requirement: to make lots and lots of money as quickly as possible. And there aren't many careers better for that than investment banking. Apart, maybe, from management consultancy. The starting salary at Bain, I've heard, is £22,000 p.a. But everyone knows – we've all become instant experts in this field, of late – that jobs in management consultancy are impossible to come by. There are about a thousand applicants for every place. Whereas banking is a doddle. Something to do with Big Bang.

So that's already two excellent reasons for becoming a merchant wanker. Minimum effort; oodles of dosh. And I've just thought of another: my new suit. My father paid to have it made for me by a tailor in Solihull so I'd look extra smart in the family photo my step-mother was determined to commission from a professional photographer. And a very nice suit it is too: charcoal grey flannel, double breasted, turn-ups and pleats on the trousers, the apogee of Eighties style. If I had a job in the City, I could wear it every day.

Plus – the reasons are flowing in thick and fast now, overwhelming any minor reservations I might have, like a total lack of interest in finance – it's a sign that I've finally grown up. I've put aside all those silly adolescent notions about writing the Great English Novel; I've stopped cruising through life expecting some plum job or vast fortune to be dropped into my lap; I've recognized that it's time to put away childish things, pull up my bootstraps, push the envelope and stake a proactive claim in my gilt-edged future.

Plus, I'll be 100 per cent, cast iron, guaranteed socially smart. I won't be the minor-public-school-educated son of a Midlands businessman with a Black Country accent. I'll be a plummy-voiced merchant banker with a huge house in London and another one in the country with a tennis court and a swimming pool (probably indoors), skiing holidays, long summer vacations, a company car, a pension plan, company health scheme, free gym membership, share options, cheap mortgage facilities, a drop dead gorgeous wife, smart kids put down at birth for Eton, a Labrador, a stake in a shooting syndicate, stables, half a dozen hunters, a string of polo ponies, a fine wine cellar, a yacht, a helicopter, a private jet—

'What do I do next?'

'It's all explained in this leaflet,' says the careers adviser.

A Career In Investment Banking, it says.

*

Going to see my friend and would-be literary mentor Jackson Grunewald immediately afterwards is a stupid idea, I know it is, but I can't help it. It must come from the same subconscious urge that drives errant husbands to forget to wipe the lipstick from their collar or remove the love letters from the inside pocket of the jacket their wife is about to take to the cleaners: deep down they want to be found out so that they can be chastised and punished and mortified and forced to feel as bad as they know they deserve to feel.

Jackson does not take it well. But then, being the very antithesis of a career in investment banking, Jackson wouldn't. Jackson has a brain the size of China. He knows everything there is to know about everything. He has a work ethic that makes Stakhanov look like Al from *Married With Children*. If he'd wanted to, Jackson could be earning stratospheric sums as an LA lawyer or the VP of a Wall Street bank. Instead, he's slumming it in Oxford, pursuing the doctoral studies he can't remotely afford, using whatever little time he has spare to complete his first novel, write articles for *Sports Illustrated* and cultivate a select body of undergraduates of which I, until about ten seconds ago, was among his favourites.

'Well, you make it easy on me. It'll make one less worthless acquaintance I don't have to trouble with,' he says, his bear-like body – he resembles a cross between Orson Welles and Meatloaf – squeezed into a tiny chair before a desk piled high with half-edited manuscripts.

I reach forward and stroke his arm gingerly, like he's some enormous, unpredictable cat. 'Oh, come on,' I say. 'You know you love me really.'

'Josh, this isn't remotely something to joke about.'

I stop stroking him and pull a face that says he's a big meanie. It still doesn't work.

Jackson continues: 'The person I thought I loved – liked, at any rate, I don't think you ever quite made the love league – wanted to make his career as a writer.'

'I still do.'

'So you're not going to be a banker?'

'It didn't do T. S. Eliot any harm.'

'T. S. Eliot was a genius,' he says. 'And, I'll have you know, he contemplated suicide while at Lloyds.'

'OK, but how else am I going to support myself while I write?'

'There are other ways.'

'Yeah, but they involve being poor.'

His expression is pure disgust. Which makes me sort of disgusted with him. I want to tell him: 'Look just because you happen to feel comfortable wearing the same smelly old clothes and living on junk food doesn't mean everyone has to.'

But I don't because I know he'll only go into one of his savage lectures about the grotesque snobbery of the English and about why is it that he, an American, can be friendly with undergraduates from all walks of life but that whenever he makes the mistake of trying to get them together they all hate each other because they went to the wrong sort of school or speak with the wrong sort of accent or wear the wrong clothes and what kind of pissy little two-bit country is this anyway?

That's one reason I don't try criticizing him. The other is that he's actually quite sensitive and I don't want to upset him. I mean he's about the only real person I know. And I remember how exciting it was when first we went for coffee in the Covered Market, just the two of us. Before that, it was always with our mutual friend Marcus and Marcus, being jealously possessive of his pet American postgrad novelist, might well have preferred it to stay that way. So we had to be subtle. Like we were having an affair almost. And when we did come together, it was like your first proper date with someone you've fancied for so long but never dared ask out, where you can scarcely speak for fear of revealing yourself to be incompatible with this person you so desperately want to get on with, and where little by little you discover – oh joy – that this person and you, you agree about pretty much everything, about art and literature, about movies, about food, about work, about mutual friends, about the meaning of life, about people – the many, many people – who are Evil and Must Die, and you realize then that this one is for ever, it's a match made in heaven, it's the real thing.

Plus he's a published novelist. Or an about-to-be-published novelist with contacts and a contract which is damn near the same thing. And how many of those do you ever get to meet or call your friend? How many of them are you lucky enough to have advise you on how to write a novel of your own?

'It's not compulsory, you know,' I say. 'There are other careers besides "literature".'

'None that you'd be as good at,' he says. 'You're singularly cut out for nothing else.'

'How do you know?'

'I get it from your essays, from the way you talk,' he says. 'The way you are. Why can't you see you're absolutely useless as anything but a writer or possibly a houseboy to some old queen in Kensington who wears a muumuu and keeps lapdogs? I thought you were going to be brilliant.'

'Please. Name me one of your friends who you don't think is going to be a brilliant writer.'

'Most of them.'

'I'm flattered.'

'Why on earth would I flatter you? Your ego is colossally oversized at it is. I just want you to know what you're about to throw away.'

'I'm not throwing anything away. I will write that book, I promise.'

'By the time you do, it won't be worth reading. You'll be all used up. Do you think I haven't seen this before? "Oh, I'll just go into banking for a few years to make some money to give me the time to write." Only by the time you've made your money, you've forgotten what it was you wanted it for. And whatever imagination, whatever extravagance of thought, whatever outrageous and untenable ambitions your youth and ego and creativity could have called forth, all of that will be dulled and smoothed over and thought to be silly and impractical and you won't be worth a shit to me, as a writer or a friend. Because being a writer *is* silly and impractical! It's the very stupidest thing to do, reserved for a class of people who can't imagine themselves doing anything else. Who, if told they could never write or be a writer, would likely become a suicide or at least make a decent go of alcoholism. And clearly, sadly, you *can* imagine doing something else, so I radically misjudged you, which is my fault.'

As he speaks I search his face for some indication that this is all an elaborate joke. I mean friendships, surely they don't end so suddenly over an issue quite so trivial. Do they? And surely, I ask him, surely he must have at least a handful of stockbroker, banker, lawyer friends who have slipped through the net?

'I don't need, and the world doesn't need, any more of them,' he says quietly. 'If you go to the City I won't even know you in five years. And neither of us,' his voice falters, I think, 'neither of us will think that a shame.'

'Oh, Jackson. Please. Can't we talk about something else?'

'What amusing trifle would you care to discuss instead?'

'Your book. You said you were going to let me see what you'd done to that last chapter.'

'I was,' says Jackson pointedly, gathering up his things to leave. 'I was.'

*

'Obviously an understanding of finance would be helpful,' says the well-scrubbed young head prefect from Barclays de Zoete Wedd, standing in front of his white projection screen in a plush, high-ceilinged conference suite at the Randolph Hotel. 'But what we're really looking for are proactive team players who are keen to take on new challenges in a dynamic business environment . . .'

I'm about to light a cigarette, to keep myself awake, when I notice that no one else is smoking. Not even the people who I know for a fact smoke loads, loads more than I do. Very discreetly, I slip my Camel Lights back into my suit pocket. It's only the milk round but you never know. Maybe this is part of the test.

'At BZW, we're very proud of our graduate trainee programme. By the end, you will have had a full grounding in every aspect of your chosen speciality. So please don't worry if, at present, you don't know too much about investment banking. Nor did any of us when we started,' says head prefect, exchanging chucklesome looks with the colleagues gathered either side of him.

'In fact, if it makes you feel better, I can tell you that on day one, there's at least one graduate trainee who doesn't even know what a fax machine is for!'

He laughs and most of his undergraduate audience laughs with him. I laugh too. I mean it's pretty bloody obvious, the name's a giveaway: some sort of computery device that spills out facts – business figures, pork belly prices, that sort of thing.

About five days later the presentation ends and we can hit the free booze. Some of my rivals – as I must now learn to see them – have other ideas. They gather round each BZW representative, ostentatiously sipping orange juice, sucking up with creepy questions, looking eager and earnest. It's scary. And it's not just here, you can feel it all over the university. Like some evil witch has waved her wand and turned a whole year of reckless hedonists into earnest, grey old suits.

I stand near a potted palm with my housemate Duncan the Snake, one of the few others to have risked a glass of wine.

'I'm gagging for a fag,' I tell him.

'Why don't we?'

'What do you reckon?'

'I reckon what they're really looking for is people who can be themselves.'

And while the bug concealed in the palm fronds records every word of our conversation, a tiny BZW video camera concealed in the hotel wall zooms in to catch us lighting up.

*

Banking jobs, I learn, fit into two broad categories. Total bastard ones. And marginally less unpleasant ones.

The total bastard ones divide into two sub-categories. Those at Japanese banks, where Europeans are considered a sub-human slave species to be worked like prisoners building the bridge over the River Kwai. And those at American banks, where you can't leave your desk before midnight and where you have to spend your only free time on Sunday mornings playing softball in the park with perky Harvard Business School graduates in blue button-down shirts and chinos. In return for your life, youth, energy and personality, both American and Japanese banks pay unfeasibly vast sums of money.

The marginally less unpleasant ones are mostly English and all crap. They know they can't compete with top players like CSFB, Goldman Sachs or Nomura, so they don't pay as much and are happy to employ less able candidates.

All my research energies are dedicated towards finding which firms are crappest and therefore easiest to get into. Like Oxbridge entry, all over again.

*

Some of my contemporaries are taking this whole business far too seriously. My housemate Warthog, for example.

At the beginning of the spring term, I wander into his bedroom for an idle chat, as you do with close friends that you haven't seen after the Christmas vac.

'Hi, Warty,' I say. 'How've you been?'

Warthog doesn't reply. He carries on silently unpacking his clothes, arranging his records, stacking his pile of new books about economics, the stock market and finance on his shelves.

I watch him, quietly amused. He's got a kind, generous side, has Warthog. But he can also be rather wild, sociopathic, and unpredictable, hence the nickname.

'God, you're not actually going to read them, are you?'

I say. 'I've spent five minutes on that Tim Congdon and I didn't understand a word.'

Warthog continues with his arrangements, for all the world as if I'm not there.

I linger with more intent now. To bait him. It's quite fun, warthog-baiting. He hates his nickname, hates being teased about his eccentricities. And simply by being here, I'm training a spotlight on his foibles so that he can see how stupid they are and annoying and pathetic.

And rude. I mean I am one of his best mates. I've stayed at his house, I get on with his parents; we've got hogwhimpering drunk together, shared most of our darkest secrets. So this is hardly what you'd call an acceptable response to a civil question.

Eventually I get bored.

'Let me get this right. For some weird warthoggish reason, you've decided you're not going to speak to me. Yeah?'

Naturally, he doesn't respond.

Nor does he – and you'll hardly believe this but it's true – for the rest of term. Not until he has been offered a job by whatever firm he'd decided he wanted to join, Warburgs, I think.

When it's all over, I ask him to explain himself.

'You were competition,' he says.

*

Surprisingly, I get through to the second-round interview stage with only one bank of the umpteen I applied to join. It's called Robert Fleming and I know as soon as I walk in that I'm going to be happy there, because it has a sexy glass atrium with jungly foliage and an aura of big swinging-dick kudos; because it has lots of modern art by painters I've heard of on the walls, which must mean it's interested in other things besides boring old finance.

I'm given a badge to wear with my name on it (not handwritten but pre-printed, which shows how seriously they're taking me) and I'm escorted by a friendly graduate trainee to meet different people in different departments, so I can get an idea as to which area of investment banking might suit me best.

Everything's so much easier than it was in the first-round interviews. Then, you were grilled by a professional interviewer from the personnel department, who asked you searching questions about your CV.

Now though, it's less a case of you trying to impress them than of them trying to impress you. It's great. They're all over me: the friendly graduate trainee who assures me that if you've got this far, it's pretty much a shoe-in, and yeah, he thought banking was going to be piss-dull too, but it has its moments; the smoothie from fund management who, noticing that 'cooking' features on my CV, waxes lyrical about his trade's unrivalled lunching opportunities; the baby-faced balding jack-the-lad who discovers I'm quite fond of gambling and assures me that trading stocks makes roulette look like My Little Pony.

My favourite is the middle-aged toff from corporate finance. He has one of those double-barrelled dynasty names I recognize – not Lane Fox or Sebag-Montefiore or Hanbury-Tenison, but something in that region. And he's very old school: florid; paunch; braces; ultra-polished shoes; perfectly cut chalk-stripe suit; indolent air – the type I'd feared that the post-Big Bang invasion of workaholic Americans had driven out of the market.

We sit in his not-very-big office and talk of anything but

banking. I speak in my poshest accent and somehow work the Christ Church beagles into the conversation.

Then he glances at the clock, yawns and swings his feet on to his desk.

'So,' he says, stretching far back in his chair. 'I suppose you think corporate finance is all about putting your feet up on your desk, swanning off on foreign jaunts and being paid large amounts of money to do not very much. Is that the sort of career you were looking for?'

And I can sense this a test of some sort. What he doesn't want to hear me say is: 'Oh good Lord no. I'm looking for something far more dynamic and challenging, something where I can really get to grips with the world of finance.' Because then he'll know I'm either a liar or the sort of over-reaching workaholic that could put him out of a job.

What he wants, clearly, is a kindred spirit, someone he can trust not to rock the boat.

So I give him a big smile and say: 'Absolutely.'

Peel me a grape

It's not often you get to utter a single sentence that ruins your whole life. But, God, I came close in the final stage of my Oxford entrance interviews, in the autumn of 1983. I'd done all my interviews with the Christ Church English dons; and I'd even been sent for interview at my second and third choice colleges, Oriel and Mansfield, which didn't augur well, I didn't think.

The nail in my coffin was when I was called up for interview with a panel of dons headed by the Dean of Christ Church.

'So, Mr Devereux,' the Dean asked. 'What do you plan to do if you don't get into Oxford?'

You could almost hear the thud as my heart hit the floor. After two days of interrogation, your paranoid brain grows quite expert at deciphering the subtext beneath apparently innocuous questions. You hardly needed an Engima machine for this one.

My lower lip plunged, as it does when I'm gutted beyond measure. My throat felt like the strings on a tennis racket and my eyelids begin involuntarily to quiver as I thought of all those years, days, hours, minutes, seconds and milliseconds I'd spent fantasizing about how totally ace it would be to get into Oxford, even to the extent of practising my imaginary future address out over and over again – Josh Devereux, Christ Church, Oxford, and about how in the space of a moment, my dreams had been tossed whimpering into the Isis like a sack of puppies.

I knew how I wanted to reply. 'Suppose I'll just have to top myself,' I was on the verge of croaking back, because that's what I thought and that's how I felt, and there didn't seem anything to lose at this stage by speaking my mind.

Heaven knows what miracle of self-control and maturity led me to amend it half way through to a less histrionic, 'Suppose I'll just. have to go to Exeter instead.' But I'm convinced it made all the difference. Think about it. You're the Dean of Christ Church, you're vetting borderline candidates for entry into your college, and you're confronted with one who threatens that if you don't let him in, he's going to kill himself. Do you think: Oh dear, poor chap, if it means that much to him I suppose we'd better let him in? Or do you think: Christ, we've got another wrist-slitter. Let's pack the bugger off to Exeter as soon as we can.

I've thought about this incident a lot over the years. I'm thinking about it now at the farewell dinner in the Senior Common Room which has been laid on for all the Christ Church English undergraduates by all the Christ Church English dons. To think, I'm thinking, that if I'd said what I almost said instead of what I actually said, I would have missed out on all this.

By 'all this', of course, I don't just mean the farewell dinner, I mean the whole of my three years at Oxford, from that very first night in hall when I wore my gown for the first time and heard my first Christ Church grace and got so intimidated by the grandeur of my surroundings and suddenly here I am fast forwarded to now and not being intimidated or impressed any more, just mildly sad and valedictory. It seems a shame, really, to be leaving just as I've got to know the place.

I look at the faces round the long table – undergraduates', dons', undergraduates', dons' – and wonder whether my year-mates are thinking similar thoughts. Bet they are, even the cool ones with weird haircuts who campaigned to have Anglo-Saxon pulled from the Oxford English curriculum, who always acted like there'd been some terrible mistake with their UCCA forms, like they shouldn't really have come here at all, they should have been somewhere more red-brick and credible. It's like leaving school, all over again. You hated the place; you want to tell your teachers exactly what you thought of them. But when the moment comes, you're paralysed by nostalgia. You realize you weren't nearly as miserable here as you per-suaded yourself at the time; that actually, the old dump had its good points; that, in fact, sob, you were happier here than you'll ever be again.

'Any plans after this?' asks the don to my left. She's called Petra and she's a Marxist Feminist.

'Yeah, we've got this brilliant champagne called Cremant de Cramant, which if you haven't tried you really should, chilling in Molly's fridge. Come and join us. There's still loads left after finals and after this evening I'm not sure I want to drink the stuff ever again,' I say and I'm not trying to wind her up by acting like a stereotypical Hooray Henry, it's more that I like her and it would be an enormous coup luring a Marxist Feminist don to drink champagne with you in your rooms and besides I'm beginning to realize that I'm more drunk than I thought. Obviously with so many dons around and so much potential for embarrassment I've been trying to pace myself. But this being the Senior Common Room, there's this overzealous waiter type behind my back who, whenever

I'm not looking, keeps filling my glass with rather good claret or Sauternes it is now, now that we're at the pudding stage.

'Thank you. That's very kind,' says Petra. 'I was thinking more of your plans after leaving college.'

'Oh. *That*. Real life, you mean? God, no,' I say, staring thoughtfully – well, dazedly – at my fruit plate. The grapes are delicious, Muscat, I think I heard someone say, but they've got these thick, bitter skins which are much better peeled off, if you can be bothered. 'Except obviously, whatever it is, I want it to involve being paid masses. I mean, I know it's the last thing I should be saying to a Marxist Feminist—'

'I'm a Marxist Feminist, am I?'

'Aren't you?'

'It's not how I introduce myself at parties.'

'But you'd concede you come a bit closer to fitting the bill than I do?'

'Yes,' says Petra, with a smile. 'I think I would be prepared to concede that.'

'So anyway, my point was – and I know this is disgusting but there it is – I just don't think I was born to be poor. These grapes, for example. I think it's an absolute bloody outrage, I really do, that I have to peel off the skins myself. So that's one of the things I'm going to do when I'm rich. I'll employ someone as my personal grape peeler.'

I think the main reason I'm talking like this is that I've acquired an audience. Su, the even-more-feminist-and-Marxist-than-Petra undergrad with dyed pink hair; Darius, the tall, enigmatic Old Etonian; even Mr Kurtz and Mr Maldon, my distinguished, terrifyingly diffident Anglo-Saxon-tutor-cum-unofficial-MI5-recruiter who I'm still not sure knows my name, have started tuning into our conversation.

'Do you think that's excessive of me?' I continue.

'Absolutely not,' says Petra. 'I should say with a man of your refinement, it's de rigueur.'

'Well if you're interested, I could audition you now. Petra, a peeled grape, please. And be spry about it,' I say.

As it happens, Petra already has a mostly-peeled grape on her plate. She cuts it nearly in half, scrapes out the pips and makes to put it in her mouth. Then a thought seems to strike her and she holds it out, slightly uncertainly towards me.

I open my mouth like an expectant dog and indicate with my finger where the grape should go.

Petra pops it in.

'Wow!' I say, feeling my cheeks begin to burn, because I didn't think she would do it, nor I'd guess did Petra, and everyone's staring at us and I suddenly feel like the most outrageous exhibitionist.

'When I've made it, the job's yours,' I say, blushing.

'Has he told you what he got up to in his finals?' asks Mr Kurtz from the other side of the table.

Petra shakes her head.

'Oh, I didn't in the end,' I say.

'Didn't what?' says Petra.

'I had this plan that I was going to turn up for my last exam dressed as a girl. Then I chickened out.'

'Very wise, I'm sure,' says Petra.

'Do you reckon? I've been worrying that it was a big mistake. Don't you think it would have been a good story to tell my grandchildren?' I say.

'Ah, but what if you'd flunked the exam and never become rich enough to employ a personal grape peeler?' says Petra.

'Oh dear, I was kind of hoping exam results didn't make all that much difference. They don't, do they? Not unless you want to become an academic or join the Foreign Office or something.'

'I'm sorry to hear you won't be joining us in academe,' says Mr Kurtz.

'Yeah right, like that was ever an option. Wouldn't have minded the foreign office, though. Or MI5, come to think of it, if Mr Maldon hadn't already turned down the golden opportunity to employ me,' I say, looking across to where Mr Maldon is shifting uncomfortably. 'Bet I'd have been really good,' I tell him. 'Especially with honey traps.'

'Yes and you've got just the right degree of modesty and self-effacement,' offers Molly.

'Hey you can hardly talk, and they still offered . . .' 'you a job' I was going to continue say before I check myself and continue, after a pause, 'But I do take your point. Hiding in alleys and not revealing myself probably isn't the thing I was born to do.'

'Quite the opposite,' says Mr Kurtz. 'Maybe you shouldn't even be trying to get a job. Maybe you should hire yourself a public relations assistant and just *be*.'

*

'You were on sparkling form,' says Molly, sullenly. She fills two champagne flutes and passes one to me.

'Are you cross with me?'

'No.'

'Yes you are. You're pissed off with me for mentioning that MI5 thing.'

'It was a bit hard on Mr Maldon, poor sweetheart. No one's supposed to know he's their recruiting officer,' she says.

'Everybody does,' I say.

'That's not the point. There are some things you just don't blurt out in public.'

'Why not?'

'Josh, darling, if you don't know that after three years at Christ Church . . .'

'Oh good, at least you're not patronizing me.'

'Well, it was why you came here, wasn't it? To learn how to be smart, how to do things properly?'

'God,' I say, reaching for my cigarettes, 'you really are in a bad mood.'

'Maybe occasionally you could consider other people's feelings instead of always trying to create an effect.'

'I'm sure Mr Maldon is big enough to handle it.'

'I don't just mean Mr Maldon.'

'Who else did I offend? Petra? She loved playing the grape game. Su? Serves her right for being such a fucking lefty. Mr Kurtz? He likes me. He thinks I should spend the rest of my life being me.'

'Oh God,' Molly groans, 'we're never going to hear the end of that one.'

'You've got to admit, it was a pretty cool thing to be told.'

'I think I preferred you as the sweet gauche thing you were when we met.'

'When you could control me, you mean?'

'I never controlled you.'

'Course you did. It's half the bloody reason I'm the way I am now.'

'Now you're scaring me.'

'Yeah, well wake up and smell the coffee, Dr Frankenstein. If you hadn't taken the piss so much during my tweeds and beagling phase, I might still be that meek, polite, would-be toff you apparently found so sweet and endearing.' I refill my glass. 'Oi. Have I got to finish this stuff by myself?'

Molly drains hers and I refill that too.

'When did I take the piss?' she says.

'All the time.'

'Give me one example.'

'OK. Um – yes. When my brother came to stay.' I pause, involuntarily. It's not an incident we've mentioned since, and I wish I hadn't now. 'When you said how much cooler he was in all his ethnic gear.'

'You changed your whole image, just because of me? How sweet!'

'I never said "just". There were loads of other reasons.'

'Yes, but I was one of the main ones – that's what you said.'

'You're taking it completely the wrong way.'

Molly takes a long exultant swig of champagne. I refill her glass.

'Are you trying to get me drunk?' she says.

'You're doing a good enough job yourself.'

'Perhaps we should stop now before we do something rash,' says Molly, but not as though she means it.

'I think we should be drunk all the time,' I say.

Molly gets up to change the record. More Edith Piaf. Apart from Nina Simone, and a Tom Waits record Marcus must somehow have foisted on her, it's the only popular music she has. I'm thinking she probably missed my literary joke, but when she comes back she says, half teasingly, half goadingly, 'You never did find your Sebastian Flyte.'

'Probably because they're all wankers.'

'He came to the House a social climber; he left a class warrior.'

'Then what am I doing with a filthy toff like you?'

'Maybe I'm your Sebastian,' she says.

'Wasn't Sebastian supposed to be beautiful and charming?'

'Wasn't Charles supposed to be sympathetic?'

More refills. We've now drunk half a bottle each, not counting what we had at dinner, but I've no urge to stop and nor, it seems, does Molly. Where is all this leading? Tears? Sex? Bloodshed? Definitely something in that league. The room's so charged you could power the city off it. But Molly isn't offering much by way of a clue.

I pop open the next bottle – with some difficulty: Mumm Cremant de Cramant has a special cork which is a bugger to open – and slop some in Molly's glass.

Glad you've cheered up, anyway,' I say.

'*I've* cheered up?'

'It wasn't me who got into a huff about dinner,' I say.

'It wasn't me who got so touchy about not being as cool as my younger brother.'

'Touchy? All I was saying was—'

'Touchy!' she repeats in an annoying, playground voice.

'You're drunk.'

'And you're not, I suppose?'

'Sober enough to know the real reason why you were so cross at dinner. It was the grape business with Petra.'

'I was bloody embarrassed, if that's what you mean.'

'Nothing to do with jealousy, then.'

'Why should I be jealous of her?'

'Yes, well quite, I mean putting aside the glaringly obvious facts that she's way too old for me and I don't fancy her in the slightest, there's that other small detail about you and I not being a couple.'

'Don't sound too bitter.'

'I just don't think that being my friend gives you the right to get jealous whenever I do some harmless flirting.'

'You can talk.'

'Yeah?'

'I wasn't going to mention it, but don't think I haven't noticed how you've been avoiding me for the last year,' she says.

'What? You're always in the bloody library.'

'It never stopped you before.'

'Look, one's bound to spend less time socializing in one's final year.'

'Oh, one is, is one? One seems to have found time enough to hang out almost every night with Marcus.'

'We do live in the same house.'

'And to go off on lost weekends in Amsterdam.'

'So? If you smoked dope maybe I'd go with you to Amsterdam too.'

'My point is I know exactly why it is you've been avoiding me,' she says.

I give her my most brazen look, hoping she isn't going to say what I think she's going to say.

'It's because of Dick, isn't it?'

'No.'

'Because you've never forgiven me for that one tiny remark about Dick being cooler than you.'

Bitch, I want to say. Disingenuous bitch. But I don't. I just look at her coldly, as if to ask how on earth she can say such a thing without blushing. And she looks back at me, her deep grey eyes all fluttering, Bambi innocence.

I unclench my fist and reach for the bottle. It's got us into this problem, so it may as well get us out of it again.

When I've refilled both our glasses, I look at Molly

again, and say with a calm that surprises me, 'You slept with him.'

Molly is so busy affecting shock that at first she can't answer.

'No,' she says, at last.

'Molly, I was there, I saw.' And I explain to her the circumstances in which I discovered their secret.

'And you were there in the bedroom, watching as we made love, I suppose?'

'Oh right, so what's your version? Dazzled by my brother's extraordinary intellect, you were up half the night talking to him? Go on, tell me. I'm sure I'll be really convinced.'

'God, you can sound like the most sadistic, self-righteous pig, sometimes,' she says.

'I just don't like being lied to by my friends.'

'And I don't like it when I tell them the truth and they don't believe me.'

'And your version of the truth would be?'

'Not just my version, but the thing that actually happened. I bumped into your dazzling Lothario of a brother in the quad and invited him in for a small dram of my single-malt whisky which he did, before having another and yet another and then drifting off to sleep. I thought about waking him, but decided not to because I didn't think you'd be back yet, I stayed up to do some reading – *Othello*, I seem to remember, which as I'm sure you'll agree, my dear trusting Moor, was pretty bloody apposite – until I realized how late it was and sent your brother packing while I went to bed. Alone. And if you don't believe me, I'm frankly too cross to care because for my part I think it's a damned insult that you think I'm the sort of person who goes in for one-night stands with my friends' younger brothers. Good enough for you?'

Molly lights a cigarette. I light one too.

'Oh,' I say at last.

Molly stays silent.

'Well, I'm sorry, then,' I say.

Still no response.

'Very very very sorry,' I say.

Molly regards me suspiciously.

'Beyond sorry,' I say. 'Positively prostrate with repentance.'

'I don't see you kneeling,' she says.

I get down on my knees and shuffle across the floor towards her, my hands clasped in prayer. 'Please, please, forgive me,' I say, clawing piteously at her knees. While I'm there the thought flashes through my mind of how nice it would be to bury my head between her legs. I try to dismiss the thought before it takes too deep a hold.

'Enough,' she says, pushing me gently away. 'You're forgiven.'

'Oh,' I say, resuming my seat, only slightly closer to her than I was before. 'I was quite enjoying that.'

'Enjoyment is the last thing you deserve right now,' she says.

'That's a shame. I was just asking myself whether we ought to pop another bottle. As a toast to your not being the brazen hussy I thought you were.'

'You put things so charmingly,' she says.

'Well, shall we?'

'I'm completely hammered, aren't you?'

'Yes. But I quite like this idea of doing something we might regret.'

'Go on, then.'

'What? Open another bottle or do something we might regret?' I say.

'Either. Both. I'm not bothered.'

'Seriously?'

'Only if you stop dithering,' she says.

In a second, I've closed the remaining inches between us. Our legs are touching and I've an arm draped ambiguously round her back.

'Quick enough, for you?'

'Desperate, I'd say.' She studies me with curious fondness.

I kiss her experimentally on the mouth. Her lips part, but only slightly, allowing the tips of our tongues to meet just long enough for me to taste a hint of the essential Molliness beneath the more dominant notes of tobacco and champagne acidity. I'd like to explore further, but at the same time, I wouldn't. It's like kissing your sister almost.

Molly pulls away, but gently. 'Weren't you going to open that other bottle?'

'I thought you weren't bothered.'

'Well, if you want me to do something I might regret . . .'

'Don't you?' I say, cautiously taking her hand.

'Yes.' She gives my hand a squeeze. 'I think so. It's just . . .'

'What?'

'How exactly do we get there?'

'I was slightly wondering that myself.'

'I mean, it's not that I can't conceive of us, you know, doing it.'

'No, quite. I'm sure it would be great.'

'Me too.'

This might be the cue to thrust my tongue down her tonsils, put one hand down her bra and the other into her knickers. Instead, I find myself, locked into an exchange of sweet but gormless smiles.

'Do you think a joint would help?' she says, after a time.

'Maybe. But it might make you sick if you're not used to it. Especially after champagne.'

'I have tried it before.'

'And?'

'I found it quite relaxing.'

For one so drunk, I skin up with amazing dexterity and speed. But I'm still not quick enough to catch the tail end of the mood. Molly has got up to change the record and fetch some water. I've lost the bulge in my trousers. We're not even sitting bang next to each other. We're very nearly just-good-friends again.

Which is why I've taken care to make the joint – hash, unfortunately, not grass – extra strong. And why I hold in for as long as possible the three deep hits I take before passing it on to Molly.

Molly passes it back to me. I take some more. It's not particularly pleasant – there's that sickly sweet sausage taste to contend with – but it will no doubt serve its purpose. In Molly's case, it already has, for she shakes her head when I try passing it back and collapses dreamily in my arms.

I look down at her upturned face. Her eyes are closed. I would try kissing her again, except my head's spinning too much. Give it a few minutes, maybe. Try thinking about what's going to happen very soon, you know it's going to happen because she's already said that she wants to do it as much as you, and you both know it's going to be great, so there's no need to rush things now. It's going to happen.

'Molly.' I stroke her hair – as much for my own comfort as hers, because the head-spin's getting worse not better. I think I was going to add that I love her, but I can't get it out, what with this heaving motion I'm now feeling in my chest.

'Josh.'

'Mm?'

'I think I'm going to be sick,' she says, springing up from my lap and staggering towards her basin.

I rise stiffly to comfort her, but as I stand there, numb and tingling, rubbing her back, the smell from the basin brings me on too.

Once we've wiped our faces, cleared up the mess, drunk some water, we look at one another half amused, half appalled, suddenly very sober.

'Do you think someone up there is trying to tell us something?' she says.

'I do,' I say with a pale smile. 'And if you ask me, he's a rotten, rotten bastard.'

My brilliant career

Once the Warthog has landed a better job than anyone else, he invites a few of his closest rivals down to his parental home in Herefordshire, as he has every summer for the last three years. We play boules on the gravel drive, tennis on the scurfy courts beyond the kitchen garden, and mini-golf and croquet on the sloping lawn with views across oak-studded pastures towards the western edge of the Malvern Hills. In the evening we get drunk on real ale at the Green Dragon; drunker still on aperitifs in the sitting room with the fireplace so big you can stand either side with your head up the chimney while swaying in time to the muffled sounds of Harry James and his Big Band inflicted on us by Warthog Snr.; and quite paralytically drunk in the dining room with the Tudor ceiling rose mentioned in Pevsner, where Warthog makes sly digs at his mother's cooking, while Warthog Snr. treats us to endless refills of claret and port and even more endless tales of national service japes and scrapes with the London fast set in his Chelsea days with the legendary Rawlings Street Gang. 'Showing form' is what it's called.

Next day, we do it all over again, only with worse headaches and less energy. In the evening, we gather on the steps by the lawn, smoking Turkish cigarettes, downing Warthog Snr.'s obligatory white ladies as a flotilla of hot air balloons drifts over British Camp in the dying sun.

Warthog bum-shuffles next to me on the lichen-dappled flag and nudges me in the ribs. 'Chin up, Pleb,' he says. He's the only person who calls me this and I only include it for reasons of strict accuracy.

'Who says I'm down?'

'Aren't you?' he says with a warmth and sympathy I haven't heard him employ in a while. Of course I'm down. We're all down. It's the Last Summer of Our Youth.

'Yeah. A bit.'

'If you hadn't tried to post me—' he says.

'You fat cunt, you know it's got nothing to do with the croquet.'

'Good Lord, is that Devereux still banging on about the croquet?' booms Warthog Snr. jovially, bearing towards us with an overspilling jug.

'It's your arse of a son who can't stop talking about it. Is he not used to winning or something?'

As he tops up our glasses Warthog Snr. laughs. Teasing is another sign of 'showing form'.

'I'll have you know I haven't lost at croquet here since summer '83,' declares the Warthog.

'Yes, well, we know why,' says Duncan.

'Bugger off, Snake,' says Warthog.

'Yeah,' I say, 'because the second anyone else looks remotely viable, you start handicapping them with all these ludicrous House Rules like – what was today's again? – no croqueting the host unless the red ball is lying perpendicular to the third daisy on the right of the—'

'Dad. Defend me here.'

'Nor,' chips in Duncan, 'shall any player be permitted to

beat the host, unless there are three Rs in the month, not counting Leap years, Olympic years and any others which the host in his wisdom—'

'Dad!'

But now everyone has joined in. Warthog Snr. Mrs Warthog. Anna. Susanna. Marcus. Johnnie. Duncan. I wish we had a camera to capture it. It would be like those fading black and white snaps you see of Bright Young Things with tennis racquets and centre partings and silly expressions disporting themselves at grand houses in the Thirties. You look at these gilded youths, looking so much older than their age as people did back then, and you wonder who pulled whom, or whether maybe they were too buttoned-up to have sex in those days; and how many of them survived the war; and whether any of them had any inkling of what was to come, the deprivation, the destruction and death, then afterwards the end of their social order. I doubt it. You don't think these things at the time, do you? You think it's all going to go on for ever – that these people you're with, they'll always be your friends, you'll grow old together but never age, you'll share the same interests, be the same people, remain in the same income bracket, marry one another and have children who'll go to the same schools and the same colleges in a country which looks the same, where values don't change, where time stays frozen on this perfect day in this perfect English summer because that's how life is going to be for ever because you're young and you're beautiful and how could it not?

It's a shame you never really met these people. You would have liked them. Elegant, devious Snake with his Byronic curls and diffident manner. Or Anna. No way could you have not fancied Anna, that face of hers, really I think she's too implausibly lovely even to consider having sex with. No, on that front,

I think Melissa might have been a better bet – not that I would ever have dared myself, too experienced, too over-powering, but blimey you would have learned stuff. Bright too. Starred first from whichever weird college she was in, Mansfield, maybe? Swung both ways, I think, in case you're interested.

Warthog, too. This is the last you'll be hearing of him. He'll go his way, I'll go mine and though it's not the last we see of one another, God no, we'll spend many of the next few years flat-sharing, first just off High Street Ken, later in these truly extraordinary digs near Baker Street, like an Arab harem almost, which you'll get to peek at right at the end. So you might think it unfair to have him written out so early on. But that's how these things work. Some characters you keep, some you expand on, and some you have to kill for reasons of space. Same as with real life, in fact.

The laughter has begun to die now and Warthog Snr. looks at his son and says: 'How heartwarming it is to see a man command such respect and love from his friends.'

'Oh, I can understand it,' says Warthog. 'The resentment of the unemployed.'

The Snake grins. Last week he accepted a job offer from BZW, starting salary £15,000 p.a.

'Sod that,' I say. 'It's you and Snake I feel sorry for.'

'Hear, hear. Bankers are wankers,' says Marcus.

'Yeah, yeah, you say that now,' says Warthog.

'Yes, you think the milk round's not going to get to you but it does,' says Duncan. 'You go in there a dope-smoking Sandinista-loving hippy; a term later it spits you out with a briefcase and a pin-stripe suit.'

'It didn't with Josh,' says Marcus.

'Maybe he wasn't good enough,' says Warthog.

'Maybe he sabotaged his own interviews because he realized what a bunch of tossers you all are in the City; maybe he realized that there's more to life than trading in your personality for lucre', I say.

'Sounds a fair trade-off to me,' says Warthog.

'God, he even admits it,' says Marcus.

'Yes, well not all of us are in the fortunate position of having daddies who own half of Radnorshire,' says Warthog.

'I just think there've got to be more important things in life than money, that's all,' says Marcus. 'Melissa, Anna, what do you think?'

'Oh, as if they're going to give you an honest answer,' says Warthog.

Melissa breaks off her girlie chat with Anna. 'What was the question?'

'Which is more important: willy or wallet,' says Warthog.

'Both. Either. Depends,' says Melissa.

'Do we really have to choose?' says Anna.

'We were talking about jobs,' says Marcus.

'Good, just so long as we don't have to join in,' says Melissa, turning back to face Anna.

'They've got the right idea,' says Marcus.

'Only because girls don't need jobs. They just have to marry someone with one,' says Warthog.

'Or become their kept woman,' I say.

'Or go on the game,' says Warthog.

'Yeah, and when if they do get a job and they make a mistake or they're about to be sacked all they have to do is burst into tears and they'll end up with a pay rise instead,' I say.

'And our orgasms last ten times longer,' calls out Melissa.

'Fuck it. I'm getting a sex change,' I say.

'You could be the new Jan Morris,' says Warthog Senior.

'Who's Jan Morris?'

'Writer. Journalist. Used to be called James Morris,' he says. 'It's what you should be doing.'

'What? Chopping my goolies off?'

'Writing, you bloody fool. You ought to, you know. You write such damned good thank-you letters.'

'Or maybe you could find work for him, Dad, as your personal arse licker?' suggests Warthog.

'Journalism, that's what you should be aiming for.'

'Really?'

'You sound horrified.'

'Oh, it's not that, it's just – isn't it supposed to be one of those jobs that are really hard to get into?'

'You mean unlike investment banking?' says Warthog.

'I mean aren't you supposed have done loads of hacking on *Isis* and *Cherwell* and have all sorts of contacts?'

'If it's contacts you need, I've plenty of those,' says Warthog Snr.

'Well, that's very generous but um— aren't you supposed to experience a sense of vocation about these things? When I come to write my autobiography, say. Mightn't it look a bit crap if I go: Oh. Yeah. I was pissed on white ladies and a friend's old man thought I wrote nice thank you letters and oh goodness look where I ended up?'

Just a gigolo

Sometimes I look back mournfully at my past and think: 'If only I could have you all over again. I'd do it so much better.'

Like the time in my gap year when I headed off for the island of Spetses, which is where you find me now, lying prone on my beach towel beneath the August sun with my Rayban Wayfarers and my statutory copy of *Zen and the Art of Motorcycle Maintenance*. I'm twenty-two and the future is as golden as my skin: I'm in perfect health, my body ought to be at its physical peak, I have completed my education and earned a good degree, I have no financial commitments, my parents love me, and I can do what the hell I like for as long as I like because for the first time in my life I am free.

But as I sprawl on my towel beneath a perfect blue sky I have no time to think how lucky I am to be sprawling on a towel beneath a perfect blue sky because my mind is continually being assailed by nagging distractions of the sort you often forget years later when you're looking back on your gilded youth and wondering why you didn't enjoy it more.

Foremost among these is the dull, generalized ache of Protestant guilt – my awareness that some time this has all got to end and better sooner rather than later because there is work to be done.

Then there is Spetses. I came here because it's the island

in John Fowles's *The Magus*. So I was kind of expecting something mysterious and unspoilt, with tiny white houses, none of them less than a century old and a picturesque harbour with craggy Greek fishermen in brightly painted boats and weird millionaire magician types who invite you to their homes where you get involved with mysterious beautiful women and witness bizarre illusions involving Nazi soldiers.

But Spetses is not like that. It's a dumping ground for package tourists. And I'm really pissed off with my Lonely Planet guide for not having made this clearer; and for not having steered me towards one of the dozens of other islands that are still mysterious and unspoilt with tiny white houses none of them less than a century old etc. I can imagine them all now, floating in their wine-dark seas, taunting me with their pristine loveliness. And all the people who've gone to visit them congratulating themselves on how clever they were to have ended up there instead of Spetses.

Money, of course. You can never forget money. You haven't got much and the longer you'll stay the less you have. Unless you try earning some, but for the kind of work you're qualified to do – washing up, waiting, picking grapes – you're going to get less than nothing in a place like Greece. So this idea you've got about being able to stay here as long as you like – basically, it's bollocks.

And why would you want to stay here anyway? It's not like you're enjoying yourself. You don't know how to. Like, what did you do when you came to the beach? Did you position yourself near an attractive young female and attempt to chat her up? Of course not. You were too scared. You went and sat miles from anyone, so you couldn't even ask anyone to put suncream on the unreachable part of your back. Which is why you're now slightly burned and having to cover the sore bit with your T-shirt. As you'll continue to have to do for days now, thus denying yourself the perfect all-over tan you've spent so much of your life hankering after and are probably never again going to have an opportunity as good as this to acquire.

And *Zen and the Art of Motorcycle Maintenance* is shit. You thought it was going to change your life and it hasn't. You hoped there wasn't going to be any motorcycle maintenance in it but there is. More than you'd need, even if you had a motorbike. Besides, you're sick of reading.

What you want is a swim, but you daren't leave your stuff untended. You'll just have to leave it with the barman on the other side of the beach. But the barman won't let you till you've bought a drink. And you can't afford one yet because you're budgeting on only one cold drink per afternoon and you only had lunch three hours ago. In fact you might not even have an afternoon cold drink at all, because then you can allow yourself two beers in the evening instead of the usual one, enabling you to get mildly intoxicated rather than just frustrated and sleepy enough not to be able to read or write postcards.

You reach for your bottle of mineral water, wipe the sand from the rim and roll the lukewarm liquid round your mouth. You try to avoid tasting it as you do so, because it's probably stagnant. All that backwash, fermenting in the heat. But think of the money you're saving.

From the corner of your eye you see movement. You turn, squinting because it's directly into the sun, and see two girls approaching. Tanned, slim, possibly quite attractive though you can't be sure because of the glare. Not that it matters because they're not going to come anywhere near you. No reason. The beach is half-empty. There's loads of space.

They're quite close now, so you look down intently at your book, in case they see you looking at them and get scared off. If you were Greek or Spanish or Italian or French, you'd brazen it out and keep staring at them until you got a response. If you were Greek or Spanish or Italian or French, you'd get a lot more sex.

You're looking at the pages but you can't take in a word. It's like this in films where the escaped POW is hiding in a ditch, and he can hear the guards getting closer and closer. Now there's a pair of boots just inches from his head. The POW shrinks in desperation and terror.

'Excuse me?'

I look up, as if surprised. The two girls are standing above me. Both in brightly coloured bikinis with sarongs knotted around their waists; both clutching expensively-cheap-looking beach bags. The one who has spoken is more tanned than the other one, like in the Bergasol ad with the two blondes with their backs to you and the plaited hair. She is wearing pink-framed Lolita sunglasses and talks in a posh, husky voice.

'Do you mind if we sit here?' She gestures to a spot nearby.

'Er, no,' I say, meeting her gaze for as long as I dare. Which isn't very. In the dying moment before I look down again, I try to find an additional phrase which will indicate how utterly I don't mind if they sit there. But all I can manage before I pretend once more to be engrossed in the book I don't even like is a 'No. Go ahead.'

The girls go ahead.

Yet again, I've blown it. It would have been so, so easy to follow up with a 'So you're English too?' or a 'Hot enough for you?' Now the moment's gone and I'm never going to get it back. They've reverted to two-girlie-friends-on-a-beach-enjoying-each-other's-company mode; I'm the socially inadequate, bookish lone male who from now on they can ignore. If I try making conversation with them at this point it will sound strained; desperate, even. The sensible thing, really, would be to pack up, go home, have a wank. Staying here, I'll only torture myself with bitter thoughts of what might have been.

But I do stay to torture myself. Mainly because that's what I deserve; but partly also because of the tiny imbecilic voice squeaking that all is not yet lost, something might turn up.

'Yeah? Like what?' I ask it.

The tiny voice isn't sure. Maybe the girls have forgotten their fags and will need to bum one off me.

Seconds later, the posh dark one reaches into her bag and withdraws a bulgingly full packet of Marlboros, which she proffers to her friend. And yes, they do have a light.

I ask the tiny voice if it has any more bright ideas.

What if one of them goes to the loo, it suggests, and the other suddenly realizes that she needs her back rubbing with sun cream—?

Die, voice, I tell it. And I try to drown out its words with those of Robert M. Pirsig. 'Quality,' he keeps banging on about. Apparently, it has something to do with pondering things long and deep, doing them slowly. Like I sodding care. It's not going make me any better at picking up birds, is it?

I look up again and, sure enough, dark posh one is rubbing sun cream into light one's back. Then light one returns the favour. Maybe I should go and have that wank now. While the inspiration's still fresh.

It occurs to me that with an attitude like that, wanking may be the only sex I ever get for the rest of my life. If I want to get the real thing, I've got to be decisive; to be prepared to risk rejection. What I must do is think of cunning ways of resuming the conversation.

My first idea is to huff loudly at intervals, putting the book down disgustedly and then picking it up again with a 'Right, *Zen and the Art of Motorcycle Fucking Maintenance*, this is your last chance' expression on my face. Perhaps one of them might ask, 'Not enjoying your book then?' and I'll be in.

But either I don't do it ostentatiously enough. Or they're not interested in talking books. Or they think I'm mentally defective – my God, that's most likely isn't it? – they think I've got Tourette's syndrome.

My second idea is more successful but not a great deal more productive. I ask them if they'd mind looking after my stuff while I go for a swim. The dark one looks up from her book and goes, 'Yes. Sure,' which doesn't really invite further conversation, so I just say: 'Thanks' before heading off for my swim. And 'Thanks' again when I've had it.

'No problem,' says the dark one.

'Bloody is,' I'm thinking. 'That's just exhausted the last of my chat-up lines.'

It's at this point that a small miracle occurs. The light one asks me whether I'd mind looking after their stuff while they go for a swim; and the dark one says, 'Actually, babe, I'm going to stay here'.

And suddenly the dark-skinned one and me, we're alone. Whether she is the prettier of the two, I'm not sure because as usual I haven't dared look at them except indirectly or in the brief moments when we've talked. I daren't look at her now either. I'm just going to storm in there blind, hurl myself at that enemy machine-gun nest and whether I take the position or end up riddled and twisted on the wire I don't care any more, at least I'll have tried.

I decide not to act immediately: otherwise she'll get the impression that I've been waiting till she's alone so that I can take advantage of her. But suddenly, as if by some elemental force beyond my control I find myself pulled to my feet and saying: 'Excuse me—'

And then realizing that I haven't a clue what I'm going to say next.

She's lying on her back reading.

'Mmm hmm?' she says, barely moving. Just a slight tilt in the book so she can examine more clearly from behind her shades the specimen standing before her.

'I was wondering whether you'd mind putting a bit of cream on my back. It's just that I can't reach the middle bit and I think I might be getting a bit burnt,' I say.

If she wanted to destroy me she could. All it would take is a: 'Funny you didn't ask me that earlier, when my friend was here' or a 'Maybe you should put your shirt on, then.'

She sits up, draws her long, tanned legs towards her and says: 'So long as you don't have too many spots.'

'Oh, er, no,' I say, blushing. 'I don't think I do.'

'Just teasing,' she says. 'Come. Sit.'

I do as I'm told. She takes the pack of Ambre Solaire from my hand.

'You are terribly young, though,' she says, beginning to rub the cream into my shoulders. Not in an erotic way, I'm relieved to find, because I don't think I could cope with the embarrassment, but more with that brisk, determinedly professional manner that strangers properly adopt in these situations.

'Am I?' I'm not fishing for compliments. I'm genuinely surprised.

'Early twenties was Sara's guess. Mine was late teens.'

Strange girls talking about me unprompted. Wow!

'Oh,' I say, my throat going dry. 'Sara was right. I'm twenty-two.'

'Twenty-two!'

'Come on,' I say. 'It's not like you two are much older – er, assuming you even are older, I mean.'

'Wait till I tell Sara you said that.'

'Well, are you?'

'Didn't your mummy tell you it isn't polite to ask a woman her age?'

'OK. But if you are older than me, you don't look it. Seriously.'

'Thanks.' She gives me a light slap on the shoulder. 'There. All done. You might want to be careful with that middle bit. It does look slightly pink.'

'Oh. Right. Thanks. I'm Josh, by the way.'

'Charlotte.'

Now I suppose I could have found a way of prolonging the conversation. But that would be hubris. It would be like saying after sex with Meg Ryan, 'Now how's about we call up Julia Roberts for a threesome?'

Because haven't I already achieved far more in these last few minutes than any boy could dream? In the face of the most terrible anxiety, I have approached a beautiful stranger and engaged her in conversation; I have proved myself sufficiently undisgusting for her to be able to face rubbing cream into my back; I have discovered that she and her friend have been talking about me; and, finally, as I retrieved my sun-cream, I felt emboldened enough to meet her gaze for such a long time – at least two seconds and very possibly three – that her image is now indelibly printed in my brain.

If I had trouble reading *Zen and the Art of Motorcycle Maintenance* before, it's quite impossible now. All I can think is how clever and bold and manly I've been. I mean, Jesus! This is going to keep me in wank fantasies for months and months and months!

And here's Sara coming back and I know what they're talking about because there's a 'Did he really?', followed by a laugh and that queasily wonderful (and totally novel, it must be said) feeling you get when you're pretending not to notice that two beautiful women are looking at you, admiring your youth. This is all getting too much. I'll have to make a tactical roll on to my front.

Bugger. It's bloody uncomfortable, prodding the sand like that and being unable to have a rummage down your trunks to free things up a bit. And unless I can devise some sort of remedial action, I'm going to be stuck like this all day. I might even have to wait until they've gone. Which could be embarrassing. What if they come and say goodbye? What if—?

'Josh?'

Shit, fuck, bollocks, what do I do, what do I do?

'Mm?'

'Fancy joining us for a drink?'

'Er—' Down, Ponto! Down! Down, sir! DOWN.

'Only, if you don't, we could leave our bags here with you.'

'Oh right. Um—'

Was ever a man undone more comprehensively by his cock?

Of course, I want to come for a drink. OF COURSE I FUCKING DO.

'—Um—' I continue

And so embarrassing too. I must look bloody odd, stuck on my front like this. I wonder if they've guessed.

'Um. Sure. I'll look after your stuff,' I say.

'OK. Thanks. See you in a while.'

'Sure.'

Thanks, God. Thanks a lot. This one's going to haunt me for months, I'm thinking, as I watch the two girls recede, unless – will nothing rid me of this turbulent boner? Try to remember a very boring Greek lesson at school? Imagine French kissing my grandmother? Concentrate really hard on a page of *Zen and the Art of Motorcycle Maintenance*?

Worth a try.

They're in a pine forest on a camping expedition and Pirsig is going into great and unnecessary detail about how the pine needles feel and what the wood looks like and—

Eureka!

*

The girls are sitting at a round table, smoking fags and admiring the view of the young waiters. I dump their collection of heavy beach gear at their feet.

'Bored of *Zen*?' asks Charlotte.

'A bit, yeah,' I say, flopping into the chair opposite.

'What are you drinking?' asks Sara.

'Um, oh, thanks. Coke?'

'Coke?' says Charlotte disdainfully. 'It's almost gone five.'

'I know but if I drink before nighttime, I just get sleepy.'

'Darling, that is rather the point. We're having ouzo. Do you like ouzo?' asks Charlotte

'Yes.'

Charlotte waves to the barman. She indicates: 'Make that three.'

Sara pushes the Marlboros towards me.

'Thanks, I'm all right.' I say, reaching for my Golden Virginia. Important to show a bit of independence.

Charlotte becomes suddenly animated. 'Oh look, darling, he's got all the kit,' she giggles to Sara. '*Zen and the Art*; sweet little ethnic ankle bracelet; rolling tobacco—'

'Only because I like the taste.'

'Now you're not to be offended—' says Charlotte.

'I'm not.'

'—but there's something I've got to ask you,' she continues. 'Do you have in your rucksack a copy of *The Diceman* or *The Glass Bead Game* or very possibly both?'

'Neither.'

'Damn!' says Charlotte.

'Yes!' says Sara, punching the air. 'Your round, hon,' she adds, as the waiter puts on the table three glasses, a jug of water, and a large plate of calamari.

'Chin, chin,' says Charlotte, chinking glasses.

'Oh look, poor thing,' Sara says to Charlotte, with a pitiful eye on me. 'He's all confused.'

I draw for succour on my fag, then on my barely-dilute ouzo.

'I don't even like *Zen and the Art of Motorcycle Maintenance*. I think it's bollocks. And I think it's jolly unfair trying to write me off as some sort of stereotypical Euro backpacker, when you don't know anything about me. For all you know I might be fucking talented and clever, just down from Oxford and about to become incredibly famous and successful.'

'Is that true?' asks Charlotte.

'The Oxford bit anyway.'

'He's right, darling,' says Charlotte to Sara. 'We've been terribly unfair.'

'Cheer up, have a calamari,' Sara says.

'Yes, have a calamari,' agrees Charlotte. 'It must make such a change from tomatoes and stale bread.' She pinches my arm teasingly.

'Actually you're right,' I say. 'I can never afford calamari.'

'Darling. We must build this boy up.'

The way back to town is by bus. Charlotte squeezes into the seat next to mine and I don't feel awkward as I might have done earlier because we're proper mates now, not pathetic little boy v. grown ups, and anyway I'm sloshed.

I've got *Zen* open in front of me — not really taking anything in, it's just something to look at, while Charlotte looks at hers. I doubt she's reading either. I think, like me, she's a bit hoarse from talking and chain smoking. I like to think also that she's feeling slightly dejected. We've got on so well, but this bus ride is the last we'll see of one another. Tomorrow they fly home; tonight, they've got some un-get-out-of-able dinner arrangement with this rich local.

'Hey, can he conjure up visions of German soldiers and stuff?' I ask.

'God, that isn't why you came too?'

''Fraid so.'

'I'd say the Spetses tourist board owes John Fowles a fortune.'

'I'd say he should be sued under the Trades Descriptions Act.'

That's another thing I'm going to miss about my new friends. They've read stuff. You don't need to explain your jokes.

And they are both, I can now officially confirm having

spent a good couple of hours making full-on, unbridled eye-contact with them, very attractive. Charlotte especially. Charlotte whose long, suntanned arm is now resting against my own bare skin, jogging to the rhythm of the bumpy bus. Nice. Too nice. I think I may have to concentrate on *Zen* again.

Problem is, matters aren't being helped by Charlotte. She has shut her book now and one of her hands has drifted casually off her lap towards my outer thigh, resting on the skin just below my shorts. Whether it has been put there deliberately or accidentally, it's hard to tell. It's not doing anything. Just staying there. And if that's what it wants to do, I'm certainly not going to stop it. But it does mean having to press my book hard down on my crotch.

Now the hand has moved upwards. Again so subtly, almost imperceptibly, that it's still hard to be sure whether its owner is aware of what it's doing. If she were, I think she might be quite shocked. For the hand has now strayed far enough up my shorts for the tips of its fingers to reach the sensitive skin of my inner thigh. I don't want to but I can't help it: I grow suddenly very tense. The hand retreats.

'FUCK!' I mentally curse myself. 'Fuck fuck fuck fuck fuck.'

Then there's warm breath in my ear and that musky scent of tobacco mixed with alcohol.

'I'm so sorry, I should have asked,' murmurs Charlotte. 'Would you mind awfully if I seduced you?'

I try to gulp.

'Um no. Not at all.'

'Thanks.' She leans across slowly, kisses me gently on the side of the mouth and then withdraws, smiling.

Lightheaded, I step off the bus. I still can't believe this is happening. I keep having to look to reassure myself that it really is a woman's hand that I can feel in mine, that she hasn't run away since I last checked.

Dazed and malleable, I let her steer me through the streets, past head-swivelling, taverna-owners touting for early evening trade, round pale fat families, troops of dirty slappers and sunburned lads, through narrow alleys where funereal crones lurk in doorways and skinny cats prowl the gutters.

The girls' hotel is classier than the crumbling affair a few blocks away on whose roof I am sleeping. It has whitewashed walls, a small courtyard planted with cacti and succulents, and the bedrooms – I know this because I'm now in one; I am actually in Charlotte's bedroom – have large double beds and en suite bathrooms.

This is where it all goes wrong. I've just got her bra off when a man with a camera jumps out of the cupboard: 'So sorry,' she says, dressing, 'but my husband will insist on grounds for divorce . . .'

Or I tear off her knickers to reveal a set of dangly giblets. 'But I thought you must have realized,' he says tearfully.

Or I'm just about to shag her when there's the padding of naked feet from the direction of the bathroom. 'You don't mind if Stavros joins us?' she says, as a swarthy satyr bears down on my upraised arse.

She leads me by the tips of my fingers towards the bed.

'Well,' she says.

She might well be about to say something more, but it's too late, I've got my tongue deep in her mouth, I want to eat her alive, and I'm forcing her back on to the bed, one hand reaching behind her bikini top, the other diving under her sarong, between her legs.

There's just a moment as I'm pushing her down when she

tries to resist, 'No wait,' she tries to say, and tries to stay on her feet, but I'm not having it, she may have the experience but I have the strength, and now it's me who's in charge not her, and I can tell that she likes it, because she's not resisting any more, she's gorging herself on my lips and in my mouth and on my tongue as desperately as I am on hers, and she's rubbing her crotch against my fingers and reaching back to undo the bra clip, so that her breasts plop free.

As I caress one of her nipples, she moans so I bring up my other hand to feel her other one. They're not like any breasts I've felt before – not that I've felt that many, but they're not. The flesh is more yielding, the skin around the nipples more lumpy and bumpy, more sensitive too, to judge by her gasps as I tickle an erect nipple with the point of my tongue and then circle round the edge then draw it inside my mouth and suck. Older woman's breasts, I'm thinking smugly.

'Gently,' she says.

I suck more gently.

'Gently!' she says, so sharply that I draw back.

She strokes my hair, then draws the back of her hand down my cheek.

'So eager!' she chides.

She makes to slide off the bed. But I'm pinning her down, smothering her mouth with kisses, then her breasts. My hand has wormed beneath her bikini bottoms.

'No, wait,' she commands, pulling my hand away.

She slips out of her bikini, then she takes my hand and guides it back to where it was. 'There!' she says. So I slosh my middle finger aimlessly round the bit I think she meant. 'No, there. Can you feel it?' she says, this time guiding my fingers between the slippery folds until, yes, that bit does feel slightly different from the rest – harder, like a pearl in oyster. And just as elusive. As soon as I think I've got the hang of it, I lose it again, so that she keeps having to guide me back.

Why can't she just lie back and take my incompetence like any normal girl?

Then she makes it even more complicated. It's not enough that I stay on target; now I have to approach it in a particular way – not too gently, not too roughly, not too slowly, not too fast, not too close to the tip, but not too far away from it. Then, just when you've found your rhythm, the rules all change and she wants it done differently. This isn't sex. This is helicopter training.

'It's OK,' she says. 'You're doing well.'

'Oh, yeah. *Very* well.'

Then later. 'Very, very *very well.*'

And later: 'Oh God, you're good. Oh God, you're so good.'

And still later: 'Oh God, fuck me, please. Fuck me now.'

But when I try fucking her, she's suddenly changing her mind. 'Bad boy.' She hops off the bed. 'You nearly made me do something silly.'

I grin wolfishly.

When Charlotte returns from the bathroom, she's holding a small, flat plastic case that I guess may be a powder compact. 'Do you know how to fit a cap?'

'Not really.'

'You should learn.' Here, you squeeze the edge like this—' She demonstrates and then passes the diaphragm to me. It reminds me of the sort of thing a performing gerbil might burst through at the circus. I'm at once fascinated and appalled. On the one hand it looks so desperately unsexy, so clinical, so gynaecological; on the other, it's quite a privilege to be entrusted with an item which has been up this woman's cunt dozens of times. Perhaps hundreds of times. Which rather begs the question, how many different penises have at one time another shot their load towards this thing I'm holding. Which rather begs the answer, don't even think about it.

When I squeeze the edge it twangs out of my hand on to the bed.

Charlotte looks unimpressed. I retrieve it quickly and assume an eager-to-learn expression.

'OK, so you squeeze it with some of this,' she says.

'Lubricant?' I ask.

'Spermicide,' she says.

I have to say this is all getting a bit off-putting. More *Carry On, Doctor* than *Emanuelle III*. Like, here I am looking at a woman's splayed legs and I'm getting no erotic pleasure out of it whatsoever. All I can think of is angles of entry, how to get it in without hurting her or losing too much of the spermicide or losing my grip on the springy sides, and how I really don't think this a man's job at all. It's her vagina, for God's sake. Why should I have to deal with it?

When I've finally done it, though, I have to admit that I do feel a mild flush of pride. Like when you've ironed a shirt. Like how Andy McNab feels at the end of *Bravo Two Zero* after he's been frozen and starved and had his teeth smashed in and been tortured half to death by the Iraqis. It's not something you'd like to do all that often. But now it's over and you've proved you can do it, you're glad the opportunity arose.

'Now—' she says, feeling for my willy which inevitably has gone limp after all that technical work. Not that she's remotely phased, she just dives down straight for it. But instead of putting it in her mouth, as I expect, she gives the tip one teasing flick of her tongue before moving on to my lower stomach, and my inner thigh, and my balls which she massages gently while my cock's growing so fast it feels like it's going to burst out of its skin like a frying sausage. I want her to put it in her mouth, but she doesn't. Not for a very long time. And when finally she does, I have to beg her not to. I'm too close to the edge, one more lick and I'll explode.

She swallows every drop, tugging softly at my scrotum like she's milking a cow.

I try to lick her tits but she's not having it. She presses her mouth against mine, forcing me to taste the residue of my own sperm, though not much of it, I don't think, God I hope not, I think most of that stuff in her mouth is just saliva, and the bit that is semen, well it's not that noticeable, or if it is I'm going to choose not to notice it. (Salt? Fish? Must?)

But the thing I'm most aware of is the shaming fact that I've come and she hasn't; that she's ready for action and that all that I've got between my legs is a shrivelled, salted slug that despite all this kissing (or even because of it, especially the taste-your-own-sperm bit), the prospects of my getting another hard on in the next half hour are—

Blimey, what's this?

Bloody hell, the dirty, filthy whore, she's got her finger moling up my arse.

Mighty effective though, because in seconds I'm primed and ready once more. And I fuck her. And fuck her and fuck her and fuck her. I'm so good at it, it doesn't even feel like it's me. It's more like a pumping automaton; like some metaphoric train from a Jean Renoir movie; a sex machine with the controls set to eleven. In the distance, I can hear her gasping and begging for me to do it harder. At the base of my cock I can feel her fingers, working at her clitoris as my balls bang rhythmically against her arse, thrusting in till I can feel the rubber of the diaphragm against my tip. She's screaming now. Screaming for mercy and for more; thrashing her head from side to side in ecstasy. I don't stop.

When finally I withdraw, she's just a heap of limp, sweaty, perfumed flesh.

What the fuck has got into me? That wasn't me back then. That was Arnie; John 'King Dong' Holmes; James Brown; Barry White.

And it's not even me now. I want more. I want to fuck this girl until she's turned to melted butter.

'Oh dear,' she says, when I draw her attention to the problem.

'I'm sorry,' I say.

'Don't apologize,' she says.

We're lying there later, amid the twisted sheets, discarded clothes and damp stains, chain-smoking fags, touching sweat-sticky skin in shagged companionship when there's a knock on the door. By this stage Charlotte's told me how old she is – thirty-six – and what she does for a living, which is lecturing in sociology at University College London. I'm not sure whether to feel hurt or pleased. Hurt because chances are she does this thing all the time – she knows what students are like, how easily seduced. Pleased because I've done the thing you're supposed to do when you're a graduate. I've slept with a woman old enough to be my mother. Well, feasibly, just: if she'd had me when she was fourteen. I have been seduced by my very own Mrs Robinson; and learned from it; and enjoyed it; and though I say it myself done really, fucking well at it. So well, that I wouldn't mind trying it again back home. Except that when I tried asking for her number just now, she didn't respond. Maybe she didn't hear.

Before the knocking stops, I'm out of bed and halfway to the bathroom. It strikes me as the proper thing to do.

'Come back,' she hisses.

She makes me lie down, props up my back with a pillow, and rearranges my limbs until my position is aesthetically pleasing.

She studies me as a sculptor might her creation. Then she arranges the sheet so that it just covers my crotch, leaving the rest of my naked body exposed.

She nods and goes to the door.

'Not interrupting anything, I hope,' smirks Sara.

'Not at all,' says Charlotte.

Sara gives me a friendly little wave.

I give her one back.

'We ought to get going,' says Sara. 'Iannou's expecting us in ten minutes.'

'I'm there,' says Charlotte. 'Just let me grab a shower.'

She makes towards the bathroom and then turns to me, almost as an afterthought.

'You can let yourself out, when you're ready.'

Charlotte dresses quickly. Then, with barely another word, the girls are gone.

'Wait!' I want to call after them. 'It can't end like this. Surely there must be more than this . . .'

But their footsteps recede and I'm left alone on the bed of a woman who has already forgotten my existence. I smoke a slow fag lying on my back, staring at the ceiling, not too worried where the ash falls because I'm cool, I'm a man, I'm beyond all that. I try thinking triumphant, post-coital thoughts but they won't come. I feel empty and bereft; and I wonder what I can do to prolong the almost-vanished moment.

Maybe, I think, maybe I could have a rummage through her things, see if there are any letters, photos, or better still a diary, so I can get inside her head and create the illusion that she's still with me.

Or maybe I should go into the bathroom and have a sniff at that bikini she's just discarded, the one stained with juices that I personally aroused.

But I don't, perhaps from instinctive prudery, perhaps because I know it won't summon her back, it'll be like kissing a corpse.

So I take a shower and after nothing more intrusive than a fond farewell scrunch of those dirty bikini bottoms on the bathroom floor, I shut the door of her hotel room behind me and drift into the night.

She has used me. I was nothing more than a piece of meat to her. A cock on legs.

Ah, but if only girls would treat me that way more often!

Miss out Monday but come up smiling Tuesday morning

'St Paul's Road – is that a good address?' I ask my cousin who's not really a cousin, not a blood one anyway. We grew up together and we're related by marriage, that's all. And I only call her cousin when we're getting on well, which we're not at all on this particular phone call because she's making out that she's doing me this hugely big favour by lending me her flat for six months and I know she's only doing it because she needs someone to guard her sublet and pay off her rent.

'If five minutes' walk from Highbury Corner is good, yes,' she says, like I'm supposed to be impressed.

'And is it?' I say, mainly to wind her up because it's pretty rich, coming from a fellow Midlander, this 'God-you're-such-a-hick-don't-you-know-anything-about-London?' routine.

'Jo-osh! It's bang in the middle of Islington.'

'And that's a good thing?'

'You don't know where Islington is?'

'Well excuse me, Miss Pearly Queen Gorblimey Luvaduck Darn The Apples And Pears: nor did you a year ago.'

'Exactly. I had to find out. By using my initiative.'

'And I'm using my initiative. I'm asking the person most qualified in all the world to tell me whether or not the flat

I'm about to rent is a palace in central London or a shithole right on the outskirts.'

'A shithole now, is it? If that's your attitude I'll just have to let someone else have it.'

'I didn't say—'

'There's thousands who'd leap at the chance, you know. I only asked you because—'

'And I appreciate it, coz. Really I do—' No I don't you fucking bitch I hate you I hate you and what I hate most of all is having to pretend I don't hate you just for the privilege of spending six lousy months paying way over the odds for a flat I'm almost bound to hate even more than I hate you which is pretty damned hard you evil, evil cow.

'Do you want this place or not?'

'Yes!'

'Fine. I'm leaving Heathrow first thing Sunday morning. Key under the brick on the right-hand side of the pathway as you go in. And if anyone comes sniffing round from the housing department, for God's sake don't mention you're renting it. Just tell them you're a friend. OK? See you in six months.'

I'd like to ask whose friend. In fact I'd like to ask loads of things. But the phone's gone dead and I daren't ring back. Vicious cow might change her mind.

*

Surprisingly the flat is not a shithole. At least not by my twenty-two-year-old standards. Today I'd no doubt see it differently. I'd be horrified by how poky it is: a narrow room about the length of one and a half mattresses with a tiny, partitioned-off cooking area, and a shared bathroom and loo outside. And I'd notice the tall, sash windows and absurdly high ceilings and I'd curse the vandal who'd divided up a finely proportioned Victorian house into a series of cramped cells fit only for the impoverished and the desperate.

But that's not how I see it when I first walk in. I see golden motes dancing in the three huge shafts of yellow light which stream on to African carvings, Indian print fabrics, old wine bottles dripping with candle wax, and lush, healthy pot plants which the note by the cooker tells me I'd better look after or I'm dead. I see the mattress laid on the floor, as is the practice of people who are young and free and have lots of sex. I see, perched on a wicker table at the pillow end, a telephone: my telephone; the one I can pick up whenever I want to ring my friends; the one I'll do clever journalism things on and make money with; the one which, when it rings, I'll pick up and know the call's for me because it's my phone, I'm a grown-up. I'm a Londoner.

The thrill doesn't last, though. Especially not after I've dialled all my London friends and told them my new phone number and not one of them has got remotely excited about my having become one of them, let alone said: 'Hey. Let's celebrate! I'm on my way . . .'

Once I've unpacked my stuff – not much: the only portable thing I own apart from clothes and a few coffee cups is my hi-fi – and bumped into the slightly older bloke who lives next door ('Hi—' I say. 'Hi,' he says back, apparently having missed the '—' at the end of mine), I flop on the mattress, stare up at the cobwebs, and feel the slow creep of disillusionment.

'I'm a Londoner. I'm a Londoner. I'm a Londoner,' I try reminding myself under my breath. But it only makes me feel self-conscious, like a character in a book who has just moved to London.

Except, if I were a character in a book I'd be having a much more interesting time. Important, symbolic things would be happening to illustrate the massive life-significance of Moving To The Big City For The First Time. I'd meet new people, make new friends, like Mary Ann does right away in *Tales Of The City*. I'd get a freshly made joint taped to my door by my kindly but mysterious new landlady.

All my landlady has left me is a long, depressing note saying stuff like 'Bins WEDNESDAY' and 'Please DO NOT bath after 10pm' and 'Please LEAVE FLAT AS YOU FOUND IT' and 'Paul the hairdresser: mention my name and you might get a discount.' And a third-empty bottle of Campari. Which depresses me so much I'm almost tempted to drink it.

The hippy mattress is a motivation vampire. It's sucking out my desire to do anything other than lie there, maybe read a book, maybe have a wank, maybe something less energetic. I let my eyes close, teasing myself with those micro-sleeps like the ones that kill you on motorways if you don't pull in at the next service station; seeing how deep under I can travel while yet remaining conscious; jerking myself reluctantly back again whenever I get too close to the edge. Like you're supposed to when you find yourself freezing to death in a snowdrift and you hear those siren voices saying: 'Go to sleeeeep! Go to sleeeep!' Which is something I've often wondered: would I be the sort that struggles and struggles and struggles till the rescue party arrives and then gives interviews from his hospital bed, frost-blackened stumps swathed in bandages, saying: 'I wanted to sleep but I knew I couldn't let myself or I'd be a goner'? Or the sort that says 'Sod it' and just drifts off?

The natural thing, I suppose, is to wish yourself in the position of the person that survives. But I wonder. Would I really want to spend the rest of my life with half my fingers and toes missing? And anyway: do I really want to be the sort of person who has the sort of mind that enables you to stay alive in snowdrifts? Because you'd need to be a bit of an uptight git, wouldn't you? The muscular Christian type who relishes a struggle and thinks life is a gift from God, not something to be cast aside lightly. The sort that never takes drugs or smokes cigarettes or gets too drunk because they're bad for you and temptation is something to be resisted. Whereas if you were the sort that hears those siren voices, goes 'What? You mean I get to choose between a) shivering here miserably while my extremities slowly drop off and b) deep, blissful, endless sleep? No contest!' and promptly succumbs, that would make you a pretty groovy kind of guy. I mean, how cool and decadent can you get, throwing away your whole life for the sake of a few minutes' extra kip?

What worries me is that I think I'm the uptight, puritanical sort that survives. I can tell by the way that whenever I play this almost falling asleep game, I never actually do fall asleep because of the prissy little voice in my head saying: 'You can't sleep in the day because there's stuff to be done and your enemies will creep up on you and your rivals will steal a march on you and you'll only wake up feeling groggy and miserable.' Like it's saying, now, for example.

The question is: what do real Londoners do? I know what non-Londoners do. They queue outside the Hard Rock Café and Madame Tussaud's or go shopping in Oxford Street or wandering up and down the King's Road or bopping in The Hippodrome, all of which I've done, except The Hippodrome part because I'm not even that trendy.

But real Londoners?

*

One thing they don't do, I learn on my mission to pick up a *Time Out*, is give each other the time of day. Everyone I pass en route to the newsagent completely blanks me when I try catching their eye, including the haughty old woman with a pair of black pug dogs who doesn't know what she's missing because I like pug dogs, we used to keep them ourselves, and I could have chatted to her happily for several minutes about such puggish trivia as the way their tails uncurl when they're unhappy, which is more than most people can because they think pug dogs are ugly and pointless. And maybe then she might have invited me back to her palatial Victorian villa for tea because I seem such a nice young man and asked me whether I'd mind housesitting for her when she's wintering in the Cap d'Antibes which she'd worried she might be unable to do this year, what with those terrible quarantine laws and her housekeeper gone . . . I've just reached the bit where the letter comes telling me that the pug dogs and I are the sole beneficiaries of Lady X's obscenely enormous estate when I hear her calling back to me.

I wheel round, half smiling at her.

'Jock!' she repeats to one of the pugs, who has stopped to sniff at a turd. She gives me a look that says I'm worse than the turd. I walk on.

In the newsagent I'm hyper-polite and friendly to the Pakistani woman behind the counter, asking for my Camels in a big smiley voice, 'Oh and one of those lighters, please, if you wouldn't mind. Yes. *Thank* you', thanking her again when I give her the money and again when she gives me the change. Partly it's race guilt. Mainly it's so that she can say to me: 'I haven't seen you before,' and I can reply: 'Just moved in,' and she can say: 'Nice to meet you. Look forward to doing business with you and would you like me to keep you a paper in the morning?' Which she doesn't.

I hover by the door in a stagey, bumblingly comical way which is supposed to make me look loveably scatterbrained.

'Ah yes. Milk,' I say, spinning on my heels towards the refrigerated cabinet. 'Milk', I repeat, holding the carton, scrutinizing the label as if it were some pricey bottle of wine, then grinning back to check she's still enjoying the show. Her expression reads boredom or indifference, and I wonder whether there's a question I can ask to make her feel charitable, bring her onside. 'Is half-fat the same as semi-skimmed?' 'Any idea what homogenized means?' But the moment's gone. She has been distracted by a lean, unshaven man in an overcoat.

She's still looking at him, over my shoulder, when I hand her the milk.

'Just moved into the area, you see,' I say.

The woman nods, puzzled and hands me my change. The man in the overcoat regards me with disgust, as if I've suddenly announced: 'I fuck puppies.'

*

Time Out recommends I should see a film called *Withnail & I*. It's on at this arty cinema called The Screen On The Green: the sort of place where the cashier has long straggly hair, glasses and a PhD and instead of popcorn and synthetic orange they sell dried organic banana chunks, home-made samosas and Fair Trade Nicaraguan coffee. Almost everyone in the audience looks like I want to be: slightly older, more dishevelled, knowing and sophisticated. They all know one another, calling out greetings to mates in distant rows, giving each other high fives and double kisses in the aisle, like there's a Sunday matinee cool person's club that I've accidentally gatecrashed.

I position myself next to a party comprising one boy about my age and three ridiculously pretty girls. Well, not dead next to because as I approach, the dark-eyed girl nearest me looks up and I lose my nerve. But two seats away, which I still think is quite brave. Their conversation is mostly in-jokes or gossip about people I don't know. Whenever they make a joke I understand, though, or when the adverts come on and they start talking about how crap they are or how brilliant, or better still when they start reminiscing about great, cheap, local cinema ads of yesteryear like the cartoon one, crackly and dusty from overuse, where a little man with stick legs comes on and says: "Ere Bert. This is the place,' I smirk and flash little glances in their direction, as if to say, 'I'm not just a strange person sitting two seats away from you in the cinema, you know. I'm a human being just like you, with the same sense of humour and the same outlook and I'll bet if we got to know each other we'd really get on, so won't you please be my friends, oh won't you, please?' It's like casting for trout, I guess.

When I realize they're not going to bite, that maybe worse they're thinking: 'What's with the weird, grinning geezer on the left?', I curse my cowardice in not having moved just one space closer to the seat that might reasonably have made them consider me more like part of their group. Maybe I still can. I've got an excuse now. Some annoying tall person with a birdsnest head has sat down bang in front of me and whenever I think I'm safe, he's slumped down low enough for me to almost see without craning my neck, he pulls himself erect again.

'Is that seat taken?' calls a bloke standing in the aisle to the pretty, dark-eyed girl who I would have been sitting next to if I'd moved quicker. He doesn't even bother asking me. Is it really so obvious that I have no friends?

'It's yours,' says the girl with a smile on which the bloke immediately capitalizes by telling her 'just in time', that he's been so looking forward to this film and he's heard so many good things about it. The girl and the rest of her party respond with instant bonhomie, and offer him some of their Bombay mix. Then they ask him what he's doing afterwards, they're having some friends round for an orgy, and does he like drugs and is there one of the girls he particularly fancies or would he prefer to have sex with all three?

*

Afterwards I feel even more depressed. Not about the film, which has immediately jumped ahead of *Brazil* as my official all-time favourite movie, but about everything else: it's raining, there's that miserable fssssshh of car tyres on wet road and I walked here without an umbrella; my brain thinks it's night but it's still light, a watery grey Sunday afternoon light; I'm living in London and I haven't got a job; nor any friends; nor woman neither . . .

That's what's most depressing. All those incredible lines of dialogue and no one to misquote them at, no one to reminisce with about the best bits like, 'We're not from London, you know'; or when Uncle Monty tries to seduce Marwood; or Danny the Drug Dealer; or – well, it's no fun on your own. You need someone else to keep trumping you with a 'yeah but what about the bit when . . .?' so that then you can trump them with one of your even better bits.

Clearly, the only way of dealing with all this is to get off my face as quickly as possible on drugs and alcohol. But where to procure them? It's approaching 5 p.m. – still over two hours to go before the pubs or off-licences open. I don't have a drug dealer. I don't know anyone who knows where I could find a drug dealer. And even if I did, they'd never get to me fast enough because I need my hit of unreality right now.

Having changed out of my wet clothes, and searched the recesses of every pocket, knapsack and suitcase for one of those tiny lumps of hash I might have overlooked on all the previous occasions I've been in this situation, I realize that desperate measures are called for.

I will invite my next-door neighbour in for a drink . . . No, can't do that. Not when all I've got to offer him is Campari.

I'll knock on his door, introduce myself and just ask him by the by whether he's got any hash spare. And I'm not going to stop and consider the potential repercussions of this because if I do, I definitely won't get any hash whereas this way, there's just the slimmest chance I might.

OK.

Knock knock.

No answer. But soft music from within.

KNOCK KNOCK.

My neighbour peers through the crack, looking pissed off and half asleep.

'Um. Sorry to bother you but I just thought I'd say hello, I'm borrowing this place from my cousin for a few months, so I'm your new neighbour.'

'Oh right yeah. Hi.'

From behind him, a female voice calls something.

My neighbour turns round and calls back to her. 'It's OK. Just the guy next door.' He turns back to me. 'So anyway, nice meeting you,' he says, preparing to close the door.

'There was just one thing,' I force myself to gabble, before the voice of reason advises me otherwise.

'Yes?'

'Drugs.'

'What?'

'I was wondering whether you had any.'

'What sort of drugs?'

'Smoking drugs. Hash. That sort of thing.'

'You're asking me whether I've got any drugs to sell you?'

'Yes. I suppose. Unless you just want to lend me them.'

'Sorry, mate. No.'

'Oh.'

The whole scene seems so unlikely that once back in my flat, I try persuading myself that it never happened. But then from next door I hear peals of laughter.

I vow never to do anything so brazen ever again. Until I remember that it was my very lack of brazenness a couple of hours ago which got me into this mess in the first place, because if only I'd sat right next to that girl instead of two seats away from her, I wouldn't be here now, I'd be at their sex and drugs orgy, probably.

Now I'm getting desperate. Not Campari desperate, but desperate enough to investigate a rumour I heard at school: namely, that if you want to get stoned, the thing to do is smoke grated nutmeg or those little stringy bits you find attached to the flesh of a banana.

Impressively, I have both. While I'm waiting for the stringy bits I have collected from the two blackened, inedible bananas which were rotting on top of the fridge to dry in the oven, I get myself in the mood by putting on my *Best Of Jimi Hendrix* LP and playing 'All Along The Watchtower' over and over again because it's the only song I own from the film. Then I lay the stringy bits along the bottom of my three skins, sprinkle them with about the same quantity of nutmeg as you'd use if it were hash, and crumble the contents of a stale Camel on top of them. *Et voilà.*

The taste is not as rebarbative as I'd feared. Quite sweet and spicy. But then come to think of it, it would be, being nutmeg. So I'm able to burn through my schoolboy special in only a few quick, deep drags. Afterwards, I feel nothing but a sense of tobacco-induced giddiness, which gradually develops into nausea, disorientation and a splitting headache. I take out the headache with a couple of paracetamol; I attack the nausea – which I put down to hunger – with the remains of the inedible bananas, fished from the bin, because I can't face shopping for real food in my current state; and then I attempt to make the most of the disorientation, which seems to be coming on quite promisingly.

Or is that just wishful thinking?

No. I don't think it is because one effect it has had on me is to make that bottle of Campari seem suddenly less unattractive than it was half an hour ago. Desirable even.

I stumble towards the bottle, twist off the lid and sniff the contents.

Yup. Bitter and disgusting. Just as I remember from the days when my grandfather used to drink it and gave me a sip and I went: 'Yeuuch! How could you drink this stuff?' and he said: 'It's an acquired taste.'

I glance at the clock on the oven. Ten past six. Still far, far too long to wait till the pubs are open. Looks like I've no choice.

I would drink it out of a glass with ice, soda and a twist of lemon but I don't have any and besides, you don't want to dilute this stuff, you want to get it down as quickly as possible so that your tastebuds have less time to register the full horror.

Glug.

Ugh.

Glug glug glug glug.

Ugggh.

GLUG.

More bearable now.

GLUG GLUG GLUGGLUGGLUG. GLUG.

Done.

*

Quite what happens next isn't immediately clear. I'm slumped in the only chair, applauding myself on how clever I am – not just clever, but FUCKING FUCKING CLEVER for having triumphed over the dread forces of sobriety – and got myself really, really, God I'm so wrecked, so numb, so slippery swimmy and gone, such a bum when I'm suddenly assaulted by the sour taste of puke at the back of my throat and up my nostrils and a massive throbbing in my temples. And when I've finally made it to the kitchen clock, noticing en route that my legs don't work properly and that my shirt's all wet and smeared with chunky bits, I see that it's now gone eleven o'clock. Which is a massive pain, because it means I'm too late to catch the pubs and God do I need a drink right now.

Next thing I know I'm soaking in the bath and there's a tremendous banging on the door which at first I think is my headache but which is actually someone knocking.

'Come in,' I say, automatically.

It's the bloke who gave me that funny look in the shop.

'It's you,' he says, crossly.

'It is.'

'You'll be Susan's cousin, then.'

'I will.'

'Didn't she tell you about bathing after ten o'clock? I have to work early shifts and when the heating pipes bang it ruins my sleep.'

'Oh. Sorry.'

'And another thing,' he says. 'Next time you have a bath, you might want to think about taking your clothes off first.'

I look down. A good point, well made.

Rhymes with slut

Flat 3, 88 St Pauls Rd,
London N1

September 1987

Dear Molly

How is Yale?

But enough of you because it's me I want to talk about
and since none of my other so-called friends seems to give
a toss about my thrilling adventures since arriving in
Londinium, I thought I'd better tell you instead. And
please don't think that the inordinate length of this letter
has anything to do with the fact that I'm trying to write
my bloody novel and that I'm badly in need of a
displacement activity.

The annoying thing about writing novels, I've
discovered, is that you can't just sit down and dash them
off. I tried and managed six chapters with some quite funny
jokes in and some OK dialogue and characters based
totally on everyone we know including you, I hope you
don't mind, I've just borrowed your house and your
general background not your looks and personality and the

sex scenes aren't too embarrassing. Well, actually come to think of it they are. Fucking embarrassing. But perhaps they will serve as a salutary lesson as to what an enormous mistake it would almost certainly have been had we gone ahead with our plan to do something we might have regretted.

Meanwhile, the not-novel-writing part of my career seems to have got off to an even worse start than the novel-writing part. First I had this interview with this ultra-snobby type at *Harpers & Queen* who's bound to be a close personal friend of yours so I shan't mention his name. He's dressed in a zillion-pound Savile Row suit and I can see him looking at my clothes and thinking: 'I thought that being fresh up from Oxford and, having the same surname as the Earls of Essex, this Josh Devereux would be a smart young fellow but I see now that he is a total oik.' And then he came over all faint and had to be revived with smelling salts by a minion in a powdered wig.

The nail in my coffin, I reckon, was the bit where he asked me about my favourite sort of architecture. Well as you know, this is a subject on which I am a total expert and which I care about enormously. If I'd thought, perhaps I could have come up with something arsey like 'Ah the cloistered splendour of my beloved Christ Church.' Instead I gabbled about being quite fond of Lutyens, not that I knew the first thing about him except that on the tube I happened to have glanced at an article in the *Evening Standard* about something he'd built, so I thought I was being topical. 'Ah. Lutyens,' he says, disdainfully, as if I'd just said: 'Oh the thing I like most are houses made of poo.' Also, I noticed that he pronounced the Lut bit to rhyme with 'Slut' whereas I'd pronounced it to rhyme with 'soot' because I thought he was Dutch.

Of course, what I should have said was 'Georgian.'
I know this because when I went for my second interview
with a similarly buttoned-up toff at the *Spectator*, there
was a framed quotation behind his desk saying about how
Georgian architecture was the only right and true form for
London buildings. Or some such bollocks. I can't remember
much that was said because I lost interest from the
moment when he said, 'You do realize that we don't have
any job vacancies?'

I remember the end bit, though. He asked me did I
have any features ideas. And I replied that I'd heard it
wasn't a good idea for novice journalists to give editors
their ideas because quite often other, more experienced
journalists ended up being commissioned to write the piece
instead. Apart from the fact that it was better than
admitting I didn't have any ideas, I thought he'd be
impressed by my directness and honesty. But instead all I
got was this weedy laugh. Like I'd personally insulted him.

The last interview went much better, though. It was
with the chap who edits the Londoner's Diary, which, as you
probably know, is the gossip column on the *Evening
Standard*, and the best thing about it was that it didn't
happen. He just rang me up and said: 'Come in and do a
day shift.' So that's what I'm going to be doing tomorrow
morning and I think I get paid something like £60 which,
if you came in every day, would work out at about £15,000
a year, which I realize is next to zilch in your plutocratic
terms, but for an humble Midlander like me is a king's
ransom and – more to point – even more than the starting
salary of all my wanky friends in merchant banking, most
notably the Warthog who I believe is on a mere £13,000.

Am I sounding chippy and embittered? *Moi?* Well this

may not be unconnected with the fact that for the last few months (I would count but I don't want to depress myself further) I have been about as sexually active as Mother Theresa of Calcutta during International Chastity Year. Perhaps it's because I'm living in Islington, which is so remote from anywhere civilized I might as well be in fucking Lapland. Perhaps God is punishing me for my hubris in having assumed that this amazing fling I had with an older woman on a beach in Greece that I might or might not tell you about sometime was how my sex life was going to be in the future. Perhaps I'm in fact a hideous troll with no personality and no chance of ever scoring ever again.

At which point you're supposed to come in with a 'No actually you're very handsome and one of the most interesting men ever and if it weren't for the fact that we're sexually incompatible I would definitely, definitely shag you, you quivering hunk of manhood.' So can you say that please, only in such a way as to convince me that you mean it.

Oh, and if you have been having sex at any kind at Yale, not that I imagine you'll have had time if that reading list you showed me is anything to go by, I do not wish to hear, OK?

Good.

Do please write back the very instant you get this letter because I don't write letters often and I need encouragement.

Yours in the ranks of death,

Josh xxxxxxx

No man but a blockhead ever wrote, except for money

Everyone apart from me on the southbound platform of Highbury & Islington tube looks miserable, and I understand why. It's how you're supposed to look at eight o'clock on a Monday morning at the start of yet another working week. Tragically, though, I can't get the expression right. The corners of my lips keep drifting upwards and my happy thoughts sometimes seep out as delighted snuffles. God, I must be annoying. I know I'm annoying, I can see it in my fellow commuters' eyes. 'Fuck off,' they say. 'Mind your own business. Don't you know you're *never* supposed to make eye contact with *anyone* on the tube?'

And I do know this rule, of course I do. It's not like I'm some hick from the sticks on the tube for the first time. It's just that normally when I've done it, it has been at the weekend or during the day or late at night. Never during an actual rush hour. Never on my first official journey to my first official day as a fully-fledged member of the rent-paying, career-building, economy-boosting, tax-paying classes.

Not that the white-haired Nazi behind the desk appreciates this. If I were a foul-smelling tramp who'd staggered up to him to ask for the price of a bottle of Thunderbird he could scarcely treat me with more contempt. I tell him why I'm here and he picks up the phone, wearily shaking his head. The phone isn't answered for ages. The Nazi glares at me like it's my fault.

'Got a Mr Devereux here. Claims he's been asked to do a day shift,' he says. 'Yeah? All right.'

'Third floor,' he growls. 'Someone will meet you at the lift.'

The building seems to get scummier the deeper inside you venture. Its entrance on Fleet Street is newspaper baron grand – all fascist Thirties porticos and stonework and 'Behold the power and the majesty of the fourth estate.' So too is the courtyard which leads to the Art Deco reception area. It all makes me think that I have come to the right job: one with high pay, generous expenses and excellent prospects; where you are treated with respect and travel first class as a matter of course.

Inside, though, it's a wormhole of endless peeling grey corridors and sub-corridors and ante-rooms and nooks and crannies full of horrid gnome creatures who hiss when you ask for directions and send you the wrong way just to be spiteful. Because, of course, when I emerge from the lift – one of those whirring old-fashioned jobs with the hand-operated grille – there's no one there to meet me, not even after I've waited, so eventually I give up and have to find my own way.

The diary editor, Lucian Mildmere, looks not much older than me, with floppy hair, basilisk eyes and a cruel mouth. His voice is silken and educated. You could imagine him playing Mr Nice in an interrogation duo. Then later you'd discover that he was even nastier than Mr Nasty.

'You're very early,' he says.

A beautiful young woman next to him looks up curiously from her typing.

'Sorry, I thought—'

'No matter, we're on edition, you'll have to keep yourself amused—' he looks distractedly towards one of his minions, a middle-aged man with a beard. 'Tom, have we had that Archer story legalled yet? Yes, yes, I know he fed it to us but I'm still not sure he's going to appreciate the spin we've put on it.'

Having issued several more directives in this vein, he notices that I'm still standing next to him.

'Look, I really haven't time now,' he says. 'Try to find yourself a phone and work on whatever stories you've brought in.'

'Um. OK.'

'You do have some stories?'

'Not really, no, but—'

'Hermione, could you be a sweetheart and sort this boy out with a desk and some trade papers? He appears to have come in without any stories.'

The young woman rises from behind her typewriter. She floats towards me in a cloud of loveliness. She's explaining something but I don't take it in. I'm thinking of a poem by Betjeman. I'm thinking: how does anyone get any work done?

This is the last human contact I have until lunchtime. It's like the scene in *Aces High* where the fresh-faced young flier straight out of school walks into the officers' mess and no one thinks it's worth getting to know him – they don't want to upset themselves when he dies.

When I look up they're gone: Hermione the secretary, Tom the bearded number two, and the three others whatever their names are, I never did find out, because I've been buried in the *Church Times, Motorcycle News, Practical Fishkeeping, Soldier Of Fortune, Campaign, PR Week, Ariel* and *The Stage.*

'Well?' Lucian asks over my shoulder, which makes me jump because I'd thought he'd gone.

'Um, nothing as yet.'

'Did no one explain to you what this job involves?'

'Not exactly.'

He pushes a newspaper clipping towards me. 'See what you can do with that.'

I skim it quickly. Something to do with a place called Keats' House. Apparently there's an ongoing row about its future. Maybe Lucian has views on where the story should go.

But he's gone.

'Still here?' says another voice, sometime later. It belongs to one of the Diary people whose names I don't know. Well-spoken, male, about my age.

'Where am I supposed to be?'

'Not here, definitely. Lucian hates anyone to be in the office at lunchtime. Terribly bad form for a diarist.'

'Where should I go then?'

'You can come for a drink with me, if you like.'

My eyes have gone watery, which is utterly pathetic. Except it's the first nice thing anyone has said all day.

His name is Dominic and he hasn't been at this game much longer than me, I learn at the Old Cheshire Cheese. A bit like the Bear or the Turf at Oxford, this is a pub which is very aware how famous it is. There is sawdust sprinkled nostalgically on the floor and much wooden panelling in its maze of rooms so small that you only have to exhale to spill someone's pint. It's swarming and booming with middle-aged cunts with pale-grey polyester suits and florid faces. Journalists, presumably, getting off on how traditional they're being quaffing ale in such an old established haunt, like generations of pissed old hacks have been doing since time immemorial. There's nowhere to sit and by the time we get to the bar, they've run out of food, so we have to make do with cheese and onion crisps.

'So was it like this on your first day?' I ask Dominic.

'Like what?'

'You know. Not knowing what you were supposed to be doing. Everyone ignoring you.'

'I don't think it's deliberate.'

'No?'

'You shouldn't take it personally. It's just, you know, they get a lot of young hopefuls passing through, and if they stopped to change everyone's nappy, they'd never get the column out.'

'Just a bit of normal, human courtesy was all I was hoping for.'

'Ah, but that would spoil the creative tension.'

'The what?'

'I think it started at the *Mail* but now everybody's doing it. The theory is the more unhappy you are, the better you work.'

'But that's rubbish. Surely? All it makes me want to do is never come back here again.'

'Maybe that's the idea. Maybe they want to drive you off to one of their rivals, where the regime isn't quite so tough.'

'OK. So where's nicer?'

'*Guardian*, possibly, except the money's dreadful and you don't get paid for months. *Telegraph*'s OK. It's still run like a sort of gentleman's club and the pay's better than *The Times*, which is also OK-ish apart from the Murdoch factor. Unlike the *Sunday Times*, which definitely isn't, because they're even more into their creative tension than the *Mail*,' he says. 'And the *Standard* – hey, if we're quick we might just have time for one more round.'

I'm feeling pissed enough already, but I sense that it is my duty as an authentic working hack, just as it is my duty to order by the pint when all I can really manage is a half. I try to sop up the excess alcohol with four more packs of crisps.

'Why does anyone stick it out?' I ask Dominic.

'Hermione?'

'So I'm not the only one?'

'You're at the very bottom of a very long queue.'

I pull tragically on a cigarette, 'I suppose I was just banking on the vague possibility that you might all be gay.'

'Because we never look at her, you mean?'

'Well, I did wonder.'

Dominic assumes a doom-laden voice. 'We know that to look is to torture ourselves with what we cannot have.'

'Has no one tried?'

'Would you?'

'God, no. She's way out of my league.'

'She's out of everyone's league.'

'So why do you all work here?'

Dominic thinks for a moment.

'Money?' he says.

'Money?'

'Well don't sound so surprised. You know what Dr Johnson said.'

'Yeah. But aren't there more important considerations?'

'Like what?'

'I don't know. Being allowed to write what you like without having to turn everything into tabloid-ese? Developing a style, maybe?'

'Blimey. Are you sure you've chosen the right profession?'

By the time we get back to the office, everyone is at their desks looking harrassed, barking down phones and typing aggressively. Lucian gives us a significant look.

Having picked up the newspaper clipping about Keats' House and stared at it sightlessly for a long time, it occurs to me that I am drunker than I thought. In the pub, I felt confident that I could take whatever creative tension Lucian and his henchmen cared to throw at me; that I'd wrap up this Keats' House story in no time, writing it in prose so fine and witty that everyone would suddenly worship me and want to be my friend. Now I'm back, the plan just isn't working. The newspaper story has grown even more opaque and uninspiring than it was last time I stared at it. And I daren't ask anyone what my angle should be, in case I get my head bitten off.

Every few minutes, I have another fag or another cup of coffee. Each time, I persuade myself that this will be the one that triggers the synapse that makes the mental connection that finally steers me out of the mire. All I get, though, are palpitations and a worsening headache.

It's the same with the phone. If only I make just one more call, I persuade myself, I'll finally get hold of the person who can explain everything. Instead, all I get is information. And I haven't got room for any of it. I'm only allowed three paragraphs – pars, they're known as – and that space is there for jokes, catty asides, sneering conjecture, and vicious punchlines not for boring information about what an impressive number of visitors Keats' House gets or whatever other propaganda the person I've just called has chosen to inflict on me.

What's worse is that never having written to this length before, I have no idea how much verbiage I can pack in.

My first few attempts are stuffed with literary allusions and biographical details clearly indicative that the author of the piece is a jolly clever young man who studied Keats somewhere really posh, Oxford or Cambridge, almost certainly. But when I stop to count the wordage, I'm already three times overlength and I still haven't got to the bit where I say what the story is.

So I try making a few cuts and it's still way too long.

So I ruthlessly excise every single joke, allusion or pleasing antithesis that isn't absolutely necessary. And still, it's twice as long as it should be. With no newsworthy angle.

So I bring what was to have been my concluding paragraph to the beginning, to see whether that makes any difference. It doesn't, not really. The story still has no point and it's still too long. I like the second sentence, though.

So I keep the second sentence and lose the first. Now I'm only 180 words overlength instead of 200. Except that I still haven't found room for the story, yet.

'How are you getting on?' asks Lucian.

'Almost there.'

Which might be true if we were working on wordprocessors. Problem is, we're still stuck in the days of typewriters. Each time you want to write a new piece – each time you want to write a new paragraph, almost, because the paper's very small and you're typing with triple line spacing – you can't just highlight, delete and replace, you have to insert a whole new piece of paper. The paper doesn't go in at all easily because it's special journalist paper, a thick wad of sexplicate or whatever the word is for six sheets of paper, so that the various relevant departments – which ones I don't know and don't care – each get a copy. And having gone through the business of aligning and scrolling, you then have to type on top your name and your department and the subject of the story and page number. So that's another five minutes gone before you can even start writing.

'Are you sure you're cut out for this sort of thing?' says the silken voice.

I blink to clear my eyes. I've been staring so hard I've lost all track of space and time.

'I don't know,' I croak, noticing all of a sudden that the desk has emptied. It's dark outside.

'Show me what you've written,' says Lucian.

I hesitate. Then show him the least bad effort so far.

'There's no story,' he says.

'No.'

'Perhaps you had better go home.'

On the tube back, I have no problem identifying with the battered, sullen exhaustion of the other passengers. No one looks me in the eye, which is just as well. If they did, I think I would kill them.

Up Christopher Biggins's bottom

St Pauls Road etc
December

Dearest Molly,

I have arrived. And to show you just how arrived, here are
some of the people I have met since starting on the diary
job: Jenny Seagrove, Michael Winner, Gareth Hunt, Darcey
Bussell, Vera Lynn, Reg Varney, Su Pollard, Auberon
Waugh and Christopher Biggins. Yes, I have turned into a
bit of a star-fucker. Not literally, obviously, which is probably
just as well in the case of Christopher Biggins, but not just
as well in the case of Darcey Bussell who is this up-and-
coming ballerina and really quite fanciable in a hair-tied-
severely-back ballerina-ish sort of way and I think it's
about time I got to sleep with someone famous, don't you?

Oh dear. It suddenly occurs that you probably haven't
a clue how famous these people are. OK. So I don't need
to explain Vera Lynn because, knowing your taste, you
probably own half her records; and I seem to remember
Bron Waugh's your godfather or something, isn't he?, so I
kind of wish I hadn't mentioned him because now you'll
be going: 'Fancy getting excited about meeting Bron.

M'dear, simply everyone knows Bron' and you won't take the rest of my list seriously, which you should because it's sodding impressive.

Right. Jenny Seagrove is this well-known English Rose type actress who I think was either a werewolf or a vampire bride in that brilliant series *Hammer House of Horror* which was on when we were teenagers but which you're bound not to have seen because you were probably reading Proust. Michael Winner is the director responsible for three of my favourite Charles Bronson revenge movies, *Death Wish I*, *II* and *III*, which your secret lover Dick and I have seen at least a dozen times each on video. Reg Varney was the chirpy one in the classic Seventies sitcom *On The Buses*, which you're probably the only person in England not to have seen. Su Pollard is in the equally classic Eighties sitcom *Hi Di Hi*. And Christopher Biggins is famous for what I'm not quite sure but there's this rather good memory game you play called Christopher Biggins's bottom, where one person says 'I was up Christopher Biggins's bottom and I found a banana' and the next person says 'I was up Christopher Biggin's bottom and I found a banana and Richard Gere's pet hamster,' and so on, adding to the list all the time until someone forgets and loses a life.

But how, I'm sure you're gagging to know, have I found myself in such august company. Well, what I have to do is this. On Friday afternoons I'll ring up the Diary and they'll go through all their invites, tell me which parties they haven't got anyone going to, and then I'll go to them. It could be anything – a book launch, a restaurant opening or best of all a first night, where even though you're only there to pick up gossip from the celebrities at the party afterwards, you get given two free tickets (really good ones, usually. If you're ever over here, you must come to one: loads of free booze etc) to see the play as well. The idea is to go up to anyone you see who's famous and get them to say something vaguely interesting. Then, when you've got enough quotes, you spend the rest of the evening snaffling up canapés and getting pissed on free champagne.

I probably sound a bit blasé now but at first, I was absolutely shitting myself. You've no idea how horrible it is going into a room full of people you don't know, most of whom don't want to know you. It's even more horrible when there's no one famous there because then there's no story and you don't get paid. That's why I was so incredibly lucky at my first party – some bash at the Orangerie in Holland Park organized by Leith's, for what purpose I never could quite work out – when just as I was giving up ever talking to anyone worthwhile, who should I spot but Michael Winner and his girlfriend Jenny Seagrove, who I've always found extremely fanciable.

Anyway, the point is I didn't at all expect people in that league of famousness to give me the time of day. But they were really nice to me. Gave me some quotes. Said they were old friends of Londoner's Diary. Almost like they were desperate for the publicity, which I can't believe they were, even though that's what some cynical bastard on the desk said when I rang in to see whether they were going to use my copy. I think they say these things just to spite us tyro hacks (as we're always described in books, though I've never heard anyone use the term in real life). And I learned quite a valuable lesson from this which is: don't be intimidated by famous people because deep down, they're exactly the same as you.

Meanwhile – I wasn't going to tell you this but with you mooning over your hideous-sounding preppie Yale pretty boy Dale (Dale? What kind of crap name is that anyway?), I think it's only fair – I have fallen tragically and hopelessly in love with an unattainable beauty called Hermione. She works at the Londoner's Diary office where everyone apart from my mate Dominic hates me, so I hardly ever get to see her except when my infatuation gets the better of me and I go in to do a day shift. Day shifts are horrible and I don't know why I do them – well I do, obviously, but you know what I mean. The only things that make them bearable, apart from the fragrant presence of the Divine One (whom no one is allowed to look at, ever, it's like the Court of the Sun King) is Dominic Barsford, who sits next to me and spends the whole time being cynical because he hates the job even more than I do. Recently, to torture me, he has started telling me that Hermione is talking of leaving, possibly to move abroad for ever. If ever she does I shall, of course, be forced to kill myself.

I'll tell you what Hermione reminds me of. That Betjeman poem that goes: 'Isn't she lovely, the mistress, with her wide apart grey green eyes . . .?' I should know the words off by heart now because it's on this great album called *Banana Blush* where Betjeman's poems are set to jaunty music which even you would like I reckon. My favourite bit is when it goes 'And the sound when she speaks is as rich and deep as the Christ Church tenor bell.' Because, do you know what? Now that I've left that dump I actually feel quite misty-eyed about it.

Meanwhile, please send me lots more amusing letters about the evils of American academe. Perhaps, with luck, you'll be able to tell me about the hideous penile injuries your friend Dale suffered while being inducted into the Phi Delta Kappa frathouse.

Oh and thanks for the Boswell tip. I look forward to checking him out. If he turns out to be as like me as you say he is then truly he must be worth reading.

Shit, must go. Off to this party at the the Savoy where John Mills is supposed to be and it's black tie and I'm not changed and I've lost the invitation, fuck . . .

Lots of love,

Josh

Celebrities are cunts

'Cunts', I say.

'Fucking cunts,' agrees Dick.

'Fucking bollocking wanking cunts,' I say.

'Bastard bollocking fucking twatfaced cunts,' he says.

'They are though, aren't they? We're not exaggerating.'

'God no,' he says. 'You couldn't.'

Dick and I are back at my place in Islington, consoling ourselves over a bottle of Jack Daniel's after possibly the shitest evening ever.

I take another slug.

'I guess deep down, though, we always knew,' I say.

'Did we?'

'That time with Rod Hull, remember?'

Dick doesn't, which is odd, because he was there. One man's formative experience is another man's irrelevance, I suppose.

Anyway, the story is that it's the mid-Seventies, I'm eleven, so Dick must be nine, and we're queuing up outside the backstage door of the Alexandra Theatre in Birmingham to get the autograph of the celebrated glove puppeteer Rod Hull.

His name doesn't mean much now – still less, I imagine, if you're American or German or Italian or something not British, preferably reading this book in translation, that would be better, because I haven't yet been translated and it would be so exciting if I were – but in his heyday he was enormous. Quite possibly the most famous person in Britain, especially after the celebrated incident in which he attacked the second most famous person in the country, chatshow host Michael Parkinson, with the comedy emu he wore attached to his arm.

People were more innocent and easily pleased in those days. They must have been for, let's be honest, there's only so much uproarious mirth you can derive from watching a dishevelled middle-aged man shoving his hand up a puppet's arse and pretending it's a different person.

So here we both are outside the Alexandra Theatre. It's cold, it's blustery, it's starting to rain and we'd like to go home but we can't, not with all the other children around us waiting so determinedly. Not when I've brought my autograph book specially.

It used to be my father's. There's no one really famous in it – it's family stuff mostly, comic rhymes, cute pictures – barring one exception. On one page, his very own special page, is the signature of heroic record-breaking speed ace Malcolm Campbell. I'm terribly proud of this and ever since my father gave me the book I've been showing it to anybody who's interested (and an awful lot of people who aren't) and, wait, here's Rod now, I'm going to hand him the book, open at the special page, so that he'll go:

'Wow! You've got Malcolm Campbell's autograph. Are you really asking me to sign my humble name next to his?'

and I can go:

'Yes, Rod. Because you're famous too.'

But the way things are looking, I'm not going to get an autograph at all. Rod, much more haggard than he is on TV, like a sick pigeon, is clearly in no mood to hang around.

'Just the last few now,' he says, hunched, scowling, scrawling distractedly. In the squash of autograph hunters, I feel the panic rise. I try to catch his eye but he's scanning his escape route. 'That's it, now,' says Rod, but not before I've thrust my book into his reluctant hand. The very hand that just half an hour ago was up Emu's bottom.

He looks at the page with Malcolm Campbell's autograph, tuts and says: 'This is no good. I need a clean one.' And he's so mortally offended that he makes to hand it back to me, until, shaking his head to indicate that, in his supreme wisdom and generosity he has deigned to give this worm-child a second chance, he flicks to a cleaner page and infects it with his mark which I can never look at thereafter without writhing at the memory of how I got it.

'And do you know what I really hate about that incident?' I say to Dick.

'What's that then?'

'Ever since, I've always thought it was my fault, never Rod's. You know, like I blamed myself for having been so stupid and naïve as not to give a busy important man a clean page to sign. Just like now, deep down I'm blaming myself for having interrupted those cunts' conversation, wondering whether maybe they were right and I was being intrusive, whether maybe—'

'I was there and I saw it,' says Dick. 'They were cunts, Josh. Definitely cunts.'

*

Our cunt encounter is at the launch of a film called *Torrent of Arse*. Obviously I've changed the name for legal reasons, but I'll give you a few clues. It's one of those sturdy, worthy, quite well acted, reasonably well done but ultimately pointless historical costume dramas that we British used to make before smile-through-your-tears comedy dramas about people up North suffering in the Thatcher years proved more profitable. And it's about, let's say, a dysentery outbreak during the retreat from Kabul. Up and coming male lead Ben Cheekbones is the idealistic young lieutenant. Scouse character actor Dave Chipp is the cantonment's roguish medical officer.

The party is at the gentlemen's outfitters Gieves & Hawkes in Savile Row (which is where the original historical characters bought their pith helmets and cleft sticks) and by now I know the drill pretty well. You go in with your notebook tucked discreetly in your pocket, sidle up to anyone who looks vaguely famous and extract tame anecdotes from them along the lines of: 'How I upended my boots one morning and a scorpion dropped out' or 'How I researched my part by deliberately contracting amoebic dysentery'. It's a symbiotic relationship: they get to plug their latest project; you get a story to put into tomorrow's diary. That's how the publicity circuit works.

All this I explain to Dick as he cowers near the drinks table, terrified on my behalf at what I'm about to have to do. 'Don't worry, you almost start to enjoy it after a while,' I say.

'God, do you really?' he says.

'Actually no,' I say, pulling on my third fag in as many minutes.

My technique is to start gently, working from the minor players to the screenwriter, the director and the producer, leaving the stars till last. That way, by the time you reach the big names, you're not so awestruck that you lose the power of speech. It happened to me once with Roger Moore, which is odd because I'm not even that big a fan. It's just that in real life Roger Moore is so amazingly, preposterously Roger-Moore-like, quizzical eyebrows and all, that you think he must be some kind of imposter. It's like watching his dummy at Madame Tussaud's suddenly come to life.

You wouldn't have thought Chipp and Cheekbones would present nearly the same problem. They're B-list stalwarts or C-list up-and-comers, not A-list superstars. But when I try hovering on the edge of their circle – they're talking to a thin, elegantly dressed baldie with a camp, catty voice who appears to know them both from way back – they won't acknowledge I'm there. Almost like it's a game. Let's see how long we can completely ignore this person for.

Dick watches from a safe distance. As I've explained to him earlier, once you've moved in you can't chicken out. So I wait and wait and wait for my entrée.

Chipp, Cheekbones and the bald one are having a chat about whatever it is that actors talk about. I try to adopt an expression which simultaneously conveys rapt, intelligent interest in their amazingly funny, clever, fascinating conversation and the fact that of course I'm not listening to a word they're saying, not without their permission, that would be rude. I turn my eager, puppyish eyes towards whoever is speaking. 'Oh, please like me, please,' my expression says. 'I'm ever so nice and I'll do you no harm and just you watch me wag my little tail'.

But they don't like puppies. Not even a puppy who, when one of them asks for a light, immediately proffers a cigarette lighter in his cute fluffy paw. The light is accepted but not the puppy's plea for an entrée. 'Sod this,' thinks the puppy.

'I'm terribly sorry to interrupt you . . .' I say, in my most achingly love-me-do ingenuous yet charming voice, eyes describing a tactical 33.33-per-cent-attention-per-person arc so as to be sure none of them feels dissed.

'Then why are you doing it?' bitches dapper baldie. Let us call him Queen Cunt.

That put-down has been used on me before, when I telephoned an irascible old author for a quote during his afternoon nap. The harshness of it stung me for hours. But when someone says it to you in the flesh, it's ten times nastier. It's so sudden and shocking and unexpected, it's like running flat out into a tree. Your face collapses for a moment as you think: 'Was what happened then as horrible as I think it was?' Then collapses a fraction more as you think, 'Blimey, yes, it was.'

Then somehow as soon as you can you have to twist your face into a semblance of grin. You can feel your jaw trembling with the effort. But under no circumstances can you respond to Queen Cunt in kind because you'll only give him a better excuse to do what he already wants to do, which is ignore you completely.

'Yes, piss off and leave us alone. We're having a private chat at a private party,' says Chipp.

'Not that private,' I say, with what I hope is a jaunty laugh.

Chipp treats me to the sort of look Caligula might have given to an impertinent servant before having him tossed to the crocodiles.

'Bloody well is. It's a private film party for *Torrent Of Arse*,' says Chipp.

'Yes, I was at the screening this afternoon, it's really good,' I say.

'We don't need you to tell us that,' says Queen Cunt.

'Aye. What are you? Some sort of journalist?' says Chipp.

'Yes I'm covering it for the Londoner's Diary. In the *Evening Standard*.'

'We know what the Londoner's Diary is. Didn't they once do a number on you, Ben?' says Queen Cunt.

Cheekbones nods. 'And they're not doing it again.'

'Hear that Mr Londoner? They've done their interviews and they're not doing any more,' says Queen Cunt.

'It wasn't an interview I was after. Just, you know, a few jolly quotes to plug the film.'

'He still here?' says Chipp to Queen Cunt.

'Maybe he can't take a hint,' Queen Cunt replies.

Cheekbones gives me a half smile. 'I'd go if I were you,' he says, not without warmth.

'Aye, piss off,' says Chipp.

'All right, but before I do, can you just tell me one thing.'

'No,' says Chipp.

'What?' says Queen Cunt.

'Why are you being so horrible to me?'

Queen Cunt lets out a shriek of laughter and pretends to be doubled over with mirth. Chipp decides to join in. Cheekbones shakes his head.

'Oh, that's the funniest thing I've heard all day,' says Queen Cunt to his friends. 'A journalist asking a question like that.'

'I reckon we've let you off bloody lightly,' says Chipp.

'He doesn't. Look at him, I think he's going to cry,' says Queen Cunt. 'Have we been too horrid to you, Mr Londoner? Are we going to make you cry?'

I bite my lip.

'Just leave, mate,' says Cheekbones, softly. 'It's not worth it.'

I turn towards him pleadingly. 'But surely you understand. Just a bit. I mean if people treated you this way, wouldn't you try standing up for yourself?'

'He has been treated this way. By a journalist,' says Queen Cunt.

'We're not all bad, you know.'

'And that's the second funniest thing I've heard all day,' says QC.

'Well we're not.'

'Parasites that's what you are. Parasites. Feeding on other people's misery,' says Chipp.

'We do nice stuff as well. I mean, what about when you get good reviews?'

'Don't read reviews. Load of bollocks,' says Chipp.

'Ooh, you big liar,' says Queen Cunt.

'Hey, don't help him out!' says Chipp.

'I think what we're trying to say to you, Mr Londoner, is that if you don't want people to be horrible to you, don't be a journalist.'

'So you never read newspapers, then?'

'My private life is my own affair', says Queen Cunt.

'He wouldn't understand that. Being a journalist,' says Chipp.

'All I'm saying is that it's a bit hypocritical if—' I say.

'Oh, so we're hypocrites now, are we. That's nice. First he interrupts a private conversation. Then he starts insulting us,' says QC.

'If he wants to trade insults, he's picked the wrong man,' says Chipp.

'Please. I really didn't come here for an argument, I'm just trying to do my job.'

'That's what the guards at Auschwitz said,' says QC.

'Fine then, if you want to twist everything I say.'

'Being a journalist you'd know all about that,' says QC.

I crawl back to Dick, mashed and bloody, like a hedgehog that has been sideswiped by a pantechnicon. I can't look him in the eye because if I catch a trace of sympathy it might just make me cry, which you really don't want to do in front of your baby bro.

He thrusts a glass of fizz in my hand. I down it almost in one.

*

After a while, we agree there's no point dwelling on it any longer and I put on *Strangeways Here We Come*, skipping straight to track five.

'Ah yes, this'll cheer us up,' says Dick, possibly sarcastically, possibly sincerely, because they are a bit like that The Smiths – so insuperably miserable you cannot but be uplifted.

I motion to him to be quiet. The doomy, rainwashed, minor-chord intro to 'Stop Me If You Think You've Heard This One Before' is my favourite bit of the whole album, especially when it changes key just before the vocals start. I catch myself doing that embarrassing music-aficionado-in-ecstasy thing, where you bite your lower lip with your front teeth, and jerk your head dreamily in time to the beat. Looking across, slightly embarassed, to see whether Dick has noticed, I catch him doing it too.

'You like?' I say.

'Or what? I play it all the time,' he says.

'What?' I say, mildly outraged. 'When did you get it?'

'Week, ten days ago, maybe? You know – it was after that South Bank Show special.'

'God, me too. Sad, isn't it?'

'Is it?'

'Well yeah – the fact that it takes an old fart like Melvyn Bragg to tell us what's cool and uncool. I mean, shouldn't we have been into The Smiths already?'

'Probably,' says Dick.

'Actually the seriously annoying thing is that I kind of was. This mad girl Amanda on my Africa trip had their first album and I was really quite into it. And that was in '84 – right at the beginning, when hardly anyone knew about them. And suddenly, here they are splitting up and it's all too late.'

'They're not?' says Dick.

'They fucking are, it's why I'm so pissed off. I think of all the times I could have seen them and didn't. Like when they came to the Oxford Playhouse. Norton saw them, I didn't.'

'Hey, how is Norton?'

'Poor, struggling. The usual. He's got this squat in Brixton he's keen to drag me down to and he keeps having these shows with all these other crusty South London types. But you do kind of wonder what the point is. I mean, if he were any good shouldn't he have been discovered by now?' I say.

'What is he? Twenty-two? Twenty-three?' says Dick.

'He was born in 1964, a year before me. Same year as Stephen Conroy.'

'You know about Stephen Conroy?' he says, impressed.

'Only 'cos I'm jealous. Don't you do it too, that thing where you're constantly measuring yourself against people the same age as you, well nearly the same age, because I've still got a year to be as famous as Stephen Conroy?'

'I think it's just one of your problems.'

'Well it should be one of yours too. Seriously, Dick. How are you ever going to achieve anything if you're not eaten up with self-hatred at not having done as much as your age group? Like Keats, for example. You realize by my age, he'd written half his great poems. Or Martin Amis. He was twenty-two when he published *The Rachel Papers*. Which must mean he started writing it when he was at university. And he'd done more sex than us. And more drugs.'

'Now that does worry me.'

'So it bloody should. I can see us both in twenty years' time, still never having done coke or heroin or acid, unhappily married with a mortgage and kids, wondering what the fuck happened to our youth, why it was we missed out on every single cool trend that ever happened. You know, like how we were too young for punk and not quite poofy enough to be New Romantics and not grim or leftie or Northern enough to get into that whole New Order/Smiths scene?'

'Until it was too late.'

'Yeah right, and by the time the next scene comes along, we're going to be too old. I already am too old. Twenty-two. Twenty-fucking-two. That is completely off the scale as far as any youth trend is concerned.'

'Do you reckon?'

'Well, that's the annoying thing. Do you remember how we felt when we were sixteen or seventeen or eighteen or however old you need to be to be the right age for these youth trends?'

'Too young.'

'Exactly. We thought we were still too young and it would all start happening when we got older. And now we are older look what happens. It turns out we needed to be younger all along.'

'God, you're depressing.'

'So tell me I'm not right.'

'That's what's so depressing.'

Max Factor

Darlingest Molly,

No, of course I'm not pleased that Dale turned out to be
such a shit and no, of course, I don't really think you're
an outrageous whore who slept with my brother nor a
distant, clueless, out-of-touch toff who doesn't know the
first thing about any pop cultural development since 1950.
Just because I imply these things doesn't mean I mean
them and surely you know me well enough to know that
by now. Also, I think it's important to remember that just
because you're unhappy that doesn't mean other people out
there aren't unhappier still. Me, for example.

Indeed, I have so much shite news that I'm not sure
where to begin. By telling you that Dominic was not lying,
Hermione really is leaving the country, probably for ever?
That the late nights and non-stop diet of canapés and
champagne are making me seriously ill and weak, so ill
and weak that I went to see the doctor in case it was ME
or something I picked up in Africa and all the fucker said
was, 'Try cutting down on the drink, cigarettes and late
nights'? That I can't stop doing it because I badly need the
money and what I earn isn't nearly enough in any case
(£25 for a down-page diary story and £75 for a lead don't

go very far when you only get in, at most, three stories a week)? That I may have no choice in the matter, anyway, because after this terrible thing that happened to me last week I'm probably never going to get any diary work ever again. Yes, why not let's start there.

It happened at this place called Vintners' Hall, which, as you probably know, belongs to one of the City guilds, and is so incredibly posh that this jobsworth at the door very nearly didn't let me in because it said Lounge Suits on the invite and I wasn't wearing one. Eventually I'm rescued by this scary PR woman who glares at me like it's my fault and it turns out I'm the *only* journalist there who isn't a famous columnist like Auberon Waugh or the editor of a national newspaper like Charlie Wilson and Andrew Neill and Andreas Whittam Smith. And I realize there's no way I'm going to get any gossip because you don't go up to newspaper editors and say: 'Hi, I'm from Londoner's Diary: got any stories?' because if they have they're not going to give them to one of their rivals, are they? But I can't just stand around there like a spare part, so I go to your godfather, Bron, and say: 'Excuse me? Are you Auberon Waugh' and he says: 'Yes I am, thank you' and carries on with this conversation to this tall man with glasses who I suddenly realize is the editor of the *Telegraph*.

Obviously what I desperately need now is some Dutch courage and I spy a silver tray with six glasses of what looks like sherry on one of the side tables. So I grab a glass and down it in one, which is I think what you do with aperitif sherry, though it doesn't much taste like aperitif sherry, this stuff's sticky and sweet. I'm about to grab another when there's this strangled scream from this bloke in poncy Vintners' Hall regalia and he comes rushing towards me saying 'Those are for our VIP guests.'

'Oops. Sorry,' I say.

Then he sees the empty glass and says: 'Good God, have you already drunk one?'

And I say: 'I think so, yes.'

To which he replies: 'Were you aware that you have just consumed one-sixth of the world's remaining supply of 1782 Imperial Tokay?'

And now a scary PR woman is on to me and hissing: 'That invitation was addressed expressly to the Editor of Londoner's Diary and was *not* transferable.'

'I'm sorry,' I say. 'But what do you want me to do?'

'I expect you to write a very, very, *very* good story about this event.'

So I promise I will. And I mean it too. What I've failed to take into account, though, is the alcohol factor. Now, to be honest, I've become sick of champagne because what they invariably serve at these press dos is cheapo stuff that strips the enamel off your teeth and burns the back of your throat and turns your stomach to acid and fills you with gas so that you keep having to light cigarettes and scurry to different bits of the room to escape your farts. But when I see that what they're serving is Bollinger NV, I think I'll make an exception here.

Then, just when I've decided to slow down a bit, they start serving up vintage Bollinger instead. And obviously, I don't want to miss out, so I have a glass of that – just the one and it's going to be my last, until the next thing I know they're serving this stuff from the 1950s. And I think, well when do you ever get to drink Fifties vintage Bollinger for free?

Pretty much the last thing I remember is having a piss in these spectacular urinals. I'm admiring the porcelain and the polished brass pipes and probably trying to see whether I can get my piss stream to the top (quite impossible because these urinals are enormous) when I'm aware of this presence next to me. Well, by this stage, a sort of we're-all-pissed-together camaraderie has set in and all the age, class, and hierarchy barriers have come down, or so I think, so I say to this bloke: 'Bloody amazing, these urinals, aren't they?' He grunts something I take for a yes, so I glance across to see who it is and it's Max Hastings, liberator of the Falklands and editor of the *Daily Telegraph*. And I think: 'Shit! Have I just made a huge gaffe or have I been merely sociable?' Well there's only one way of finding out and that's to carry on the conversation. Fortunately, he has started peeing after me so while he's trapped mid-flow, I've just enough time to think up something apposite, and not too creepy. So: 'Can I just say, Mr Hastings, how much I admire what you did in the Falklands' is out. But: 'Expect the sanitation facilities in Port Stanley were a sight more primitive, eh?' might just be the one, if only I can convey my message with the right degree of manly bluffness, waggishness and carefully, but not too carefully, concealed arse-lickiness.

Which, is quite a difficult trick to pull off when you're so seriously ratarsed you can scarcely enunciate. 'And while we're here, would you mind awfully giving me some advice as to how I might obtain some work experience on the *Daily Telegraph*?'

'Try not making an ass of yourself in public lavatories,' he barks. Then he tells me my editor will be hearing of this, and that if I attempt to apply for any job on the *Daily Telegraph* he will personally ensure that I do not get it.

Um. God. Writing about it has so depressed me that I'm not sure I want to tell you about the throwing-up-over-the-PR-as-she-poured-me-into-the-cab aftermath. So I won't.

Oh, yes, one good thing. You were absolutely right – Boswell is my new hero and I totally adore him. It's like reading the thoughts someone wrote down yesterday, not two hundred years ago, in fact it's changed my perspective on the whole of the eighteenth century. You'd think because it was a crueller, more primitive age that people thought and felt differently, but they didn't, they were just like us and I wish I'd known this when we were at Oxford because I think it might have been the thing that tipped me towards a first. The other bummer – and it was very cruel of you not to warn me of this – is that just when I'd started identifying with him and thinking, 'Yes, if I could have been anyone in history, Boswell's the man,' I discovered what a miserable life he in fact had, how poor he was and unfulfilled, and how everyone apart from Dr Johnson seemed to think him a bit of a buffoon. And I suddenly thought: Fuck. Maybe that's how people see me. A total buffoon. And maybe I'm going to die poor and unfulfilled too. Oh fuck, oh fuck, oh fuck!

See? Your problems ain't got nothing on mine. So cheer up at once, you cradle-snatching, brother-stealing, completely-out-of-touch, snooty, tarty toff, or there'll be trouble.

Write back soon.

Lots and lots of love

Josh

PS as from the end of this month my new address will be 89 Hazlebury Road, London SW6. It's in Fulham, which is the place to be, I'm told.

Lara's theme

'Maybe we should go now,' I say. 'Before we get too depressed.'

'There's a place I know in Chelsea,' says Dominic. 'We could drink to forget.'

'Forget? Shame on you, man! How could we ever forget?'

We both gaze longingly towards Hermione – what very little we can see of her through the encircling fins of male hacks and executives vying for a Parthian shag. You'd never believe how many people have turned out for her party. Well, you would, but it's still pretty amazing. I mean how many secretaries get lent the executive dining room for their leaving bash? How many get a personal appearance from the proprietor and the chairman? How many get a speech from the editor?

They're all after her. The happily married ones, the deter-minedly celibate ones, even the gay ones. It's like *Kind Hearts and Coronets*: if you had to murder all the people ahead of you in the queue by dint of their being richer, more powerful, better-connected or better-looking, there'd be no one left alive.

'God, will you just look at her, Dom! Did you ever see anything quite so—'

'Fragrant?'

'Yeah. That might be it. Because she's no page three

stunna, is she? I bet your average bloke could pass her in the street without even noticing.'

'You reckon? I don't,' says Dominic.

'Alluring, that's the word I was after. Hermione is Allure personified.'

Dominic rolls the word round his tongue. 'Allluurrre.'

'And you're right. No way could you pass her in the street without noticing. It's like, you know, the way girls are so much sexier with their clothes on than off?'

'No.'

'No, but you know what I mean. It's this thing Hermione's got. She looks all demure and 1940s – prim almost – but you just know that if ever you got to grips with those tonsils—'

'Or those sweet, melonesque breasts—'

And I'm suddenly aware that Hermione is looking right at me.

'I'm getting out of here, before I explode,' I tell Dominic.

'You're not going to say goodbye?'

'Too painful.'

On the way out I stop for a lengthy pee. The men's executive toilets are out of order so I have to use the women's instead, which is embarrassing. Especially when I hear someone waiting outside, causing me to lose my concentration and dribble over the floor. I mop it up guiltily.

'Urrgh, you just pissed all over the floor, didn't you?' says Hermione. Well, what she actually says is: 'Dominic told me you'd gone.'

'I had almost.'

'Weren't you going to say goodbye?'

'Oh. Sorry. It's how I always leave parties.'

'Isn't that rather rude?'

'It's not meant to be. Quite the opposite actually. When

you're having a good time, the last thing you need is someone coming up to you and reminding you that it's all finite.'

'What if you're not having a good time?'

'Do what I do.'

Hermione shakes her head. She's about to go into the loo, but then she checks herself and says, 'Do you think I'd get away with it?'

'Why not?'

'They'd be awfully cross. They've booked us a table at Simpsons in the Strand and everything. Then we're off to Lucian's club.'

'Do you want to go to Lucian's club?'

Hermione thinks for a moment.

'I'll need your help,' she says.

I'm not sure how much is at stake here – at the very least, Hermione's undying gratitude; possibly even her phone number – but I do know that the mission I am about to undertake is one of the most delicate and vital of my life. I must steal back into the executive dining room and, from under the very noses of the enemy, I must remove Hermione's bag and her fake fur coat and hat ensemble. The one that makes her look like Lara out of *Dr Zhivago*.

'Devereux!'

'Shutupshutupshutup, Barsford, I am not here,' I say through clenched teeth. 'I'm on a secret mission.'

'Excellent. What's the mission?'

'It's secret and you're not even to look at me because then you'll know what it is.'

But I can see recognition has already dawned, for his expression is one of horror, outrage and the bitterest jealousy.

I pat him consolingly on the arm. 'Look, I promise, Dom, if anything happens, you'll be the first to know.'

'That's just what I'm afraid of.'

But I don't think it's going to come to that, I really don't. Not with so many obstacles to negotiate. Here's Roger, the Diary's bearded number two, who has barely exchanged two words with me during all the time I've been coming into the office, but is suddenly all smiles as he asks whether I really did throw up over the PR at the Vintners' Hall bash. And just as I'm denying it, two more diarists chip in to enquire whether it was true I interrupted Max Hastings mid-stream to ask him for a job. And, no sooner have I escaped them, than Lucian pounces.

'You still here?' he asks.

'Not really.'

'Never were, were you?' he says, which is fine by me because he's too busy thinking up insults to notice that I'm leaving the party with a woman's handbag, fur coat and hat. And thank God he hasn't because I've been trying all this time to think of what I'd say if anyone noticed and I just can't think of anything plausible.

I'm nearly through the door when I hear someone behind me say: 'Those are Hermione's, aren't they?'

I walk on, pretending not to have heard.

But there's a tap on my shoulder. It's Roger the beardie.

'What are you doing with Hermione's things?'

'She asked me to fetch them for her.'

'Oh dear. Is Hermione leaving?'

'Not yet, I don't think. It's just . . .'

Now Lucian is listening in.

'Roger thought I was pinching Hermione's coat,' I explain.

'And are you?' says Lucian.

'Oooh, yes, because I look soo chic in fur.'

'So where are you taking it?' he asks.

'To Hermione.'

'She's going?'

'She just wanted her cigarettes.'

'But she doesn't smoke.'

'She does. But only when you're not there. Knows you don't approve.'

'Silly girl. Tell her to come back here and smoke as many cigarettes as she likes. No. I'll tell her myself—' he strides forward purposefully. 'Where is she?'

'Outside. In the street somewhere. It's hard to describe exactly. Maybe I'd better go.'

He looks at me shrewdly.

'Just tell her not to be too long,' he says.

Hermione is hiding in the loo.

I tap on the door three times.

'Is it OK?' Hermione calls.

'Yes – no. Wait.'

There's someone behind me. I look round.

It's Dominic, beaming and giving me extravagant thumbs-up signs.

'Fuck off,' I mouth.

He nods, winks and gives me more thumbs up signs.

I wave him away. He leaves, sniggering.

Hermione and I make it to the lifts unnoticed. But as we're waiting for the lift doors to close, we hear approaching voices.

'Oh, please, God, please let the lift doors close and I'll do something you'll really like, I'm not sure what, but something good,' I'm thinking as the voices get closer and closer – one of them belongs to Roger the beardie – and I'm jamming my thumb against the door close button even though I've read somewhere that it's not connected to anything: the button's there purely for psychological reasons.

Hermione must be thinking similar thoughts because as soon as the door does close and the lift is heading indisputably downwards she releases a long, musical sigh. I think: 'God, I wonder if that's a preview of the sound she makes when she c . .', when I notice she's looking at me – reading my thoughts probably – and to cover my shame I say the blandest, least erotically-charged thing I can think of which is: 'Phew, that was close.'

'Yes. It was.'

The 'it was' comes after a slight pause, in which she has clearly been trying to find some way of extending that particular conversational line and then realized it isn't possible. I give myself a mental kick and think of all the more promising things I could have said, like, 'You know that scene in the lift in *Fatal Attraction* . . .?'

But the moment has passed. She's staring serenely above the door at the descending numbers, which enables me to glance in the mirror, first to give myself a triumphant grin, second to check that there are no hanging bogeys or nasty little whiteheads in the recesses of my nose, third to give myself another triumphant grin and fourth to gaze in wonder at Hermione's reflection, so thrillingly close to mine, and think: 'This is unreal!'

The bit that's going to make it more real, of course, is the one when Hermione goes, 'Thanks for getting me out of that little scrape,' pecks me on the cheek and takes the next cab home. Which is why I'm in no hurry to ask her what she plans to do now. Rather, while I still can, I'm just going to luxuriate in the remote-but-not-yet-totally-beyond-the-bounds-of-credibility possibility that she might agree to

accompany me out for a drink. Or maybe even dinner. Or –
well no, that really would be beyond the bounds of possibility.

For I think I ought to make it absolutely clear, here, just
what sort of girl we're talking about. If I go into too much
detail about her pre-Raphaelite looks you might think she's
not your type and lose interest, which would be a mistake
since she is your type, she's everybody's type, even if you're a
woman she'll turn you lesbian. Suffice to say she is the sort
of girl so ravishingly gorgeous, so stunningly sophisticated,
so out-of-your-league, so perfect in every way that in the
extremely unlikely event that she were to allow you anywhere
near her bed, even for just one night, you would be congratulating yourself for the rest of your life. You'd be Guy Ritchie
after he first dated Madonna. You'd be thinking: 'God! I owe
you for this.'

Hence my pre-emptive strike, as the lift door opens with
a, 'Look, God, I'm really grateful for the way you got the lift
door to close like that, but would you mind doing me another
favour? When I ask her out for a drink could you please,
please, please let her say "yes"? If you do that, I'm yours. I'll
do anything you want me to. Within reason, obviously. I
mean, I'm not promising to be born-again. But I'll see you
right, just you see.'

And there's a taxi approaching now with its orange light
on, so I'd better get in there quick but, oh God, this is too
awful, what if she says no, what if I ask in the wrong way,
what . . .

'What do you want to do now?'

It's not me who's asking.

'Er. How about a drink?' I say.

'I don't think so. I've already had a bit too much champagne. Where do you live?' she asks.

'Islington.'

'That's more or less in my direction. Why don't we go there for coffee or something.'

Or something?

Her palm is soft as I help her into the taxi. It makes me feel like the debonair hero of some Forties' movie.

If I were really debonair, of course, I'd use these precious early seconds to slide across the slippery mock-leather and insinuate myself right next to her, as if some imaginary third person were about to join us on the back seat. Being me, though, I behave more as if she were suffering from anthrax, squeezing myself primly against the far window.

I daren't say anything. I daren't even look at her, lest she suddenly realize it's me sitting next to her not Tom Cruise. Instead, I pretend to be enthralled by the business adverts on the partition in front of me, while fumbling in my pockets for a nerve-calming fag and plotting how best to cross those vast arid wastes that stretch between us.

The sensible thing, it seems to me, is to use the motion of the cab when it corners to accidentally on purpose slide sideways until, oops, goodness me, our elbows appear to be touching, Hermione, and – well I never – my right arm seems to have leaped over your shoulder while my fingers are brushing gently against the nape of your neck.

Before I can put any of this into practice, the cab takes a sharp right corner and I feel the weight of Hermione's fur-clad body pressing against my arm. I freeze. She stays where she is. I wait, just to make absolutely sure that this isn't an accident. Then, with the slow, disbelieving awkwardness of the sole survivor stumbling from the wreckage of a Jumbo jet, I jerk my arm over her shoulder and pull her more tightly towards me.

She nestles her head against my neck.

I smell her hair, her warm skin and the traces of some impossibly sophisticated scent so rare and perfect it probably doesn't even have a name.

I want to kiss her. I want to ask her: 'Why me?' But I'm paralysed with the terror that any second I'll wake up and it's all going to end.

Please, God. I know you're not a huge fan of pre-marital sexual intercourse but if you can somehow see your way to letting us – you know – then I'm yours for ever. I'll go to church next Easter. This Sunday even, if you like. I'll give a tenner to charity. I'll say my prayers every night for the next month. I'll, look if it's really that important to you, I'll even marry the girl, if she's willing. Just please, God. Oh please, please, please let me get my end away.

I stumble from the cab, dizzy with pre-sex adrenalin. The driver gets a huge tip. 'Have a good one, mate,' he says with a wink.

It's nearly dark now. I steer Hermione through the gate and along the rough, ill-lit pathway to the squalid side entrance. I'm worried about the stickiness I can feel in my pants. Just anticipatory lubrication, I hope.

'So, this is it,' I croak as I fiddle with the lock.

'Mm.'

Arm in arm we climb the stairs.

It's a wonderful moment, this. The one where you know for absolute certain that in seconds you're going to be seeing this person you've always fancied naked for the first time. And that they're looking forward to it as much as you are.

You ready your key to open the door . . .

When suddenly you realize . . .

It's already open.

Burglars.

You've been burgled.

Still, nothing to panic over. You've nothing worth stealing and provided they haven't done anything really offputting like crap in your bed, you can still go ahead with what you were planning to do without too much trouble.

Unless, of course, they're still in there.

Which, they are. You can hear them, bumbling about.

Shit!

'Stay back,' I mouth to Hermione.

I knock on the door.

'Hell-ooo,' I call.

The door is opened by a heavily suntanned young woman in yellow rubber gloves.

'About bloody time,' she says. 'You can help me clear the rest of this filth which I've spent half a day cleaning already. You've murdered the plants, you've wound up the neighbours, you've drunk my Campari—'

'Er. Hermione, this is my cousin Susan. Susan, Hermione.'

'—You've been here six months and did you ever bother to clean it in all that time? The dust on the window sills was an inch thick! The cooker – well you're going to have to get all those burn marks off the top because I've tried and I can't. But first I'd like you to—'

'Maybe I should just—' says Hermione.

'No. Let's have dinner,' I say.

'If you think you're buggering off for dinner—' snaps Susan.

'Look, I'm tired. I really ought to be getting home,' says Hermione. She pecks me on the cheek. 'And thanks. For everything.'

For a long time I cannot move, so stunned am I by the

outrageousness of my terrible ill fortune. And when I do and hurl myself downstairs and through the gate and on to the street and discover that she's disappeared, I realize something still worse. I never even got her phone number.

I Never Got Her Fucking Phone Number!

So I shan't be going to church next Sunday.

Nor at Easter.

Nor sodding Christmas neither.

Hugh Massingberd's hat

Dearest darlingest Mollsy babes,

Sorry for not having written in a while but too much exciting stuff has been happening, not least the possibility that I might be getting a real job.

It's at the *Daily Telegraph*, which you probably think is a bad thing, I know I did till quite recently because obviously no one but old colonels reads it, the print's all dense and gothic, and about the only interesting things in it are the court reports on page three where you get more juicy detail about sex and murder cases than even the tabloids. But actually I think its old fartishness is a huge bonus because it makes all the executive types paranoid that their readers are dying faster than they can replace them, i.e they're desperate for younger readers and they think the way to get them is to have younger writers. Which is where I come in.

It all came about after this lunch I had with this cadaverous chap called Evans the Death, who works on the obituaries section. I didn't know him or anything. Nor do I nurture any massive ambition to spend my life writing about dead people. He's just a friend of a friend who said,

'Why don't you give him a ring? He's really nice and he might help your career.'

Lunch was great. We had it in this restaurant on a boat and got drunk. Two bottles drunk, which is a lot for me. I was quite surprised because I'd been expecting lots of serious questions like: 'And what special qualities do you think you can bring to the *Daily Telegraph*'s obituaries column?' (I'd even prepared an answer: 'I'm terrified of dying so I think I can empathize with people who have.') Whereas all we actually talked about was Oxford (Evans the Death was at Univ about five years before us) and how drunk we used to get and what drugs we took. I've since realized that, of course, he was interviewing me all along. It was a bit like those tests they give you at All Souls where you have to demonstrate at dinner that you can peel a grape with the correct fish knife or that you won't discuss politics or the Queen until the third don on the college president's left has been sconced. Apparently I passed.

All my job involves is thinking of fun people who are likely to die and then writing their biography in the house style which is based on Aubrey's *Brief Lives* (i.e. you pick out all the weird and wacky detail from their lives, go big on that and ignore all the worthy stuff they print in all the other newspapers). I started with Freddie Mercury because they've hardly got any rock people in their files and because there's this rumour that he's got AIDS. At least I hope he has because if he ends up dying of old age fifty years hence I'm buggered. Just in case, though, I've done several oldsters more in tune with our readers' tastes: Barbara Woodhouse (dogs), Norman Parkinson (snobbery) and Simon Raven (cricket, booze and buggery).

I could do them at home but actually it's quite nice going to the office which is this huge blue glass building in the Docklands with vile open-plan workspaces that you reach via this crap railway which always breaks down. But at least you get free light, heating, phone calls, stationery and decent company. I doubt the rest of the *Telegraph*'s like that, but obits are run as a private fiefdom by this splendid fellow called Hugh Montgomery Massingberd. His *Private Eye* nickname is Massivesnob, which is jolly unfair because even though he's obsessed with genealogy, he's one of the least snobbish people I've ever met. (Though obviously, he did notice that Devereux was the surname of the Earls of Essex.) Hugh thinks having to work for a living is a terrible injustice and spends the whole time trying to pretend it's just our hobby. When you hand him in another obit, for example, he acts like you've just done him the most tremendous personal favour. He has lent me his old grey fedora, which is initialed HMM on the hatband and comes from Locks. I'm not sure whether it makes me look raffish or a prat. Both, I suspect.

But this job I mentioned. I think it's going to be on Peterborough, which is like the *Telegraph*'s nursery for young graduates. Tragically, it is a diary which means I'll be doing more of the same shite I did on the *Standard*. But since the starting salary is £18,000 who sodding cares what I have to do – poking the eyes out of kittens, unloading babies from lorries with pitchforks, I'll do it.

Why do I need the money? Well, I have started to acquire some expensive vices. This weekend I am going to be taking my first Ecstasy tablet and they cost £35 each, which is a lot, I agree, but you can't get hold of them anywhere, this batch has come over specially from California, and they're supposed to be so brilliant that they'd be cheap at twice the price.

What's cool is that no one I know has ever tried one. Not even the bloke who's selling me the stuff, he's just my coke dealer. (Or rather, the bloke who sold a friend of mine a gram of coke which I ended up going halves on – I don't want you to get the wrong idea about my drugular sophistication.)

This is probably going to sound too extreme for you, but just in case you meant what you said in your letter about being sick of being a bluestocking, well, maybe I can help you. There's loads of room in this new house in Fulham where I'm renting, so, if you like, next time you're over you can come and stay and we'll find some drugs to do. Or we could even go to a club. There's one I checked out the other day called Enter The Dragon. I only went for work purposes because I was researching a piece for *Tatler* on King's Road groovers, which I decided could be stretched to encompass Kensington High Street. But I got the impression that something quite cool was going on – everyone was sucking lollipops and smiling, and the music was incredibly simpatico in a weird, bleeping, pulsing sort of way.

Then again knowing my luck this new scene will turn out to be a really crap one that fades in about a month and everyone gets embarrassed about having been involved in. I mean, constant smiling and lollipop-sucking aren't very punk rock, are they?

So, please, the second you're next over, come and see

me that very instant. Preferably before my ashen, drug-filled body is found in a pool of vomit.

Lots and lots of love,

Josh

Blessing serpents

I'm wading through my usual pile of office post and it's all quite uselessly dull – press releases for events I'd never dream of attending, grumbly letters from cranky readers and invoices from lunatic contributors for stories they filed but which we never actually ran – except for the promising-looking pink envelope which I've saved till last.

Everyone else on the desk is watching me surreptitiously because they all know. They've probably been tipped off by Violet, our secretary, who clucks over us all like a mother hen and is no doubt delighted to have uncovered some small piece of evidence that at least one of her boys may possibly be heterosexual, though God knows none of us looks it, least of all me. For this is me in my Veronica Lake phase – as one admiring queen will later put it at some showbiz party – which is to say I've got my hair cut into a bob. Combined with my still-boyish looks, my line in those wide, colourful ties which seem terribly outré at the time but which within two years everyone will be buying from Tie Rack, and my extremely gay, black Venetian wool suit with its high-crossed tulip lapels, ultra-broad shoulders, nipped waist and its arse-baring bum-freezer cut which positively screams for immediate anal entry, it must be said that 'straight' is possibly not the first word that would spring into the mind of the casual onlooker.

As I look up, the others glance quickly at their screens then back to me again, by which time I've secreted the pink envelope in my jacket's inside pocket.

'Oi, Josh, innit. You going to open it?' squawks Millicent, the secretary of the letters section, whose desk is adjacent to ours.

'Sorry, Millie. It's private,' I say. And then realize what a prig I sound.

'Oh, Josh, I do think that's terribly unfair,' says Violet. 'We've been waiting all morning.'

'Since when did my private life become public property?'

'Since you started writing about it in intimate detail in your party column?' suggests Crispin.

'Since you started telling every celebrity you meet so much about yourself that you've no time to find out anything about them?' suggests Charles.

'Quite, Devereux. You weren't back from the Caprice till four yesterday. Then you were straight off to that A-list celeb-fest that urgently required your presence because only you were on intimate terms with the veritable galaxy of stars. So where are my yarns?' barks the editor, who's the same age as me but acts like he's fifty. We call him the Rottweiler.

'All right, all right, I'll open it,' I say, withdrawing the card from my pocket. 'I just hope you can all live with the shame of being such prurient scumballs.'

'As diarists I expect we're going to find that quite a struggle,' says Crispin. The card shows a soppy cartoon bear clutching a big red heart. Inside it says simply 'Be my Valentine', underneath which someone has written an X and a '?'.

'Good Lord, I'd know that handwriting anywhere,' chortles Quentin, the city diarist. 'It's Robin's, from the canteen.'

Everyone laughs. Robin is widely known as the Bender in the Hat, because he wears a gay hat and because, since he speaks in a fruity voice and loves opera, he's obviously a huge bender.

'Looks more like Hilda's shaky hand to me,' says Lucian, with a mischievous nod towards the myopic old crone on Court and Social.

'Oh, you're too naughty,' says Violet. 'I'm sure it's from someone very lovely.'

A few days later a girl I've never met before accosts me in the lift. She's dark-eyed and really quite pretty and despite her strong Essex accent, naff haircut and suspiciously Top-Shop-looking attire, I'm thinking: 'Blimey, if it's her I'm well in.'

'Hi,' she says.

'Hi.' And already I'm mentally undressing her and taking her right there against the wall of the lift with one finger pressed against the 'door close' button while the doors go 'bang bang bang' as they do when there are people on the other side trying to get in.

'You got the card, then?'

'Er yes. Yes, I did. Thanks.' Flash forward to our first date in – a nightclub called Jingles or Tiffany's in somewhere like Romford where everyone's staring at me because I dress funny and talk funny but that's OK because she's all in Mandy-Smith-goes-to-Marbella white, looking really dirty and up for it, and now it's time to drink up and go back to her place and—

'—didn't get it.'

'I'm sorry?' I say.

'Carol was,'

'Who?'

'You *know. Carol!*' she says.

She's still giggling at what she seems to imagine is my very funny joke, when the doors open and Quentin the City diarist walks in.

'Going up?' says Quentin fruitily.

And I can't get out now even though it is my floor and I badly want to because if I do I might never know.

It takes eons of embarrassed silence for the door to close and eons more agony – during which Quentin teases me over the girl's shoulder with various incomprehensible gestures which may mean: 'Coo! Wot a stunna!' or 'Steady there, old man. Slumming it a bit, aren't you?' – before Quentin reaches his destination and it's safe to talk once more.

'So,' says the girl. 'Are you going to keep playing hard to get?'

'That very much depends on who the fuck this Carol person is and whether or not she looks like the back end of a bus,' is the answer that immediately springs to mind. The one that comes out is: 'I don't even know her . . . extension.'

'7723. You'll phone her, then?' she says.

'But what if she's a dog?' I ask Violet in the canteen at lunchtime.

'Oh, Josh, that isn't a nice word to use about a pretty young girl.'

'Violet, if she's pretty, I won't need to use it.'

'Just ask her out for a drink. What harm could it possibly do?'

What harm? I could try telling her but she'd never understand. Old people don't. It's what happens to you after a certain age: you stop being embarrassed by things. If you feel like doing something, you do it. Being that much closer to the grave, you know you'll probably never get a second chance.

In your twenties, though, you will get a second chance. And a third, fourth and fifth one probably. Which should make you feel free to make as many mistakes as you like. But oddly it doesn't. You'd like to be reckless and impulsive. That's how you're always being told that young people are supposed to be. But the people telling you this are older people and they're not to be trusted. Their memory of what it's actually like to be young has been warped by nostalgia. Or they're simply urging you to make a complete dick of yourself because that's what they did when they were young and they want to even the score.

But you know better. You know that every decision you make in your twenties could change the whole course of your life. Especially if it's something as delicate as an office romance. Whatever you do, everyone will know. Everyone! If your date comes to nothing you'll be known for ever more as a sexless crypto-gay. If you fuck her and chuck her, you'll become the office bastard. If you start going out with her, your every intimate secret will be round the building like wildfire – from your penis dimensions to the frequency and pungency of your bedtime farts, your whole life will become part of some terrible intra-office soap opera. If you do nothing . . . Yes. That really is the only sensible answer.

'We're being watched,' says Violet.

'What?' I glance over my shoulder. 'Ohmygod, it's her.'

'Which one?' says Violet.

'How do I know?'

'They're jolly nice-looking, all three of them. The dark one especially,' says Violet.

'That's the friend who's definitely not her.'

'Even so, the others—' says Violet.

'You sure? The mousey one looked pretty rough.'

'You can't have seen her for more than a second. And if it's her beautiful blonde friend who sent you the card . . .'

'What if it's not? Check out the mousey one again, will you. Just how dog-like—?'

'Hello!' Violet smiles as the girls walk past our banquette in line abreast.

I feign sudden and intense interest in the remnants of my lunch, and don't look up until the girls have almost disappeared. But I'm still in time to catch the blonde one giving me a coy and very lovely smile.

'Blimey, did you see that?'

'I think we have our answer,' beams Violet.

'Yeah, you know what, though. She's bound to be too stupid or too common. Or both, probably.'

'Faint heart never won fair maiden,' says Violet.

'Maiden? Now that's one thing we can be sure she isn't.'

Still, you can't be too careful. Just to make sure, I send Violet upstairs on a couple of vital missions. On the first, she will ascertain more or less where extension 7723 is. On the second, she will hover subtly in the vicinity while I dial the number from below at a specific time. In this way, we will know that whichever girl picks up the phone is Carol.

Both missions are a success. Violet assures me that the girl who picked up the phone is the one I fancy. And as an added bonus, the voice I hear at the other end before I quickly replace the receiver, sounds reassuringly educated. If you can tell such things from three-quarters of the word 'hello'.

Later, in a halting, awkward phone conversation, we arrange to meet near work, at one of those riverside pubs in Narrow Street, in a week's time. I could have arranged it for earlier and I rather wish I had, if only so as to have avoided all the penile damage I've done tossing myself raw with a series of increasingly fervid anticipatory wanks. But I didn't want to sound as desperate as in fact I am. Which is very. Very, very, very. I haven't had sex in Christ knows how long and this date is surely about as close as a man can get to a 100 per cent surefire thing.

The only things in any doubt, it seems to me, are the tiny details, like whether or not to use eau de cologne and which suit to wear and whether or not to bring my car. The last one's particularly tricky. If I don't, it means I'll be able to drink more, thus giving myself some Dutch courage, providing an incentive for her to get drunk too, and ultimately giving me the chance if anything goes wrong to blame it on alcohol. If, on the other hand, I do bring my car, I can gamely offer to drive her home, thus cutting out that awkward bit at the end of the evening where you've just hailed her cab and she has to make that nerve-jangling snap decision as to whether or not she's going to ask you back for coffee. It's a measure of my confidence that I plump for option two.

Carol clearly isn't quite so sure though, because on arriving, I find she has invited one of her mates along for moral support. Carol's mate smiles at me from the bar and I smile back my recognition, which I think is quite clever of me given that I've seen her only once before, that time in the canteen. In the second before I join her, I'm assailed by a moment of terrible but ill-defined doubt. But it soon passes as I try to concentrate on the job in hand: viz, demonstrating to this girl that I'm a nice guy who's safe in taxis so that she feels confident enough to fuck off home and leave her pretty blonde friend to my tender cares.

'So,' I say when I've ordered us both a drink. 'Still no sign of Carol?'

At first she doesn't reply. But the baleful look she gives me is charged with such awful meaning – accusation, terror, despair, guilt, confusion – that she really doesn't need to.

'I am Carol.'

I take an extra deep drag on my cigarette, partly out of dire need, partly to buy time. I've got, what?, a couple of seconds at most in which to think up a convincingly self-exculpatory reply. Any longer and she'll know I'm lying.

If I need to lie, that is.

Why do I need to lie?

Why can't I just come clean and tell her I'm sorry, there's been an awful mistake, it's her friend I fancy not her? Why can't we just drink up, head our separate ways and spare ourselves a long miserable evening spent discovering how incompatible we are? WHY?

'Of course I know who you are,' I say with a rictus smile. 'What I meant was: the Carol I saw in the canteen the other day, what on earth's happened to her? You look so different. So—'

Oh God. If I say so much prettier, she'll think that when I first saw her I thought she was a complete hound and then she'll get all upset because she'll know that I only came here out of duty.

But if I don't show enough enthusiasm, she'll know my heart's not in it and then she'll lose interest herself, causing our evening to flatline and reducing to zero any remaining chance of it all leading to the frenzied sexual encounter I've fantasized about for the last week. Not, on first impressions, that that's necessarily what I want to happen. But you never know. It pays to keep your options open.

'—So – you *know*.' I say, as if the breadth of my smile expresses far more than mere words ever could.

She doesn't look as if she does know. Her eyelids flutter as if she's on the verge of tears, but her voice is strangely collected.

'If you want to call it off now, I really won't mind.'

'What? Why do you think I'd want to do that?'

Her eyes are an eerie, watery blue. I'm reminded of Carrie. Does Sissy Spacek have watery blue eyes? I don't know. But she spooks me.

'I'd just rather we were honest with each other, that's all.'

I look her straight in the eye and enunciate each word firmly. 'I want to be here.'

'That's very nice of you. But it's not too late to change your mind. Please—'

'I'm not going to change my mind,' I say, hoping that if I keep looking at her hard enough I'll find something about her that I fancy. 'I came here for a nice evening with you and that's what I'm going to do. So let's drink to that, shall we?'

I chink my glass against hers.

'To a nice evening,' she says.

'God that sounds lame, doesn't it?' I say.

We chink glasses again.

'To a brilliant evening.'

Yeah, right.

It's not exactly outdoorsy weather, but I suggest we go outside anyway and sit on the balcony which overhangs the river. That way, we'll have something to talk about; we'll be less likely to be seen together by someone from work. And it'll be too dark to see her properly.

It's not that she's pig ugly. I mean, I'm sure in the right light with the right clothes and the right make up on the right day she'd look quite OK. Unfortunately right at this minute none of those conditions stand. Apart from her eyes – her second-best feature provided you can somehow ignore the sinister Carrie effect – the most noticeably attractive thing about her is her lustrous hair. And when the best thing you can find to say about your date's looks is that her hair's lustrous, well—

Oh, and I quite like her clothes too. She's wearing thick black tights, a black polo neck and a jacket and matching skirt in pale grey Prince of Wales check. Her and a zillion other PAs, account executives and upmarket secretaries. But that's what I like about it. When I look at her clothes and mentally detach the head, I can kid myself I'm with one of the prettier girls I've at some time glimpsed in the same kit.

Once we've exchanged the inevitable banalities about ourselves – she's twenty-two, read social sciences at Manchester, works in marketing, lives in Camberwell, doesn't smoke, not even dope, so bang goes another opportunity for us to get so out of it that we're really not responsible for our actions – we start exchanging banalities about our surroundings.

Like, Oh look there's a police boat, wonder why he's circling like that, do you think he's found a body, that would make our evening wouldn't it, if we saw him find a body.

Carol isn't sure that it would.

Well, not make our evening, maybe, but when you see a floating object in the river don't you always find yourself wishing it's going to be a body? No? God, I do, though preferably a fairly recent one because they get really bloated and foul after a while, don't they, so wrinkled their finger prints have peeled off, you have to go by the dental records. And the smell, can you imagine the smell?

Carol would rather not.

That's the thing I often wonder, though. Suppose you wanted to commit suicide and you threw yourself in the Thames and then changed your mind, do you think you'd be able to scramble out or do you think the currents are so strong you'd never make it? Or what if you just dived in for a bet, do you know I've been really tempted sometimes. It's a form of vertigo, I suppose, like when you're on the edge of a cliff and you just can't resist going closer and closer to the edge – No? Maybe it's just a boy thing. God it's weird, sometimes the urge is so intense, I could almost do it now.

Carol thinks that wouldn't be a good idea.

Sorry, am I freaking you? Don't mean to. See that house there. That's where Ian McKellen lives, went to a party there once, he's got a garden right on the river, or am I confusing it with David Lean, not sure, I never actually went outside. What's he like? Oh nice, nice, if you're young and male and he doesn't know you're not gay which obviously in my case . . .

Carol confides that quite a few of her friends suspected I might be.

Oh God [shudder: she talks about me to her friends; whatever I do tonight is going to get straight back to them] I know, I know, even I'm not sure myself sometimes.

No?

Well, maybe I'm exaggerating. But how do you know, how does anyone know? I mean have you never been tempted by the idea of having sex with another woman?

And I see what I'm doing here, it's what I always do when I can't deal with a situation normally, I change myself into a different person so that it's not me experiencing it it's someone else. I've become this brash, unpleasant, cartoonish hyperperson whom with luck she'll realize she doesn't much like, thus sparing me the need to hurt her feelings because it'll be she who decides to reject me rather than the other way round. At least that's what she'll think.

So now I've moved on to the inevitable bit about how, God, I wish I was a lesbian and how fabulous it must be to be a woman having your very own pair of tits to play with – and it's as if the more disgusted with myself I feel the more suicidally outrageous I have to become in order to punish myself for being so horrible, which means I'm going to get ghastlier and ever ghastlier in a spiral of self hatred – when suddenly I notice that she's shivering with cold and probably has been for quite some time.

'I'm sorry—' I say. Which is an understatement because at last it has occurred to me just what a shit I'm being. It's not her fault I don't fancy her and it's not as if she didn't give me several chances to pull out at the last minute, so why am I treating her like some ravenous maneater who has lured me into a trap? '—you must be freezing. Shall we go indoors?'

I offer her another drink and she says no, she ought to be getting off now and thanks very much for the drink, it's been lovely talking to me. She's just popping off to the loo and then we can say goodbye.

I shouldn't but I can't help it, as she sets off I watch the tight, swaying cloth of that Prince of Wales check skirt and I think of the naked flesh of her buttocks underneath and of the bare skin beneath her black woollen tights. And then I kill that train of thought before it goes any further because I know that this is the moment, it has all been set up perfectly, the mood is right for a clean departure with no hard feelings, it just didn't work out, that's all. When she returns, I'll kiss her warmly on both cheeks and maybe mumble something about being sorry if I seemed a bit offhand, I've got a lot on my mind at the moment, followed by a vague 'See you, sometime . . .'

Now she's coming back, not looking at me, mildly crest-fallen clearly but there's no point worrying about that now, I know what I've got to do and I mustn't make things worse than they already are.

'How're you getting home?' I ask.

'Oh. I should get a taxi easily enough,' she says.

'Let me drive you. It's hardly out of my way.'

'It's miles out of your way,' she chides, with the first genuine smile I've seen all evening.

'Come on. I've bored you rigid and half frozen you to death. It's the very least I can do to make it up.'

It takes less than twenty minutes for us to get from Dock-lands to Camberwell: more than enough time for me to ruminate on the idiocy of my offer. I try distracting myself by driving extra-fast, but Carol's palpable terror only increases the tension. I try turning the radio up loud so we don't have to speak, but because she feels obliged to find new things to say and I feel obliged to reply, I spend half the time driving one-handed, twiddling the volume up and down. Which makes Carol more tense still. Occasionally, when I think she isn't looking, I steal glances at her out of the corner of my eye, to see whether she's got any better looking since last time I checked. Each time I do, it triggers a new bout of guilt and remorse.

It's during one such bout that I hear myself saying: 'Do you think we should maybe grab a bite to eat?'

'No really, there's no need,' she says.

'Aren't you hungry?'

'A tiny bit but—'

'Great. Where do you fancy?'

Our conversation during the long wait for our pizza is even more studiedly formal than the earlier one about our family backgrounds and educational history. All around us, on candlelit tables, are couples about our age spoiling for a shag. Yet here we are talking about the routes we take to work and the slowness of the Docklands Light Railway and thence to the quality of the food in the canteen. Not at all bad, considering, we decide.

'Fuck, this is ridiculous,' I say, sticking my hand in the air. It's not really the service I have in mind. I'm thinking: I'm desperate, she's available and provided we can keep the lights down low . . .

The bottle of red I've just ordered comes long before the pizza and I insist we both down our first glasses in a few swift gulps.

'I think we need to relax a bit,' I explain.

'Maybe,' she says. Tensely.

Now I need to up the ante. Asking whether she's got a boyfriend seems the obvious route. But I can't just ask her out of the blue. It would seem too pointed. Better to wait for her to say something relationship-related. Then I can segue in smoothly with a:

'You don't have a boyfriend then?' or a 'Going out with anyone at the moment?' or 'So tell me. Is there a man in your life?' or 'God, it's a relief being single, don't you think?' or—

But if she ever does say something relationship-related I don't hear it because I'm too busy running through the options of what I'm going to say when she says it. And the longer I deliberate, the harder it gets. What originally seemed like a reasonably innocuous enquiry as to the current state of her love life now seems almost tantamount to asking: 'You up for a fuck or what?'

It's like standing on the edge of a millpond on a hot summer's day. You know the water will be lovely once you're in and you know there's no way you're not going to jump in eventually because you'd regret it too much afterwards. But that doesn't stop you delaying the moment as long as possible. What about that freezing shock when you first hit the water? What if it's shallower than you think? What if there's a pike in there? Or leeches?

Time and again I take a long running jump at the question only to pull up at the very last second. Until, finally, I blurt out—

'Do you have a boyfriend?'

– suddenly aware, as I'm saying it, that she's in the middle of telling me something deeply personal and poignant about a late and cherished aunt.

Which would explain the puzzled silence before she answers: 'No. And you?'

'Not really, and I'm not sure I'd like to be in a relationship right now. Not a serious one. You know, there's so much going on in my life at the moment, and I just don't think it would be fair if I put someone in a situation where, um, they expected something from me that I wasn't capable of giving.'

'Commitment?'

'Uh. I guess. Do you think that's terribly immature of me?'

'Yes.' She gives me a hard, meaningful look. 'But I can't say I blame you. To be honest, that's exactly how I feel myself right now.'

'Uh huh?' I say, unable to meet her eye. It might, of course, be that she's saying that she's not up for any kind of relationship – one-night stands included. But there's something in that eerily intense blue Carrie gaze, something animal and predatory, that tells my delicately wine-pickled brain otherwise. 'Lick me, fuck me, do what you please with me,' it seems to be saying. 'I don't care about tomorrow and I don't care if we never see each other again. Let's just do it now.'

When I glance up for confirmation, her eyes are still saying the same thing. I've gone weak with lust, I can feel my legs turning to jelly. I want to speak – to tell her 'Fuck the pizza. Let's get you home right now!' – but first I have to clear the lump in my throat and—

'One pizza pomodoro. One American Hot,' announces the waiter, brandishing his risibly enormous pepper grinder above Carol's plate.

And the spell is broken. The magic has gone. The police have burst in on the orgy and we're like 'Who? Us? Never. We were just having dinner.'

We both chew in silence.

'Bit stingy with the pepperami. How's yours?'

For just the briefest instant our eyes meet. 'Phew. That was close,' they seem to tell one another. But whether with regret or massive relief, I'm not quite sure.

I'm still not sure when I'm standing at the foot of the piss-ridden, graffitoed, stained concrete stairway which leads up to her flat, wondering whether or not to accept her invitation to come in for a coffee.

And I'm no more sure when I'm inside, cupping a mug of nasty instant between my palms while trying to find a comfortable position on a giant beanbag – the closest thing she's got to a chair. Carol sits on the floor opposite me, legs chastely crossed, nothing in her demeanour suggesting that she invited me in for anything more than a restorative caffeinated beverage followed by a polite goodnight. Which is annoying, because if only she were a bit more forward, I might be able to resolve my dilemma.

On the one hand, here I am, sex-starved and fancy-free, in the unusual position of being alone with a young woman who has given me the vague impression that if I made an advance on her it would not be wholly unwelcome.

On the other, I have my credibility to think of. And the near certainty that whatever I do will be reported back in juicy detail to all her friends and thence to everyone else on the newspaper. And the fact that I don't fancy her. And the terrifying possibility that she's up for a longer-term thing; that she has no intention of putting out on the first date; that by making a move on her I will be simply committing myself to yet further dates. Which isn't what I want at all.

What I want is—

'Can I ask you something?' she says.

'Sure.'

'Why did you come here?'

'What? Um – well, it just, you know, I thought it would be nicer for you than coming back by taxi.'

'Is that all?'

'Um. And I thought it would give us a chance to get to know each other better and that sort of thing.'

'That sort of thing?'

I nod weakly and fumble for a fag.

'Tell me what you really came here for,' she says. I notice she's shaking, as if she's fighting hard against her natural reticence.

'You really want to know?' I light the cigarette, inhaling hard.

'Yes.'

'Can't. Too embarrassing.'

She leans towards me, stroking her hair away from her ear. A pretty ear. 'Whisper it, then.'

'Can't.'

'Don't you want to tell me?'

'Yes. No. Maybe.'

'If you tried writing it down. Do you think you could do that?'

'Not sure.'

'Let's try.'

She eases herself off the floor, in a pleasingly fluid, gymnastic movement that gives me pause: is she more lissom than I imagined or has my mind been warped by lust?

She returns with a felt tip and several sheets of paper.

'Oh God,' I say, blushing. 'Do I have to?'

'You just do whatever you want to do.'

'But I don't know what to write,' I say. What I'm hoping for, obviously, is that she'll respond with something safe and predictable like 'Well, you're the journalist' and the tension will vanish and everything will return to normal. Except at the same time, of course, it isn't what I want. More intense would be better.

'Write down the thing you most want to do. With me. Here. Now,' she says.

'I WANT' I write and then stop, unable to go on. I look up, grinning sheepishly. 'Do you think maybe I should write "Dear Santa" first?'

She doesn't answer. Her expression is almost contemptuous.

'—TO FUCK YOU,' I add very quickly, as if speed will somehow serve to diminish the awkwardness of the sentiment.

I hand her the note. As she holds it in front of her, I notice her hand trembling. She won't meet my eye.

She writes a note of her own.

'WHEN?' it says.

'NO—' I write. I'm about to complete it with a 'W' when I think better of it, suddenly aware of the shift in the power balance, rather enjoying it. '—T YET' I add.

The cigarette I was smoking has burned down to the butt. I smear it against the ashtray and light another one, coolly, sadistically observing Carol from my beanbag throne.

She is sitting below me on the floor, back straight, legs crossed, eyes downcast – some sort of yoga position. I continue to stare at her, waiting for her to crack and look upwards so that I can see in her eyes that she wants me as much as I want her. Because she knows and I know – and I'm going to tease out this delicious anticipation for as long as possible – that any time soon I'm going to be fucking her so hard . . . or maybe so gently . . . or . . . And I sink deeper into the beanbag, my eyes wandering languorously between her lips, her tits and her crotch, in sweet contemplation of the myriad ways in which I could possibly fuck her.

Still she does not look up.

I stub out my cigarette and reach for the pen and paper. After a moment's thought I write: 'TAKE OFF YOUR TIGHTS.'

She considers the note and, with a faint show of reluctance, shuffles them off. She crosses her legs self-consciously, but I can still just make out the indentation of creamy dampness creasing her white knickers.

'TAKE OFF YOUR KNICKERS,' I write.

She gives me a brief, accusing look. Then she does as she's told but draws her knees towards her, clasping her arms chastely round her legs. I leave her like that, watching her shiver. I regard her curiously.

She reaches impatiently for the paper: 'NOW!' she scrawls. I shake my head.

'STAND UP,' I write.

As soon as she does I take her hand and draw her closer, so that her pubic mound is just a few inches from my nose. I smell the scent of cunt and I want to bury my face inside but somehow I contain myself just enough as she whispers, 'Now. Please. NOW!' to reach for the paper and write: 'WRITE ONLY.' She reads the note and lets out a yelp of frustration.

But now it's her turn to punish me, or so it seems, for to retrieve the notepaper she doesn't dip down on her knees as you might normally. Rather, she swivels round so that her buttocks are almost in my face and she bends at the waist slowly and ostentatiously, to reveal by teasing degrees in all their exquisite raw rudenesss every inch of those sweet-scented parts which I'd so dearly love to lick and probe and penetrate. But when I make to seize her hips, she straightens once more and turns to face me with a triumphant smile.

'NOW?' she writes.

'NOW!' I write.

She nods and I take her by the hips and turn her gently round and she knows what to do.

'No,' she murmurs, less out of any reluctance, for she's evidently more than willing, than out of disbelief that something so extravagantly naughty could really be happening. And it's true, it's what I'm thinking too as I ease apart her buttocks still further, the better to reach the deep wet gash which I can feel growing wetter with each deep probing lick, as I inhale the smell of cunt mingled with sweat and shit, the ecstasy of whose perfume drives me ever more drunk with desire so that whatever I do is not enough, I want more, I want all of her in my mouth, I'm licking this crack now and she's screaming that she wants still more . . .

Until I whip out my hot hard prick and it slips in with such ease.

Then out again and in as I pump and I pump

'Oh, God, I want more . . .'

As I thrust it in deeper, my hip bones hard against her buttocks

'Yes yes yes! Oh God you're the best. This is the best oh God it's the best.'

And maybe it would have been if it had ever actually happened. Which of course it didn't because these things never do. In reality, after that strained cup of coffee over which I'd been too dilatory and she too demure to allow the evening to have panned out as it should have panned out if only we'd seized the day, we bade each other a cordial goodnight and promised to see each other sometime.

Which we did and still do to this day. But only in my imagination as I shuffle towards old age like some ancient masturbator, a rotting handkerchief round my neck, doomed to repeat the same old tale which grows ruder with each telling as the memory fades and what little factual basis there was acquires so many fantastical accretions that nothing of the truth remains.

On one

There's this tiny club in Cheltenham, more of a café with a sound system really, and my brother Dick, his latest girlfriend Saffron and I are dancing pretty manically to this not very good dance music. In fact it might not even be dance music, it might just be frug-along indie stuff, but we're not particularly bothered either way because we're all E'd up and being as it's the very late Eighties when the E quality control has yet to drop too far, the pills are strong enough for you not to care.

I'm wearing this purple tie-dye hooded top made of soft, slinky cotton that clings pleasingly to your arms, so you look wasted and skeletal. On the front it has a crescent moon motif.

Earlier, in the shop (packed with Indian print dresses, ornamental jos stick holders, rave paraphernalia etc.):

Me: What do you reckon. Sun or moon?

Dick: Moon.

Saffron: Yeah. Moon.

Me: But don't you think the orange on the sun one's jollier?

Dick: Why did you ask, then?

Me: So you reckon definitely the moon?

Dick (exchanging glances with Saffron): If you like the orange go for the orange.

Me: Yeah. But I see your point. The moon is a bit clubbier. A bit more – nocturnal.

Dick (to girlie shopkeeper, who thinks it's funny): That's what three years at Oxford does to you.

Me (afterwards): I hardly think 'nocturnal' is an especially difficult Oxford word.

And I'm still not sure I shouldn't have got the orange one.

I'm not sure I should have gone for either of them, actually, because I'm a bit too old for this sort of thing. Twenty-four. Nearly middle-aged. Whereas all these kids around me are twenty, twenty-one, twenty-two at most.

But no sooner have I thought this worrying thought than it's magically erased as worrying thoughts are when you're on E and I look round and think: 'No, this is nice, this is really really nice. The people are nice. The vibe is great. The music's top, well no, it's probably crap, but what do I care, I'm on E.'

I look round at the other faces and try to tell who's on one and who's not, which is hard because there's so much E around these days, people are downing them like peanuts. I smile at my brother's girlfriend Saffron and I smile at my brother and I smile at the other people I know got pills from the same batch as us, can't remember their names, but they're really nice obviously, and I smile at the girl who wasn't part of our group earlier but is now, she's dancing with us, dancing with me mainly and she's smiling at me as much as I'm smiling at her. Definitely on one, got to be.

Now she's enticing me towards her like some enchantress, like some young beautiful enchantress and I'm not going to resist, why should I resist, she's young beautiful and enchanting. And she wants me, I can tell. I can see right inside her thoughts, it's like telepathy, her thoughts are beaming straight from her eyes into mine.

'I want you,' they say.

And I can't see much point in going through all the preliminary stuff. We're already way past that. So I say, and it's quite hard because I'm still rushing big time, I say: 'Do you want to go somewhere else?'

'We can go back to my place, if you like,' she says.

My brother and Saffron and the rest of our E circle look really sad when I tell them I'm going because obviously it would be so much nicer if we all stayed together for ever. But the look they give me says: 'We understand.' Because they do. You understand everything on E.

So I'm back in this girl's bedroom and I'm not telling you what happens next, not yet because we've jumped the gun. First, I want to put everything in context.

*

So.

It's November 1987 and I'm lounging around my mangy Islington pit when I get this call from Martin, a coke-dealing friend of a friend from Oxford.

Martin says: 'I said I'd get in touch when we're having another one and we are this Friday, so if you're interested come on over.'

I am interested. It's still at an early stage this E thing, so early in fact that I don't think we even call it E but MDMA maybe or Ecstasy. But I've read enough about it to know that it's very much my kind of thing and I'm dying to get hold of some before there's a massive clampdown or it goes out of fashion.

The party is to take place at Martin's home in this drab street in Sands End, an area of Fulham which will soon become as overpriced and yuppified as the rest of the borough but which at the moment is mainly white working class. Exceptions to this rule include the middle-class family next door, the father of whom is a major league coke dealer (no connection with Martin, strangely). One day, a few months after this E party, he will get into trouble with one of the Colombian cartels for having reneged on his debts but by then will have had the good sense to flee abroad. His wife and children will not be so lucky. Not long afterwards, they will disappear permanently.

I suppose the big difference between my first E experience and most other people's first E experiences is that when I do it nobody really knows what to do. Ecstasy culture doesn't exist. Dance music is only just being invented. So instead of boshing our pills in a club, gurning at strangers, and dancing our tits off at four-to-the-floor bass-in-your-face anthems, before mellowing out in a specially allocated chill-out room, and then coming down at home with spliffs and ambient music and trippy rave videos designed specifically for E heads we have to approach it in the clinical spirit of experimental scientists voyaging into the unknown.

Which maybe explains the atmosphere when I arrive. On first glance, it looks just like the normal parties I'm used to – people jostling for drinks in the kitchen, people skinning up on the stairs, people queuing for the loo, people smoking and chatting. When you look more closely, though, you see that for every normal person there's another freaky one grinding their teeth and staring vacantly through massive, dead, black pupils or heaving like they're going to be sick or shaking their head very slowly in apparent wonderment. There's a charge in the air, a subdued hysteria at once thrilling and scary.

'So what do I do?' I ask Martin, examining the capsule.

My palm is hot and sticky. I've got palpitations. I want to go home and pretend this never happened. If it weren't such a waste of £35, I think I would.

'Just swallow it.' He's smiling reassurance but he looks as if he wants to go away, talk to someone else, sell them some drugs.

'Just swallow it, like on its own?'

'It's best if you haven't eaten. It works better.'

'Yeah, I know. I haven't.'

'So.' He smiles more broadly and turns away.

'With water?'

He turns round.

'With water,' he confirms.

'And then what?'

'You won't notice anything for an hour. Maybe longer if it's your first time.'

'How will I know it's working?'

'You'll know.'

'But how?'

'You get this rush.'

'Rush?'

'Like, I don't know. A heroin rush?'

'Fuck, it's like heroin?'

'No. Don't worry. It's not at all like heroin.'

'Then—?'

He rests his hands on my shoulder. 'Just swallow it. It'll be all right. If you have any problems, ask him. He knows the score.'

Martin nods towards a tall man with a ponytail and sunken cheeks. He does indeed look like someone who knows the score.

I nod, swallowing.

An hour later, every one of whose passing minutes I have tracked obsessively on my black and yellow Swatch watch, I am both relieved and concerned to notice that nothing has happened. Well, not unless you count the sundry mini-trips – swimming vision, vague dizziness, mild sense of dislocation – which I have experienced en route and which I have come to suspect are just psychosomatic symptoms of my desperation for something to happen.

When not looking at my watch, or experiencing imaginary trips I have been trying to find people to talk to, as you would at a normal PBAB party. But I don't know anyone apart from Martin, who seems to find my clinginess tiresome. And people are more jittery and stand-offish than usual, either because they're waiting to score, waiting for their pills to work or just because they thought this was going to be a normal PBAB party and are a bit freaked out by the general weirdness.

Then there are the people whose pills are actually working, and they're the worst of all. You know those nightmares where you're walking through a graveyard past midnight and these hands start clawing at your feet as the undead burst from their graves? Well, that's how it feels. These strange people with blank eyes and jaws macerating like locusts and little bits of white gunk on the corners of their mouths, they want to talk to you meaningfully and bond with you intensely and stroke your hands with theirs which are – urrggh – all clammy and warm. And you just want to get away.

Well, not totally. At the same time as you're repelled by these clammy Morlock things you're strangely drawn to them, partly out of grim fascination, mainly out of karmic self-interest. Because in a few minutes' – hours'? – time you're going to be in the same position as they are, wanting desperately to commune with strangers and if all these strangers do is think 'Run away! Run away!', it's not going to be very nice for you, is it?

So what I do is end up in this half-way house position, where I'm sitting on a bed near to where a floppy Ecstasy casualty is lying but not actually engaging with him. He's quite happy enough, anyway, having his feet massaged by the drugs expert with the sallow cheeks and the pony tail, who turns out to be American and says foot massages are good when you're on E.

'Mmm,' goes the Ecstasy casualty.

'You've done this before, then?' I ask the American.

'Yes,' he says, not looking at me, still kneading. Then, sensing my hurt at his curtness, he looks up and adds: 'Many times.'

'Have you had one tonight?' I say.

'No. Tonight, it's enough for me to see other people enjoying it for the first time. It's very special, your first time.'

Half of me thinks: you pathetic hippy. The other half thinks: sweet.

'Is it your first time?' he asks.

'Yes. No. I mean, I've taken a tablet. I'm just not sure if – is it possible that you get one or two duff ones in each batch?'

'You're worried it's not going to work, right?'

'A bit.'

'It'll work.'

'Oh good.'

'When did you drop?'

'An hour and – fourteen minutes ago.'

'It shouldn't be long now. It's only your anxiety that it's not going to work that's holding you back.'

'Or maybe, it's started working without me noticing it working?' I suggest.

'You'll know when it's working.'

From the bed comes a voice like a single played at 33 rpm. 'You'll know when it's working,' confirms the casualty.

'But how will I – oh! I got something just then. Do you think . . .?' I feel my mouth expanding in an enormous smile and bile rising from my stomach. 'I think—' I'm really heaving now. The smile's so strong it's as if my face is going to split. The whole of my spine and the back of my head feels numb and tingly. I'm detached, remote, soaring through space. And it's getting more and more intense all the time. I'd like to fill the American in on all this, but I can't, because my grin's getting tighter and tighter and I'm stuck too deep inside my head and it's all I can do to keep the contents of my stomach down.

So this is what it's like, a small part of me is thinking. A very small part of me, because the majority of my brain is way, way too far gone to analyse what's happening. It just is. And I just am.

But the part, the very small part that wants to analyse is doggedly resisting. Because after all, I'm a journalist, aren't I, and what else do journalists do but stand at one remove from experience observing and analysing, never quite participating? And how can you not analyse, anyway, when something so amazing is happening to you. I mean, surely, the unexamined life is the life unlived. And I know what hippy over there—

He's smiling at me.

I smile back, what else can I do, I've got the oral equivalent of an uncontrollable erection.

– I know what he'd say, he'd say: 'Don't fight it. Go with

the flow.' I know he would because I've heard him say it to other people. But I'm not like—

Oh yes. Oh yes. Oh yes. I see what rushing is now, I see what—

Stop analysing. Go with the flow.

Go with the flow, that is such a beautiful concept. Go – with that lovely round O sound. And flow – with also that lovely round O sound. It rhymes. It rhymes exquisitely. There has never been a more perfect rhyme. Well, maybe there has. All rhymes are perfect, aren't they? Except for the ones that aren't perfect. Like – too difficult. But that's OK. Everything's OK. We're flowing with the motion of the ocean. That rhymes too, another perfect rhyme. He is so clever that man so clever for telling me you have to go with the flow when you're on E because I am I'm going with the flow I'm flowing and surging like a huge wave and here comes a big one.

Unnhh! Like the bottom of my stomach is being sucked through my mouth. Temples and the back of my head paralysed. But I'm cocooned and shimmering and warm and

Oh! Too much. This is too much.

Bigger and bigger. Can't think. Beyond thinking. Just feel. Feel good.

God I feel good.

This is the best I've ever felt.

Ever.

Ever.

Ever.

Ever.

EVER.

And it's a drug that's doing this. One tiny pill. One tiny pill that I love, that's so clever, that I want to tell the world all about so that they can all feel just as good as me. God, wouldn't that be great? If we just took this drug all the time, every day. We'd be laughing, wouldn't we? There'd never be any more war. Just peace and love all round.

Economy would struggle a bit, mind. With people doing nothing but loll around smiling, loving one another.

Oh dear, if you're thinking thoughts like that the drug can't be working as well as it was.

And you'd better stop thinking that thought too because if you start thinking that the drug isn't working as well as it was then it means it isn't working as well as it was because if you're capable of rationalizing it means the—

Josh. I love you very much and you're a very beautiful person and there's no one else I'd rather be right now not now not ever but God, you are so fucked up. Can't you just relax and

Go with the flow, like the man said, like the man who's looking at you now saying:

'Need a foot massage?'

'Yes. Please. If you don't mind. If you're sure you don't mind.'

My voice sounds hesitant, cute, desperately polite, like that of a well-brought up child who has just mastered the art of speech. I feel all fuzzy at the edges and remote, as if I'm communing with the world from the wrong side of a telescope.

Very awkwardly I take off my shoe. My co-ordination has gone, but more obstructively, I've been distracted by the incredible sinuousness of my shoelaces, the way they dive in and out of the eyelets like wormy snaky diving things. And the feel of the leather. It's so – leathery. Why did I never notice how leathery leather was before? Supple and stretchy like the wings of a bat, yet tough like the skin of an ox, which is funny because it is the skin of an ox, well, a bull anyway.

And that's just for starters. Because what about the no-less-amazing stretchiness and woolliness of my sock, the coarse brushing sensation as it slides off my cold, damp foot, like, well, like wool against bare flesh, really, only more so.

'You're very nice,' I tell him as he massages my foot. The massage is good but what's better is the physical contact with another human being.

'So are you.'

'Am I? Do you think so?'

'Everyone's nice,' he confirms.

I look around the room. Very, very slowly, like I'm watching it through one of those heavy old pay-per-view panorama devices you find at beauty spots. And I see that he is right. Everyone is exceptionally nice with warm beatific smiles and beautiful faces radiating happiness.

'Only—' It's a sinful thought, so I stop myself. But I can't because the drug is compelling me to tell the truth. 'Only, do you think it would be that way if we hadn't taken this drug?'

'Maybe what you see on the drug is the truth.'

'Yeah!' I go, not caring to think about this one too much because it's what I want to hear. 'Yeah you're right – what's your name?'

'Aaron.'

'That's a nice name. He was the Moor in – *Titus Andronicus*. Have you read it? It's a great play. Everyone dies horribly. Which is sad. Awful in fact. And it's all Aaron's fault. But you're not like him at all. You're a nice Aaron.'

I want to squeeze his hand. To hug him. So I lean forward and do just that.

'A really nice Aaron,' I say, enjoying his stubble against my face, his boniness, his male smell.

I pull away. Suddenly concerned.

'You don't mind me doing that?'

'No. You can do that.'

'Even though you're not on E?'

'Don't worry about me. You just do whatever you want to do.'

'Only I really like you. Like I've known you for ever. Like, almost like we're in love.'

Aaron nods.

'I'm not gay or anything,' I say.

'No,' he says.

'Not that I've got anything against gay people. I really like gay people. Some of the nicest people I know are gay. And I did wonder sometimes whether or not I was gay. Especially at prep school. Do you have prep schools in America? Like boarding schools?'

'We have boarding schools, yes. But they're not as common as they are here.'

'Am I talking too much? You don't have to stay here if you don't want to. Obviously I'd like you to stay here though because— it goes in waves, doesn't it? There was a while back there, when I felt a bit – sad, almost. Like it was ending. And I didn't want it to end.'

'It's not over yet.'

'But when it is, will I be OK?'

'You'll be OK.'

'And I'll get more good bits?'

'You'll get more good bits.'

'Yeah.'

'Yeah.'

'I meant – I – think – one's – coming—

*

And there's much more of this, of course there is. Four more hours of rushing, hand-holding, carpet-stroking, and exchanging of eternal verities, punctuated by those shaky comedown bits which are what make your E trip so fragile and poignant.

Personally, I could do without them. Just as I could do without death. I was railing about this to my friend Tim once, saying, 'But why do we have to die, why? It's so horribly unfair.' And Tim replied, 'If we weren't going to die, life wouldn't be so special. Death is what gives our lives meaning and it's what makes us do otherwise pointless things like art in order to try and transcend it.' (Tim doesn't really speak so stiltedly, by the way. I'm just conveying the gist.)

Anyway, the point is that the very thing that makes E so wonderful is also the thing that makes it so terrible – its built-in obsolescence. The moment you become aware you're experiencing your trip is the moment when you know that the effects are starting to wear off.

It goes something like this:

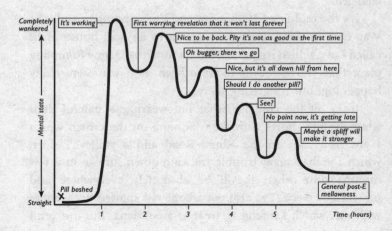

And though you know after the first (and heaviest, most headfucking) rush that you've several more such treats ahead of you, you also know the best has already been and that from here on, it's pretty much down hill.

What's more, you know that however many pills you take in the future, they're never going to recreate the magic of your first one. Because that's another of E's sod's laws. Diminishing returns.

Mind you, I don't think the comedown is as bad as everyone says. Maybe if you've been stacking them up on a Saturday night, then your Wednesday blues can be really bad. But often, the day after Ecstasy is almost the best part. You feel so comfortable, so benevolent, so insulated from reality.

One amusing side effect is this obsession you get with repetitive beats. It's more than easily sated nowadays because they're everywhere – in shops, on the radio, on children's TV. But if you needed repetitive beats in 1987 you had to make do with police sirens and pneumatic drills.

So let's flash forward six months and see how things changed.

It's the middle of 1988, now, and I'm standing outside the Wag club in Soho, waiting to get in to an acid house night called Love, which isn't as cool as Shoom, the Danny Rampling place that you're meant to have been at if you were really happening, but it's getting there.

It's a bit too cold for what I'm wearing: a pair of tight white cycling shorts with the Madonna on the crotch which I got from Boy in the King's Road and a smiley T-shirt, which I've had great trouble tracking down, unlike in a few months time when they'll be absolutely everywhere and unwearably passé. I've also got a large red spotted neckerchief with me, which I intend to wear as a bandana. But not until

I get inside the club. Outside, it would make me feel too self-conscious.

On the walk from the tube to the club, I get quite a few looks from the Friday night crowds. From elderly diners and theatregoers; from middle-aged couples; even from people my age and younger. They've read about my sort in the newspapers: shock horror stories about this new designer drug we all take and this acid house music we listen to. No one has ever looked at me this way before, like I'm part of some strange new menace to society. It makes me a feel a bit self-conscious. But also terribly smug. Now I know how the punks must have felt in 1976, with their safety pins and bondage trousers. Except I don't feel as if I'm part of any revolution. I don't want to change the world. I just want everyone to be on the same trip as me.

And I've tried, I really have. It must have been a bit like this for the disciples, after Jesus had risen from the dead. You've got this incredible news: the Lord is risen; He has come to redeem your sins. And no one's really interested because so far as they've noticed nothing's changed – they've got the same job, live in the same house with the same people, are getting the same amount of sex – so what difference is it going to make? How do they know you're not just part of some weirdo here-today-gone-tomorrow cult?

This is what my housemates think. They view this acid house thing I keep banging on about rather as one might Civil War battle re-enactment or line-dancing: perfectly agreeable activities for those who like that sort of thing, but not something that's ever going to catch on.

Occasionally, though, you do find people who'll listen. Tonight's recruits are Molly and her boyfriend Tom, whom I think she met at her new job at *The Times*. Yeah I'm as surprised as you are that she's up for it, but I think it's Tom we have to thank. I was all ready to hate him – especially after I found out he was another fucking old Etonian, I mean is there some sort of upper-class law that people like Molly should only date Etonians? – but actually he's pretty cool. He's into the right kind of music and he's got his hair cut into a bob just like mine. So I don't feel jealous. I just feel that paternal glow you get when you're about to introduce two novices to their first E.

'Let me get you a drink,' says Tom, once we've checked in our coats.

Molly looked a bit nervous in the queue. I don't think she's ever been to a club before, apart from Annabel's, which doesn't count. But now all three of us are buzzing with that 'hey, we got past the doorman and we're definitely in the club and we're going to have a great time' feeling, checking out the faces, the bustle and the dance floor which is pretty empty at the moment because it's still quite early and nobody's Es have kicked in.

'What are you going to have?'

'Corona,' says Tom.

'Spritzer for me, please,' says Molly.

'Uh uh. You're having a Corona,' says Tom.

Really water's the thing when you're going to take E and though I'm becoming a bit of a purist, it doesn't go nearly so well with your pre-match fag as ice-cold lager and a segment of lime.

'Same for me then, cheers,' I say. Besides, I need a bit of alcohol to calm my nerves. I won't feel safe until I've found The Man and scored some Es. I've just had a butcher's and he doesn't seem to be where he usually is, in that shady alcovey bit near the left-hand speakers.

By way of distraction, we all head up to the next floor, which is smaller and more drinksy and chatty than the main one. Molly and Tom are trying to make conversation with me, but I'm not really there, all I can think of is the score. Every now and then, I lurch from our circle towards anyone vaguely likely, and say: 'Know where I can get any Es?' But all I get is stuff like 'Sorry, mate. We came sorted,' and 'Naah, mate. Our first time here,' and 'Yeah there was a bloke. About half an hour ago. By the dance floor. With this kangaroo pouch type thingy.'

Kangaroo pouch type thingies. I'm not sure what the correct term is but all the club dealers wear them in 1987, almost vauntingly, as a sort of badge of office: hence the uselessness of that last direction. This, remember, is a time before the big anti-E clampdown when dealers can sell pills almost as openly as the barman sells lager and when you know there's going to be no problem with quality control because the scene's still too intimate and the vibe too right-eous for it yet to have attracted rip-off merchants selling cat-worming pills at £15 a throw. Even so, you can never be 100 per cent sure you're going to score. Supply is limited. Ninety-nine out of a hundred people in this club want their pills just as badly as you do. What if they get there first? What if – heaven forfend – every single person in the club is off their head on E and all you've got to keep yourself going are alcohol and nicotine?

Where is he where is he where is he?

Molly and Tom are starting to get anxious now. Each time I come back upstairs from another abortive drug quest, I try reassuring them that it's all perfectly normal, it's still pretty early, it won't be a problem. But I've never been good at hiding my feelings, especially where something as important as drugs is concerned, and they're looking at me like two small children who've started wondering how Father Christmas can really squeeze down a chimney when the flues are so narrow and there's a fire at the bottom and how could you, Daddy, how could you tell us such fibs?

But then, as if by magic, he appears. What he looks like, I don't remember, so I ring up my brother for clues.

'Hey, brother, I'm trying to put some vague facts into this book I'm writing. Can you remember when you did your first E?'

'With you, I think. That time with all your Oxford friends in Fulham.'

'Oh. Yeah. Then. I'm not doing that one—'

Largely because there isn't much to say. It's just me, my brother, his girlfriend and a couple of pretty girls I know from Oxford – Karin and Samantha – and we spend an evening in my dingy basement sitting room cooing and billing, exchanging the occasional snog but nothing more dramatic, before coming down with a few spliffs and going to bed. Why do none of us have sex? I don't know. It's bloody annoying. The only memorable part is the horrible bit at the beginning where Samantha starts gagging and heaving like she's going to die. We're already up on our pills by then and it's not what you need at all: having to think about procuring medical care and what lies to tell should the police get involved when all the pill is telling you to do is don't worry be happy. It makes you realize how bad it must be for the kids at parties where somebody does actually die from E. Sure it's bad for the victim and worse for the parents but the people I feel sorriest for are the friends who supplied the pills. I mean, when you buy Es you never buy them singly, do you? One of you gets in the order and then collects the cash and divvies them all up, which technically makes you a class A dealer liable to lengthy imprisonment but which is no more than what thousands of otherwise law-abiding people do every weekend. But just think if it went wrong: you'd have your friend's death on your conscience; you'd be branded murdering scum by their parents; you'd be named and shamed in all the newspapers; and you'd almost certainly end up in prison. Plus, you'd have your E trip completely ruined. And why? Because your bastard, tossy, useless mate selfishly decided to have a one in a million reaction to a drug which statistically kills fewer people than peanuts. But they never brand the greengrocer who sells the fatal packet of KPs murdering scum, do they?

'—I'm doing the Wag. Did you never come there with me?' I say.

'I think so, yes. Yes, I did. Sharon from Staines,' says Dick.

'God. Wow. Yeah, that rings a vague bell. But I'm not doing that time, sadly. You'll be in loads elsewhere, though.'

'I know. It's what's worrying me.'

'The thing I wanted to know, though, was: what did the dealer look like?'

'He wore a white hat. Like a fez. A white fez.'

'A white fez? That is cool. I'll have to put that one in. Thanks.'

So this dealer, when I find him, he's wearing a white fez.

'How many?' he says.

'Three,' I say. I've got my £45 all ready and I try slipping the bundle into his hand in a way which is supposed to indicate discretion and vast drugs-buying experience but which in fact indicates enormous cackhandedness because I fumble it completely. Anyone watching would know that this is not two old mates shaking hands in a club, or whatever implausible thing it is that we're pretending to be doing. A light bulb would appear above their head and in the thought bubble it would say: 'Drug deal in progress.' When our hands brush, I fail to make the transfer – the money, now painfully visible, gets stuck to my palm – and when he passes me the pills it's almost as bad. He tuts as I study them under the light for way too long and then retreats, irritably, into the shadows. Or is it always like that with dealers: this thing they have of making out like it's they who are doing you the big favour.

Tom and Molly watch me approach. I'm trying to pull a long face to tease them but I can't sustain it.

'Hey!' says Tom.

'Should we—?' asks Molly.

'Bosh 'em now, I should,' I say. Except I probably don't say 'bosh' because the word hasn't entered popular currency at this stage. More likely, I say something like 'swallow' or 'take'.

'Will you?' asks Molly.

'I'm leaving it half an hour. Once you've done it before, it comes on quicker. I want to be up there smiling the same time as you.'

'How sweet.'

'It's a sweet drug.'

With the nervous sidelong glances of E beginners, Molly and Tom slip their pills discreetly into their mouths. They wash them down with beer.

'No going back now,' says Molly, brightly, as if fighting to persuade herself that she has done the right thing.

'Not really,' I say, because I can't think of anything cleverer. It's always like that before an E for me. I find it impossible to concentrate, I get all jittery, not because I'm scared of doing a Leah Betts. It's just that expectation thing of knowing that your brain is about to go through this massive transcendental shift and that really you'd like to get it over with and be up there instead of having to endure all this queasy dead time.

So we'll skip the next hour, during which little occurs save the boshing of my E, much teeth-grinding tension and the consumption of many fags, and move on to the moment where Molly feels a twinge and then Tom thinks he might have got something too but he's not sure.

'Better get you down to the dance floor. Work it up a bit,' I say. Though, by the time I've said it, I can tell by Molly's startled grin – like a happy shell has just exploded in her cerebral cortex – and the way Tom's eyes keep flicking meaningfully between mine and Molly's as if to say there's no need to work it up, no need whatsoever.

'Can't – we – just – stay – here – a – bit?' says Molly.

'You'll like it more on the dance floor,' I say. And I'm right, of course I am, but I can't pretend there isn't an ulterior motive here. If I don't work up a sweat and boost my metabolic rate, by the time I'm coming up they'll be coming down and that won't be nearly as much fun. Trips are like orgasms: best when simultaneous.

Molly looks panic-stricken. As panic-stricken as it's possible to look while being as happy as you've ever been in your life.

I take her hands in mine and she squeezes them gratefully. Tom – who can't bear to be left out, naturally – joins his hands with ours and our all for one one for all gesture—

I think Tom actually says it: 'Hey, we're like the Three Musketeers.'

—turns into this big mutual hug.

'We should just stay like this,' says Tom.

No fear, I'm thinking, because unlike them I happen to be in full possession of my faculties. And one of those faculties is my sense of embarrassment, which leads me to look to see if anyone's watching. (Which no one is, or not consciously.) Another is my sense of fair play, which tells me, 'They're having fun and I'm not and it doesn't matter about them, they'll be happy wherever they are, it's my needs we should be thinking about.'

'I'm taking you to the dance floor,' I say.

I can feel Molly resisting.

'I promise it will be better,' I say.

'He's right, Molly. He's our E guide. Remember?' says Tom, who seems to have mutated from a languid Etonian into a little boy called Tommy.

Molly and Tommy would like to maintain this mutual hug all the way to the dance floor, but frankly this isn't realistic. You can't push through crowded clubs when you're a six-legged love machine. So I take Molly's hand and Molly takes Tommy's hand and clinging on very tight—

'You won't let go?'

'I won't let go, Molly. You're safe with me.'

—we stretch out like paper cut-outs and weave through huddles of clubbers all doing very similar things to the ones we've been doing, surreptitiously inspecting and then consuming pills, chain-smoking fags, making group declarations of eternal unity and so on. Sometimes the crowds grow quite thick, especially as we reach the stairwell and try forcing our way down while other parties, also holding hands – everyone who's moving is holding hands – are trying to force their way up. No one shows any ill-grace as we squeeze past one another. It's not like later when people start wising up and getting cynical, for this is the spring of 1988, the prelude to the Summer of Love, and everyone's on the same trip, everyone wants a good time, and just as importantly they want everyone else to have a good time because this is what it's all about. Each person you pass, you check out their face, especially their pupils, and you exchange a look of recognition which either says: 'Don't worry mate, I'm tripping,' or 'No worries, mate. I soon will be.'

Sorted, that's the word. Everybody's sorted.

What with the crowds and everyone in this mongy, floaty state it takes about five times as long to get to the dance floor as it should do. By now, the whole downstairs area has been transformed. It's incredibly hot and very humid. There are no gaps any more, the whole floor is taken up by throbbing, sweating, up for it clubbers. Clubbers in bandanas. Clubbers with their shirts off. Clubbers in surf shorts and surf longs in acid pinks, acid yellows, acid greens. Clubbers in smiley T-shirts. Clubbers with whistles hanging from their necks. Sweltering clubbers. You could poach an egg in their sweat.

And the music.

The music beckons you towards the dance floor, the basslines throbbing beneath your feet, the ethereal melodies shimmering and fluttering in your brain like birds of paradise, for this is like no music you have experienced before. Well, not since the last time. It glows, it pulses, it invigorates, it inspires, it feels like the very essence of happiness is being pumped hot and sweet into your veins so that it courses through your arms and into your hands, your hands with their amazing fingers, so sinuous and dextrous and perfectly formed, so—

So the hand obsession, this is good, this is very good, for unless I'm very much mistaken – and I could I suppose, it could just be the vestigial memories of previous Es brought on by the music – but unless I am, I have a sneaking and excedingly pleasant suspicion that I might I just might be—

Molly has caught my eye. Just a shy exploratory glance first, as if to ask 'Are you—?'

Tripping.

'I reckon,' I reply. Telepathically, of course, because we're communicating purely with our eyes, sucking one another into the black vortices of our pupils.

She grins and I grin.

And I realize how strikingly, stunningly, amazingly beautiful she is. Though obviously it's something I must have appreciated once before, you tend not to notice these things after a time. Suddenly I'm aware of every detail: her cropped chestnut hair, her wide forehead, her intense grey eyes, the aristocratic pallor of her skin. Should I tell her how gorgeous she is? Would she be embarrassed? Would it be rude in front of Tommy?

'—'

She's saying something but I haven't a clue what, except that it's nice. She says it with this delirious smile.

'What?'

She says it again. I still can't hear.

She reaches over my shoulder and pulls my ear towards her mouth.

Her breath is hot, her voice booms.

'Thanks.'

'What for?' I yell back.

'For this,' she gestures around the room.

'My pleasure.'

She seems to find this very very funny.

'Your pleasure!' she says, smiling, smiling, smiling.

I'm smiling.

Tommy's smiling.

Everybody's smiling. Catch their eye, that's all you've got

to do to get that grin of recognition. I'm on one. You're on one. We're all on one. Sorted.

And the DJ. Is this guy brilliant or is this guy brilliant? He's brilliant. He's a god. He's very possibly God. Because it is quite like a church this place. Not to look at maybe, but the atmosphere. It has the atmosphere of this massive, fuck-off cathedral with vaulting Gothic arches and this rumbling pipe organ like something out of Captain Nemo sending shivers down your spine, while your brain soars towards heaven. And the bells. Church bells. Recordings – samples, the term is – of Ibizan church bells, or so I heard. It's the Balearic sound.

Bong bong bong bong bong bong bong bong bong bong.

I know this one. And it's bloody unusual, that. To know the names of any of the nameless songs by nameless outfits the nameless DJ is playing.

'De Testimony' by Fini Tribe.

I'd love to impart this fascinating information to Tommy and Molly. But I'm speechless. I'm still rushing and all I can think is

The bells! The bells! Those chiming bells!

And grin as the DJ starts dropping in these bits of another tune I recognize.

But he's toying with us, this DJ. Like a kitten with a mouse.

Sometimes, you can feel the pace slacken as he winds everything right down. And what he's doing here – though you're probably not aware of it, you probably just think hmm, I don't seem to be having quite as brilliant a time as I was ten minutes ago – is mimicking the chemicals in your brain, the way the euphoria comes in waves. If you were rushing before, you're not any more, and though part of you is still very much in that cosy, private pilled-up headspace, another part is dimly aware that things are not as they ought to be. You're not beyond consciousness any more, you're in a club, you're on a drug called E and you know from experience that it gives you lows as well as highs and you rather wish it would just hurry up and get this low bit over so you can move on back to the high. If you've been on the dancefloor some time or you're quite far down the line of your trip, this is the bit when you suggest to your mates that you all head off to the chill-out room. Except there's one, there's always one, who's at a different stage of the trip from you. They're still buzzing. They want to stay. And there follows this agonized debate as to who's going and who's staying, and 'Do you mind? Are you sure you don't mind? I'll come if you like, it's just—', because what everyone would really like is for everyone else to be doing the same thing as they are, so they can all be one big happy family like they were at the beginning.

Luckily, I'm not there. I'm at that brilliant stage where you're still sufficiently fucked not to really care what you do, but not so fucked that you're incapable of making clever choices like:

'I'm dehydrated. I think I'll get my posse a drink, and while I'm on the way, I'll go for a piss, which will be really fun because toilets always are when you're on E, and I'll make lots of new friends and then I'll come back to a tumultuous welcome from my family just in time to catch the moment when the music starts building again and I can enjoy another huge wave secure in the knowledge that I haven't wasted the interlude and that we're sorted for important things like water. And gum.'

Gum, terribly important that one. It's a rare and valuable commodity in clubs, what with everyone having the same problem: i.e. this desperate urge to chew and chew, which can give you awful jaw ache the next day if you're not careful, not to mention the damage it does to your teeth, with all that grinding. But they don't sell it behind the bar. Or if they did, they've run out long ago, so that's another mission for you – it's nice to have missions when you're on E. Gives you a sense of a purpose and later a sense of achievement. Find some gum.

First stop is the bar to get some water. The bar staff have this pissed off air about them. Or am I being unduly E sensitive? No. I don't think so. The problem, I reckon, is that they're all straight and their customers are all off their faces, which the bar staff consider unfair. And it's not as if they're going to get any tips. Not when all anyone wants to buy is water, because it's not something you give a tip for, water, is it?

The barman nearest me – young, blond, short hair, Australian-surfer-type – is leaning back against the floor-length fridge containing the many cans of Red Stripe he has failed to sell, his arms folded, his eyes pointedly not looking at me.

I want to show him that I sympathize with his plight: not just because I'm on some stupid drug which would make me radiate peace and love to anyone, even to Adolf Hitler if I bumped into him, but because I genuinely care.

The best way to do this, it seems to me, is to pretend I'm not on E.

I stretch out my arm towards him, a tenner between my fingers. I'm not going to call out or anything. Just wait until he feels ready.

Someone else joins me at the bar, someone taller than me who doesn't look like a raver. He's wearing normal person's Friday night clothes – pleated trousers and a patterned shirt.

I'm not consciously staring at his face but I must be because he nods briskly and says: 'All right?' rather as you might to humour someone mentally subnormal.

'Yeahhh.' It's not so much a word as an exhalation.

He turns to the barman.

'Two Red Stripe, please.'

The barman snaps to it.

'Oh, sorry, mate, was you being served?' asks the normal man.

'Not yet.'

'Oi, mate,' he calls to the barman. 'Do you want to do this geezer first?'

'Um three—'

'Mineral waters,' says the barman, taking the money, thrusting the bottles into my hand and giving me the change in what seems like one swift movement.

'Thanks,' I say to the nice man. 'That was really nice of you. You're not on E, are you?'

'No, mate. But you are.'

'Yeah,' I concede with a big sloppy grin.

'Nice one. Take care.'

Which is sweet. But not quite as sweet as the sort of conversation I'm really after, where you meet a total stranger and five minutes later are vowing eternal friendship. It won't be long, though. Never is.

I swig down one of the waters on the way to the bogs. The journey is a huge adventure, because you don't walk when you're on E, you just sort of float and shimmy and pulse, like some gossamer undersea creature, a jellyfish maybe. A jellyfish on springy marshmallow legs, which are bouncing in time to the beat. So not like a jellyfish at all really. More like – oh, fuck knows. The point is, it feels great. Looks great too. All these faces to gurn at. Beautiful, beautiful faces. Such clear skin, such shining eyes, such white teeth. It's like I've arrived at the paradise island where the Bounty hunters live. And everyone's my friend. Beautiful girls included. These girls – really, model-standard girls – so way, way out of my league that I wouldn't dream of even looking at them under normal circumstances, I can look at them, talk to them, stroke them, maybe even kiss them and they won't mind because we're all friends. I'm not going to, though, obviously. I just know that I can, that's all.

One thing I like about going into the toilets at clubs is the dramatic change of environment: from dark and loud to quiet and bright. You couldn't call it a haven exactly: not with that sick, flickering yellow fluorescent lighting; with the hard surfaces which make every noise – the shhhpp of taps, the creak and swish and poo-scented tailwind of the swing doors, the click of cubicles being locked and unlocked – sound harsh and brittle; with the continual flow of bombed-out human traffic filling water bottles, splashing faces, snorting lines, emptying E-loosened bowels, pissing, chatting, trying to remember precisely which of the above they came in here to do. But it does give you the chance to put the evening on pause; to assess where you've just been, where you're going, how big your pupils are, how fucked and pale and smiley you look in the mirror, how fucked everyone else is.

Only one of the cold water taps is working and a queue has developed. A solidly-built, crop-headed geezer who looks like he might be a builder has elected himself official water dispenser: you pass him your bottle, he fills it for you.

When it's my turn, I say: 'So you'll be the official water dispenser, then.'

He says: 'Eh?'

His strong London accent, his build, the swiftness of his answer, the way he cocks his head as he gives it, they're all a bit scary and if I hadn't been rendered so innocent and trusting by the drug I probably wouldn't repeat myself. But since I have, I do.

'Right mate,' he says, with some enthusiasm. 'Yeah. Yeah, I'm the water dispenser. What's your name?'

'Josh,'

'Nice one, Josh. Nice one. I'm Andy.'

He shakes my hand but then – with a sudden forward lurch – corrects his gesture to a full on hug.

'You're all right, mate,' he says. He's beaming, fixing on my pupils.

'You too. Matey.'

'Safe.'

'Or what?'

Someone else comes in with an empty bottle and makes for a different cold water tap.

'They're all knackered, mate,' says Andy. 'Give it here.'

The punter looks uncertainly at Andy.

'He's the official water dispenser,' I explain.

Andy fills up his bottle.

'Nice one,' says the punter.

'Nice one,' says Andy.

'Hey, Andy,' I say.

'Yeah, mate? Sorry, mate. Forgotten your name.'

'Josh.'

'Yeah, Josh. Sorry, mate. Josh.'

'You haven't got any gum, have you?'

'Naah, mate, sorry, mate. You can have some of this if you want. All I've got.'

He extracts from his mouth some white and very well-chewed gum and breaks me off a half. I remember how first time round someone did that for me I was a bit shocked. Not so shocked that I didn't go ahead and chew it, because you lose a lot of your squeamishness about oral hygiene when you're on E. But shocked enough to register the extreme weirdness of accepting a manky old piece of gum which has spent the last hour being ground into the teeth and bathed in the saliva of a person who for all you know could be Typhoid Mary's more contaminated younger brother.

'Cheers.' I pop it into my mouth.

'Quite speedy this stuff, innit?'

'Gets your jaw, definitely.'

'Probably from the same batch. You get yours here?'

'Yeah.'

'White with speckles.'

'Yeah. But they're all like that, aren't they?'

'Yeah. Yeah, you're right there, mate. Josh. It is Josh?'

'Yeah. And you're Andy, right?'

'Right. Eh, I was meant to be getting water for my posse. You want to meet my posse? You'll like them, I reckon. Fucking nice, all of them. Like you, mate. Josh. They might have some gum.'

'Yeah. Sure. Why not? I'd like to meet them. Andy.'

Andy's posse are in the upstairs bar, seated on the floor in a circle by the far wall. They greet the returning hero with upturned faces and warm smiles. Andy crouches down to dispense the water, hugging the people nearest him as he does so.

'Everybody, this is Josh,' announces Andy. 'Josh: Trish; Mark; Darren; Kelv; Mand; Beck.' Hands are raised in greeting, teeth flash, heads nod as each one is introduced.

Andy and I sit between two of the girls.

'Hi,' I say to the girl next to me. Blonde, pretty, natch.

'Hi,' she says.

'Come here often?'

'First time. You?'

I try to think of a clever, witty answer which, without sounding boastful, arrogant or misleading, will indicate that yes, I've been quite a few times now and I did start coming before the herd. Unfortunately, I'm still pretty fucked and what comes out in a bilious, breathy gulp is: 'Not my first time.'

One of the boys calls across to Andy.

'How many pills you got left?'

'Three. No, two. You want to do a half?'

'Yeah.'

As Andy and his mate split their pill, there are desultory negotiations for the remaining one. It ends up being divided four ways, which means that everyone has had a top-up apart from me and the girl next to me. But she's too bombed to care.

'Sorry, mate,' says Andy.

'No worries,' I say. 'I'm still up on this one.'

'Me too. But it's nice to have insurance.'

'Yeah, I know what you mean. It's like, you need something for the – what are those down bits called you get in waves?'

'Dunno, mate.'

'Yeah but you know what I mean. You need something to fill in the – the troughs, that's it. The troughs.'

'Yeah.'

'Except I've sometimes wondered, if you fill in the troughs, maybe the peaks wouldn't be so good. Maybe you'd be back to normal.'

'Yeah.'

'So maybe, somehow, what you really want to do is time it so that your second pill kicks in while you're peaking on the first and you get a double peak. Which would mean you'd get a double downer too. So then what you'd have to do is take another pill, which brought you up just as the other pills were bringing you down. And so on and so on.'

'Yeah.'

'Or am I talking shit?'

'No, mate.'

'You're not just saying that? Only – I really like you. And the last thing I'd want to do is bore you by talking shit.'

'Mate, you're beautiful. Even if you were talking shit, I could sit here listening to you all night.'

'So I am talking shit?'

'Mate—' he drapes an arm over my shoulder, pulls me towards him and holds me there for a while in a tight hug. And I feel my paranoia draining away.

I clasp his hands in mine. They're big and rough. Labourer's hands. I gaze adoringly into his massive pupils.

'Andy. You are a fucking top geezer.'

'You too, mate. You too. So where do you learn to talk like that, then?' says Andy.

'Like what?'

'Posh.'

'I dunno. School maybe.'

'You went to one of them public schools?'

'Yeah.'

''Kin' 'ell.'

'Does it bother you?'

'Mate, nothing bothers me. It was more, I was thinking: you and me. We'd never be talking to each normally, would we?'

'I dunno. Kind of depends what you do.'

'Do?'

'As a job.'

'Oh. Right. I'm a plumber.'

'Well. There you are then. You might have come round to my place to fix my – plumbing.'

'Yeah, mate. But I meant talk, like in really talking. Like we are now.'

'Yeah. That'll be the drug, won't it?'

'Yeah.'

'Fucking brilliant, that, isn't it? I mean what a fucking brilliant invention. A drug that brings everyone together, makes everyone mates. I mean don't you think we should be taking it all the fucking time.'

'All the fucking time, mate.'

'And it's like – apparently, it's having this amazing effect on society. I hear this stuff 'cos I'm a journalist and like, on the football terraces—'.

'You're never a journalist?'

''Fraid so.'

'Who for?'

'Um. *Telegraph*, mainly.'

''Ere guys, listen to this. My mate here – Josh, isn't it? – he's a journalist from the *Telegraph*.'

Everyone is most impressed.

'You doing a story, then?' someone asks.

'What? In this state?'

There's laughter.

'So you were saying—?' prompts Andy.

'Was I?'

'About the football terraces,' he says.

'Oh. Yeah. Well that's it, really. Just, the football terraces

are a lot friendlier these days, I've heard. 'Cos they're all doing
E instead of violence.'

'Like me.'

'Yeah, and me.'

'Naah. I meant the violence. I used to be well into it.'

'What, you mean, punching people and stuff?'

'Stanleys, mainly.'

'No.'

'Straight up, matey.'

'But wasn't that quite – horrible?'

'Was meant to be, mate. If the opposition's horrible, you've
got to be more horrible, ent cha?'

'I suppose.'

'Have a butcher's,' he says. He pulls down the neck of
his T-shirt, the better to show a long deep white scar. 'Inch
lower and I'd be dead. That's what they said at the hospital.'

'Blimey,' I say.

'It's OK, mate. You should have seen what I done to the
other bloke.'

'I can imagine.'

'But I shouldn't be talking about it, really. It happened a
long time ago and I don't want you to think I'm like that any
more or nothing.'

'No. That's OK. I was just thinking how amazing it was.
Me talking to a real life football hooligan. Ex-hooligan.'

'And you from the *Telegraph*. That's what does my head
in.'

'And all thanks to one small, speckledy white pill.'

'Three and a half.'

'You've had three and a half? Blimey. Why aren't you
dancing?'

*

Hand in hand my tough new friend and I ease and squeeze our way back to the bit of the dance floor where Molly and Tommy last were. Horrifyingly, they have moved. My whole world has begun to collapse when belatedly I realize that the brown-haired girl whose bare back and midriff I can see swaying in front of me, the one who reminds me of Molly, is in fact Molly. I just didn't recognize her without her top, which she has now wrapped around her waist. In my absence she has turned into a full-on raver. Her body shimmers with perspiration, she radiates luurve, she can now do all the clever body popping moves that only rave chicks can do and she greets every new tune – or 'choon' as we will one day learn to spell them – as if she's known it since her grandma used to hum it while dandling her on her knee. I'm so proud to have provided the pill that engendered this transformation. Like a father on his daughter's wedding day.

I tap Molly's glistening shoulder. She turns round. Her eyes burn with fierce joy. Were this our first encounter after six months lost in the jungles of the Amazon we couldn't be more pleased to see one another.

'Where's . . .?' I mouth, because the volume now renders all speech inaudible. The DJ is cranking things up for the next big wave.

But Tommy has already leaped on me with a pre-emptive hug, shirt drenched with sweat, face flushed and dripping. I hug him back, thinking: 'Uurgh. Bit sticky,' and 'He needs some water, quick.' Which practical thoughts must mean I'm on a different stage of my trip than they are. They've kept their highs going by dancing. I need to work on mine a bit.

I introduce Andy wordlessly to Tommy and Molly. They welcome him instantly to our circle. He gives them the thumbs up.

I can't resist pulling at Andy's shirt to show Tommy and Molly his scar.

'Why are you showing me this?' says Molly's look.

'Because it's interesting and fun,' reply my upraised thumbs.

Smiling, Andy makes a 'he's mental' gesture.

I grin. Now that I'm on the floor, it's all coming back to me.

I have timed it well. The DJ has reached that stage of his set where things have been slowed down for a while now and people have started to notice. The ones who have stayed on the floor are getting edgy. The ones who are back from the toilets or the bar want to know why nothing is happening. Whistles are being blown. There are hopeful trills of 'Aciied.' Knowing looks are being exchanged. The tension is palpable. And – was that our imagination? Or did the DJ just drop in a sample of an anthem we all know, one of those really big choons that brings you right up again, where everyone goes mental?

More tension; more working of the jaw; more whistle-blowing; more expectant whooping. If this foreplay goes on much longer, we'll be driven insane.

But wait. There it was again. The vocal sample. And a few recognizable beats this time which the DJ is now mashing with the current track, flipping back and forth, teasing us with a little bit more of the new one each time.

Now we're all turned towards the glow of the DJ booth, arms outstretched, palms facing upwards, making upward-pushing gestures which say: 'Crank it up, Mr DJ' or beckoning ones which say: 'Come to us, good music. Come to US!'

And it does come.

Roaring down upon us in a pyroclastic flow.

The crowd on the floor surges upward as one. The whistle blowing explodes in a shrill fortissimo.

'Aciieeeeed,' someone chants.

'Aciieeeed,' comes the choral reply.

And as if transmitted by some exceptionally virulent happy virus, the smile goes round the floor from face to face to face.

As the music builds, my pill starts coming on again, coming on strong. And where a few minutes ago, I was plotting my dance movements with a certain care – am I moving my legs too much? how do I get my hips to waggle? are there any cleverer things I can do with my arms? – I simply don't give a toss any more, I'm lost in the music, no longer a solitary individual but part of some massive Gaian whole, this radiant, pulsing entity where everyone's happy and everyone's moving in time to the same beat and everyone's on the same trip.

In those rare moments when I do become self aware, like, say, when Molly catches my eye and dances just for me – gosh I love Molly so much, she's my bestest bestest friend – and I want to dance back for her to show that I'm with her, I notice my feet are glued to the floor, it's just my knees and my hips and my arms doing all the work, making these cunning and sinuous hieratic gestures signifying maybe bounteousness and love and rays of light, which look especially fabulous I can't help noticing, when viewed in slow motion when the strobes come on. I like this thing we're doing. I like it a lot. As do Molly and Tommy and Andy, and yes, those two gorgeous girls who were dancing next to us a moment ago but have now been sucked into our circle by this huge loving vibe we're emanating and are now dancing with us, smiling at us, mirroring our moves, sharing our water, exchanging gum, like we've known each other for ever. We all like this thing a lot lot lot and if it carries on like this until the end of time you won't hear any complaints from us.

It doesn't though. Nowhere even close to the end of time does this beautiful thing go on, and though we manage, exhaustedly, to dance our way through the next trough and enjoy – more or less, because it can't match the previous ones – the next peak, by the time the DJ starts winding things down once again, we know there's no point in waiting for the next build. Not without another pill. We're out of here.

Andy's back with his group. And Tommy and I are queuing for our coats while Molly queues for the loo. We're still feeling fuzzy at the edges, our teeth are grinding, we're desperate for some gum and preferably a strong joint, but the best of the pill is over and the club is starting to thin.

Joint back at Tommy and Molly's place maybe? Well, I'm tempted. A bit of company's what you need while coming down, as of course is some strong weed, and I love those post-E conversations. But Tommy's place is in Camden which is completely the wrong way for me and anyway they're an item and have got better things to do right now than talk, which is fine, I'm not jealous, I love them both so much that all I want is for them to be happy. We'll do it some other time.

'Some other time,' says Molly. 'That would be good.'

Sure enough, over the next few weeks we keep bumping into one another for various reasons. And every time, we remind ourselves what an incredibly good time we had that night and how we really must do it again.

*

But you'll want to know what happened with that girl, I expect, the one in whose bedroom I find myself after dropping that pill on a visit to see my brother in Cheltenham.

Well, it's pretty simple really.

We have sex.

It's fairly typical one-night-stand-in-untidy-student-bedroom sex and I only mention it for two reasons. First, it turns out this girl isn't on E at all, she just collects Devereuxes. She has already slept with my brother, and she has taken advantage of my innocent E'ed-up state to seduce me. Not that I'm complaining.

Second, though she's a nice girl and everything, there comes a point after about half an hour's urgent thrusting where I have to haul myself off and say: 'Look, I'm really sorry about this but the way I am at the moment I could go on for ever. All that's going to happen is that we'll end up feeling very sore because I just can't come.'

Which isn't something girls are used to hearing, I imagine. Nor is it something I'm used to saying in my early twenties: God no, far from it.

But that's the other thing about E. It keeps you up all night.

A boy's own story

I have a photo in front of me that makes me want to weep: grainy, black and white, cunningly lit, arty, it's a close-up of me in my mid-twenties taken for a picture byline that was never used on a column I once had when I was a reasonably handsome young man about town.

The saddest thing about the picture isn't that this youth is so much more louche than I can afford to be and more beautiful than I'll ever be, but that the boy in the picture isn't aware just how lucky he is.

He has been on the staff of the *Telegraph* for almost two years now and if he continues on this trajectory (which he won't, but he doesn't know that yet) he'll become very nearly as famous and successful as his insane ambition tells him he ought to be.

Besides his overpaid job on the Peterborough diary, on which his main role is to gossip and joke and sprawl foppishly while his colleagues do the work, he has acquired two more columns than a callow twentysomething has any right to expect. One is as the *Sunday Telegraph*'s radio critic; another is a weekly diary called Party Piece, in which he has to attend showbizzy parties, make a fool of himself and then write about it amusingly and self-deprecatingly afterwards. All this brings his income to more than £30,000 a year, which he spends on champagne, designer drugs and eau de nil Jasper Conran suits with nipped waists, flared pockets and enormous late-Eighties-style power shoulders.

He thinks this is normal, though no way is it normal, not when you're only three years out of university, not when you're out-earning your contemporaries in law and banking who work ten times as hard for half the kudos and none of the perks.

But this is what I mean. Instead of enjoying the present, all this boy can think of is how much better things are bound to be in a few years when he gets a bigger column or a fatter salary or a proper girlfriend or indeed any girlfriend or the courage to quit his job and write his novel or whatever it is that needs to happen before he can start enjoying life, he's not sure what it is exactly, he just knows at the moment things aren't quite right.

Maybe, this boy is thinking – I'm thinking – maybe today will be the day that makes everything change. I'll get in to work half an hour early, I'll write up my review, my first ever rock review and then I'll, I dunno, I'll get to do whatever it is you do when you're a rock critic. Go to gigs. Hang out with rock stars. Take drugs. End up with their surplus groupies, maybe.

The office looks quite odd at this time of day. Odd enough for me to waste most of the time I've gained by arriving early just gawping at the goings-on: the cleaners giving the desks and screens a final wipe; secretaries from far-flung departments gathering to pool gossip before their bosses arrive; sporty tossers on their way to the gym; the workaholic with the pipe – Education, I think – already at his desk, beavering away. It's like one of those undersea documentaries where you discover what happens on the coral reef after all the fish have gone to bed; or when you're leaving a club at 5 a.m., and you notice all the milkmen, cabbies, street cleaners and stall holders for whom being up at this hour is completely normal.

Then I notice that twenty minutes have gone by and I've still got nowhere with this piece, possibly the most important of my career. I consult my notebook. Green-red, it says. Blue-yellow. Violet-penile? Puerile? Purple I guess it must be, though it doesn't quite make sense because why would you have two colours so close together? Wouldn't it have been something a bit more contrasty? Did I perhaps, in my enthusiasm, accidentally describe the same colour twice? Does it matter.

No, I decide on my return with a mug of coffee-flavoured cancer juice from the Girovend machine, it doesn't. Or even if it does, I think as I stoke up my second fag, it doesn't matter at this moment. At this moment, what I need is an arresting intro. The bit about the colour-changes is just filler stuff for the middle. Maybe if I'm clever, I'll even be able to work in a joke about a colour also being the name of their new album.

So, this intro. This arresting, clever intro. The one that's going to impress the rock editor so much he's going to send me to lots more gigs. The one which I can't afford to get wrong because if I do get it wrong – well that's it, curtains, my rock-reviewing career will have ended before it even began.

Fuck. No wonder I can't think of a decent intro if I keep thinking thoughts like that. And it's not just the pressure. It's this silence. I'm not used to working when the office is all quiet like this. If only a few more people would arrive; a few phones would start ringing, then maybe I could concentrate.

Ring ring. Ring ring. Ring ring. Ring ring.

Is someone going to answer that?

Ring ring. Ring ring. Ring ring.

For fuck's sake.

'Hello, dear. You're in terribly early,' says Violet, hanging up her coat.

'Yeah, well. I've got this bloody rock thing to write up, haven't I?'

'Your concert. Yes. How was it?'

'Great. I think.'

What spoilt it slightly was that I was there as a critic, not just as a fan. I do definitely remember the fan part of me feeling suitably tingly and elated when they did classic early stuff like 'Perfect Circle', and my favourite track from the new record. But the bits I remember far more intensely are the ones related to my role as a reviewer. Like: being incredibly self-conscious about holding my notebook – half wanting people to go 'Wow, you're a critic.' Half wanting nobody to notice in case they think I'm a wanker; studiously jotting down the new colour combinations every time the lighting changed; trying to think of some clever technical observation I might be able make about, say, Bill Berry's drums or Mike Mills's bass, realizing I didn't know enough to make one, then worrying about it; asking the person next to me what the title of the song was; them telling me, after my second request, 'Look do you want me to do this review myself?'; me badly wanting to have a joint but not daring to, because it's hard to smoke discreetly at an all-seater affair at the Hammersmith Odeon and I can already see the headline '*Telegraph* critic in marijuana bust'; wanting to leave early so as to beat the rush, but being unable to do so, in case Michael Stipe died or announced he was gay or something; hardly getting any sleep through being so worried about writing a good enough review.

'Actually, Violet, I think I may have hated it.'

'Oh, well, never mind. You won't have to do it again.'

'But that's the terrible thing. I do want to do it again. Badly.'

'What do you want to do again badly?' asks the Rottweiler, dumping his briefcase on his desk. He lights a cigarette and makes urgent coffee-drinking gestures to Violet.

'Nothing.'

'You've always been good at that,' he says

'Nothing you'd understand, I'm talking about popular music. And this rather wonderful beat combo I saw last night,' I say.

'Ah yes. REO Speedwagon.'

'Very nearly. If you replace the O with M and remove the Speedwagon.'

'Before you get too cocky, you're talking to a man who actually owns an REM record.'

'Really?'

' "*The End of the World as we Know It*". That's one of theirs, isn't it?' he says.

'One of their singles, yeah,' I say.

'Oh I see and only albums qualify, do they, now that we're a professional rock critic?'

'Well, I'm hardly that, am I?'

'Professional enough to have got your review written before I arrived. Well done.'

'Actually, Robert, I was wondering . . .'

'No.'

'Please.'

'Mm hmm hmm—' the Rottweiler has started humming '*Clair de Lune*', as he always does when he catches his team moonlighting for other sections of the newspaper.

'But if I don't get it in before twelve—'

'I've got a diary to fill and, as of this moment, no stories to fill it with. So, what yarns have you got for me?'

'I'm still chasing that one about the General Synod and women priests,' I say.

'Ah yes, the one that got the biggest yawns in conference yesterday. Anything else?'

'Um—'

'Where is everyone, anyway. Violet?'

'Lady Waters called a moment ago to say that Clytemnestra might be a little late.'

'Too windy again?'

'Something about having a new dress fitted.'

'Oh well, as long as it's not something incredibly trivial that she could have had done any time . . . Crispin, there you are. What you got for conference?'

'I think the General Synod may be about to—'

'No women priests,' says the Rottweiler.

'That's the gist,' says Crispin.

'I mean I never want to run another story about bloody women priests. I don't care. Our readers don't care. Yes all right, maybe they do care, but if we paid any attention to what they think all we'd ever be writing about is Stannah stair lifts and zimmer frames and send in the teams of highly trained killer bees to sort out the mess in the Colonies. McDougal, where the hell have you been?'

'Oh, the DLR was absolutely—'

'The Docklands Lighthearted Excuse For A Railway is no excuse. It always breaks down, you know that, so you have to leave earlier. Now, please. Give me a decent yarn for conference before I'm forced to sack the lot of you.'

'Well, there was that story I thought I'd follow up about the Muthaiga allowing female members.'

'The Muthaiga being an obscure club that no one gives a damn about apart from a few old colonels?' says the Rottt-weiler.

'Perfect for Peterborough, then,' observes Crispin.

'It was in *White Mischief*,' I say. 'Maybe we could slip in some reference to Greta Scacchi's breasts?'

The Rottweiler frowns. Everyone else sniggers then stops when they see the large and terrifying Foreign Editor looming over Rottweiler's shoulder.

'Sydney, what can I do for you?' he says.

The Foreign Editor murmurs in his ear.

'Really?' says the Rottweiler, glancing in my direction, then looking quickly away. He stands up and walks with the Foreign Editor until they're out of earshot.

'What's eating him today?' Crispin asks.

'Cirrhosis, I'd imagine,' I say.

Now the Rottweiler is easing back into his chair.

'*What* were you doing last night?' he says, frowning.

'You know what I was doing,'

'Not all of it, clearly. Not according to Sydney.'

'What did he say?'

'Bearded men in leather ring any bells?'

'Er—'

'I'll press him for more detail after conference. Probably got you confused with someone else. What was that club's name again?'

'The Muthaiga,' says McDougal.

'It's in Nairobi. I've been there, actually,' I say.

'And that's not the only exotic place you've been, is it, dearie.'

'Piss off, Crispin.'

While the Rottweiler is away in editorial conference, I try to bash out my rock review. They only want 350 words, but writing short is even more difficult than writing long. There's no room for flannel. And it doesn't help that every few seconds there's another Message Pending signal flashing on my screen. Most of them are from Crispin.

'Well?' says the first.

'Come on, you can tell me,' says the second.

'No more secrets from me, then,' says the third.

'Ever,' says the fourth.

'Just got a very interesting message from Godfrey. About "the floppy fringed ephebe who sits not unadjacent" to you,' says the fifth.

Godfrey is the *Telegraph*'s official homosexual. He used to work on *Gay Times*, which seems to make it all right.

'What?' I write back.

'I'll show you mine if you show me yours,' comes the reply.

When I look up Crispin is smirking.

'Send it on to me now or you're dead, Crispin,' I say.

Message pending flashes again.

It's from Godfrey. 'Welcome to the club. (And what took you so long?)'

Without thinking, I type back: 'I AM NOT GAY.'

Now they're coming in droves.

From Julia on the fashion desk: 'Tell me the rumours aren't true? All replies guaranteed to be kept in the strictest confidence.'

From Quentin on City diary: 'Don't let the bastards grind you down, old boy. If you need a consolatory drink at lunchtime, I'm available. (Available for food and drink, that is. Not – ahem . . .)'

From Godfrey: 'Understand your confusion. Friends of mine have found this helpline no. very useful . . .'

From Crispin: 'Car park last night? Young man with long hair in dark suit? Other man in leather? Witnessed by security guard? Caught on surveillance camera? Now please, Josh, deny it no longer. Tell Uncle Crispin all!'

'Right that it is sodding well it,' I announce, rising from my chair.

'Dear, Josh, what is the matter?' asks Violet.

'I'm sure Crispin will explain. If the Rottweiler wants me, tell him I'm in Sports.'

The spare desk near Sports is where we all go when we need to write articles in peace. You log on to your computer as a visiting freelancer and you don't get disturbed by any flashing messages. The Sports desk, of course, are all animals. When you arrive you have to put up with a few quips about rolling out the red carpet, Lord Fauntleroy's here etc, etc. After that they normally get bored and leave you in peace. Today, however, they don't even notice my arrival. They're gathered round their TV screen, watching some sort of grainy, pirated video. Schoolgirls and donkeys, maybe. Or is it the true life death one, where you see that journalist being shot in Nicaragua?

I try focusing on the screen but I've left my glasses back at my desk and I daren't attract the mob's attention by going closer. It seems to involve a trouserless man standing by the boot of his car. He fumbles about a bit. Then there's a shot from a different angle of the man in the driver's seat. Next to him is a leather-clad man with a beard. It seems strangely familiar. Now the sports hacks are laughing heartily because the driver has disappeared. Occasionally, you glimpse the top of his head, bobbing up and down, directly over the passenger's lap.

'Bloody hell,' I think, and my instinct is to join the mob for a closer look.

'BLOODY HELL,' I think, again. This time because I've realized who the protagonists are.

'Hey!' I hear someone call behind me. 'Hey, look, it's him!'

'Oi, Gaylord, what's the matter? Aren't none of us your type?'

''Ere, Gaylord, 'ere's a tenner. You'll do French for a tenner, won't you?'

I slump back at my own workstation, flushed and furious. 'That is it! That is it! That is sodding bloody it!' I say, smashing at the Read Message button and then instantly deleting all seven or eight newcomers.

'Oh, Josh, do tell me what's going on, Crispin's being all coy.'

'Yes, well he's all excited because he thinks I'm a toilet trader like him, that's bloody why.'

'A lot of the greatest men in history were bisexual, you know,' says Clytemnestra.

'Listen, Clitty,' I say (I gave her that nickname myself. She doesn't like it), 'I'm quite capable of being great without doing any uphill gardening.'

'Get her!' shrieks Crispin, making scratchy claws gestures.

'OK. Just so that I don't have to put with any more of this stupidity, I'm going to tell you exactly what happened. The man in the video—'

'What video?'

'Oh, God, Clitty, you are so— the surveillance video in which I was supposedly caught giving a man a blow job—'

'Steady,' says Violet.

'Was in fact my brother. As you all damn well know because you've all met him, he has a beard and likes wearing leather because he rides a motorbike. I went with him to last night's gig, as you all also know, because you'll remember reception calling up to say he was here.'

'I don't remember anything of the sort, do you, Violet?' says Crispin.

'Don't be naughty, Crispin. This must be very upsetting for him.'

'Aye, Caliban's rage on seeing himself reflected in the glass,' says McDougal.

'The reason I took off my trousers was so I could change into my jeans for the gig—'

'I have to say, the alternative version sounds much more plausible,' says Crispin.

'And the reason I was bobbing up and down like that was because I was scrummaging around on the floor trying to find the REM cassette, so that I could get into the songs on the way to the gig.'

'Right,' says the Rottweiler to me briskly as he arrives back in his chair. 'I've got a few more details. You sure you wouldn't rather discuss this in private?'

'It's OK, we know the whole story,' says Clytemnestra.

'Apparently,' says Crispin in a voice oozing scepticism and mirth, 'it was his *brother.*'

*

But it does get me wondering. A day or two later it's London Fashion Week and I'm at this aftershow party at Marshall

Street Baths thrown by Lynne Franks for Katharine Hamnett. It's terribly *Ab Fab*, though none of us knows this because the comedy series has yet to be invented.

Everyone here is young, beautiful or at the very least extremely fashionable, the drink flows, Silk Cuts are chain-smoked, the queue for the loos is a mile long, the music is spun by top DJs on a small, crowded floor where at one stage I find myself dancing next to and possibly even with Neneh Cherry, and there are lots of dinky little side shows like the room where these Victorian school desks have been converted into pedal-powered bumper cars which nobody is quite sure whether to drive ironically or sincerely.

And there's Katharine Hamnett herself. She'll be good for a few amusing quotes.

So I sidle up to interrupt this earnest conversation she's having with some other fashion female of a certain age and compliment her on the bumper car school desks.

'Who are you?' she says.

I tell her.

'Right. Would you mind fucking off?'

I fuck off, hurt, but mildly consoled by the thought that I can now write about how Katharine Hamnett told me to fuck off.

The woman who was talking to Katharine Hamnett follows me.

'Who are you?' she says.

I tell her.

'Do you have an invitation?'

Yes.

'May I see it?'

What is this, Nazi Germany?

'I'm Lynne Franks, Katharine's publicist.'

'Ah. Then you might want to advise her that when people come to write nice, tame, puffy stories about her parties, it's a good idea not to tell them to "Fuck off"'.

'Look you have to understand, fashion week is a very fraught time for designers. These parties are their only chance to relax. They're private events. The last thing anyone wants is to be hassled by journalists.'

'So why invite journalists, then?'

I would feel mildly triumphant, except that I don't think I actually said all the things I've just reported myself as having said. I think my real responses were far more conciliatory, because that's how you are in your early twenties. You're not quite sure of your place in the scheme of things, what your rights are, when you're being unfairly treated. Instead, you just let yourself get shat upon.

Anyway all this is just scene setting, the real point is a conversation I'm about to have with this Irish photographer that I haven't seen in some time. His name's Terry Grogan and I worked with him on one of my earliest features, a piece for *Tatler* on the King's Road, which was never used — rather stupidly, as it transpired, because if it had been, it would have been one of the first articles to describe the new acid house scene.

Terry and I talk stiltedly about this and that, am I still living in the same place, how's the job, what parties have I done so far, what am I doing later.

'Stick around here and try to pull, I guess,' I say.

'Boy or girl?' asks Terry.

'Er, girl.'

Terry eyes me shrewdly. My bobbed hair, my stripy sailor shirt, my World Service strawberry linen jacket and my grey jersey cotton palazzo pants so baggy they look like a skirt:

these, his don't-bullshit-me-I'm-a-shrewd-Hibernian look is saying, are not the most obvious indicators of rampant hetero-sexuality.

'Is that so?' His voice has an edge now, quite aggressive.

'Why shouldn't it be?' I say, not as confidently as I'd hoped.

'You know you're gay really.' To get the full effect of this, try saying it with a sneering, Bono-style accent. And he does look quite like Bono in his early U2 days: jet-black hair, designer stubble, leather biker jacket, brooding expression, very Pictish.

'Oh, I don't think so. It's girls I fancy,' I say. Limply.

He gives me his searching, don't-bullshit-me look again and his voice swells with that poetic resonance which the Irish turn on like taps and use like shillelaghs.

'But who is it you think about when you're lying alone in bed? Who is it you dream about? Who is it you fantasize about? Don't tell me it's girls, I know it's not girls. Look into your heart and tell yourself the truth. You're gay, Josh. You're gay.'

At which point I say that I really must circulate. I slink off, pursued by his horrible jackal grin.

'Fuck!' I say to myself when I'm out of his sight. 'Fuck!'

I light a cigarette. I'm trembling. With shock, no doubt. Or rage, maybe. Or possibly even exhilaration.

God yes, why not? Maybe I'm trembling with the exhilar-ation of a man who has finally discovered his innermost secret. Yes, it's a cliché. But the reason clichés are clichés is because they happen so often. Could it be that I have travelled the whole wide world but never been to me?

For the first time – or perhaps it isn't the first time, perhaps I've been doing it my whole life without being aware of it – I try concentrating on the men in the room rather than the women. It's quite encouraging because they're all having an outrageously good time, as gay men do in party mode. A much better time than I've ever had at a party. But perhaps that's because I've been in denial. Maybe if I came out it would change everything.

Except I don't fancy any of them. Not the hunky worked-out ones, nor the slim, graceful ephebic ones and definitely not the shrill, effeminate, catty ones. Surely if I were gay, I'd find myself drawn to at least one of them. I mean these boys are models. This is as good looking as gay gets.

Ah, but hold on. Maybe the reason that I don't fancy other men is that I've conditioned myself not to? You read of all sorts of men who get married, watch their children grow up, and only realize in late middle-age that they're gay. Which, clearly, is a fairly crap time to discover it. If you're going to discover you're gay, you want to do it when you're still young enough to pull. It's a very age-sensitive thing, homosexuality. So all my gay friends say.

And there's a pointer if ever there was one. Why are so many of my friends gay? Why do I always seem to gravitate at showbiz parties towards gay celebrities like Stephen Fry and Ian McKellen and Simon Callow? And why do they seem to find me so simpatico? Because they've spotted a kindred spirit, that's why. There was I thinking I'm a heterosexual flirting with homosexuality when in fact I'm just a homo deluding himself that he's straight.

Unless—

Oh, stop trying to wriggle out of it, you're gay, you're gay, like the man says, you know you're gay.

OK. But these models. How come I'd much rather shag the girls than the boys?

We've been through this. Because as a self-hating gay you've conditioned yourself to prefer women.

Well, now that I do, can't I stick with them? Then I wouldn't have to change my lifestyle, I wouldn't have to make painful confessions to my parents and live a lie for my grand-mother, I wouldn't have to worry about losing my friends, I'd stand a smaller chance of contracting AIDS, I could go on sleeping with girls who are so much softer, more curvy and generally better designed for sex than knobbly, bony men.

You could. But you'd never be happy.

Is it really so stark a choice?

Yes.

Are you sure?

Yes.

How do you know?

You're gay you're gay you're gay you're gay you're gay.

It's a shame there's not some sort of Gayness Tester Kit that you could pick up over the counter in Boots. Think of the agonizing it would spare so many confused young men! As it is, after days of turmoil, I seek the counsel of Crispin.

'You're not,' he says.

'Then why is this bloke so convinced I am?'

'Because he's gay.'

'How do you know he's gay?'

'Isn't he?'

'Yes.'

'There's nothing an old queen likes more than telling a pretty boy he's gay. Well, apart from when he convinces him.'

'He wasn't trying to get me into bed. I'm not his type.'

'So he was telling you out of the goodness of his heart?'

'Crispin, if you met him, you'd realize. You'd never even know he was gay.'

'Josh, he's a cunt.'

'How does that help me?'

'It makes me right and him wrong because he's a cunt. Seriously, only a cunt would tell you something like that. And even if you were gay he shouldn't have said anything because it's for you to decide not him.'

'So I might be gay.'

'Do you feel gay?'

'Not especially.'

'Then you're not.'

'Is it that simple?'

'Yes.'

That night, in the bath, I give myself a final test. I try to see if I can make myself come using nothing but homosexual fantasies. And a little friction, obviously. I mean, if I was capable of coming on homosexual fantasies alone I would hardly be needing to conduct experiments to find out whether or not I was gay, would I?

After much fruitless abrasion, I cheat by thinking about girls. Then, when I'm reasonably hard, I try moving on to men, racking my brain for possible scenarios in which I might enjoy having sex with them. It isn't easy. The last time I was aroused by a bloke was when I was thirteen, at prep school, when males tend to look a lot prettier and girlier and more fanciable than they do after puberty. I try to picture all the boys I tossed off and to decide which one was the most attractive. But frankly, after so long, it's hard to remember one from another. And anyway, isn't it a bit paedophilic of me to be trying to wank over twelve- and thirteen-year-old boys?

Only having resumed thinking about young naked girls who want me deep inside oh God how they want it up them right now etc. do I reach a sufficient state of hardness to risk thinking about men once more. I try conjuring up my ideal fantasy male. It turns out that he looks exactly like a pretty girl, the only difference being that he isn't one. Like the beautiful creature I saw in Africa once. Central African Republic, I think it was. At a border crossing.

We were waiting in a corrugated hut for our passports to be processed by corrupt officials wanting baksheesh. It took a very long time. As the afternoon wore on, we were joined by a middle-aged Belgian who'd clearly been ravaged by malaria and his young charge, a pubescent girl with fluffy blonde hair, babysmooth skin and quite the most angelically beautiful face I had ever seen. It had been some time since I had had sex. (To the extent that I didn't have wet dreams any more. After a while, you just dry up.) In an instant I was infatuated.

And I wasn't the only one. Sometimes, when they thought they weren't being watched, I would catch the other males in my party gazing at this vision in tongue-lolling wonderment. Or their eyes would rove across the customs hut's interior as if at random only to settle on that exquisite piece of flaxen gorgeousness for just a fraction longer than true randomness would have allowed. Or they'd stare blatantly in her general direction but slightly to her left or right, as if it weren't the girl they were focusing on but the fascinating makeshift barrier on the road outside or the truly amazing border guard slumped asleep under a tree. We all realized, I think, that there was something slightly predatory and unwholesome about our feelings towards this creature. This girl – if it was a girl, because I'm sure we all had our doubts – can't have been more than thirteen. Jailbait. And particularly cherubic, innocent-looking jailbait at that.

But how could I approach her? It should have been easy. Here we were in the middle of nowhere, the only white people for miles around, waiting in the same customs hut to get our passports stamped. Quite a few things in common, there, you might have thought, to help us break the ice. And so we might have done had it not been for the antisocial vibes emanating from the gaunt, disease-racked Belgian. Obviously when he came in he gave us a brief nod and grunt of acknowledgement: not to have done so would have attracted more of the attention he so clearly didn't want. What he determinedly wasn't going to do, though, was give us enough of an entrée to find out who he was and what he was doing and who this cute fluffy thing next to him was – the one now smiling across the room at me, with its big blue bushbaby eyes, like it wanted to make friends with me even if its surly keeper didn't.

The most sensible thing, I decided, would be to win the keeper's trust. So, once I'd plucked up sufficient courage, I sidled with tropical languor across the hut and said to the Belgian: 'Salut. Ça va? Vous êtes en Afrique depuis longtemps?'

Yes, he replied. He had been in Africa quite some time. Then he made a half smile and gazed into the middle distance.

Normally, I might have taken the hint. But my curiosity was insatiable. I began telling them all about the adventures we had had; about the civil war which had forced us to take a thousand-mile detour via Central African Republic, about the rebel plane which had bombed Khartoum the morning we arrived, about the starving villagers in the west who'd pressed a scrawny chicken upon us, about the Sudanese army officers who'd offered to take us gazelle-hunting with Kalash-nikovs in the desert—

'Ah, la chasse. Moi, j'aime bien la chasse,' squealed the companion in a voice that still didn't offer much clue as to whether it was male or female. And oblivious of its guardian's reproachful glances, it began telling me that its personal ambition was to go monkey hunting with the pigmies said to live in these parts.

When it wondered how hard blowpipes were to use, I replied that I didn't think they used blowpipes – that was in South America – they used bows and arrows instead. Ah, well, if it's bows and arrows, that'll be easy, I have one of my own at home in Belgium, said the pretty thing, adding that it really was too boring sitting in here and did I want to go with it outside.

Why not, I agreed.

The Belgian grunted something about not straying too far.

Outside, beneath an intense blue electrical sky, the beautiful thing grew more radiantly lovely still. Its blonde hair glowed halo bright, its tanned cheeks shone, its pretty little teeth gleamed white.

And of course it turned out to be the thing I hoped it wouldn't be.

A boy.

His name was François and the Belgian, whom he called Uncle Jacques, wasn't really his uncle he said but a friend of his father's who had agreed to act as his guardian while his parents were sorting out some sort of unspecified trouble at home. He was travelling in Africa for his 'education'.

There was no guile in his voice, which I suppose could have meant that what he was saying was true. Or that, in his warped imagination, it was what he'd come to persuade himself was true. Or that months of deceit had turned him into a practised liar. Or, simply, that he had abandoned all sense of morality.

In my more optimistic moments I would convince myself that his relationship with the sick Belgian was as innocent as he claimed. In my more cynical ones, I would torture myself with visions of what they might be getting up to in the camper van they had parked on the edge of our encampment.

They went on to travel with us for several days. The roads were bad, we were going the same way, and in dangerous countries it's always better to drive in convoy. Mostly, they would eat apart and sleep apart from the rest of us. But just occasionally, François would wander over to our camp fire for a chat and cup of tea. He'd sit by my side, often so close that the bare flesh of our legs would touch, and while he chattered away, I'd dream of how we'd steal away in the night and begin a new life together. Because it struck me as quite outrageous that this filthy old man should have sole access to such ephebic beauty.

When I was at prep school, tossing off my mates, I never failed to feel absolutely shit about it afterwards. I remember coming home one weekend and my mother telling me that a friend of hers who had a son at the same school had learned from her boy that homosexual activity was rife. 'Have you ever done any of that sort of thing?' my mother asked. 'Because you know darling, if you did, I'd love you just the same.' 'No,' I said, praying that my cheeks weren't burning as visibly as they felt they were burning.

And I hated everyone. I hated that bastard boy for telling his mother something that no boy should ever tell his parents. I hated mother both for her indelicacy and for her blanket love and forgiveness which only made me feel worse than I did anyway. Most of all, I hated myself for being such a hideous, revolting pervert who was doomed to spend the rest of his life as an outcast. A bender.

Except that isn't how things have turned out. I can't pretend I didn't enjoy my sessions at prep school and I can't pretend I didn't fancy that Belgian boy. But what I've never been tempted to do in the years since is to have a sexual relationship with another man. And it's not that I don't like the idea of it – I mean, what could be more cool and liberated? – it's quite simply that I have finally realized that I don't fancy blokes and I don't think I ever have.

Those boys at prep school and François – they weren't really men, they were girls in disguise. It was their prettiness that appealed to me, their feminity – not their grubby boy hands, and their dirty boy smells and their rancid little boy willies. It was the fact that, faute de mieux, they were sexually available.

Here's the sad thing, though. Now that I've reached an age where I'm no longer confused about my sexuality, I do miss the time when I was. Life may have been harsher and more anxious; but the possibilities were so much more interesting.

One, two, three with Ant and Bea

There are lots of things you should have done by the end of your twenties and having a threesome is one of them. But the annoying thing about girls when you raise the subject is that they always say: 'Sure. Who's the other bloke?'

And I don't believe them. I don't think they really want to have sex with two blokes at all, I think it's just a cunning strategy to ward you off and make them seem liberated all at the same time. Because what you inevitably say is: 'Urrgh. No way am I going to have sex with another man.' Which enables them to say: 'Well, what makes you think I'd want to have sex with another woman?'

But it's not their real reason. The real reason is that women prefer their sex to be an exclusive thing, a special moment between two people, not some debauched shagfest involving simultaneous penetration of multiple orifices. If they're making love to a man, they want to be able to persuade themselves that he has eyes only for them, because this, after all is what they're biologically designed for – finding a single mate, enticing him with sex and then trapping him so that he can look after the resultant sprog.

Men are the opposite.

So naturally when one summer holidays I find myself in the South of France with two teenage girls who claim to be

307

up for having a threesome with me, I light another fag and say: 'Fine. OK. You're on.'

This might sound a nonchalant response to so generous an offer. But the last thing you want to do is show such enthusiasm that the girls start thinking: 'Hang on. What are we getting ourselves into here?' You want them to think that what you're about to do is about as uncontroversial as eating your croissant with apricot jam; dipping your brioche in a bowl of hot chocolate; mixing your pastis with water; that sort of thing.

It being the South of France I've been doing a lot of these lately. I'm staying in this ancient stone-built Provençal *mas*, belonging to Molly's and Marcus's rich grandmother, and there's not much to do in this heat except eat, slump by the pool and get drunk.

The drinking starts around lunchtime – earlier, if we have particularly bad hangovers – and because Molly isn't around, just me and Marcus, we can really go for it. Marcus is quite fond of the pink semi-fermented piss sold in plastic cartons as Vin du Pays Rosé by the neighbouring cooperative, I find that pastis gets you there quicker and isn't quite so brutal on the head.

We've been at it for two, three, maybe four days when the girls appear, seemingly out of nowhere. We're lounging in the garden as per usual, trying to make sense of the swimming words on the pages we've no doubt read and re-read about half a dozen times, when they materialize on the lawn with their sunglasses, towels and pasty English schoolgirl skin.

'Hi, we're here. Any idea which bedroom we're supposed to be in?' one of them asks.

Marcus barely looks up from his book. 'Grab any one that looks free, I should.'

When they've gone I glance across at Marcus. If only I could learn to be as offhand with girls, maybe I'd get as much sex as he does.

'Were you expecting them?' I ask.

'I think so.'

'So?'

'Oh, you know, they're just friends of my baby sister's. InterRailing across Europe, I think.'

'You might have told me earlier.'

'How's that?'

'So I could have been a bit more prepared. I mean, what's the situation here? Do they have boyfriends? Are they up for it?'

'Josh,' chides Marcus, who in the four years I've known him has shagged more girls than I will in a lifetime.

'What?'

'They're friends of Poppy's, for God's sake. They're still at school. They can't be much more than seventeen.'

'Oh, right,' I say. Like I've any problem with any of that whatsover.

*

I'm crap with girls and always have been. The pat explanation for this is that I spent ten years in all-boys boarding schools, but then so did Marcus and it doesn't seem to have done his bird-pulling skills much harm.

What I think it really is is a class thing. I'm middle and Marcus is upper, which means that while I'm constantly vacillating between wishing I were posher and wishing I had more proletarian street cred, he has never doubted his place in society. He was born to look on the whole world as his as of right. Including all its women.

You'd think women would be repelled by this proprietorial arrogance but they're not, not remotely, they find it wildly attractive. It signifies strength, charisma and alpha-sperm superiority. It means he might not love you in the morning but at least he's going to give you a proper seeing to. And if by some lucky stroke, you do manage to keep his interest for more than a night, well, you're laughing, aren't you? You've landed exactly the type of man girls are supposed to land: ones that make good breeding stock, ones that will bring home the mammoth chunks and ward off dinosaurs with their powerful spears.

At least that's how I think girls think. It's certainly what I think they're thinking now – Beatrice and Antonia, their names are – as they re-emerge from the house to parade themselves in their bikinis towards an uninterested Marcus.

I too try to show no interest but it's quite hard when there's all this nubile flesh you've never seen before being exposed in front of you. Harder still when you've had a few drinks, and haven't had sex for weeks, as usual.

But I know I mustn't stare. I mustn't, *mustn't* stare. Because if they catch me looking at them with anything more concupiscent than polite curiosity they'll run a mile because that's what girls are like. Especially teenage girls. They only want what they think they cannot get.

Marcus, for example, who rises dutifully to kiss them on each cheek, and asks after their brothers – who, of course, were at Eton with him – and keeps them up to speed on those recent family developments Poppy has neglected to mention. And I'm reminded of yet another thing I find so envy-inducing and alienating about the upper classes, this languid ease they all have with one another, the way they've been to the same schools, know the same people, own houses in the same places, go to the same parties, holiday together and sleep with one another, almost as if the normal world, the non-upper-class world, the one I mostly inhabit except on occasions like this, simply didn't exist.

'Do you know, Josh?' Marcus asks them.

'Oh, hi,' they say turning to scrutinize me just long enough for their memory banks to whirr through all the myriad acceptable social connections of which I might be part until they conclude that, no, I am not One Of Them.

'Hi,' I say with a casual wave, and would leave it at that, except if I don't do something to make them vaguely interested in my existence they might carry on ignoring me for ever. 'I was just going to fix another drink. Anything you fancy?'

The offer is a mistake. It gives them the opportunity to say no, which means that a) I have been implicitly rejected and b) I have to spend the rest of the afternoon pacing my drinking, lest I end up jeopardizing my chances later.

Mind you, I think we should be clear about what we're discussing here. I don't know about you, but when I read in a book the phrase 'teenage girl' I immediately think of blue eyes, high cheekbones, pert breasts, lithe, tanned legs up to the armpits, but with these two that isn't quite the case. They're just OK-looking, upper-class English girls.

Which in a way makes it more difficult. If they were completely out of my league, I wouldn't bother. Whereas, as it is, I'm trying way, way too hard.

Like at dinner, I decide it would be a good idea to impress them with my cooking. Nothing that complicated, just a spaghetti all'amatriciana, with a green salad, but it goes down really well and Antonia asks me how it's done.

So I tell her about frying the chilli with the garlic to bring out its flavour, and how pancetta's good but you can just as easily use bacon, smoked for personal preference, though purists insist it should be green, and how I normally reserve the bacon/pancetta/whatever once it's cooked and only put it back with the tomatoes right at the end, otherwise it goes soggy; about how it's one of those useful pasta dishes where you don't need parmesan because it tastes just as good on its own.

And through all this, as we sit outside beneath the vines under a full moon on a perfect Provençal summer evening, the girls are looking really quite interested – like all of a sudden they've understood the point of my existence.

But then there's a slight pause, which Beatrice fills by saying: 'And your salad dressing's great too. How do you do that?'

And I explain, in perhaps a little too much detail, because half way through I notice Antonia turning her head distractedly to locate the cicada chirruping nearby, and though I cut myself off with an 'and that's pretty much it', Marcus prolongs the agony with a: 'Yes. When we were living together at Oxford – five boys and Josh was the cook – all our mothers used to complain that our palates had been ruined because Josh's cooking was so much better than anything they could do.'

I try to bury it quickly: 'Yeah, well, it wasn't that complicated. Just roast meats and basic stuff like stews and casseroles.'

'Still it is nice when a man can cook,' says Antonia.

'Yes, makes a nice change,' says Beatrice, looking at Marcus, 'I'll bet you can't cook a flipping thing.'

'Too right,' Marcus agrees. 'I'm absolutely hopeless.'

By now, I can feel my laurels turning to dust, because what the girls have clearly decided is that my interest in cooking is actually a bit precious, a bit anally retentive, not the sort of thing a proper bloke should be doing. What a proper bloke should be doing is what Marcus has been doing while I was in the kitchen: slouching on the patio with his kir and his fags, serenading the girls on his guitar with his creaky but unabashed 'Wish You Were Here', making them laugh, making them even more eager to sleep with him than they were already. Me, I'm just some culinary poof.

Then it could be worse. At least they're both conversing with me now, at least they're getting stuck into the booze and generally acting less stand-offish than they were this afternoon. And later, when I tell them a bit more about what I do they start getting interested again. Especially when I start mentioning – at this point I catch Marcus rolling his eyes – all the celebrities I've met and telling them what they're really like.

'Beats covering Algeria,' says Marcus, who reported from there quite recently, and is clearly dying to tell the tale about the time in the souk when he was chased into a blind alley by a dagger-wielding mob of FIS supporters only to be dragged into a doorway by some merciful rescuer at the very last second.

Unfortunately for Marcus, the girls aren't much interested in Algeria and almost certainly haven't a clue who the FIS are or what it stands for. They want to know about Rob Newman; about Tony Slattery; about Mike Edwards from Jesus Jones.

Quite how I manage to drag the conversation towards sex and threesomes I really can't remember. Some tenuous connection with 'Bonnie & Clyde', maybe?

'Bonnie & Clyde' – the Serge Gainsbourg and Brigitte Bardot version – is one of only three records in the house. The others are an album called *Songs For Gay Dogs* in which a fruity-voiced thirties toff called Paddy Roberts croons ditties like 'Oh Dear What Can The Matter Be?' and 'Don't

Use The WC While The Train Is Standing In The Station'. And the Yardbirds single 'For Your Love'.

Naturally since 'Bonnie & Clyde' and the Yardbirds are the only things you can dance to, we play them an awful lot. Especially late at night when we're drunk, like now.

The bit I particularly like on 'Bonnie & Clyde' is when the young Brigitte whoops sex-kittenishly 'oo ooo oo' in the background.

'God, he was a lucky bastard, that Serge,' I yell to Marcus, above the record – which we're playing for the fifth or sixth time, loud to the point of distortion – 'she must have been so shaggable, in those days.'

'Definitely a lot more than she is now,' calls back Marcus.

'Yeah. Right. Leather-faced old puppy-rescuer.'

'No bone structure, that was her problem,' says Antonia, jigging besides me.

Aha, I'm thinking. A girl who can keep her end up in sexist male conversations.

'Unlike Serge,' says Beatrice. 'Serge just got sexier the older he grew.'

'It's why a man should always smoke,' I say, smiling and waving my cigarette in time to the music. 'Smoking makes you more like Serge.'

'You'll need more than fags to turn you into Serge,' says Marcus.

'Marcus, my friend. Compared to me Serge Gainsbourg is a fucking eunuch.'

'Oh really? Tell us more,' says Beatrice.

'Mm, do,' agrees Antonia.

Which would normally be the point where I'd run away screaming. Fortunately, I'm sufficiently laden with pastis. 'You'll just have to find out later,' I say.

'What both of us?' giggles Antonia.

'Hey. Normally, for me a foursome's the bare minimum.'

'That's OK, we've got Marcus,' says Beatrice.

'Keep me out of this,' says Marcus.

'Three girls, I meant,' I say.

'But you'll make an exception just this once, for us?' says Antonia.

'Fine, OK. You're on.'

What I haven't worked out at this point is whether any of us means it. I'm not sure they know either. But I try to keep the temperature at a suitable level by proposing a spot of moonlit skinny dipping.

Marcus isn't keen. The girls will do it, but only topless, not fully nude.

'OK,' I say. 'We'll do it topless too, then.'

'That's not fair,' says Antonia. 'If we take off our bras, you have to take off your trunks.'

'I hope you're not suggesting that my lovely breasts aren't as important as yours,' I say.

'If you won't go bottomless, we won't go topless,' says Beatrice.

'Fine. Who cares? Let's just swim,' says Marcus.

After that, the evening sort of peters out. We have a swim. I cheekily remove my trunks because I like the feel of water on my goolies. Then, to much screaming, I help the girls remove their tops. But not long afterwards, everyone starts feeling the cold. We pad, shivering, across the lawn into the house. We have one final fag and night cap. Then we all head off to bed.

Luckily, there's only one bathroom, which enables me to accost Beatrice and Antonia while I'm queuing behind them to clean my teeth.

'So, girls, are you ready?'

'Oh gosh, our threesome, yes,' says Beatrice.

'You are still on for it, aren't you?'

'Are we?' Beatrice asks Antonia.

'I suppose,' says Antonia.

'Give us five minutes,' Beatrice says to me.

Much, much longer than five minutes later, I'm propped up in bed with an unread book, trying to keep myself awake on the vague off chance that they might yet do as they said. Not that the omens are all that promising. The way Antonia said 'I suppose', for example. It didn't sound like a rampant nubile teenager gagging for hot deviant sex with an older man. It sounded more like a reluctant but dutiful child being dragged to the nursing home to receive sweets and gummy kisses from her ninety-seven-year old great-grandma.

And, to be honest, I can't say I'm feeling desperately horny myself. I try to think rude thoughts about a pair of teenagers, moaning and snogging one another, one sitting astride my tongue, the other bouncing up and down on my mighty organ in wild abandon. But somehow I can't quite picture it. Stodgy English girls with pallid skin and giggly, public school voices just aren't cut out for that kind of behaviour.

Suddenly the door's open and they're here, in the room, wearing nothing but their knickers and shirts buttoned loosely to cover their breasts.

'Sorry we're late,' says Antonia.

To which I suppose the correct response would be: 'You'd both better bend over while I give you a good spanking.'

But I don't, I say: 'Hi, come on in.'

The girls perch on the bed, either side of my legs which are under the sheets.

'So, where do we go from here?' says Beatrice.

'Uh, not sure. Do you think maybe you should take your shirts off?'

'Not with the light on,' says Antonia.

'With the light off, then,' I say.

Beatrice turns off the light.

'Now,' I say, unbuttoning Antonia's shirt. 'That's better, isn't it?'

'What about me? What am I supposed to do,' says Beatrice.

'Just let me play with Antonia's breasts for a few minutes, then I can do yours.'

'*Do* mine? He's got a sexy way with words, hasn't he, Ant?' says Beatrice.

'Oh all right, caress, fondle, stroke – er – titillate. What do you want me to say?'

'Not titillate,' says Antonia, 'that's seriously unerotic.'

'Anything so long as I don't just have to sit here like a gooseberry,' says Beatrice.

'Excuse me for a minute, Antonia,' I say, transferring my attentions to Beatrice's breasts.

'But you didn't even get started,' protests Antonia.

'Yeah, well, Beatrice was feeling left out, wasn't she?' I say.

'Don't make out like it's my fault. You're the man. It's your job to keep both of us happy,' says Beatrice.

'Look I've only got two hands. I can't be everywhere all at once. Why don't you take care of each other's top bits, while I take care of your downstairs bits?'

The girls look at one another.

'You can't,' says Beatrice.

'Why not?'

'Why do you think?' says Antonia.

'I dunno. You don't go all the way on the first date?'

'We're on the rag,' say Beatrice and Antonia together.

'No!' I say.

'We thought you'd realized,' says Beatrice. 'In the pool when we had to keep our bottoms on.'

'But that's *so* annoying.'

'Sorry,' says Antonia.

'But . . . but . . . how are we supposed to have sex if you're on the rag?'

'Well, we could always – do – you,' suggests Beatrice.

'But that'll be no fun for you.'

'Yes it will,' says Antonia.

'Yes, we don't mind,' says Beatrice.

'Well, I might. If I'm going to get turned on, I'd like you to be turned on too.'

'We will get turned on, a bit,' says Antonia.

'Yeah, but not very much,' I say.

'We may as well try, though. Now we're here,' says Beatrice.

'Oh, all right,' I sigh. 'And I'll take a breast each. How's that?'

'Sounds fair,' says Beatrice.

While I have a breast in each hand – quite interesting, one's broad and squelchy, the other's much smaller and firmer – I feel the girls hands creeping under the bedclothes on either side of my legs, guiding themselves upwards towards my crotch. When the hands meet, they both recoil in shock. The girls start giggling. Their hands meet again, and this time, they start attacking one another, like wrestling tarantulas.

'Do you mind?'

The girls giggle even more.

'Do you think we should bother?' I say. To judge by the state of their nipples, neither girl is even the slightest bit turned on.

'OK, we'll be serious now, won't we, Bea?' says Antonia.

'We will,' says Beatrice.

Their hands work their way up again towards my crotch. This time one of them reaches the end of my penis, and roughly squeezes the foreskin together with a pinch of pubic hair, and begins tugging cackhandedly. The rival hand forages around for something else to hang on to, realizes there's no spare willy left, and so contents itself with clawing at my balls.

'Are we not doing it right?' says Antonia.

'The thing that will turn me on is when you're turned on. Are you sure there's absolutely no way round it?'

'It's no good. We only came on this morning,' says Antonia.

'Can we maybe lift up the sheets, so we can have a better idea what we're doing?' says Beatrice.

'Sure, if you think it will help,' I say, pulling back the sheets.

Both girls crouch intently over my penis.

'Do you want to go first?' says Antonia.

'I don't mind,' says Beatrice.

'Isn't it sweet. Is it a roundhead or a cavalier, I can't tell?'

'Cavalier, I think, look, there's quite a bit of foreskin, have a pull.'

'Mm, it's quite clever that isn't it? Much better with than without. Gives you something to hang on to.'

'Er girls, look, I'm sorry. But this really isn't going to work.'

'Bea was only being complimentary.'

'Yes, I'm sure. But the thing is, I feel like a frog in a biology class.'

'Maybe if we put it in our mouths?' suggests Beatrice.

'Look, I'd love to, but not tonight. Maybe when your periods have finished.'

'But we'll be gone before then.'

'Guess that's the end of our threesome, then.'

'Gosh, that is so unfair. We've never had a threesome before.'

'No. Me neither.'

*

'Er, Marcus,' I say at breakfast. 'You won't mention anything to Molly, will you?'

Mr Migarette stole my soul

It happens in one of those stone-built two-word villages half way between Cheltenham and Oxford but I'm a bit shaky on the exact details for reasons that will become apparent. The bloke who's holding the party is called Saul, has a beard, florid cheeks and is something to do with the scaffolding industry; and the pub opposite may or may not be called the Red Dragon (my guess would be not because it's too big a coincidence).

But there are other bits seared on my brain. Like the grimy yellow of the bouncy castle, where the madness started; the cobwebs and odour of musk in the red phone box; the cheap modern furniture and cheap fitted carpet in the room where we watched *Dougal and the Blue Cat* on an expensive television; and the narrow passage by the back door with the boiler and the coats and wellies and the butler's sink over which I clutched a pint of salty water and tried to make myself puke.

Let's start with the pub. That's where we decide to take our blotters – me, my brother Dick, his girlfriend Saffron, and two or three other heads, let's call them Jenna, Dave and Pete – over a pint of rustic ale. Thus can we attempt to delude ourselves that this is going to be a normal Friday evening out on the piss with our mates. Rather than the night of weirdness, abandon, manic laughter and terror we all know it's going to be probably, depending on our state of mind and how it reacts with the psychedelic chemicals with which we're about to dose ourselves.

Red Dragons, they're called, which is why I have my doubts about the pub's name. Not just ordinary Red Dragons, either, but double-dipped ones – so theoretically they should be twice as strong. We know quite a bit about this sort of thing, by now, or think we do. Batmans (which have a picture of Batman or the Joker on them) are so mild you could drop them at a drinks party with your parents; Purple Oms (which have a purple om symbol on them) represent five hours' guaranteed wipe out; and microdots and Red Dragons are hide-the-knives, lock-all-the-windows and make-no-plans-for-the-weekend, all-out brain-fucks.

So if we're feeling a little queasy as we down our squares of blotting paper with a beery gulp, it's because we all know there's no turning back now. From here on in until the moment the carpets start to swirl and the curtains to breathe, we're stuck in the waiting place. It's like that scene in *Gallipoli* where they're all preparing to go over the top: the officer listening to *Au Fond Du Temple Saint* on the gramophone in his dugout; men grabbing their final fags; scrawling letters home and then sticking them to the trench walls with their bayonets; each man responding in his own way to the awful knowledge that there's precious little time left before the whistle blows and you climb the ladder that leads to certain death. Except our situation isn't quite as poignant or life-threatening, obviously.

"Nother pint?' asks Dick.

'Don't know,' I say. 'What do you reckon?'

'I reckon – why can't you say yes or no like everyone else?' says Dick, glancing for theatrical effect at everyone else.

'Maybe you should run the pros and cons by me,' I say.

'OK, well another beer will relax you more but it might also get you drunk. While not another beer won't do either.'

'Hmm. What do you think I should do?'

'I don't know what's going on in your head.'

'You must have a rough idea, being my brother and all.'

'Oh. God. I knew there was something I had to tell you. Ma rang me the other day and said there'd been a big mix-up at the hospital. It turns out you're the child of a really neurotic professor who has to analyse everything for hours and can never make up his mind and can't just simply enjoy himself without asking all these complicated questions about the nature of enjoyment and stuff.'

'Wow. Suddenly it all makes sense.'

'So you having this beer or not?'

'Dunno!'

The pub regulars are starting to trickle in. As they enter, their eyes sweep the interior, pause on our alcove just long enough to let us know they've seen us, before settling on their fellow regulars at the bar and by the shove ha'penny table. They exchange greetings in thick accents. Sometimes they look with studied leisureliness over their shoulder and mutter something that is invariably followed by a sinister chuckle.

'I've suddenly worked out why I didn't want another pint,' I say.

Dick begins craning his neck round to see what I'm looking at.

'No, don't. They'll know.'

'Not coming on already, are you?'

'I'm quite capable of being paranoid without the aid of drugs.'

'What's this about paranoia?' asks Saffron.

'Josh is coming on,' says Dick.

'I'm not coming on. I'm just worried what will happen when we do start coming on. I mean, a pub's not exactly the best place.'

'You mean like when the horse brasses start climbing off the walls and the pint pulls grow heads and you realize the dart board's this alien vortex?' says Dick.

'Don't give him ideas,' says Saffron. She looks at me, whether sympathetically or disapprovingly it's hard to tell. 'You want to go somewhere else, then?'

'Only if everyone else does.'

'That's so you, that is,' says Dick. 'You make everyone do what you want to do and then pretend you're just going with the flow.'

'No. What I want is for us to be all on the same trip, that's all.'

'Right. So long as it's *your* trip.'

'Forget it. Let's stay here. All I say is, you've all seen the end of *Easy Rider*.'

'Oh God, I love that scene. In the cemetery. Right?' says Pete. 'That just has to be the best acid trip sequence ever.'

'So your trips are all in black and white slo mo? Very interesting,' says Dave, sarcastically.

'I think he meant the very end,' says Dick. 'Where the freaks get wasted by the rednecks.'

As one, everyone looks towards the bar.

As one, the yokels at the bar all look at us.

*

At the house things aren't significantly better. Saul has decided to stage two parties simultaneously: one with kegs of bitter and boxes of wine and Marks & Spencer snackettes for straight people in rugger shirts or frumpy dresses who sound like they might be junior management trainees or high street bank clerks or accountants or valued clients and senior colleagues from the scaffolding industry who have clearly come with the intention of conversing with one another until they are sufficiently plastered to broach the disco room where they will jiggle with decreasing self-consciousness to three-year-old chart hit collections while hoping to pull a member of the opposite sex whom they can then snog or perhaps even shag somewhere in the bushes outside or in one of the bedrooms upstairs should there be any that has not already been commandeered by the stoners; and one for Us.

Since the Them party has already captured the kitchen and the middle room with the hi-fi in it, the Us party has no option but to take the only other ground-floor one, at the far end with the TV in it. It is here, as we slump on cushions while skinning up and watching *Dougal and the Blue Cat* on the video and waiting for something to happen, that the something we have been waiting for starts to happen. So surreptitiously that by the time we've realized it's happening, we're already beyond any objective take on it. We just are.

What I'm being right at this moment is a character in *The Magic Roundabout*. Almost all of them, in fact, at various times, apart from Brian the Snail whom for some reason I really hate. It's funny, I used to think that they were just a bunch of cardboard cut-outs — well, wood, wool, felt and papier mâché cut-outs, if you want to be pedantic — but suddenly I've started to identify with them. I feel their pain.

Dougal, for example. He's really, really stressed. He's

paranoid. He's a control freak. His fur is much mankier than you remember it being when you were a child. Underneath that fur, he's all skin and bones. I think coke is his drug of choice. I'd worry if I were him. Which I am sometimes.

Except when I'm Florence. Florence's big problem is her hair. It's frizzy and unmanageable, with more than a suspicion of ginger. All she can do is tie it back with a ribbon and hope. Dougal fancies her, of course, but I don't think, being a dog, he's really suitable. Florence is a bit prim but I think she'd be up for doing drugs if everyone else was. Later you'd see her crying as it all went horribly wrong and you'd feel bad that you hadn't tried harder to dissuade her.

The Magic Garden's chief pusher is Mr Rusty. You can see it in the wild eyes and top hat, as sported in the high Sixties by foppishly low-life purveyors of rare herbs and proscribed chemicals. His cover is the handcranked musical box on wheels which gives him the perfect excuse to hang around playgrounds and which doubles as his mobile stash container. All the children gather round his box and leave with big smiles on their faces. We like Mr Rusty.

Dylan is a stoner and a waster, but I don't find it as easy to empathize with him as I should. It's a bit anti-social, the way he just sits under that tree, off his face. I've met his sort before. He's like those multiple pill-boshers who keep taking more and heading off on their own to the dance floor, while everyone else has got to the stage where you want to bond and mellow out.

Zebedee. I would never dare be Zebedee. He is far too all-mighty and powerful. He is the *deus ex machina* who controls your trip. 'Time for bed,' he says. And off you go. Just as well he is benign.

Brian. What is it about Brian that I hate so much? His

snailiness? His rosy cheeks and pointy nose? His hat? His suburban, Home Counties busybody voice? His—

'Hey. Tricia. Come and see what's on TV.'

Even before I hear his voice I sense his presence, the way the room's energy, its balance has suddenly shifted. Before, everything was enclosed, hermetic, secure, like a big comfortable box. Now that reassuring solidity has been ruptured. There's a hole in one of its sides. Someone has walked in. Someone who isn't meant to be here.

I try not to look. Immersed in the world of *The Magic Roundabout*, where the colours are so much more vivid, the narrative more involving, the people more real, I don't want to go back to that other world where everything's beige and grey and uncertain.

'Wow! *The Magic Roundabout*. Haven't seen this since I was a kid,' says a female voice.

'Boing! Time for bed. Boing. Time for bed.'

'Shhh. They're trying to watch.'

This conversation, this annoying conversation, all seems to be taking place at one remove, like one of those nagging exterior noises that insinuates itself into your dream and becomes an unbidden part of the plot.

'Do you think they're on drugs?'

'Jason!'

'Some people here are, apparently. LSD. They probably don't even know we're here. They probably think I'm a giant spider or something.'

'Jason, you're pissed.'

'Come on. Let's leave the weirdies to their children's TV.'

'Sorr-ee', says the girl to the room with a cartoon smile and a cheery wave.

During the brief moment of lucidity in which I realize I

am not a character in *The Magic Roundabout* but that I am sitting in a room watching it, I notice that there are several other people in a similar predicament. One of them is my brother. Though I had completely forgotten, he is sitting right next to me.

I open my mouth to speak.

Then close it. Dick's skin is orangey green. His pupils are black saucers.

'Yeah,' he says.

'Did I say it?'

'What?'

'The thing I was going to say.'

'What were you going to say?'

'Um—'

My eye has been caught by the blue bright pulsing radiance of the television screen and as I look I feel myself being sucked back into Dougal world—

'Hang on', I would say to Dick, but the tiny part of my brain that is still with him, waiting to finish that sentence just isn't powerful enough.

—where everything makes so much more sense, the issues are clearer cut and the colours – rich blues and yellows and reds and greens and pinks, at least until that bloody cat comes along, ah the cat, the blue cat, I've seen this before, it gets quite scary soon – are so much more intense that I can't think for a moment why I left this world that time a while ago whenever it was, or perhaps that was my imagination, no I don't think it was because I do remember something annoying, something very annoying, something never mind but I do mind well try not to mind OK I'll try I'll concentrate on what's happening what's happening? Dougal's trying to tell Brian something and Brian of course being the fucking annoying red-cheeked stupid-hatted pointy-nosed snail he is, Brian that's it. Brian is like the people who came into the room who were really annoying, the straight people. Them.

With some effort I heave my self from Dougalworld and twist to face my brother.

He looks at me. His face is still greeny orange, his pupils are blacker yet.

'Them,' I say.

'Yeah,' he goes.

'Those people.'

'Yeah.'

'Was it my imagination or were they really horrible?'

'Really horrible.'

'Do you think we should escape?'

'I think we're safe here.'

'But what if they come back?'

Dick turns to Saffron.

'What if they come back?'

'We'll be OK,' she says.

'But it gets quite scary soon,' I say.

'It gets quite scary soon,' Dick tells Saffron.

'What does?' she asks.

'What?' Dick asks me.

'This. *Dougal and the Blue Cat.* The bit with the heads, remember?'

'The bit with the heads,' says Dick.

'Right,' says Saffron.

'Stay here if you want but I think we should go and check,' I say.

'I think we should,' agrees Dick.

'Check what?' says Saffron.

'Just check, you know,' I say. 'Just in case.'

'We'll be back,' Dick tells her.
'We will,' I say.

*

Outside, the ground is crisp with snow which you can't see, obviously, it being a mild late spring. You can just sense it, like you can sense the view that isn't there of the white fields and hedgerows which lead to the church while the robin perches on the gatepost reminding you of the perfect Christmas you remember dimly from childhood which never actually happened you just got it from a card.

There's a laurel hedge and beyond it an animal flitting. You hear a rustle, a sussuration, which may be a couple snogging, may be people like you just walking, you don't want to find out, you don't. Or maybe you do.

What's Dick doing? Dick's walking with his thoughts.

Now there's gravel underfoot, bad gravel, worn gravel crushed into dry mud and a car nearby, a car parked with the engine still warm and the smell of car engine still there, just faintly but enough to make you think of travel, logistics, mechanics, getting home, we have to drive home when this is all over, we'll never drive home, never, not in this state, when will this state end, not yet not for a very long time yet.

Retreat from the gravel and the car, we don't like the gravel and the car, we want roses, herbiage, lush, sparking memories of summer, Burnt Norton, unheard music, that's better. Much better.

A scream.

Woahh. We don't like that.

Another scream.

Maybe it's OK, it's a happy scream.

Now we can see its source. A bouncy castle. Wow. They've

got a bouncy castle. How cool is that? Got to have a go on the bouncy castle.

The couple on the bouncy castle look at us, they're about to say something, when they look back at one another and smiling awkardly, not looking at us, they slip off and put their shoes back on.

'What did we do?' I ask.

'Don't know,' says Dick.

Telepathically.

The bouncy castle is much more difficult than I remember bouncy castles being. So, for that matter, is taking off shoes. It's not like you're doing it yourself, it's like some total incompetent has taken over your body and is doing it for you, while your brain sits on top just observing. Maybe there's not enough air in it, maybe we're too big, but when you try standing up, your foot gets sucked in too deep and you collapse almost instantly. But you have to keep trying to stand up because then you get to fall down, which is the fun part – that cushioning whumph as you hit the rubbery floor and the pleasantly unpleasant rush of stale, rubbery air forced from the vent holes by the impact. When we can take it no more we look up at the stars. It's a clear night, a clear beautiful night with thousands of stars, almost too many to be able to deal with in a state like this. So many, in fact, it's funny, you've got to laugh. Look at them all. This is just absurd. Look at them all, it's a joke, it's a cliché, you're tripping your face off and there are so many stars it's . . .

Hahahahahahahahahahahahahahahahahahahahaha

Dick's laughing too.

Hahahahahahahahahahahahahahah

'Tell Saffron,' he heaves. 'Got to tell Saffron.'

'Yeah, Safhahahahahahahahahahah.'
'Come on. Let's tell her.'

*

Saffron isn't in the TV room. No one is. It has been taken over by Them. But at least it's safe now in the music room – no more chart hits but proper dance music being spun on decks by a proper DJ I think but I'm not sure, it could just be what I want to think, I saw someone out of the corner of my eye bending meaningfully over a record player and just assumed he was a DJ but he might just have been someone putting on a record and I don't want to check because I'd rather not know, but anyway

There's Saffron.

She smiles and beckons us towards her, she has got something to show us. There's this man. He's got a beard and straggly hair, he's standing in front of her, showing her something. He's a wizard, I think. Definitely some sort of wizard. You can tell from the aura he's emanating. And the beard.

'Are you a wizard?' I ask.

He bares his teeth, flashes his wild eyes at me and laughs.

'Yeah, that's me. I'm a wizard.'

'Yeah, you can tell,' I say.

'Look what he's got,' says Saffron.

The wizard closes his hand around whatever he was showing her.

'Ah but would they appreciate it?' says the wizard, appraising me and Dick with eyes so shrewd and shiny set into a face so etched with bony fairy tale character, so grotesque – just watch his chin lengthen, his nose sharpen and wartify, his stubble ooze as we watch – that you know he's not really real, he has crept straight out of some Brothers Grimm story, maybe to test us, like some sort of trip test, like we're on a grail quest and he's a wodwo* like in *Gawain*, a wild man of the woods.

'Oh, I think so,' says Saffron. 'It's the sort of thing they would appreciate.'

'Oh, we would,' I say. 'We definitely would, wodwo.'

The wizard/wodwo unclasps his fingers, slowly, like he's trying to let out a spider which is what I think it is at first, but when his hands are opened I see it's a—

Well I'm not sure what it is other than that it is quite definitely one of the most incredible things I have seen. It glows and shimmers and sparkles with kaleidoscopic colours that burst outward, like shooting stars. And the more you look at it the more you want to look, it sucks you in, almost like your mind is trapped inside this beautiful, glowing thing, whatever it is, crystal maybe or some sort of mystic amulet, or computer-generated, 3-D graphic, techno something. Oh what do I care it's just . . .

'Wow!'

'Wow!' says Dick.

We stare. For what may well be a very long time.

'What does it mean?'

'Mean?' says the wizard.

'He's my brother,' says Dick. 'He has to know these things.'

'Ah. Like that is, he?' says the wizard, craftily, like some pointy, subterranean, treasure-guarding hobgoblin thing, touching the side of his warty nose. His accent has gone all

---

* Middle English scholars please note: I am aware that the correct singular is wodwos not wodwo, which was based on a mistranscription in the original MS, later corrected by Tolkien. But I only discovered this in 2002, while reading one of the many articles about the film version of *Lord of the Rings*, a good decade after this acid trip sequence.

cockney. He seems to know much more about this whole scenario than we do. I'm not sure I trust him. I never did.

'Are you tripping too?'

'He asks a lot of questions, your brother,' says the wizard.

'That's what he's like,' says Dick.

'Are you?' I ask him.

'Too many,' adds the wizard and I'm getting uncomfortable now, I sense I'm being criticized, got at, just for being me.

'He is, look at his eyes,' says Saffron.

'Do you think that's wise?' I say.

'He's the Lord of the Flies,' says Dick, on the exact moment that my pupils meet the wizard's and I see—

Eyes, marbled yellow like a goat's with that sinister black line drawing me into an endless vortex of pure evil. I see misery, despair. I see death. I see fear. I see madness.

'That'll learn you,' cackles the wizard.

'Can we see your Thing again?' asks Dick.

'We've got to go,' I say.

'Can't we just see his Thing again?' asks Dick.

'We've got to go.'

'Let him go,' says the wizard.

'He's with us,' says Dick.

'Not for long,' says the wizard's voice, pursuing me through the door and into the garden.

*

'Feeling better?' asks Saffron, as the hot sweat on my back turns to ice and the leaves high up crackle like crisp packets.

'Fuck!'

'You look terrible,' she says. 'What happened?'

'Didn't you see? He was the devil.'

'I thought he was a wizard,' says Dick

'He was. But then he changed. He was evil!'

'I think he was a bit gone, that's all,' says Saffron.

'I liked his Thing,' says Dick.

'It was a lure. To lure us in. And trap us.'

'God, do you reckon?' says Dick.

'He's just a friend of Saul's. A bit weird. He didn't mean us any harm,' says Saffron.

'You wouldn't say that if you'd seen what I saw.'

'Well, it's all OK now,' she says.

'Is it?' I ask. 'I'm not sure I can cope with much more of this. How long do you think it will be before it's over?'

'A while yet,' says Saffron.

'You sound pretty straight.'

She makes an iffy motion with her palm. 'Comes in waves.'

'Yeah,' I say. 'Except the peaks seem to be getting higher and higher. And if it gets any more intense, I don't think—'

'Bouncy castle,' says Dick.

*

On the bouncy castle it all gets better again. Lying on my back enveloped by stars it's as if the goat-eyed devil-wizard never happened, it's like last time I was here and I couldn't be happier if I tried. I mean trips, what is it they say about trips? You connect with the universe, don't you? You see God and this is what I'm doing, sort of. Except if I tell myself I'm doing it I won't be doing it because what you have to do with acid is let the mind go, let it go, soaring up to the stars above you, that velvety twinkling canopy, you can see them, see them all, so many stars, big, bright ones that twinkle, that could be planets, little shy ones that recede as you try to focus on them, drawing you back and back into an endless perspective of tinier and tinier stars so small but so numerous they merge together in a pool of milky light, yes, like milk, like the Milky Way, that's why it's called the Milky Way and you never realized that before it's just one of those phrases you took for granted, but now you understand, now you understand Everything. And there are so many stars – yes, you've been here before you have, you have – so many stars that you've really got to laugh because it's such a cliché, this seeing stars on acid thing, it's like a joke, the best joke anyone ever told you, no, funnier . . .

You're laughing, really laughing now, you can tell by the silent heaving of your body and the vibration in your throat, it's pouring out of you, like a burst water main. But you can't hear yourself, inside your body, it's as quiet as the padded interior of a coffin, all plush white silk with those indentations like spiders' traps. Only outside is the noise. Outside, the noise is awful. Deranged. Abandoned. Almost inhuman. God you wish they'd stop, it's worse than the howling of dogs, the screaming of cats, it's like someone possessed by demons, someone tell them to stop.

'Stop it,' says Dick.

I'd tell them myself but my mouth's stuck open and all this stuff is spurting up, right up towards the vastness of space where my head is, where my brain has just fused with the universe.

'Shut up, Josh.'

It's not me, you fool, I'm a constellation. It's him. I've seen him, he's wearing a tall black hat.

'You're ruining it for everyone. If you don't stop, we're going.'

'Josh, can you hear us?'

A million miles away there's a squeeze on the arm of the body that used to belong to me.

'Let's leave him, he's freaking me.'

'Don't leave. Please don't leave. I want you here with me, sharing this moment, sharing my happiness. If you go you won't be on the same trip, you'll have different adventures and I want us all to have the same adventures,' I would say if I had any control of my former body which I don't, not remotely. And it's a shame, because where I am now is a good place, well at least an interesting place, I'm picnicking beneath the stars on this gingham table cloth with the man in the hat who reminds me of something—

'Is he going to be all right?'

'Course he is, but not before he's spoiled it for everyone else. He's so selfish.'

'Josh, we're going. Do you understand? We're going. See you later.'

When the laughter stops they're gone. I'm alone and I'm scared but when I try moving, my body won't respond. I'm stuck in the same position, looking at the stars but they're no longer funny and I'm no longer part of them, they're glowering at me, ridiculing me for having ever considered them a form of solace, they look down on me, cold, merciless and uncaring. I'm just a meaningless speck, I'm nothing. A small voice is telling me not to go down this road, it's just paranoia, it's not real, you can fight it if you want. But I don't feel big enough to fight it. I feel hopeless. Overwhelmed. And though the feeling has started to come back to my lifeless body – I can lift a leaden foot, wiggle my fingers, turn my head so as to see how I might get off this thing I'm lying on – it doesn't feel like my body, it's just a husk.

What really scares me, though, is this: there's a tiny part

of my brain, a very, very tiny part which knows how things ought to be and that how things currently are is very, very wrong. But it's helpless. The bulk of my brain has been taken over by this madman. He doesn't care about the rules. He doesn't care about anything. He's like a monkey let loose in a car, twisting the steering wheel this way and that, pulling gears, accelerating, decelerating, according to his whim. I'd jam on the brakes but someone has cut the cable.

Need a cigarette. In fact I don't need a cigarette but that is why I must have one. Because that's what I would have done before this happened. If I can try to do the things I would have done before this happened, maybe I'll become the person I was again.

But oh God, it's hard, it's so hard. How to function when the synapses are going off like flashbulbs blam! BLAM! BLAM! blam! BLAM! How can you think, how can you hear, how can you see when you're blinded and deafened by these cameras, where do you begin?

Pocket. In the pockets of your jeans, but they're so tight, you can barely squeeze a single finger in. And they're bulging with so much – *stuff*. Smooth stuff, rough stuff, papery stuff, hard stuff that chinks together and cuts into your skin, and it's all slipping out now, half slipping out, half stuck to the strandy tendrils that extend from the inside of that tight, awful crevice, so that you have to stuff it back in, in case it's important stuff, some of it is, that stuff you keep in your pockets.

Pause to recover. Remember your mission. You need to smoke a fag, you don't want to smoke a fag, but you must because then you have a purpose. Otherwise, you know where you'll end up, don't you?

DON'T YOU?

You're close to it now. Just peer over. Deep, isn't it? Compared to the vastness of the cliffs which plummet below you, you're the tiniest speck, a flea on an elephant. From here to there is but the smallest step towards, well you know what lies below, you can already see it, the men in the ambulance taking you away, you strapped beneath a blanket, are they wearing white, of course they're wearing white, because that's it, you're gone mate, you're going to stay like this for ever.

For ever.

It's so unfair you want to cry, how can things like this happen, how can things turn from good to bad so quickly? I was such a nice boy I was doing so well I know I never admitted it to myself but I was I had a good salary a great salary for someone not even twenty-seven and a job what a brilliant fucking job I had a job where you get paid to drink champagne with starlets and pose at first nights in the very best seats and hang backstage at gigs and interview your idols and entertain imaginary contacts on lavish expenses at unaffordable restaurants and turn up to work no earlier than half ten and write whatever drivel takes your fancy and get it printed in a national newspaper with your name in big letters and sometimes your picture too, and for all this I was never grateful, not for my career, not for the family whose love and support made it possible, not for the friends all those wonderful friends who have chosen to like me for who I am or rather who I was for I'm not that person any more and never will be again that's what so sad you only appreciate what you had when you've lost it all those things I might have done but will no longer be able to do the book I'll never write the girl I'll never marry because no one wants to marry a madman do they look at poor Syd in his Cambridge garret he had it and he blew it and I have too and it's so unfair I don't deserve this, I want to cry and I would cry too if I had control of my body if it weren't in the charge of this this fiend—

'That'll learn you.'

—who's talking to me, God I hate him, I hate him, I must have a cigarette, if only I can smoke this cigarette.

Try again. Second pocket. If this one doesn't work, I'm not sure I can cope with any more. Squeeze, squeeze, cottony material no good, hah!, something squishy, half metal half paper, that's it, out and – yes! Tobacco in hand, in left hand, now find paper. Down again, down, so deep, like the abyss I stared into, God not the abyss, don't think of the abyss, down, crumbs under nails, tightness against fingers, strip, strip of shiny cardboard. Papers.

Swollen, frostbitten fingers clumsily pinch and fail, pinch and fail, till at last a paper is free. Then gone. Stolen by a cruel gust.

Once more. Concentrate this time. Take paper and squeeze, squeeze, so hard it hurts, so it can never be stolen.

Now tobacco, the awkward folds of metallic paper, so hard to pick and prise with puffy forefinger. And the springy, brown strands, too moist, all uneven as you lay a pinch on the creased, scruffy skin now cupped in your dead left hand. You try rolling it into shape but your fingertips won't obey so you bring it towards your dry mouth regardless, only to find as you run your sore, bumpy tongue the length of the paper that there's no moisture there, at least not on your tongue now dotted with vile flecks of bitter brown, just enough on from the new baccy or the clamminess of your hands to make the adhesive strip stick to your fingers and this will never work anyway, you've got the paper upside down.

But it *has* to work.

Frenzied, desperate now, you push and squash and fold

the bristling, bulging paper envelope, now one end, now the other, as more and more tobacco tumbles out, you could scream, now, you could weep, why won't the tears come, when will you be released from this hell?

'You OK there?'

'Uh?'

'Would you like a real cigarette?'

In my hand, a perfect tube. How?

'Better do it for him. He's fucked.'

'Here.'

My hand is empty again. I feel the cylinder between my lips.

A sulphurous flash; a burning roar; an acrid chemical stench that claws the back of my throat.

'Take care, mate.'

Dancing spots, burned on the retina. A glow beneath my nose, now close, now receding, now close, now receding. It's my hand, automatically drawing a cigarette to and from my lips. I'm smoking. I'm not quite sure how I got to this state but I am and even if it doesn't feel good it feels right.

That glow! The grey so ashen and crumbly, the orange so molten and hot, like a volcano. Except you can see that it's an extension of the tube, that this glowing tip is perfectly cylindrical. Except for the man at the end. You can't see all of him – just his head, his tall hat and the pipe he is smoking. I know at once with absolute certainty who this man is and what he has done. Mr Migarette has stolen my soul.

I flick off the tip, but Mr Migarette remains. Tall hat. Pipe. Just the same as before, only taunting now, smiling at my predicament.

I grope forward through the murk. My eyesight has all but gone. There was a stream not far from here, maybe I should be there. I could plunge my head under and see if that worked. Drown myself like Ophelia. Anything to make it stop.

Garden. Remember this bit. T. S. Eliot. Hidden laughter. Came here when I was normal, well, not normal but not like this. Gravel underfoot. Bad gravel, squashed into dry mud. And the car. Warm engine now cold, if the engine were warm it would be better because then it would mean I was closer to the time when things were happier. Got to get my life back. Got to get my old life back. Talk to someone who understands . . .

*

Red phone boxes have heavy doors which are hard to open and then, when you close them, they stink, stink of all the thousands, hundreds of thousands of people who have been here before you, breathing into the mouthpiece. Do they disinfect these things. Ever? No never, you see the yellow crust of their solidified breath gumming the little holes, don't look, just make the call. Shaky finger aims for wobbly metal numbers, this can't work, this will never work, I'm too fucked to make phone calls surely?

'Hello?' says an irritable voice. Posh, male. I hate him instantly.

'Who's that?' I say.

'Who's that?' says the voice.

'I asked first.'

'Jake,' says the voice.

'Is Molly there?'

'Who shall I say is calling?'

'It's important.'

I wait. Muted conversation in the background.

'Hello?'

'Molly. 'Sme.'

'Josh. Are you all right?'

'Molly, it's horrible. There's this bastard at the end of my cigarette called Mr Migarette and he's stolen my soul.'

Pause.

'Darling, it's very late.'

'But can't you do something?'

'There's a man on the end of your cigarette?'

'Yeah. He just sits there smoking his pipe, chuckling about it. And you can't flick him off, he just stays there. With his hat.'

'Sweetheart—'

'He's like, you know, that Van Eyck picture of the couple with the round mirror in the back and you know the tall hat the man's wearing?'

'Yes.'

'Well, he's wearing a hat like that. Or maybe one of those Welsh eisteddfod hats. Whatever, it's tall and black and it has something to do with picnics. I keep seeing these gingham table cloths, only not seeing them, you know what it's like on acid, well you don't, but they're just this image in my mind more real than the things you do see.'

'Darling, if you've been taking acid there's really not much—'

'Molly, I don't think I've ever been so scared in my life, I think I'm going mad.'

'You're not, of course you're not.'

'You don't know what it's like in my head.'

'You don't sound that mad.'

'That is the whole problem. There's part of me that's all cold and rational, but it's not the one that's in charge, it's this fucking lunatic.'

'Mr Migarette?'

'I think he just stole my soul. I think it's someone else that's in charge, maybe more than one. Like those compartments inside your head in that comic. Like the Numskulls.'

'Is there no one else with you?'

'They abandoned me. Just because I was laughing too much in the bouncy castle.'

'Then you must go and find them and tell them to look after you.'

'But they won't. They're evil.'

At the other end of the line, here is more background male chuntering. 'Yes, yes. I know,' I hear Molly say.

'Darling, you've got to understand,' she says to me. 'I'm in London, you're wherever you are it's terribly late and—'

'You wouldn't say that if he wasn't with you.'

'Josh, I'm really going to have to go now.'

'He's a bastard, Molly. He's evil. You should find someone better, he—'

Beeeeeeeeeeeeeeeeeeeeeeeeeeeeep.

*

How long is it before I find my brother? An hour? Three hours? Time seems simultaneously to have stretched and contracted and I don't go looking for him, I don't want anyone's pity, I'm way beyond help. Sometimes I'm outside in the dark. Sometimes I'm inside, passing people doing stuff, not wishing to find out what, not meeting their eyes, just skulking past, head down, like I'm invisible. Then I'm upstairs in a room with no ceiling, just the eaves of a roof and a mattress on the floor, with people sprawled, sitting, smoking, telling stories. I listen to the stories, uncomprehendingly, for by the time we're in the middle I've forgotten what the beginning was and by the time we've reached the end I've forgotten both. Sometimes, people hand me a spliff or don't hand me a spliff, I don't care either way it's not me this is happening to it's someone else. Sometimes people look at me nervously; it's the deadness they fear, I think, the emptiness behind the eyes like that shell-shocked GI in the Vietnam photograph.

Then, for no particular reason, I find myself going down-stairs. I want to feel something, anything, even if it's bad. I want to feel some connection between my brain and my body. In a cupboard I find a packet of salt. I pour half of it into a pint glass and fill it with lukewarm water from a butler's sink in the corridor, outside the kitchen, where the coats are and the boiler is, where straight people in rugger shirts are talking, half watching me curiously, but I don't care. I stir the salt round with my finger. Then I drink a third of the glass in one go – it would be more, but I'm retching now, gagging over the sink. Hardly anything comes out.

I take a match from a box someone has left on a side-board. I strike it and mercilessly bring the flaming head to the palm of my hand, where I hold it, until I feel a distant hot pain and smell a faint smell, and someone says: 'You can't do that!'

And I stop.

'You'll regret that in the morning,' chides a girl.

I look at her and I see her recoil at the blankness. But she collects herself and steers my hand under the tap, immersing it in cold water.

'Does anyone know him?' she asks.

'I think he's one of the acid lot,' says a rugger shirt.

'I think I'd guessed that,' says the girl.

'Here's Saul, I'll ask Saul. Saul! Can you come here a minute. Guy here, needs your help.'

Saul's red cheeks. Saul's beard. Saul's curiously full lips. Saul's eyes looking at me.

'You look fucked, mate.'

I nod.

And I'm Derek Elms

There are, what? – no, I'm not going to count – let's say, twenty people round this table in a private dining room at the Groucho Club and at least one of them, me, is having quite the most tedious evening of his life.

Which is annoying because it was meant to be a fun evening, to celebrate one of my best friends' twenty-fifth birthday. And it's not like the grand cru booze isn't flowing or the food isn't super-edible because the whole thing is being financed by this best friend's big brother, who happens to be the most discerning foodie and oenophile.

So at least this wine won't give me quite such a bad hangover. And at least if I do have to do a tactical chuck, well the fine cuisine that re-emerges will surely leave a marginally less disgusting taste in my throat than, say, an Oxford-style kebab with chilli dressing. And at least – no, that's the end of the at leasts. There are no further saving graces.

Kate. It's probably just wishful thinking but I thought for a moment there when our eyes met, I thought maybe I detected just a glimmer of sympathy. Empathy. Martyrly one-upmanship, even. Like: 'You think you're having a bad time? Try being me, try being birthday girl.'

I'm reaching towards the white – Chassagne-Montrachet: stick to that and I should be safe – when the male member of the couple to my left that I've been trying to ignore ever since they were offended by my remarks about Northampton- shire, like it's hardly my fault if they live in the middle of nowhere, is it? – says something.

'Oops, sorry, after you,' I say and recharge his glass, or try to before he puts his hand in the way – rather pointedly, I think.

'I was asking how you knew Kate,' he says. How did a nice girl like Kate get chummy with a scumball like you, is what he means.

'Oh, you know,' I say.

The man's girlfriend, in this taffeta evening dress designed for women twice her age, leans forward. 'Did you meet her here? In London?' The way she says London makes it sound as exotic and licentious as Babylon.

'Oh, London, yes. Do I look like one of her Daventry friends?'

Which is meant to be a sort of joke at my expense, like: 'Goodness they'd never tolerate my sort there,' but it doesn't come out quite as I intend, it sounds more like: 'Christ, I hope you're not suggesting I'm a bloodless provincial like you.' There's an uneasy silence so I have to add: 'Yes. On the party circuit. Through Julian. I was covering the first-night party of a play he was in and we got chatting. Kate was with him and, well, we just bonded really. How about you?'

'We met her through Orlando,' says the girl. Orlando – yes, this is a Significant Point – is Kate's husband, a scientist and government adviser who seems to spend most of his time on business abroad.

'Ah, Orlando,' I say.

'You know him?' says the man.

'Not really. Only met him once. But I'm sure he must be a nice chap. Or Kate wouldn't have married him.'

The girl and boyfriend exchange a meaningful look.

'He's a very nice chap. You'd like him,' says the girl.

'I'm sure. Only he doesn't come up to London all that often, does he?'

There's another exchange of glances.

'We rather feel the same about Kate in Northamptonshire,' says the girl.

'Oh dear, is it a problem?' I say.

'Not a problem, no,' says the girl hastily. And her boyfriend's expression suggests she has already been far too indiscreet. 'It's just—'

But now Kate's brother is rising to make a speech.

With perfect comic timing Julian chinks his glass to get everyone's attention and allows it to ring in the most elegant yet funny way any wine glass has ever rung, before arresting it with all the panache of an unexpected and brilliantly delivered punchline. Julian has done this before.

'Ladies and gentlemen,' begins Julian in that arch, plummy voice which can make even words like 'Ladies' and 'Gentlemen' sound like 'merkin' and 'dildo'. There is much laughter. Even more when he continues, with a look towards the male in the room with girlishly long hair – me – 'And those as yet unsure . . .'

I laugh too. Obviously, I'm slightly more blasé than most about hearing the wit and wisdom of TVs Julian Trent for real, in person, privately and just a few feet away from me, because I've done it quite a bit already. But that doesn't mean I'm not still amused, impressed and pathetically grateful that I actually know this guy.

On his speech goes. Far cleverer than I could write. Or

indeed remember. Jokes are made. Warm but not mawkish tribute is paid to his dear little sister Kate. At the end, Julian reads a telegram from Kate's husband saying how terribly he regrets having to be advising the minister at this international summit when he'd so much rather be with his darling Kate whom he loves for ever etc. Then he wonders whether any of his fellow celebrants would care to chip in with mini-testimonies of their own.

After ten minutes of halting, inarticulate rambling, Julian has no doubt begun to regret his suggestion. We all have. None of us is listening to a word of anyone else's tedious anecdotes. We're far too busy working out what to say when our turn comes.

No doubt the mature and dignified response to this 'Who can be the most boring?' competition would be not to participate. But I'm drunk and when you're drunk, you're not going to take the subtle option. You're going to stand up, as I do, and say in a very loud voice:

'And the thing I like about Kate—'

Pause while you try to remember what it is that you like about Kate.

'—Is her fidelity and chastity—'

And if no one was listening to anybody else's speech, they certainly are to mine. I can see them all, looking at me, every one of them apart from Kate and Julian a total stranger. 'Who is this chap?' they're thinking. 'What right has this interloper to talk about our friend? And what's his game here? What exactly is he implying about our best friend's wife's sexual mores?'

At this stage, unfortunately, it's too late to stop. I go on:

'Because when Kate and Julian and I were up at the Edinburgh Festival last month, there weren't enough beds. So Kate and I had to share one—'

The room grows more silent still, if that's possible.

'—And do you know what? She didn't even try to have sex with me.'

In the appalled silence that follows, it occurs to me that even if I'd delivered it well, which I didn't, it would still have been a piss-poor anecdote. That far from having reassured these people of Kate's fidelity to her husband, I have unwittingly indicated quite the opposite. That she is, in fact, the most outrageous slapper who leaps at the drop of a hat into the bed of louche, long-haired Londoners that she's met at parties through her pimping gay brother.

I look for reassurance at Kate, who smiles back. Very weakly. Then at Julian, who announces in a voice which manages to combine the sonorousness of a stern headmaster, with a satirist's cruel sarcasm and queen's cattiest bitchery: 'Why thank you, Josh, I'm sure we're not only grateful for that aperçu but quite astonished to learn that any woman anywhere could ever resist sexual congress with a man as attractive as you.'

Outside I'm ashen and still. Inside, my guts are squirming like a lemon-juiced oyster.

The moral, perhaps is: don't ever ever ever ever *ever* try to make friends with celebrities.

*

But at twenty-four, which is roughly how old I am when I first meet Julian Trent, I am unaware of this adamantine rule. Rather, I think that few things could be nicer than being on first-name terms with your heroes. After all, when you worship and adore someone, it's only natural to hope that in some tiny way those feelings might be reciprocated; that your idol will look beyond the annoying, unworthy, twittering fan and see the warm, witty, likeable kindred spirit within.

Which is very much how I feel about Julian Trent. By now I'm quite used to meeting famous people: Sting, Arthur Miller, Stephen Spender, Peggy Ashcroft, Angela Carter, Iris Murdoch, Tim Roth . . . But I've never felt so strongly that I wanted them to be my friend. Trent is different. It's not just that he's funny, talented, clever, witty, famous and on TV all the time. It's that he gives the impression of being so incredibly simpatico, that you can't help wanting to know him better. You don't just think of how impressed people will be when you're seen with him or you casually let slip that yeah, you don't like to talk about it but actually Julian is a pretty close friend. You think about all the great chats you'd have with him, all the wisdom he could dispense. He's going to be like Dr Johnson to your Boswell. Yes that's it. Like Johnson and Boswell.

So we meet at the first-night party of this new West End play he's starring in, something by Michael Frayn, perhaps. Because Julian's in it, pretty much le tout luvviedom has turned up. From the alternative comedy side of his career, people like Stephen Fry, Ben Elton, Rik Mayall, John Sessions. From the ac-torly side, Ian McKellen, Simon Callow and Peter Ustinov. From literature, Julian Barnes and Martin Amis. Martin Amis! Truly, a 'galaxy of stars' as my editor on the Peterborough diary will mockingly put it the next day before asking me in that case, why the hell haven't I come up with a decent story. And clearly, with all these people queueing up to congratulate Julian on the gorgeousness of his perf, not to mention all the non-famous hangers-on and diarists itching to do likewise, I don't expect I'm going to be able to get a word in edgeways.

Just in case, though, I position myself strategically against a pillar close to where Julian is standing and wait for the throng of well-wishers to thin. Once, I think he catches my eye and gives me a sympathetic smile, but half way through responding, the smile on my own face freezes and fades as it occurs that of course he's not smiling at me, why should he, it's aimed over my shoulder at some thezbian chum. What's worrying me more, though, is that I keep having to pounce on passing celebrities so as to grab a few quotes. And every time I do, I temporarily lose sight of Julian.

But he is in no hurry to move. Every time I look across he and his floppy fringe are still there, still being mobbed, still being smily and gracious. I'm thinking, maybe it's time to change tactics. Maybe if I were to get him a drink from the free bar, I could barge in and introduce myself.

When I return, flustered with the effort of having queued for hours and then negotiated the crush with two spilling glasses of champagne, I see that Julian is about to leave.

'No!' I say disbelievingly.

But he really is going. Being dragged off by this pretty dark-haired girl.

'Bugger,' I say hurrying towards him. 'Bugger bugger bugger bugger bugger.'

'Yes,' he says kindly. 'But I've always preferred Julian. Were you bringing those for me? How nice!'

'Yes, and I don't even know you,' I say, in the dry, knowing way I tend to adopt with comics. I think the intended message is: yeah, I can do funny too.

'Ah, but I know you,' says Julian.

'Really?'

'I saw you – we both did, didn't we, Kate? – leaning against the pillar. Kate thought you were a diarist, which

I thought highly implausible, given your evident coyness. I thought it was far more likely that you were a Veronica Lake impersonator.'

'Who's Veronica Lake?'

'She wore a bob, rather like yours. Only of course, she was far more butch.'

'Kate was right,' I say, reddening, wondering how best I can indicate that I am in fact heterosexual.

'Don't mind Julian, he only teases people he likes. I'm Kate by the way.'

'Josh.'

She puts out her hand, but I'm already giving her the London, double-cheek social kiss. Even as I'm doing it this strikes me as a bit forward, but there's something in the warmth of her manner, or maybe it's just an instant shared-class-recognition thing, that tells me it's all right. She reminds me a bit of Molly, only without the side, bristliness, insecurity and slavering ambition.

'Right, well, while you two eat each other, I'm off to get some dinner,' says Julian.

'I think since you've been so horrid to Josh, you ought to bring him with us,' says Kate.

'I'm sure he's had worse. Terribly thick-skinned, these diarists. They have to be,' says Julian.

'I'm not.'

'You'll be telling me next you don't print stories that people tell you in confidence.'

'I don't.'

'Have you ever asked yourself whether you're in the right profession?'

'Frequently.'

'Then I might just to be able to help. I believe that one

of the people in our party tonight works for a talent agency called Silver Screen Goddess Impersonators. Now it might just be—'

'*Julian*,' chides Kate.

'Josh. My sister and I would be more than charmed if you could join us for dinner.'

'Oh.'

'You sound disappointed. Was there an important episode of *Coronation Street* you had to catch?'

'Oh no. I meant "Oh" as in, so Kate's your sister.'

'Josh, since we're clearly going to be such excellent friends, I think it's only fair that I let you in to a very closely guarded secret.' His voice drops to a whisper. 'The females you see in my company are unlikely to be my paramours. For I am not as other men.'

'I'm glad you told me.'

'And I'm glad that you are glad. But don't, whatever you do, let this story get out. My reputation would never survive it.'

*

I expect you'll want to hear about dinner but there's really not that much to say. The thing about celebrities en masse – and apart from Kate and the odd wife or girlfriend, I'm the only non-famous person there – is they're far more interesting in the imagination than in the flesh. Down my end of the table, I've got a film director, two alternative comics, a producer and a screenwriter who isn't yet a household name but will be by the time *Four Weddings and a Funeral* comes out. But for all the difference it makes to their amusement value or comprehensibility, they might as well be civil engineers, or social workers or Sanksrit scholars.

One of them will say: 'I see Johnny's had the go-ahead for Rowan's cheese thrift.'

And I'll be sitting there – idiot grin on my face, trying to make myself pleasant yet unobtrusive, ready for anyone to make conversation with should they so wish but certainly not daring to try starting one myself in such august company – trying to decipher all this. Johnny Gielgud maybe? Rowan Atkinson? Some sort of comedy project about cheese? Something that sounds like cheese thrift but isn't, I've just misheard.

Then someone else will chip in with 'Wasn't that eight points after the dénouement?'

'No, I think it was Jake who burned the afterglow.'

'On Tonia's rabbit turns?'

'Depends whose story you believe. The way I heard it was Rupo and Werner who scalloped the chocolate ashtray. At Ken and Em's, last Thursday. Just after the mandible olm dwelling crescent.'

'Olm? If that wasn't a fucking fire salamander then I'm Derek Elms.'

Cue, much knowing laughter.

*

A few weeks later, I get to know Julian and Kate a bit better over dinner at L'Escargot. Supposedly it's my treat, I can put it down as research expenses for this new showbiz column I've been given. In fact, though, the chances of my getting a decent story this evening are about as slim as the likelihood of the restaurant's hostess not coming to our table and saying: 'Julian, Julian, it has been so long, why do you not come here any more? Last week? You came last week? Then I am right. A week is far too long.'

One reason I'm not going to get a story is because I don't like mixing work with pleasure. Another – and this is why journalists should never befriend the famous – is because I'm scared of hurting my new chums. Another is that celebrities rarely have any worthwhile gossip – it's the hair stylists, dressers, assistants and other backroom types who know all the juicy stuff.

But the main one is, I'm too busy talking about myself. I tell Julian and Kate about what my tutor said to me just before I left Oxford. 'He said: "I don't think you should try to find a job. I think you should hire yourself an agent and just *be*." And you know, maybe he was taking the piss but I don't think he was, he wasn't that kind of person, I think it's because he really saw the point of me—' I try to ignore Julian's bitchily raised eyebrows, swig drink, suck on fag, gasp for breath. 'I mean, oh God, this is going to make me sound so crap but I want to be honest with you, you know when I go to all these showbizzy parties I have to go to and hang out with people like you I just feel like such an imposter, I mean why am I there? I'm only there because I've been paid by a newspaper to find stories not because I'm special in my own right and' – swig, swig, puff, puff '—well maybe this is the bollocks all people say at my age, even the untalented ones, so how do I know I'm any different? But I look at these celebrities at these parties, not you necessarily Julian, definitely not you, but a good bunch of them and I think, "Well what exactly is it that you've got that I haven't?"—'

'Looks? Acting ability? Charm? Wit?'

'Yeah, well, um—' Very long swig, very deep drag, blush blush.

'Ignore him, Josh,' says Kate.

357

'Oh, it doesn't matter,' I say, trailing off.

'It's worth teasing you just to see you shrink, you poor delicate flower, you. Now do go on, please go on and I shan't say any more horrid things,' says Julian.

'Well, it's just so unfair, that's all, all these people looking at you like you're lower than vermin and actually, for all they know, you could be really talented, as talented as they are.' Puff puff, drink drink. 'I mean in a way, maybe it's a good thing because one of these days I'm going to say sod it, I've had enough, I'm going to prove you all wrong and become even more famous than you are. And that's when I'll finally get round to writing this book, I guess.'

'It's going to be a novel, I take it,' says Julian.

'Yeah.'

'Let me guess. An autobiographical one about life in the London fast set.'

'Funnily enough, not – that's going to be my second one or maybe my third – this one's based on an idea I had in a pub at Oxford once. About this restaurant critic who's stuck in this job he really hates—' I say

'Not entirely unautobiographical, then,' says Julian.

'Um, no. Anyway.'

'So what happens?' asks Kate.

'Are you sure you want to know?'

Julian beams invitingly. But I'm sure he's being ironic.

'I'll give you the edited version. OK, so there's this restaurant critic and he starts writing about these restaurants that don't actually exist . . .'

Next day, during the inevitable guilt-racked hangover, this becomes a prime candidate for most cringe-inducing recollection of the evening. I mean, how could I, HOW COULD I, have been so boorish, so solipsistic, so downright-squitty-jumped-up-little-runtish as to recount the plot of my novel, a novel that hasn't even been written and probably never will be, to somebody who actually does that sort of thing for real, all the time, really well. Someone who, furthermore, can probably scarcely move for wild-eyed fans trying to accost him with their own half-baked literary schemes; someone who was probably hoping that once, maybe just this once, he was in for an evening with people he could trust not to bore him rigid with their pitifully self-absorbed drivel, to talk about something interesting for a change.

I scour the recesses of my shrivelled, throbbing brain in a vain attempt to find moments where I didn't reveal myself for a gibbering fool. But all I can find are more examples of the moments when I did. Like when I tried impressing Julian with my wine knowledge only to confuse my Bordeaux with Burgundy. Like when I attempted to tell my 'Sid'll have him' joke, only to remember half way through that I was telling it to a man who knew more about comic theory than Bergson, had better timing than Max Miller and a sharper wit than Oscar Wilde and Noël Coward after a double martini and a gram of coke, realize on second thoughts that maybe this wasn't such a good idea, and completely fluff the punchline. Like when the bill came, and I ostentatiously took it with a 'No, please, I did say this was on me,' studied it for a few increasingly horrified seconds, realized there was no way on earth the expenses department would wear the gull's eggs, foie gras, two bottles of grand cru claret and three glasses of vintage cognac, turned ashen, thought of how long it would take me after tax to earn the money back, only to be rescued by a: 'I did suspect that there might have been something a little hubristic in that promise of yours. Now, would you mind passing it back to me.'

When I get to work everyone wants to know how my evening went because, of course, I've been boasting about it for ages.

'Great,' I say, dejectedly.

'So what did you talk about? What's he like? Go on. Give us the dirt.'

'Well – he's just like he is on TV, really. Only a bit taller.'

'You spend all evening with Julian Trent and that's all you've got to say?'

'What do you want me to say? We got drunk mainly.'

'Oh. Like that, is it?'

'Like what?'

'You know what they say about Julian Trent.'

'Oh for fuck's sake, it's hardly a great secret.'

'Touchy subject, eh.'

'I—' I'm about to say that his sister was there with me but instead I just say: 'You think whatever you want.' Because frankly, I'd much rather everyone thought that I was having an affair with Julian Trent than that they discovered the far more terrible truth: that I was rejected for being boring.

It does haunt me, though. I find it impossible to work. All I can think about is what a massive failure I am because what I've realized is this: Julian Trent is the embodiment of all the things I'd most like to be; so if he doesn't like me, that must mean that I have nothing in common with him; which must mean I have none of his virtues; which must mean that I am completely worthless, I haven't a hope of achieving any of my ambitions so I might as well give up now.

'Are you functioning even slightly?' asks the Rottweiler.

'Probably not.'

'Jesus, if this is what dining with celebs does, it's the last time I'm letting you out on the leash.'

'Oh don't worry,' I say bitterly. 'I can't see it happening again.'

Later at home, after several stiff gins and lime, I finally feel capable of calling Kate for a post-mortem. The fact that she has been too embarrassed to call me at work has confirmed my worst suspicions.

'Kate. Hi. It's me. Josh.'

'Sweetheart! You sound terrible.'

'Bit hung over.'

'God, me too. I've only just got up. But wasn't it the most fab evening?'

'Was it?'

'I thought so. Didn't you?'

'Uh yes. Yes I did.'

'Julian too. Had a fantastic time. I've never seen him so relaxed.'

'Really?'

'Well, he's so used to starfuckers and hangers on and all that point-scoring and one-upmanship you get when two or three famous people are gathered together. I think he found it a relief to be with someone normal for a change.'

'Normal?'

'I think he finds it quite charming the way you're so up-front that you're not afraid to make a fool of yourself.'

'Oh God, which bit?'

'You mustn't. You absolutely mustn't. Listen, Julian really really likes you. We both do. Can't quite face dealing with diaries now, but ring me later this week and we'll sort out another evening very soon. Will you do that?'

I put down the phone. If I weren't so pissed already, I

think I'd get drunk to celebrate. Perhaps even dance a little jig round the carpet.

Julian Trent really likes me.

*

Does he? Looking back, I can't recall a single moment when I was absolutely sure that he did. This is the problem with being friends with famous people. Your relationship is always going to be an unequal one.

You may tell yourself that you like them as a person. But you'll never quite shake off the guilty suspicion that you're only really in it for the reflected kudos, the name-dropping, the nights when you're led straight to the best table in the Ivy and the maître d' skilfully makes you feel like he's doing it as much for you as for the celebrity you're with.

And even if you don't have this suspicion, your famous friend certainly will. Famous people, after all, are instinctively thin-skinned and paranoid. How could you not be when almost everyone you meet is either bitterly jealous or sick-makingly overimpressed; when no one is much interested in who you really are, only your image?

It's why famous people hang out in packs. That way, they get to be with people who share their neuroses, who aren't fazed by their fame, who aren't going to spill their secrets to the press. Because unlike mere mortals, these people under-stand.

But though I don't think I can honestly say that I am ever truly friends with Julian Trent, I do get about as close to him as any non-famous person could. Like: I have his private phone number; I've had mugs of tea made by Julian himself in his kitchen and been allowed to poke my nose round the door of his bedroom; I've been for rides in his Jaguar XK120,

once to a gig by this teenband Julian liked, where I got him
backstage passes and into the aftershow, which made both
Julian and the band really happy; when I go up to him at
premières and first nights, he mostly gives the impression of
being pleased to see me, except maybe when he's chatting to
a real superstar like say Michael Stipe or Tom Hanks and he
freezes me out.

That's it, there, you've just glimpsed it: the celebrity barrier
in operation. And though I really shouldn't complain – I'm
sure I would have done exactly the same in his shoes – it's
hard not to feel diminished by these moments. For they say
more about your relationship than a thousand XK120 rides
or home-made mugs of tea ever could: you're not friend and
friend, but famous person and not-famous person, achiever
and hanger-on.

It happens again on that fateful day up at the Edinburgh
Festival, the one which will eventually yield the disastrous
anecdote about Kate. Julian is compèring some massive fund-
raising event for the Labour Party, featuring the inevitable
smorgasbord of Leftie comics, and though I've tried getting
my newdesk interested so that they'll pay my hotel bill for
one extra night they're not interested, so I have to find somewhere else to crash. Kate says it might be possible for me to
stay at their rented apartment. Julian isn't pleased.

He's civil enough to my face. But later I hear him through
the wall, telling Kate he's sorry, the spare room's taken, so I'm
just going to have to find somewhere else. Kate replies well
she's sorry but she's already said I can and if the worst comes
to the worst I'll have to share her bedroom. 'I hope you know
what you're doing,' says Julian. At which point they must
realize they might be overheard, because though the conver-

sation continues, sounding more urgent now, it's so soft the only word I hear is 'Orlando'.

What's really making him tense, though, I reckon is that he's got the leader of the Labour Party, John Smith, coming round to tea. Now obviously he doesn't know that in a few months Smith is going to keel over with a heart attack. He thinks that this man is going to be our future prime minister. A Labour prime minister. And the prospect of having tea with this man probably impresses him more than tea with, say, Michael Stipe or Tom Hanks would. Because let's face it, sucking up to American rock icons or movie stars doesn't get you a place in the House of Lords, whereas ingratiating yourself with future prime ministers . . .

Well, perhaps I'm being unduly cynical. But the vibe I'm getting from Julian this afternoon is that he doesn't want me around. When John Smith arrives, Julian steers him quickly into a sitting room and closes the door behind him. Kate's allowed in there, but I have to lurk out of sight in her bedroom, reading and re-reading an old copy of the *New Statesman*. 'Bloody hell, you'd think I was going to assassinate him, or something,' I grumble when she temporarily emerges to fetch some more tea.

'Oh it's not you, he's just a bit nervous about tonight. I shouldn't take it personally.'

But I do take it personally because I thought I'd become part of the family and Julian has made it clear that I haven't. That, indeed, I'm an encumbrance. Not the sort of person one wants sharing a room with one's baby sister, let alone breathing the same air as one's future leader.

Perhaps if I were as bad as he seems to think I am, I'd try making a drunken pass later that night at his sister. Because she is fanciable, we are kindred spirits, and if she weren't married . . . But what we actually do is keep most of our clothes on, exchange chaste good-night pecks, roll over and try to get some sleep. It would be nice to think that as we lie there, Kate too is at least toying with the idea of infidelity. But that's as close to it that either of us ever gets.

*

It all comes to an end over dinner at the Ivy. It's supposed to be just a get-together with me, Kate and my brother Dick who's up for the weekend and whom she quite likes. Julian wasn't invited, though he's said he might come, depending on how he's fixed.

Whether he does or doesn't I'm not particularly bothered. Of course, it will be nice for Dick to get to meet him, and there's every likelihood that he'll end up footing the bill. On the other hand, there's something about Julian that bothers me – something that has always bothered me, in fact. It's that whenever I'm with him, he makes me feel like shit.

When he's being nice, I feel like shit for being unworthy of his affection. When he's being catty, I feel like shit because he's so savagely eloquent. When he's being funny I feel like shit for not being as funny. When he's talking politics I feel like shit for not being a caring socialist. When he's talking books I feel like shit for not having written one. When he's talking about art, classical music, geography, history, maths, quantum physics, rocket science, marine biology, mechanical engineering, cookery or pretty much any subject on earth with the possible exception of Obscure Indie Bands 1985 to 1989 I feel like shit for not knowing as much as he does.

But here he is now, my famous friend Julian Trent, and he's got that chap thingy with him, used to share a room with

him at Oxford, one of those non-names that you always forget
– Simon? Peter?

'Julian, brilliant, just in time. There's a vital question I
need to ask and only a man of your experience and judgement
is qualified to answer: Do you think I should go for the baked
sea bass with the Thai vegetables or the sausage and mash?'

'Is that a polite way of asking whether he's paying?' says
Peter.

Reddening – it actually wasn't what I was asking at all –
I keep my grin intact, my smiling, though-not-quite-as-
smiling-as-they-were-a-second-ago, eyes fixed on Julian.

'I think a palate torn between such wild extremes may be
beyond my succour,' replies Julian.

'Yes, but you know what I mean. You know those times
when you're sort of in an exotic, fishy mood and sort of in a
plain and honest English mood? And you need someone's
advice to tip you one way or the other?'

'Ooh, I should think you're past an age when Julian's
interested in which way you tip,' says Peter.

Julian gives him an indulgent smile.

'Your butch friend, maybe,' adds Peter.

'Oh yes. This is my brother Dick. Dick, this is Julian Trent
and Peter, um—?'

'Um will do quite all right. You remembered the celebrity's, that's the main thing,' says Peter.

'So anyway, Julian, this terribly important food question.'
I'm trying to keep it light but I can hear my voice cracking
slightly.

'I should go for whatever you feel you can afford,' says
Julian.

Ow, ow and double ow. Kate looks at me like: 'Don't ask
me what this is about.'

I take a deep breath.

'It really wasn't a question of money, whatever Peter might think. It was supposed to be more, well, the sort of friendly thing people say when they're having dinner together.'

'And we all appreciate your gesture of friendship, I'm sure we do,' says Julian, all *faux*-benevolence.

'Phew. So now we're friends again, maybe you can give me an idea of what you're going to have,' I say.

'I don't think that will help. I'm ordering off menu,' says Julian.

'How very starry of you.'

'Perhaps that's because he is a star,' snaps Peter.

'How about you, Kate?' I say.

'Calves' liver, I think.'

'Oh God, now you've made it harder.'

'Oh, I'm sorry. How's that?' says Kate.

'Well, I always have the sodding calves' liver and the only reason I'm in this mess is because I'm trying to be different. But actually, I think maybe the calves' liver's what I really want. Unless – oh I don't know.'

I look across at Julian. Normally, you'd expect him to show a certain avuncular amusement. But he's sharing a private joke with Peter. Giggling together, for all the world as if it were their dîner-à-deux. Wish it were.

'Dick? How about you?'

My brother looks back at me, clearly unnerved. He thought Julian Trent was supposed to be nice.

'Oh. Whatever you're having,' he says.

'Fine,' I say.

'So long as it's not liver,' he adds.

Kate laughs. 'You're quite similar.'

'Yeah,' I say. 'We could almost be brothers, couldn't we?'

Kate laughs some more.

'It's what we tell everyone,' says Dick camply. Then blanches. He's being observed.

'Oh, so you think you'd pass as a gay couple, do you?' says Peter.

'It has happened,' I say. 'Quite a few times.'

'Like that time in Edinburgh,' says Dick. 'At the festival.'

I notice Julian's eyes flicker at the mention of the word Edinburgh.

'Oh yeah,' I say vaguely.

'Oh, come on, you remember. In that café with that comic who's always on the radio,' says Dick.

'Simon Fanshawe.'

'My the circles you move in. Comics who appear on the radio!' says Peter.

'Forget it, Dick, whatever we say is going to be shot down in flames.'

'If you will make homophobic remarks,' says Peter.

'Since when were we being homophobic?'

'Just then. Pretending to be gay in that mincing stereotypical way,' says Peter.

'Oh, for fuck's sake. Julian. Defend us here. Were we being homophobic?'

'I can't honestly say I was listening,' says Julian.

'Can't say I blame you,' says Peter.

Maybe if I just try pretending he's not there. Maybe that'll work.

'Yeah, I think I'll go for the sausage and mash. You up for that, Dick? I think you'll like it. The mash is really creamy.'

'Sounds good,' says Dick.

'And you're having the calves' liver, Kate?' I say.

'I think so. Yes. You can always have some of mine, if you like.'

'Thanks. If you don't mind. It's just that I do need a calves' liver fix every once in a while and when you do it at home it's just never the same.'

'Never quite crispy enough, is it?' she says.

'Charring, that's the problem. You can never really char anything properly at home.'

'Only when it's not meant to be charred,' says Dick.

Sorry, is our conversation boring you? Well, it's meant to. Keep it bland, quotidian, predictable, we're thinking, and maybe we'll get to the end of dinner unscathed.

Then Julian orders the wine and I foolishly mention that I've just blown quite a bit of money on some 1990 Burgundy en primeur. It's supposed to be one of the best vintages in ages, so I expect he'll have something interesting to say on the subject, whether or not he's tried it or thinks it's overrated or anything.

'How very nice for you,' is all he says.

'Yeah, I hope so. One's a Chambolle-Musigny and one's, well just half a case because it's so expensive, one's a Riche-bourg, which I can't wait to try, they're supposed to be really good.'

He doesn't respond.

'Presumably you've had it quite a few times,' I say.

'That's *his* business,' quips Peter.

'A few,' says Julian.

'Right. So would you say I've done the right thing, buying half a case of it. I'm not going to be disappointed?'

'I dare say not,' says Julian.

'I can give you the number of the *négociant*, if you like.'

'Thank you, but I may just be able to survive without,' says Julian.

I gabble on, more to fill the void of his non-answers, than anything. 'You're not into en primeur, then? Maybe you're right. It's just, God knows what they'll be charging for 1990 Richebourg in ten years' time. And I was thinking, you know, this is the chance to get it while it's still affordable. Don't you reckon?'

Julian Trent looks at me imperiously. 'It's not something I have to think about,' he says. 'I find it far easier to have sufficient money to buy the better vintages at whatever prices my wine merchant cares to charge.'

I open my mouth for a rejoinder. Realize there isn't one. That this particular conversational line is dead. Then I ask myself whether what Julian has just said really was as condescending as it sounded. And realize it was. That this is not the urbane, modest charmer you get to see being lovely on *Wogan* and *Jonathan Ross*.

When Julian pushes away his near-full plate, declares he isn't particularly hungry and asks the waiter to bring the bill, 'just for us two, the others are staying, I expect', I decide that something ought to be said.

'That was all a bit odd.'

'Odd? What do you mean?' asks Peter.

'Just, this evening generally. I thought it was a bit strained.'

'I didn't notice anything. Did you, Julian?' says Peter.

'Oh, we've been having a lovely time,' says Julian.

'Ah. Only you rather gave the impression that you didn't want to be here.'

'And whose fault was that, I wonder?' says Peter.

'But that's just what I don't get. What did we do to offend you?'

Peter tuts and rolls his eyes.

'Well, what? Come on.'

'You expect too much of Julian. He can't be on all the time you know. Sometimes he needs to relax,' says Peter.

'But he could have done. He didn't have to come and eat with us,' I say.

'That's just my point. Julian could have spent this evening with absolutely anyone he wanted to. Anyone. You don't think there's a shortage of people in London who'd like to dine with Julian Trent, do you? What do you think makes you special?' says Peter.

'Nothing. Nothing at all. He wasn't even meant to be here. He wasn't invited.'

'Come on, Julian. We've had quite enough of this,' says Peter.

'Are we going?' asks Julian.

'We are,' says Peter. 'And thank you all for your charming company. I DON'T THINK.'

When they've gone, Kate, Dick and I regard each other with astonishment.

'What the fuck was all that about?' I ask Kate.

'Not really sure,' she says. 'It seems very unlike him.'

'I'm not going to forget that in a hurry. I know I'm not. It might even have been my worst dinner ever,' says Dick.

'Yeah, sorry, Dick. Not your best introduction.'

'I can't see myself queueing up for another one,' says Dick.

'Well, I'm sorry. I'm really sorry on his behalf. I'm sure he didn't – I mean—' Kate shakes her head. 'What can have been going on?'

A few days later she tells me she's come up with a sort of explanation. Apparently Julian and Peter were on ecstasy. 'It's still no excuse but . . .'

'Bloody right, it isn't. E's supposed to make you nice, for God's sake.'

'I'm sorry. I'm really, really sorry. You know I am,' says Kate.

'Yeah but it's not you who should be doing the apologizing,' I say.

'I'm afraid he's very stubborn that way, Julian. Never apologize, never explain.'

And he doesn't.

Down on Jollity Farm

I glance over my shoulder to check that the chairman, the general secretary and the press officer have gone. Then I whisper loud enough for the hacks at the far end of the huge conference table. 'Is it just me. Or was that the most monumentally boring waste of time which has about as much chance of getting into tomorrow's paper as a close-up of our left bollocks?'

Some of my fellow arts correspondents purse their lips, some of them smile knowing smiles which may mean 'Actually there was a brilliant yarn buried in there, as you shall discover for yourself when you read my paper tomorrow' but more likely means 'This is an Arts Council press conference. What did you expect?'

I notice Jo from the *Guardian* staring at me with particular intent.

'Or left nipple', I add, to show I'm not sexist.

Then I hear someone behind me, shuffling papers and clearing his throat. And when I look round, I see what the problem is. It's the general secretary. He must have been in the room all along.

'Oh come on,' I protest to him. 'Even you must agree with me a teeny—'

But he has already gone.

I turn to Molly, who I always try to sit next to at these things. She has been an arts correspondent longer than I have, so I think it's only fair that she helps me out. 'Oh dear,' I say. 'Do you think I upset him?'

'It's a funny thing, but people don't generally like being told that their job is a massive waste of life.'

'I dunno. If you said that to me, I'd say: "Too right, baby." '

Everyone has overheard this, of course.

'Does he ever stop talking?' says *The Times* man to the BBC man.

The BBC man says something I can't quite hear. But it sounds like: 'He should if he knows what's good for him.'

They've gathered their notes and are starting to leave.

'What was that?' I call after them.

They don't turn round.

'I'd like to see you try,' I say.

Next to me, Molly shrivels like a scorched leaf.

'Oh come on,' I say. 'He's twice my age. I could have him easy.'

It would be nice to go somewhere for a coffee and a bitch but we've both got stuff to do, so we just share a cab. Molly grumbles that it's the only time she ever gets to see me these days. And I say well it's hardly my fault if she and my girlfriend don't get on.

Molly says: 'What do you mean we don't get on? I think Simone's great.'

Which is a bit like me trying to say, straight-faced, 'What do you mean I don't like being roasted, peeled and dipped in a barrel of salt?'

'Has Simone said something about me?' fishes Molly.

'No,' I lie.

'So who says we don't get on?'

'Oh, stop it, Molly. You've been a girl long enough. You know how good you are at doublespeak.'

Molly looks at me, all wounded innocence.

I say: 'You think that Simone's a bit, I don't know, possibly a bit brash and maybe not quite intellectual enough for me. And Simone, well I don't know definitely what she thinks because she hasn't said anything—'

'Of course she hasn't.'

'But you probably know, she can be a touch possessive at times and I think, you know, what with you and me going back a long way and Simone being quite sensitive and insecure—'

'Poor Simone.'

'I knew there was no point trying to be honest with you.'

'I mean it: poor Simone for being so messed up she can't differentiate between old friends and old flames.'

I turn away from her and stare huffily out of the window. In the reflection I see Molly craning forward to inspect my expression and see how cross I am.

'Press conferences have got a lot livelier since you turned up,' she says.

'Bloody well needed to, didn't they? I feel like the boy who says the emperor's wearing no clothes.'

'Darling, you know you love the arts really.'

'Yeah but the arts isn't what arts correspondents write about, is it? It's all funding crises and rows and queenie theatre directors wanting more money. Like I fucking care. Spend it on missiles, I say. At least they make an impact.'

Molly laughs.

'Really, though, what is it with these people? You give them truckloads of public money. Our money. And all they do is whinge that they haven't got enough to do all the things they want. Which are usually crap things that you'd never want them to spend money on anyway, like education and broadening access. Why are they always banging on about education and broadening access?'

'Because if they didn't – obviously – they'd be open to the charge of élitism,' says Molly in a tone calculated to wind me up still further.

'So? Isn't that the whole sodding point of any art form? To be as good as you can possibly be?'

'Honeybun, you know that and I know that. But if you're using public money you need to be seen to be appealing to as wide an audience as possible,' says Molly.

'Exactly. Which is what's so wrong with public funding of the arts. Like the Royal Opera House. All this breast-beating they have to do about how desperate they are to attract people who aren't white, middle-class, middle-aged merchant bankers. Like, somehow there are zillions of poor, disenfranchised black people out there just gagging for a spot of *La Traviata* if only it had Swahili surtitles and the seats cost 5p and they served goat curry in the bar. And it's all such utter bollocks. The whole point of opera is that its a white, middle-aged, middle-class activity for merchant wankers. So why not just scrap their funding and let them get on with it?'

'Darling, you're surely not proposing that the Royal Opera House shouldn't be open to everyone?' says Molly. I think she only pulls the leftie stuff to annoy me.

'It is open to everyone. The only barriers to entry are a lack of interest in opera and lack of money. Which is as it should be. I mean football's bloody expensive, too, but that isn't subsidized. So why should we fork out for posh cunts to watch warbling lard arses?'

'You always were more of rock 'n' roll kind of guy.'

'Now maybe. But one day there'll come a point when my middle-age instincts start to kick in and suddenly I'll be really into it. And what I don't want to find when I've got there is that the whole opera scene has dumbed down and become trendified to attract younger audiences who shouldn't be there in the first place. I want it to be difficult and élitist, like it's meant to be.'

I glance out of the window. The Embankment – wet and congested. Close to Molly's drop off.

'Fuck, you'd better tell me what your angle is,' I say.

'Haven't quite decided,' she says.

'Oh, for Christ's sake, Molly, stop treating me like I'm some kind of competition. None of our readers gives a toss about your rag.'

'And vice versa,'

'Quite. So?'

'Funding cuts, I guess,' she says.

'Yes but whose? Norwich Opera? Ballet North? Cornish Tin Museum? It's not like they're national institutions,' I say.

'There's always the RSC. I expect they're a bit disgruntled that their grant has been frozen while the National has been given an eight per cent raise,' she says.

'Theatre company gets slightly more money than other theatre company shock horror.'

'You could work it up. Prod Adrian a bit. Ask him whether it's a reflection on his poor season,' I say.

'Oh God, I do hate all that. Why can't these stories just tell themselves. Why do they have to be teased and coaxed and *wanked* into life?'

'What would be our point if they didn't?' says Molly.

The office is almost empty when I get there. All the news

hacks have gone for their regulation couple of pints – which, being as I hate drinking at lunchtime because it makes me feel all sleepy and crap, is yet another reason why I'll never fit in. I catch the deputy news editor, just before he disappears. He looks like a prize boxer and swears a lot. Quite friendly, though, by newsroom standards.

'Where've you been, cunt?' he says.

'Getting you a story, cunt,' I say.

'It better be a good one for you to be calling me cunt, cunt,' he says, index fingers poised like fangs above his keyboard so he can add it to the day's news list.

'How about major opera house threatened with closure?'

'You tried that one last week.'

'Different company. This one's Norwich Opera.'

'Never heard of them.'

'They're very big in—'

'East Anglia?'

'Yeah,' I say, a mite defensive. 'And on the touring circuit.'

'And they've closed, you say?'

'Well, they might, if they can't find funding from elsewhere.'

'Opera company no one has heard of might close. Great. Got anything on anyone we have heard of?'

'Um. The Royal Shakespeare Company?'

'I'm listening.'

'It might need firming up a bit but I think they're going to be seriously pissed off about their latest grant allocation. There's bound to be a row in there somewhere.'

'RSC in storm over slashed budget?'

'It hasn't quite been slashed, but—'

'RSC in storm in teacup?'

'Look, I'll make it work, somehow. Just leave me to it. And if it needs any adjustments I'll phone them in later.'

'What? Buggering off again?'

'I have to. I'm covering Glastonbury for you.'

*

'Lovely,' I say, examining the patch of grass between the tent and the fly sheet on to which Marcus has gymnastically emptied his beer-swollen bladder.

'Oh, and I suppose when you need one you'll be walking the half mile to the urinals?' he says, as the pitter-patter of rain on canvas intensifies into a violent thudding.

I glance towards the two boot-shaped lumps of Somerset mud concealing what until this evening were a clean pair of buckskin Caterpillars. Then I wriggle my still-frozen toes in my still-damp socks and drag resignedly on the joint.

'Jolly authentic, though,' says Marcus.

'What?'

Marcus waves the joint I've just passed him. 'This. Everything. Mud. Drugs. The full Glastonbury experience.'

'I think the a is hard,' I say.

'Eh?'

'I think it's Glastonbury not Glaaastonbury.'

'Oh,' says Marcus.

'Well, to be honest I'm not sure. I used to pronounce it Glaaastonbury myself, because it sounds nicer. But when my brother heard, he took the piss.'

'Why don't we ask the tent next door? They seemed nice enough.'

'No!'

'Why not?'

'Because they'll know we haven't been here before.'

379

'I should say that's pretty obvious,' Marcus pokes his head through the outer flap. You can hear the remains of our neighbours' campfire hissing in the rain. 'I sa-ay,' he says. Then corrects himself, 'Excuse me, mate?'

'Can we be of some assistance, old chap?'

'Yes, we were just wondering. Is it Glastonbury or Glaaastonbury?'

'All depends how posh you are,' says the voice.

'Thanks,' says Marcus.

''Ere, mate, need any smoke?' says the voice.

'Got some, thanks,' says Marcus.

''Shrooms? Acid?' says the voice.

Marcus whispers, 'How about it?'

'No. Fucking. Way,' I say.

'Why not?'

'Suppose I get paged by the news desk.'

'Not at this time, surely?'

'Especially this time. It's when the other papers' first editions come in. If they see an important story you've missed, they get you to chase it up.'

'Are we going to have our whole festival ruined by your job?'

'Don't blame me. Blame your sodding sister. She's the one who always writes these bollocks stories.'

'I can believe it.'

'Was she always this bad?'

'Did I ever tell you about the time she caught me kissing the vicar's daughter at the gymkhana and gave the story to the gossip column in the Pony Club newsletter?'

'And I'll bet afterwards she expected total sympathy and understanding like it was perfectly normal and anyone would have done the same in her position.'

'You know the rule with Molls: either you love her for her faults or not at all,' says Marcus.

'Cow.'

'Absolutely.'

'But quite a nice cow for all her essential annoyingness. Like Ermintrude.'

'Who's Ermintrude?' says Marcus.

*

Friday begins horribly. Instead of getting stoned, I have to trudge through the mud with the photographer it took me most of the morning to find, on this insane assignment to prove that Glastonbury Festival is just like Wimbledon, Henley, Glyndebourne and Royal Ascot. The idea is to interview young, photogenic festivalgoers, preferably female ones with surnames posh enough for *Telegraph* readers to identify with and faces like Princess Diana's. Unfortunately they're all in hiding.

Or rather, they're all with Marcus, as I discover towards midday after a fruitless morning's non-interviews when a slurred voice hails me near the cider tent.

Marcus is slumped on a muddy groundsheet beneath a makeshift awning, wobbly plastic pint of rat-fermented yokel brew in one hand, fat reefer in other, surrounded by half a dozen of the sort of lissom girls you see with their breasts accidentally popping out of taffeta dresses at society weddings in the Bystander section of *Tatler*.

My eyes flit hungrily from girl to girl. I'm not thinking sex – well, not mainly. I'm thinking quotes and reader demographics.

'Cheer up,' says Marcus, offering his spliff.

'Can't. I'm off to the police enclosure after this.'

'You sure he's a friend of yours, Markie?' drawls one of the girls.

Marcus introduces us. Wycombe Abbey, Cheltenham Ladies, St Paul's. Serena, Pidge, Tigger. Just what the newsdesk are after.

'I know someone who can cheer you up,' says Marcus.

'Who?'

Just at this moment, my vision is obliterated by pink as a mesh of fingers covers my eyes. Their touch is soft and probably female and I suppose I should be pleased but I've never liked it when people play this game. It's the suddenness of it and the way their hand smell is forced into your nostrils.

'Boo,' says their owner. I feel bad for not feeling quite as pleased as she clearly thinks I ought to feel.

In fact, I'm feeling quite nasty. 'OK. I give in,' I say to Marcus. 'Who is this person who's going to cheer me up?'

'Now you be nice, she's had a rough time,' chides Marcus.

'Since when did Josh care for anyone but himself,' says Molly.

Normally with Molly you can't tell when she's hurt. She has that upper-class thing of being able to look unflustered even when she's out of her depth. Now though, her insecurity shows. Her clothes are too point-to-point, her skin is too clean, her brain insufficiently addled by drink, drugs or the legendary Glasto vibe that's supposed to make everyone mellow, even straight people.

'I'm sorry, Molls,' I say, giving her a hug. 'I've had a shitty morning, that's all,'

'Try mine. I've just come back from the police compound. My tent's been stolen. Everything. Sleeping bag, knickers, toothbrush, notebook—'

'God, you poor thing. What are you going to do?' I say.

Molly appears to grow two inches. 'Oh, it's OK, I'd already filed.'

'About sleeping and stuff, I meant.'

'I thought she could stay with us, if that's all right with you,' says Marcus.

'Yeah. Sure. I guess.'

'Seriously, don't worry about me. I'm sure I can find myself a B & B.'

'Oh, don't be ridiculous, of course you can stay with us, it'll just be a squeeze is all I was thinking. Not to mention your brother's disgusting personal habits.'

'Well, it's not as though I haven't had twenty years to get used to them,' says Molly.

'Fair enough, but on one condition. This story you've filed so nauseatingly early. What's your angle?'

'Oh, just some frothy conceit I dreamed up about Glaston-bury being the new Glyndebourne.'

'You are fucking joking?'

'Well, I know it hardly stands up but Markie's friends have been very helpful and we did get some rather nice snaps so – what are you looking at me like that for?'

At first I'm so cross I can't even speak.

'Josh?'

'You came here deliberately, didn't you?' I say. She looks at me, all wounded grey-eyed innocence.

'You came here expressly to fuck up my story, steal all my quotes, lift all my ideas and just generally totally piss all over my life.'

'You don't really think that. Do you?'

'I don't know what to think. I really don't. Except it's prettty fishy that the last time we spoke not twenty-four hours ago you weren't even coming here and now here you are.'

'But – but it was a last-minute thing. The newsdesk had a ticket spare and I wouldn't have gone – except, except—' she's biting her lip now, '—I knew you and Markie were going and I thought it would be nice, that's all.'

'Yeah, come on, Josh. Chill, will you?' says Marcus, offering me the joint once more.

This time I take a long angry puff. Then another. And another. Because I'm so totally fucked off I know there's not a drug on earth strong enough to calm me. As far as I'm concerned, this is me and Molly finished. I don't care whether or not she meant it, the point is that she did. She's a walking liability. She has stolen my story. That's it. Goodbye, Molly. The End.

*

The police HQ is miles from anywhere you'd want to go at Glastonbury, unless it's the farm in which case it's right next door. Things are very different in this sterile, barricaded, hosed-down concrete zone. Down in the valley below it's a cross between *Apocalypse Now*, *Zombies: Dawn of The Dead* and *All Quiet on the Western Front*. Here it's all muscular action, clear-headedness and brisk efficiency: orders being given through walkie-talkies, stringent security checks, fluorescent jackets, roaring tractors dexterously manoeuvred; trailerloads of eager volunteers heading forth on another litter-collection mission, shit-sucker machines returning from the latrine pits, cows, harassed festival staff, Michael Eavis with his beatific smile, bald head and rustic chin beard, like one of those cartoon pictures that makes equal sense when viewed upside down. But the biggest difference of all is, down there, everyone is stoned. Whereas up here, no one is stoned. Absolutely no one. No one, that is, except the journalist in the police Portakabin trying to keep his frazzled brain sufficiently together to sustain a lucid conversation with the officer on duty.

'And those seventy-eight drug arrests—'

'Twenty-eight, sir. We haven't been that busy,' says the policeman, with a policeman's laugh.

I try to laugh with him. Marcus's reefer was quite a bit stronger than I'd expected. 'Sorry right, yeah. These twenty-eight drug arrests. Would they be mostly leaders or dealers?'

'Pardon me, sir?'

'I meant, um—' No, Josh. I don't think it's going to help explaining that at that particular moment your mind had wandered briefly off course to that poster of the alien you often find in head shops – 'Dealers. Or just, er—'

'People caught in possession?' he says, looking directly into my enormous pupils. Then downwards, with his X-ray eyes into the pocket where, oh God, oh God, why didn't I think of this before, I've still got a solid chunk of black Moroccan. Half an ounce. Getting on for dealer quantities.

'I wouldn't have any precise figures on that, sir,' he says, 'but in my experience, I would say that the majority would have been apprehended for supply.'

'Ah. Good,' I say. He looks at me strangely. 'I mean it's good that you're going for the dealers because they're the ones to go for, aren't they?'

'In all honesty, sir – and this is strictly off the record, if you don't mind – I would say that if we were to try arresting people for possession only, we'd be here till the cows come home.'

I furrow my brow, unsure what to do. If I were less stoned, I'd know exactly what to do. Laugh probably. But what I'm thinking is, if I laugh, maybe it will suggest to him that I think drugs are a laughing matter. Which will alert his suspicions because surely he will expect me, as a *Telegraph* journalist, to think drugs are a terrible terrible thing.

'I mean you yourself, sir—'

Oh God. He knows! He already knows!

'—must have noticed how many – what shall we call them? – extra-large roll-your-owns are being smoked, fairly openly, round about the site.'

'Uh yes. Now you mention it.'

And I'm suddenly possessed with an intense impulse to come clean and confess that I too have recently partaken.

Why? Probably from the same suicidal urge which strikes towards the end of the office party when it suddenly occurs that this might be just the moment to totter over to the company chairman, jolly him up a bit, give him a piece of your mind, tell him how much better things would work if only you were in charge.

'So if someone were to come in here and light up a joint. I mean – what would you do?' I say.

'The question I'd be asking is what was he doing here. Privileged access, this area is.'

'OK, suppose, um, suppose I were to light a joint. In here. What then?'

'If you were to light up a joint? In here?'

There are two sharp knocks on the Portakabin door. It opens with a nerve-jangling scrape. A walkie-talkie crackles and in steps a thick-set copper with cropped greying hair, holding a dog lead. At the other end is an enormous Alsatian, with stinky wet fur which it shakes all over the cabin floor.

I feel my hand clutching instinctively at my jacket pocket.

'All right for some,' says the dog handler. His jacket is dripping.

He nods curtly towards me.

I nod back, eyes fixed on the dog.

'He won't hurt you,' says the dog handler, 'Not unless I tell him to.'

I try to laugh. How close do the bastard things have to be before they can smell drugs.

'Gentleman here's from the *Daily Telegraph*, John,' says my policeman friend.

'Oh, ah,' says the dog handler.

'Just been asking whether I'd mind if he lit up a joint,' says my policeman very-much-ex-friend.

The dog handler's eyes flicker with suspicion.

'Hahaha. Not exactly,' I say.

'Not so much us minding, is it?' says the dog handler. 'More a question of what Stalker thinks. Don't know why it is but he seems to have a particular aversion to drug abusers. Can't stand 'em.'

'Ah yes,' I say brightly. 'I expect he'll have had something to do with those twenty-eight drug arrests your colleague here has just been telling me about.'

'As to what operations he may have been conducting, it's not my business to say,' says the dog handler.

'Quite, quite. Well anyway, thanks for all your help.'

'Not going to stay for your joint, then?' says my ex-friend.

'I— hahaha – I—' I say edging towards the door, avoiding the dog's nose and the evil policeman's eyes, trying to come up with a rejoinder which manages to be both witty and non-suspicion-allaying. 'I—'

RUUUUN.

*

'I still say you Ethereges are totally fucking evil,' I say, through a mouthful of spicy chicken noodles. I've filed my copy. I've got my evening battlekit of jumper, woolly hat, torch, waterproofs, skins, baccy, spliff all prepared. Now we're grazing in the drizzle in the market area we've named Babylon. Or maybe that's what everyone calls it. It's all starting to become a bit of a blur.

'He was only trying to be helpful,' says Molly, savaging a doughnut.

Yes. I know I said I was never going to speak to her ever again, but now I've done my work, smoked a few more spliffs and acquired a full stomach, my perspective has changed. Plus, with Marcus having abandoned me to spend the night with one of his harem, what's the alternative?

'Oh per-lease,' I say. 'You didn't seriously buy that line about making space for his darling big sister? He was just thinking with his cock. As usual.'

'Don't sound too bitter,' says Molly.

'I just happen to think that when you're in a Nam-type situation, and your buddy's lying there screaming in a pit full of poisoned punji stakes, you don't just fuck off and leave him because you fancy a shag in the fleshpots of Saigon.'

'Is that the situation?' says Molly.

'More or less.'

'Well, I shan't abandon you.'

'Only because I'm the only one who remembers where our tent is.'

'Be like that.'

'Look, Molls, it's nothing personal. The reason I left Simone at home is because I'd kind of been looking forward to a proper boysy sesh. And the thing is, well, you're not a boy.'

'What were you going to do with Marcus that you can't do with me?'

'I dunno. Take lots of drugs, I expect.'

'I can do that too. You know I can,' she says.

'Yeah, but that was E. E's a My Little Pony drug. I'm talking about hardcore psychotropics.'

'Like this?' says Molly, fishing into the pocket of her waxed jacket. She pulls out a small plastic water bottle, filled with browny-yellow liquid.

'Piss?' I say.

'It's mushroom tea, he said,' says Molly.

'Who did?'

'Marcus. I think he meant it by way of an apology.'

'And you want to do this stuff with me?'

'I don't want to, no. But I'll do it to keep you company.'

'Big of you.'

Molly grins. 'I'm a big girl.'

*

We're aiming for this space Molly discovered earlier, while watching a 'really quite nice' band whose name of course she can't remember. It's this patch of raised ground with a reasonably good view of the Pyramid Stage, on the front right of the mixing desk. The problem is, we're approaching from the front left of the mixing desk, which means that we've got half the main stage audience to negotiate first. Worse still, because Jesus Jones have come on earlier than they're meant to, their fans are dotted all over the site and are only now beginning to converge en masse on the narrow, slippery bridges which lead to the main stage area.

Molly and I are stuck right in the middle and it's evil. Crushed, confined and helpless at the heart of a seething, lumbering behemoth of bodies, leather, hair, polyester, cold cheeks, hot breath, bony elbows and pulsing flesh. Pressed so hard that at times you can scarcely breathe; unable to control speed or direction; mud sucking at your boots; the smell of fear and barely suppressed hysteria; like Hillsborough everyone's thinking but no one's saying. Like Hillsborough.

'Moo,' some wag goes because we are – we're cattle in a pen being jabbed and prodded by some unseen force, funnelled and compressed into an ever tighter space, the terror before the slaughter.

I try craning my head to see where Molly is. Then I realize she's the person whose chin is being forced into my left cheek, her skin sandpapered by my greasy stubble.

Suddenly, I feel all protective, because if I'm as frightened as I know I am, how on earth must she be feeling?

'Fuck. Imagine doing this on mushrooms,' I say, brightly.

'We are on mushrooms,' she says.

'Oh good. So does that mean none of this is happening?'

One or two people next to us who've overheard the exchange – how could they not with their ears almost in our mouths? – snort appreciatively. I would turn to smile at them, but my head is trapped like a lock's in a scrum. And ahead, my God, headlights, the mad mad bastard what does he think he's doing? No way is he he going to get a security Land Rover over this bastard bridge.

Then, at once, the slippery wood of the bridge underfoot gives way to soft mud and we find ourselves lurching suddenly forward as the crowd ahead thins while the mass behind us continues to thrust at our backs. I stumble, recover. And we're free.

Well, almost. We've still got to worm our way through the ranks of dead-eyed punters staring towards Jesus Jones's sound and light set. It's reaching its climax, which goes to show just how long that bridge nightmare lasted. And though I don't think we've missed much – let's face it, their songs sound pretty similar – I do at least want to catch them doing 'Real Real Real'.

Molly is pathfinding determinedly ahead of me. I tug at her sleeve.

'You can't see anything from here,' she says.

The people we've just stopped in front of give us looks which say: 'Yeah, yeah. You can't see anything from here, so why don't you piss off and invade someone else's space.'

'There's nothing *to* see,' I say. 'Come on. Tactical spliff.'

Reluctantly Molly stops. The people whose limited sight-lines we've stolen huff and then get used to it, as you do. Then I skin up, which is pretty damn near impossible because even with Molly holding the papers in her cupped hands, the wind keeps lifting up the edge and strewing the hash I'm attempting to crumble on top all over the place, while the lighter's so hot it's burning my fingers and flecks of rain threaten to render the paper useless and then we can't find the baccy, or rather we can, it's just buried beneath layers of rain gear which we can barely penetrate because our arms are pinned to our sides by the people next to us. Still, when you need a joint you need a joint and we manage somehow. I'm setting fire to it, just as the opening chords of 'Real Real Real' strike up.

And I think: life doesn't get any better than this.

Because here we all are, one big snug happy family. We're all on the same drugs. We've all come to hear this song. And now Jesus Jones are playing it, just for us. It's muddy, it's raining, our legs are tired and our knees are going and our backs are stiff from having had to stand up for far far too long. But none of it matters. We love Jesus Jones. We love this song. We love one another. And life is beautiful.

Like moths to a neon-blue fizzing insect-zapper – us and 30,000 others – we're drawn inexorably to the glow of the stage in the darkness, to the flashing, trippy acid explosions of blue and yellow and red, to the blue lasers cutting the air like some Jedi duel, to the:

'Real real real. Do you feel real?'

Oh we feel real, all right. Realler than we've ever felt. In a completely unreal way, of course, hahahahaha.

I smile at Molly. Molly smiles back at me. It's like Ecstasy at the Wag all over again, only somehow more meaningful this time, because anyone can be happy on E, whereas with dope and mushrooms, well they only exaggerate the state of mind you're in already. Which kind of makes this experience more real. Real Real Real, even. Doesn't it?

Ah, fuck it, who cares, the point is that Molly's having a good time and I'm having a good time – a better time, I'm quite sure than I would ever have had with her goat of a brother. God, I wish she were my sister. Well, she is my sister, almost, because that's certainly how I feel about her, not in a sexual way, more in a loving, protective fraternal way, which isn't how you're meant to feel about potential girlfriends is it, with potential girlfriends you want to have sex with them and with Molly I'm beyond all that.

And we can feel the rumble of the sub-bass underfoot and the steel of the synths slicing into our brains while our bodies are caressed by washes of keyboards and the wind across our skin and the warmth of our neighbours and we're all on the same trip and life just isn't going to be the same again.

Then suddenly – and none of us can work out exactly

when or how it happened – the stage is empty, the lights are off, the speakers are silent and everyone's just staring, aghast, thinking that can't be it, can it, surely that can't be it?

Technicians start running on stage and hauling off equipment and we realize that it really is it. There are urgent mutterings in the crowd, as plans are made, new rendezvous named. The more quick-witted members of the audience start to move on out. Then the slower ones. And the picture begins to change. No longer are we radiant beings, floating in a warm, luminous sea of beneficence and euphoria. We're a pair of bedraggled dopeheads in the middle of a vast and very muddy field strewn with empty bottles, paper cups, mangled fast food and the slumped bodies of the knackered, the wasted and the very-desperate-to-see-the-Happy-Mondays.

'Great God, this is an awful place,' says Molly.

The ground is too foul to sit down on. But we do so anyway, sacrificing the rest of the festival programme as a ground sheet. My boots are so heavy with mud, my feet so numb that when I cross them in front of me I find myself staring at them disbelievingly, unable to conceive how they could possibly be an extension of my body.

Molly hands me the joint.

'Do you think there was anything in that bottle?' she says.

'Hard to say, with all the dope. You getting anything?'

'I had quite a lot less than you.'

'Maybe the cold has slowed our metabolism.'

'Don't look at me. I'm not the drugs expert.'

I offer her the mushroom brew. She has a small gulp. I polish off the remains.

'How about we move forward. Then we'll be really close for when your Jolly Wotsits come on,' she says.

Which is a stupid idea, actually, because towards the front-of-stage area, where Molly is thinking of going, the crowd never thins. This is the mosh pit, for hardcore fans only – the sort who wave homemade banners and piss in bottles. These are the band's praetorian guard, who orchestrate the mood of the crowd, who recognize each new song a fraction of a second before everyone else does, who endure the worst conditions, who take the most drugs. And these are the people we're now trying to push our way through. Which they don't like at all. What you have to do, is be all zen. Inhabit their warped, fanatical minds and become one with them. In this way when you slip and squeeze forward they don't see you as a threat, but as a kindred spirit, trying to get back to your mates just like they've done at some time or another with *their* mates.

We're close to the front, now. Close enough to see the ranks of bouncers guarding the barrier, and the strange patch of green stuff – so that's what grass looks like – behind them and the equipment being shunted around for the Happy Mondays and the wires being taped to the floor and the mikes being checked. And John Peel, yer actual John Peel, coming on stage, to say that the Mondays are going to be with us shortly.

Which is a huge lie because the wait that follows stretches for eons and that isn't just my imagination, you can hear it in the things people around us are saying: "Kin' 'ell, 'ow much longer?' 'Coont Shaun Ryder, he's takin' the piss,' 'Maybe Bez has forgotten how to tune his tambourine,' and you can feel the burgeoning panic as the weight of the crowd behind us grows heavier and heavier, pushing us so close together we can't even move our arms.

I don't like it.

No one likes it. You can see it in the eyes of the security

guards who've given up trying to look controlled and impassive.

'Back!' they're saying. 'Back! Can you move back.' Yeah, like we're really pushing forward on purpose. Now a voice through the PA has taken up the cry. 'This is a security announcement. This is an urgent security announcement. There is dangerous overcrowding at the front of the stage. Please can everybody take a step back.'

I can feel the fear growing more intense because it's coming on, this mushroom trip's definitely coming on, and it's gorging on the discomfort, bloating on the confusion, exulting in the horror because it knows that the more extreme the emotion the more powerful it will be.

I say: 'Molly, I think it's coming on.' Mainly so she can say that I'm imagining it, it's only the dope.

She says: 'Yeah, me too.'

I try to think of the music, of how much better everything will be when the music starts. But that only makes me dwell on how frustrating – no, far worse than frustrating – how cataclysmic it is that the music *hasn't* started yet.

What's this? A commotion to our right. Heads turn. Nothing visible, just a mass of bodies. But you can feel the tremor. Then the mutterings start. Someone hurt. Someone passed out. Sirens. Blue flashing lights. The whump whump whump of a helicopter overhead like something out of *Apocalypse Now*, God it's just like *Apocalypse Now*, the chaos, the rain, the fear, the chopper blades, starlight starbright phosphorous shells reflected in blank pupils, and the fear, oh God the fear, the horror, the horror.

'When I said the Happy Mondays would be on shortly,' comes John Peel's voice through the PA, 'I was, of course, using the Manchester definition of shortly, which is however long it takes for Shaun Ryder to finish his rider. Which, I've no doubt you'll be gratified to learn, he has very nearly done. Eh? Oh. Security has asked me to ask you, would you please all take a step back right now. We've had a young lad pass out at the front. In fact from where I'm standing, I can see it's very crowded. So why not make that two steps?'

'Molly, we've got to get out,' I say, as two Baggy types in Madchester sweatshirts heave their ashen-faced, semi-conscious mate towards the security barrier.

'How?' she says.

I try to force myself to think about the newsroom. If that doesn't straighten me up, nothing will. I think of how hard it was writing my copy and how uninterested they were when I asked them whether there were any queries. How they asked me to ring in later and how I didn't because it was too hard to get to a phone and how, oh God, I'm probably in trouble, they've probably tried to bleep me, I wonder if they've tried to bleep me. If they have, there is nothing I can do, but now I've thought of it, I can't get it out of my head, I have to know, I have to know. I slide my squashed right arm down my chest and, retrieve the bleeper from my jeans pocket. I hold the screen close to my face. They haven't called. I'm safe.

Except, of course, I'm not safe, because now that I haven't got the newsdesk to worry about, I can go back to worrying about how terrifyingly claustrophobic it is, how noisy, everyone's screaming, why is everyone screaming? And it's started.

They're on stage and straight into one of the songs I know. That insistent keyboard intro and that loping, shambolic bass-line, what's it called, 'Bummed' is it?, but they're all like that Happy Mondays songs, they're all about being bummed, they're so druggy, so very, very druggy it makes you feel like—

'Molly, I have really got to go.'

Not that she can hear a word, not with the music so loud, not with us being jostled and elbowed and pogoed into by the trashing, trampolining, lager-crazed, drug-frenzied, testosteronal moshers.

'MOLLY!'

As we flee, the dam bursts and the terror comes surging after me. We fight our way back through the crush of jerking, brutish male bodies. Kicked shins, elbowed ribs, shoulder-bruised arms, smashing heads – they're like creatures possessed. I feel sweat streaming down my face. The music's – evil. And it's chasing me, booming after me through the speakers. My jacket is half torn off. My sweat is clammy. I'm sweating fear. And the music so persistently malevolent; so debauched and ugly; see what it has done to these people, as they dance and gurn and whirl in the flickering light to that primal beat with its snarling contempt for the civilized and the beautiful, it has made them evil, everyone is evil. See how they cackle at my agonies, each looming face attached to an unyielding skeletal body determined to thwart my escape, every step a battle against overwhelming odds, every inch of ground gained a small miracle.

'They are fucked.'

''Ere, mate, got any more?'

'God, did you see his face?'

I would turn round to see how far we've come but there's no time, it's still there that Satanic music, bearing down on me like an orange and grey Hollywood explosion, getting closer all the time. And these people, all these people, how could there ever be so many people? I don't look at the faces, the eyes are the worst, because they reflect your fear and make you feel worse. Worse. Some joke, how could you feel worse than this? As you move forward, no you're not moving forward, it's the other way round, like you're standing still while all these people on conveyor belts either side of you come rushing past, as this happens you see impressions of the parts that form the whole – yellow teeth, bony fingers, soft tapering hands pale with cold; bin liners, lots of binliners tied around feet, patches on jeans, a smily badge, a red anorak like in *Don't Look Now* or was that yellow?, joined together they make a person, lots of people, thousands of people, the part for the whole, what's it called, synecdoche, I think, like a sail meaning a ship, and I hate that word, not once in my life has it ever been useful, just think of all the better words I could have berthed in its space, and I would have forgotten it, of course I would, if my English teacher at prep school, Mr Manson his name was, as in Charles, only less psycho-pathic, not at all psychopathic in fact, really gentle, if Mr Manson – Midder Man, we called him – if Midder Man hadn't made us all copy it from his exquisite blackboard copper-plate into our exercise books, made us copy it so neatly, this and maybe two dozen or more other of the literary terms he deemed essential to our intellectual grounding, because they believed in such things his generation of teachers, they believed in intellectual groundings, which is why he made us copy it so neatly, so that the effort involved – and it really was an effort, one mistake and you had to start all over again, you couldn't use Tippex and you couldn't rip out the pages of your book, well not if you were past the middle anyway because then you'd be taking out pages you'd written pre-viously – but that was the point, the intense concentration required to ensure that you'd never ever forget these words. Synecdoche. The first time I've used it since I was twelve. Twelve! When my future seemed so bright and my brain was so sharp and uncorrupted and look what I've done to it now, oh God what have I done to myself, look at the wreck I've become, why do I keep doing these stupid drugs, why didn't I heed Mr Migarette's awful warning, oh God, this time I promise, this time I promise not to do them again I swear as the faces, don't look at them, slide past on this endless conveyor belt, on and on and on let go of my arm on and on stop pulling my arm and on and on I turn to see who's pulling my arm and it's Molly.

'I think we've gone far enough,' she says.

*

It turns out that there are bits of the festival we didn't know about. We find them on our epic, post-trip come-down wander along the path that crests the hill above the Pyramid Stage, skirts the bottom of the farm enclosure and forks right down through a dark, Tolkienesque avenue of trees swarming with drug dealers, beer sellers and urinating drunks, round the edge of Babylon and into the less commercial realms of the Circus Field and the Green Fields and the Healing Fields where Arthur still reigns and his hand maidens serve you *chai* round camp fires while sticking *bindis* to your forehead and giving you Indian head massages. A crusty plays a didgeridoo. Someone else thumps out a rhythm on some African drums. A barrel-chested man with matted grey hair and a grizzled beard gazes into the flickering fire with burning intensity. He's called Uther, apparently.

'We like it here,' I tell the middle-aged earth mother type who's giving me this head massage. 'Much nicer than over there.'

But she's concentrating on the massage.

'Mind you, we did take mushrooms. Which may have been the problem.'

The woman is taking deep, meditative breaths.

'While the Happy Mondays were on. That was the killer, I reckon.'

'He likes to talk, your partner,' says the woman massaging Molly's head.

'He does,' says Molly, fondly.

I'm touched, not just by the way she says it but also that she hasn't bothered to correct the word 'partner'. Not that it's a term I'd ever use myself. We're not some firm of solicitors, for fuck's sake. But it is kind of sweet that people assume we are an item and that Molly's happy to go along with the idea.

Then Molly says: 'But he's not my boyfriend.'

'No, no I'm not,' I chip in quickly. 'My girlfriend's in London.'

There's a long silence, as our masseuses digest this information. They probably think they're psychic. 'Perhaps not now then one day. For so Gaia the Earth Goddess has foretold,' I half expect one of them to say. But they just carry on silently massaging our heads.

'Do you think it's bad to talk, then?' I ask.

'You should do whatever feels right,' murmurs the woman massaging my head.

'What's your name?'

'Marmion.'

'Oh. Right, well the thing is, Marmion – blimey, what a cool name – the thing is I do sort of know that the idea in situations like this is not to say anything. But when everyone else is so quiet I just can't help it. I get this terrible compulsion to fill the void.'

'It is harder to be silent than to speak,' intones Uther, gazing mystically into the fire.

'OK, I'll try.'

'Don't do it because you have to. Do it because you want to,' says Molly's masseuse.

'Breathe,' whispers Marmion. 'Breathe deeply. And as you exhale, imagine all the negative energy flowing out. And as you inhale, feel the positive energy filling your lungs and pouring into your body like rays of golden light.'

I close my eyes and try to do as she says. It's quite hard, because my brain's still racing all over the place and what I need is another joint to bring it down. Except I haven't noticed anyone else round this camp fire having a joint, so maybe it's *verboten*. That would be just our luck, wouldn't it? You find somewhere nice and warm to settle only it turns out to be the one place in the whole of Glastonbury where it's infra dig to smoke dope. Fucking hippies. They really are the end with their holier-than-thou, breathe deeply, we-don't-need-drugs-any-more-we're-on-a-higher-plane bullshit attitude, so I'm not even going to try this deep breathing thing, I'm not, I'm not, I'm going to open my eyes and, good Lord, is that a spliff I see being passed in my direction?

I draw very deeply on the spliff.

Now I'm ready to try this breathing lark.

When I breathe in, I can just imagine all those golden rays bursting out through my lungs and pouring like sweet, honey into the dark, weary recesses of my body, filling them with new life. And when I breathe out, I exhale the miseries of the day. It's amazing, the way they disappear one by one: the cold, the damp, the aches in my back and in my joints, the fear and paranoia from when I watched the Happy Mondays, the claustrophobic panic of the bridge crossing, what else . . .?

My leg twitches. There's a strange vibrating sensation in my upper right thigh – my tense muscles relaxing probably.

What else . . . oh God yes, the policeman the bastard

policeman with the dog and the tedium of having to waste
my afternoon filing copy . . .

And still, that weird vibration. Maybe if I concentrate on
it more, imagine each fibre of muscle loosening, maybe it will
go away.

But no. The more I concentrate on it, the more noticeable
it grows. I can pinpoint exactly where it is, where the inside
of my jeans pocket meets my leg. Maybe all the keys and stuff
I keep in there have stifled the blood flow. I start pulling them
out. One balled, snot-encrusted handkerchief; one pack of
hayfever pills; one mangled pack of baccy; one pen; one set
of keys; one pager.

Fuck.

My fucking fucking pager. With two new messages on
it . . .

'ROH in trouble! Please ring news desk,' says the first
one, and I know instantly what the problem is. It's the tiny
shortfall in the Royal Opera House's funding, mentioned in
that tedious Arts Council press conference. One of my
unscrupulous rivals has somehow managed to translate this
into a major cash crisis, and then held the story over for
Saturday's newpaper to make it look more important.

'Jesus,' I groan, already rehearsing my excuses. My pager
got lost; it broke in the rain; I was mugged; it was too late;
I couldn't get to a phone.

I flick forward to the next message.

'Or you're fired,' it says.

The golden rays have been consumed with darkness, the
aches are back, the dread has multiplied a thousandfold. I
stare at the screen of my pager, just to be absolutely sure it's
not an hallucination. The messages remain intact.

'You OK, hon?' says Molly.

'What do you fucking think?' I say. Because you hardly need to be Mystic Meg to guess the identity of that unscrupulous rival. Before she can follow me, I'm gone to find the nearest telephone.

Such a pity, I think, as I merge with the crowds, that she'll now have nobody to show her the way back to her tent.

Carry on up the Khyber

When it all starts getting too much I arrange to see a therapist. Actually it's not my idea, it's Simone's. I haven't told you much about Simone yet and to be honest, until she sneaked her way into the last chapter, I wasn't going to. It would only complicate matters, I thought, force me to tell you about stuff that I don't want to waste space talking about like where we met and what we argued about and what we got up to in bed and the time I took her up the arse and you just don't need to know.

All right. I'll tell you just briefly about the up-the-arse bit because it's one of those subjects – the great taboo that we all think about but never talk about because, well, basically it's so rude. Which, of course, is why so many of us are so keen to try it. It's the sexual equivalent of the nuclear deterrent, the ne plus ultra of extreme naughtiness, it involves bottoms and quite possibly poo, it's what gays do, it's illegal, it's got to be worth attempting once. At the very least.

So when one torpid summer evening, after yet another row, we're always having rows are Simone and I, when I'm on the bed about to take Simone from behind and she reaches back and takes the base of my cock in her hand and says, guiding it upwards, 'Not there. *There!*' I find myself thinking – lots of things actually, all at the same time.

One of the thoughts has to do with how uncomfortably exposed I feel. Being as it's high summer it's still very light outside and somehow buggery feels more of a nocturnal activity than a daytime one. Also because it's so unbearably close we've got the windows wide open and we're in this poky mews flat where the walls are way too thin and the acoustics are such that everyone who shares this incestuously claustro-phobic courtyard can hear exactly what everyone else is up to: everything from the screams and 'I don't believe you just said that. That's it, that is fucking it' of our recent row, to, very probably, the twang of urgently released bra straps, the zvvv of feverishly undone flies, the slurp of lubricated rubber on erect tissue and the slap of one finger, now two, now three in sloppy vagina even unto that whispered 'Not there. *There!*' which indicates to anyone who is interested in such things which of course means everyone: 'Josh is taking her up the arse. JOSH IS TAKING HIS GIRLFRIEND UP THE ARSE!'

Another thought has to do with this story I suddenly remember an Oxford friend telling me about the time, as he put it, he took his girlfriend 'up the shitter'. The odd thing was, he used to tell it in her company, both of them acting as if it were a charmingly funny dinner party piece, cheer-fully correcting one another's inaccuracies – 'Now darling, you're exaggerating. It slipped in perfectly easily,' 'That was *after* the Vaseline, if you remember' – blushing and tittering in anticipation of the hilarious pay off. And the pay off was, basically, that the girlfriend happened to have a dicky tummy at the time, resulting in a massive explosion and excrement splattered absolutely everywhere. Well, even with an under-graduate's determined open-mindedness I did wonder whether this was the sort of story one should be broadcasting among all one's friends. But maybe it was an upper-class thing I didn't understand . . .

Shit, inevitably, is another of the things I'm thinking about now.

I mean, there are few things more attractive than a pair of firm, juicy buttocks, but there's no getting away from it – at least once a day, the crack between them is the exit point for a turd. And unless the owner of those buttocks has had a wash, you know that there are bound to be a few faecal traces still in there. Some of which may end up on your willy. Which is a bit disconcerting.

Not disconcerting enough to stop me going ahead with it though. For one thing, I'm wearing a rubber poo shield; for another, it's not every day that your girlfriend – well, yours maybe but not mine – actively encourages you to slip her one up the Khyber. And for all you know it could be the last time anyone ever asks you to do it. The fact that she's even asked you this time is pretty damned miraculous. Because it's not like you were ever going to ask her, is it? You could never have stood the humiliation of her saying 'No.' Which would have meant, quite possibly, that you could have gone your whole, whole life never knowing what it's like to give someone one up the bum.

So at least that's one major worry off my list. I will not, after all, go to my grave an anal-sex virgin. Because, bugger me, I am actually doing it. Now. I am actually taking my girlfriend up the arse. And it's—

Well, to be honest, it doesn't feel an awful lot different from normal sex. A bit tighter, I guess. And you need to use more spit. And it does mean that – with a bit of contortion – you've got free finger access to the front hole, which is great for the girl – judging by the noise she's making – being pleasured through two orifices simultaneously. Wish I were a girl. Sort of. But for all this, I have to admit, anal sex just isn't what it's cracked up to be. You think you'll have a bigger orgasm, explore the dark side, push the envelope, commune with Satan, have the Vice Squad burst in and arrest you for contravening Her Majesty's laws on anal entry. And all it really is, is like ordinary fucking, only more difficult.

Maybe the secret is to be the catamite, though it's not something I've ever cared to try myself – particularly not after I had to go to the Hospital for Tropical Diseases for a rectal snip, which is this test they give you for bilharzia. What happens is that they put you in this robe which opens at the back and the doctor comes in, makes you lie face down. 'You might experience some discomfort,' he says, slipping on his gloves. And 'discomfort', as we know, is doctorese for fucking painful. So then this nurse, also with gloves on, starts smearing grease around your bumhole and you think: 'If I were a bit more kinky, I'd be enjoying this.' Then you see the doctor greasing this sinister-looking object resembling a glass dildo with some sort of metallic grabbing device inside. Not that. No. Surely not? Not up my – urrgghh. And sllrrrrp! Up it goes, like an imperial-sized turd travelling backwards. And it's like – like nothing you've ever experienced. Horrible, certainly, but a different kind of horrible. The horror of physical invasion; of something cold, hard and wrong in your tender flesh. It doesn't hurt, though. Not until the doctor tells you he's going to take a sample and, oh God yes it does hurt it does hurt it does as these horrible tweezer things at the end of the glass – or is it metal, I forget now, I've been trying to blank the full horror probably – penis thing start snipping away at your rectum, one, two, three maybe more times now, again I forget, for the same reasons. Then fllppp – out the wretched thing slips and you lie there, flabbergasted for a very long time while the doctor goes next door with the samples and the nurse goes: 'All over now. Wasn't that bad, was it?'

But, of course, that isn't the main reason why I've no wish to take one up the arse, even though I'll bet it's quite enjoyable for a bloke, what with your prostate being up there – which is the bit nurses stimulate in hospital when they need to give you an instant uncontrollable erection or produce a sperm sample – no, the real reason is that I'm too damned squeamish, so there.

Anyway, I was going to tell you about my trip to this therapist. The reason I go to see her is because I'm desperately unhappy and I'm not sure why. Actually, I think I do know why but I'd like to get a second opinion.

What I think is wrong is: 1. I've been fucked up by drugs. 2. I'm in the wrong job. 3. I'm with the wrong girlfriend.

What my therapist thinks is wrong is, well, they won't tell you, therapists. They just sit there and listen and you're supposed to work it out for yourself. Some would say this is an extravagant waste of £50 an hour, but not me. I think it's great, the idea of someone sitting there rapt while you whinge non-stop about your problems for a full sixty minutes. Afterwards, you feel purged and elated. Like having a quadruple gin and tonic only without the wobbles.

I start by telling her – Cass, her name is – the things I think she'll want to hear, like family background and recurring dreams and the terrible drug experiences which got me into this mess. '—Mr Migarette.'

'Who?' she says.

'The man on the end of my cigarette who stole my soul. That's when it all went wrong.'

She jots something down, but without much enthusiasm.

She looks up.

'Perhaps I should explain a bit more about the form of therapy we practise here,' she says.

It's called Gestalt and the idea, as far as I understand it – not that I'm listening that carefully because I'm feeling cheated here, I came to talk about me, not to listen to psychobabble theory – is that it's not about what happened in the past but about the present. Which would explain her lack of interest in my fascinating stories about how crap my parents were and about men with tall hats on the end of my cigarette. What she really wants to know is how I'm feeling this very instant. Tricky one.

'Um. Not brilliant. But OK, I suppose.'

Cass waits for me to elaborate.

I look round the room as if searching my brain. What I'm really doing, though, is taking in my surroundings, which I haven't dared do before, owing to my initial efforts not to look nosy or shifty. I want her to think I'm one of those people who looks you straight in the eye. Funny that, the way you want to present your best face to your therapist, even though it's the last thing they want to see. I take in books, lots of them; spider plants; cushions; a box of tissues. Tissues: freaky. Because it makes you think of all the people who've been sitting where I'm sitting, sobbing and snivelling and reaching for another one. And it makes you wonder whether the time will ever come when you'll find yourself doing the same thing. God, I hope not. So tacky.

'So, um, yeah. Pretty OK, all in all.'

'But things could be better?'

'Oh God, couldn't they always?'

'You said "Not brilliant." I was wondering what you meant.'

'God, I don't know. Something to do with Simone, I expect. Usually is.'

'Is it?'

'Um, no, I don't want to be too unfair on her, I mean we're really great together most of the time, it's just that I'm still pissed off at something that happened the other day, so fucking pissed off – you don't mind if I swear, do you, only – fuck it, I'm going to swear because I've suddenly realized just how fucking pissed off I still am. Not so much with her. More with myself really, for being such a fucking pathetic wuss.'

Cass holds her pen expectantly above her notepad.

'You've heard of Mariella Frostrup?'

'The TV presenter?'

'Right. Well, thanks to Simone, I stood her up for a date.'

Now I did think about changing the name here just, you know, because I've changed most of the other names – Simone's for example – but then I thought, well, Mariella's not going to mind and I don't think the story will have nearly the same resonance without it.

I mean, suppose I called her 'beautiful, blonde, husky-voiced TV presenter Suzie Starks'. You'd get the general gist but you'd probably end up with some generic bimbo in your head and care less about the story's outcome.

Whereas if I tell you the girl involved was Mariella Frostrup, you're going to be outraged. You're going to think – if you're a man anyway – 'What kind of total twat would turn down a date with our Mariella?' And you'd be right to think that because I was a twat and it's something for which I've never forgiven myself and probably never will.

And the stupid thing was, it's not like it was going to be a date date. Mariella and I were just good friends. I'd bumped into her, one drunken night, at some showbizzy after-show party. She was with Patsy Kensit, I seem to recall. We chatted; we got on; and after bumping into each other a few more times, we ended up not as close friends I wouldn't say but definitely more than acquaintances.

So what happens is that a couple of months after our meeting, I've said to Mariella, 'Darling we really must do lunch some time' (the requisite tinge of irony in our voices, obviously) and she's looked at her diary and of course it's absolutely chocka, but she can fit me in on a Tuesday about three weeks ahead. What say I meet her at the Groucho, one o'clock? Sorted.

Now the night before this meeting, I'm round at Simone's place in Maida Vale, doing whatever it is couples do once they've been together for two or three years. Cooking? Watching TV? Smoking? Drinking?

'Wotcha got planned for tomorrow, then?' says Simone.

'Not a lot,' I say, my casual tone in polar opposition to the frenzied panic attack her question has suddenly induced. 'Got your Marlboro thing at Heaven, haven't we?'

Simone is a model, you see. Not a model model – I'm not that lucky – but a promo model: one of those nice-looking girls they get to stand next to cars and bare their teeth at motor shows, or march around in bright red jump suits at Grand Prix, or hand out free cigarettes, or free shots of vodka at sponsored parties. Simone is good at this. So we get lots of free stuff; we go to much cooler parties than I'm normally invited to as a journalist; and we spend a lot of time chilling on first names with the really-quite-famous. Which I like.

'Before that, I was wondering,' she says.

'Oh you know, this and that,' I say, strain beginning to

show. 'Some sort of crappo press launch at the National Gallery. New acquisition, I think, ever heard of Lucas Cranach the Elder? I haven't, then lunch with Mariella, then I've got that bloody book review to finish and I still haven't decided whether or not I like it because—'

'Mariella Frostrup?'

'Uh. Yeah.'

'You kept that one quiet.'

I can feel myself reddening, which is so unfair. Repeat after me: you have nothing to feel guilty about.

'We arranged it ages ago. I probably told you back then.'

When Simone's cross her eyes turn dark. Like she's possessed by the devil. It's happening now.

'No,' she spits.

'No what?'

'No, you definitely did not tell me you were having lunch with Mariella Frostrup. I wouldn't forget something like that.'

'God, the way you put it, you'd think we'd booked into a hotel for the afternoon.'

'Maybe you have.'

'For fuck's sake, you've met her yourself. She's not like that. Anyway, she's got a boyfriend.'

'Bet that's never stopped her.'

'Jesus, you can be so vindictive. This is one of my friends you're talking about.'

'Oh right, so you're taking her side against mine?'

'You are pathetic, you know that? Completely fucking pathetic.'

I pour myself another drink, pointedly not doing the same for Simone, and roll a fag. I roll it methodically, with a wholly deceptive air of calm, while I try to think of a way of crushing Simone utterly. The ideal would be to do nothing. She hates it more than anything when I go cold and silent. Problem is, my brain's so clouded with fury, I'm not sure that I can.

'If this is what happens when I tell the truth, maybe I shouldn't bother next time,' I say.

'You weren't going to bother this time.'

'What bollocks. You asked and I told you.'

'And if I hadn't asked? You never would have then.'

'Oh, and I wonder why that could be? Surely nothing to do with the fact that you're so pathetically insecure and paranoid you have to turn a casual lunch with a friend into a full-blown fucking affair.'

'So you did lie to me.'

'Jesus, what is this? When?'

'You said you'd told me ages ago about this lunch. Now you admit you didn't because you were scared.'

This is the bit I hate in arguments: when someone quotes at you something you said and you have to remember instantly whether it was what you actually said or just what they say you said. Girls are really good at this trick.

'What I said was that I *thought* I'd told you,' I say.

'Funny that. You being scared to tell me about a casual lunch. Because if it was as casual as you said, what would you have to worry about?'

'I give up. I fucking give up.'

'Because you know what I'm saying is true.'

'Because you, Simone, are like the fucking Spanish Inquisition. There's only one answer you want: "Guilty". And you're not going to stop until you get it.'

The argument goes on in this stupid, pointless vein for most of the evening – pausing briefly for a pizza break; then for a slightly longer one when we decide to make it up by having sex. Unfortunately, I'm still so distracted by the unfairness of it all, so revolted by Simone's hot desperation to have all her anger fucked out of her, so pissed off at the transparency of her motives in starting this argument, that I can't get it up.

At which point, it all gets much worse. My failure to get an erection gives Simone cast-iron proof – well, limp-jelly proof – that I don't fancy her any more and that all I can think about is tomorrow's lunch when I am unquestionably going to end up having wild sex with Mariella Frostrup.

'If that's how you feel, fine,' says Simone. 'Fuck off home and have a wank, why don't you?'

'Thanks, Simone. Sympathetic as ever.'

'Sorry? Excuse me? *I'm* supposed to be *sympathetic* to someone who no longer finds me attractive enough to fuck?'

'For a girl who has slept with *so many* men—'

'Fuck you too!'

'—You've got a pretty poor understanding of male psychology. We can fuck a girl who looks like the back end of the bus and still keep an erection—'

'So that's how you've been managing with me. Great.'

'Simone, you do not look like the back end of a bus. Not remotely. In fact you're definitely one of the most fuckable girls I've ever fucked.'

'Thanks.'

'I mean it.'

'Just not as fuckable as Mariella.'

'Did I say that?'

'You didn't need to.'

'Jesus, if you're going to use even my compliments against me—'

'One of the most fuckable girls I've ever fucked? Move over, William Shakespeare.'

'It was still a compliment.'

'Prove it.'

'You know I can't. Not at this moment.'

'Yeah and I know why you can't.'

'Do you know what really pisses me off about this? What pisses me off most of all about this pointless, fucking, wasted evening? I don't even fancy Mariella.'

She shakes her head and assumes a stagey more-in-sorrow than anger expression.

'You don't fancy Mariella?'

'No.'

'Sweetie—' she's using the term of endearment in its loosest sense. 'Sweetie,' she says sweetly. 'You've spouted an awful lot of bollocks this evening. But that line takes the biscuit.'

'I do not fancy Mariella Frostrup,' I repeat.

She scans the bedroom for an imaginary audience and rolls her eyes.

'I DO NOT FUCKING WELL FANCY MARIELLA FUCKING FROSTRUP,' I lie.

At the end of the session where I tell Cass my therapist this sorry tale, she gives me a typed leaflet about what does and does not constitute acceptable behaviour in adult relationships. I've thrown it away, so I can't quote it verbatim, but I seem to remember it says stuff like: 'I DO have the right to have my feelings heard and understood; I DO NOT have the right to impose those feelings on others without their consent.' Or perhaps not. It may be that there are some psychotherapists reading this going: 'We'd never come up with guff like that! He has missed the point completely! What a wanker! We hate him!' Whatever, the point is that once I've read this list – weeks after Cass has given it to me, and extremely reluctantly because I don't like having to do this at all, it feels like homework – I realize that in her non-judgemental psycho-therapist's way, Cass is trying to tell me something. Namely: get real, you spineless, pussy-whipped wimp. This woman is walking all over you. Stand up to her or get rid of her.

Clearly, though, the first option is an impossibility. When you've been going out with someone for two or three years, and have established all the ground rules for your relationship, you can't suddenly turn round and say: 'Sorry. Just realized you're a selfish, domineering bitch. From now on you've got to completely change your personality so that I can get on with doing what the hell I like.' I mean, come on. You've seen what Simone's like. Would you tell her? You might just as well end the relationship then and there.

Which, of course, is just as great an impossibility as the first option. Sure Simone has her faults. But if she were that bad, I wouldn't have been going out with her for so long, would I? She's my first proper relationship and there must be a reason for that. She might even be The One. Fortunately I have worked out an ingenious third option.

*

From now on, in our sessions, I won't mention Simone at all. I'll talk about my other problems instead. The main one, of course, being:

'—the bloody newsdesk again. I just don't think they take me seriously enough.'

'Why do you think that is?'

'Well, it's obvious, isn't it. Because I went to Oxford, because I didn't do time on a local newspaper. Because I'm a specialist not a straight reporter. It's like that, you know. It's class war. The features side gets the officers, and the news side the NCOs and the privates. And it's just so annoying. You know the reason they're picking on you has nothing to do with how good you are.'

'Are you good?'

'Given the right subject. Like the other day, I had this nice soft piece to do on Dirk Bogarde. I just basically had to talk to him for an hour and pick out the most interesting quotes. And it was great – we got on; it made a good read.'

'But you're not always given the right subject?'

'No. Not at all most of the time. It's mainly routine diary stuff – like, being lied to at Royal Opera House press conferences; writing up PSI surveys. And I'm not going to tell you what a PSI survey is because you'll fall asleep.'

'Would it be fair to say that your attitude to the work you have to do is often – contemptuous?'

'Yeah. Yes it would.'

'And is that feeling something you ever convey to the newsdesk?'

I grin. 'A bit maybe. Sometimes.'

I've a nasty suspicion she's giving me a significant look.

'Look, I know what you're thinking, but you've got to understand: journalism's different. It's what we're all like. Everyone goes round acting pissed off and cynical. I mean deep down everyone hates their job. It's just that we're more open and honest about it.'

'I don't hate my job.'

'I'm not saying there aren't exceptions.'

'Maybe there are more than you think.'

'Maybe.'

'Wouldn't you like to become one of them?'

I curl my lip. I'm sure there's some sort of trick here.

'Well, yeah. Obviously.'

'Then maybe that's something we could work on.'

Oh, God. It's that sodding 'w' word again. It's one of the things, I'm starting to realize, that I can't stand about therapy. I mean, when you're forking out £50 a session, surely it's them that should be doing the work, not you. For that kind of money they should be giving you the answers; sorting you out; striding into your life and dealing with all your problems personally – having a word with your girlfriend about her jealousy issues, suggesting to your bosses that they give you a bit of leeway, thinking up witty put downs when someone annoys you, paying your parking fines, dealing with your taxes, flossing your teeth, cleaning dog poo off your shoes.

And what is it you get instead? Meaningful silences. Rhetorical questions. Thoughtful looks. An hour's worth of shelter, heating and bottom space in a comfy chair. And an all-you-can-use supply of tissues – which, damn it, I've never even taken advantage of.

As for the homework bit, it's so horrible that really, they should be paying you. Which is what I fully intend to tell Cass on our next session.

'So,' she says, smiling.

'So.'

'How have you been getting on?' she says.

'All right.'

She looks at me expectantly.

'If you're asking whether those exercises have worked, I suppose the answer would have to be yes.'

There are two main exercises Cass has given me. One is to view each newsroom assignment not as a chore but as a golden stepping stone on the shining path to all my worldly dreams. The other is to bite my tongue every time I'm about to say something bitchy or cynical, and try to think of something positive instead.

'That's good. Isn't it?' says Cass.

'Uh, yeah. Probably,' I reply with a rancid grin.

I'm thinking of this piece I did a few days ago that the news desk were pleased with. Basically, I had to go to the house where they filmed the new Merchant/Ivory adaptation *Howards End* and talk to the owner about what it's like living with a film crew and what the stars got up to and stuff. And the pictures worked out well and the owner came up with some decent enough anecdotes and I produced a good piece of colour writing because, as per Cass's instructions, I'd put a lot of effort into it and because I had already read most of Forster, even his gay short stories. So it ended up getting a jolly good picture spread at the top of page three, was complimented in morning conference and got me a pat on the back from the news editor.

All of which should have made me very happy. But it didn't. I thought: 'For fuck's sake, I studied Forster at Oxford and I've spent five years now honing my writing style and to what use am I putting all this knowledge, skill and energy? Why, writing up thinly disguised puff pieces about tedious costume dramas for the chattering classes to spill marmalade on today, pour shitty old cat litter on tomorrow. I'm not a writer. I'm not even a proper journalist. I'm just a professional turd polisher.'

So that's what I'm thinking about, but I'm not going to mention it to Cass. It would only lead to more bloody home-work about working out what it is I really want to do and then going out and doing it, which would involve way, way too much hassle, I'm much better where I am.

'You don't sound very sure,' Cass says.

And I say: 'We–ll—'

This be-sweet-and-nice-to-everyone business, that's the other thing that has been bugging me. Like, normally when I come into the office, I deal with the fact that it's the start of another working day and that I'm feeling insecure and paranoid by teasing my colleagues. Maybe I'll moo gently at the agriculture correspondent or compliment the mad science editor on a spectacularly bad choice of tie or disingenuously ask the really-quite-tasty media correspondent whether she's yet seen the compromising story about her in *Private Eye*. They have come to expect this of me, just as the deputy news editor has grown used to being called a cunt. In fact the first day I don't call him a cunt, he looks a bit hurt and says: 'Something the matter, cunt?' To which I reply: 'Just trying to be nice, for a change.' To which he replies: 'Stick to being a cunt, I should. Suits you much better.'

Cass's theory on this is that if I try harder to be polite to people, they'll try harder to be polite to me with the result that I'll have less to feel paranoid about. This may be true. The downside is that I find I no longer have anything to say to anyone, except platitudes. I've been turned into this Reasonable Other Person.

'I feel like all the rough edges that make me most me are being shaved off and all that's being left is this smooth, bland, characterless thing,' I say.

'That's interesting, your use of the passive. You say your rough edges are being shaved off. But aren't you doing these things because you want to do them?'

'I just don't want to end up as this person I'm not.'

'Do you want to feel better?'

'Depends what "better" involves.'

'Let me put it another way.' She flicks back through the

folder on her lap. 'When you first came to me, you said you were "very unhappy"; that you "wondered what the point of it all" was; that you felt unappreciated at work; that it was as if, "you had had your soul stolen" by – I can't read this word—'

'Mr Migarette. The man on the end of my cigarette.'

'Now do you think those are the words of someone who is happy the way they are?'

'Maybe happiness isn't all it's cracked up to be.'

'Is that what you believe?'

'A bit. Yeah. Maybe unhappiness is the spur you need to get on and do better things. You know, like, if you're living in a hovel on bread and cheese and you're radiantly happy, you're hardly going to end up with your mansion and your foie gras, are you?'

'It's an argument I'm familiar with.'

'And there's my literary career to think of too. I think you write a lot better books if you're pissed off with the world than if you're floating around on some fluffy, happy cloud. Look at any half way decent author: they're all drunks, depressives or druggies.'

'Many of my clients work in creative fields. It's a concern they sometimes express.'

'So what do you tell them?'

'That far from increasing creativity, suffering stifles it. It saps the energy which would be better spent on the creative process.'

'And do they believe you?'

Cass laughs. 'Not all of them, no.'

'You know what I think, Cass? I reckon the real problem here isn't me, it's the rest of the world.'

Cass smiles uncertainly.

'Yeah, I know it sounds arrogant. But, like, how is it my fault that the girl I'm going out with happens to have been born with domineering-bitch genes; how is it my fault that the people at work don't appreciate me? Is it really my attitude that's the problem? Or is it, maybe, that they're a bunch of losers who wouldn't know what talent was if it bit them on the arse? So what I'm thinking is that maybe it would be a mistake to change my personality because actually I'm OK. Maybe what I should be doing is waiting for fate, divine justice, whatever, to come along and give me my lucky break. I mean you do agree with me don't you. I do deserve a lucky break?'

'That's very interesting, Josh and it's something I'd love to talk about more. Would you like to book another appointment now?'

'I would, except my diary's at work. Is it OK if I ring you from there?'

'Of course.'

Which are the very last words we exchange.

Stuck with an axe

Our last night on the road is at a beachside resort called Ensenada. The hotel is much swankier than the Motel 6s we usually stay in because being as it's Mexico, even pretend Mexico like the Baja, you get more for less money. So instead of a staircase off a car park into a dingy, spartan room, you get a tiered central courtyard with palm trees and a swimming pool which I'd like to try but can't, because, quite ridiculously for Mexico, the weather isn't warm enough, and a pastelly bedroom almost big enough to be a suite and large beds and a decent-sized TV. If we were a couple, we'd celebrate by having sex. Being as we're not, we just watch lots of TV. We picked a good night. Besides particularly excellent episodes of *Get A Life* (the one where he makes a throne for his TV idol) and *Married With Children* (where Al sweats in the shape of Elvis on his T-shirt), there's some juicy news action from LA where there has been quite a bit of violence following the Rodney King verdict.

Jackson's more interested in the story than I am because it's on his home turf and in his wussie way he has got this idea that it's going to spread as far south as Laguna Beach, which is just soooo likely. Me, I resent the idea of wasting valuable trash-TV-watching time on this tedious non-event that everyone was expecting anyway, because a video of white policemen beating an unarmed black man half to death was hardly going to end in a communal outbreak of peace and love, was it?

Still, I'm keeping my fingers crossed. If, by some delightful stroke of luck, these scuffles manage to turn themselves into a full-scale riot then maybe they'll have to close the airport and I'll be forced to spend another week chilling in Laguna Beach.

Next morning I wake to find things have got much better. Gas stations have been torched, stores looted, people hurt. Jackson and I are particularly appalled by the footage of a burly truck driver being thrashed to a pulp by the frenzied mob. We keep flicking from channel to channel, hoping to catch it again. When we have breakfast, we make sure it's in a restaurant with a TV.

The rioting in LA is now officially an emergency. The National Guard has been called out; downtown Los Angeles is a war zone; in Koreatown, they're piling up sandbags and oiling their Armalites for the next wave; South Central is like something out of *Mad Max II* – or so it seems from the cameras on the helicopters, because obviously no reporter is stupid enough to go down there; there has been looting in Hollywood, violence in Long Beach.

'But it's nowhere near us, right?' I ask Jackson, as we drive north.

'Long Beach? It's just up the coast.'

'Gosh. Do you think we'll be able to get to the airport?'

'I don't know, Josh,' snaps Jackson, like some worried parent who doesn't mean to sound cross, but hey, if their kid had any idea how serious this was he wouldn't be asking these damn-fool questions.

How terrible. It seems that I shall be forced to spend a few more days in Laguna Beach, drinking iced *latte*, not working, muttering prayers of gratitude to whichever genius it was that made that Rodney King video. It's like those wondrous childhood moments when there's been some terrible disease outbreak and term has to start late. Or when your flight has been delayed and you get to spend an extra day abroad being put up in a ritzy hotel at the airline's expense and your parents look really pissed off but not you, you think this is brilliant.

The only bit I'm not looking forward to is ringing up the newsdesk to say I'm going to be back late. Knowing them, they'll be all resentful and pernickety and insist that I knock the extra time off my holiday allowance. Or maybe force me to find some tendentious Hollywood showbiz story to write – like I'm really going to be able to get hold of anyone when the whole city's under siege. Or—

Nah. Don't even think about it.

The problem with horrible thoughts is that, once thought, they're not easily unthunk.

So while my brain's busy going laa-laa-de-dee-dee-dee, you're on holiday in America and everything's OK, hum ti hum ti hum lalalaaa sunsets palm beaches blue skies blow jobs from beautiful strangers fuck fuck fuckety fuck – the knot in the pit of my stomach and the tightness in my throat are both saying: 'Don't for a moment think that we didn't hear what you just thought.'

I glance at Jackson. He's doing exactly the same thing he was before I thought the thought, listening to the radio, sucking his coffee through a straw, looking idly at the freeway ahead of us, the US Marine bases, the trucks, the cars, the twos and threes of raggedy wetbacks heading north. Bastard! Ever since I had that horrible thought, my whole world has collapsed about me. But, like a sleeping child untroubled by dreams because he has yet to learn how shit the world is, Jackson doesn't know and doesn't care.

He has noticed that I'm looking at him. He thinks I'm about to lower the tone with something rude and disgusting so we can pass the time by talking filth. He smiles lasciviously.

'I've had a horrible thought,' I say, very serious.

'A long, slow, wet gum-job from a hideous toothless crone?' he suggests.

'About work. You don't reckon they'd want me to cover this story, do you?'

'You're their showbusiness writer.'

'Arts correspondent.'

'So covering riots is not in your job description.'

We drive on in silence. The knot in my stomach has not gone. My thoughts are racing.

Then I say: 'But what if I want to cover them?'

He snorts, as if it's not an issue even worth debating.

'Well, what if I do?' I say.

'Josh, do you have any idea what these people are like? They have guns. They're in gangs. They kill each other for fun. Do you think they're going to care if some pussy white English boy gets in the way?'

The annoying thing is, he might be right. Suppose, for a moment, I did end up covering these riots and I got killed. Or worse still, maimed. Imagine having to spend the rest of your life hobbling on stumps or typing one-handed or blinded or brain damaged or – Jesus – castrated with machetes by a blood-maddened mob, and people forever politely pretending not to notice until eventually you'd have to say: 'Yeah, it happened during the LA Riots.' 'You were a foreign correspondent?' they'd go, impressed. 'Not quite,' you'd go, explaining how it all happened. And they'd go: 'What? You mean you didn't have to do it?' And you'd go: 'No.' And they'd go: 'Then why the hell did you?' And you'd go: 'Do you think that's a question I haven't been asking myself every single damned day of my life?'

But on the other hand: what if I'm not killed or maimed?

For a few delicious moments, my thoughts drift into an alternative future. I see my thrilling despatches from the heart of the LA riots, accompanied by a massive picture byline, on the front page, no, on successive front pages of the *Daily Telegraph*. In fact on the front pages of all the newspapers because my stories are so good that they've been syndicated. I see my family weeping with pride and thrusting the papers under the noses of everyone they know, saying: 'See? That's our Josh, that is.' And everyone they know going 'Yes. We'd already noticed. You must be so proud!' I see all the girls who never slept with me wondering if it's not too late; I see my rivals gnashing their teeth, my enemies inconsolable; I see my old friends congratulating themselves on their good fortune in having known me before I was famous and my newer ones worrying (unnecessarily, of course, for I shall be magnanimous in victory) whether I will still consider them worthy of my attention; I see my colleagues' jealousy turning to grudging admiration; I hear the newsdesk saying: 'He's a dark horse, that one'; I hear the editor going: 'Time we gave this man a decent job' and the foreign editor going: 'How about New York?'; I hear the proprietor going: 'I don't care how much it costs. It's imperative that we keep this man'; I hear people in the streets going: 'Blimey, is that who I think it is?'; I hear the BBC going: 'Fancy presenting *Newsnight* for a few weeks?'; I hear ITV going: 'Come and work for us, we'll pay you twice as much'; I hear literary agents going: 'A young man of your genius really should be writing a book' and anxious publishers going: 'We'll never get him for less than seven figures'; I hear Jackson going – ' . . . this stretch.'

I say: 'What?'

He says: 'Watch your speed. There's a lot of cops along this stretch.'

*

On Jackson's answerphone when we get in are six messages. Half of them are for me.

The first is an unconcerned drawl. 'Hello, we've been given this number for Josh Devereux. If he's there could you please ask him if he'd mind calling the office. Thank you. Goodbye.'

The second is shriller and a little more clipped: 'This is a message for Josh Devereux. Please could he ring the *Daily Telegraph* foreign desk as soon as possible. Thank you.'

The third is a *molto agitato*, banshee shriek: 'CanJosh-Devereuxringthe*dailytelegraph*foreigndesknow.'

Jackson looks at me

I look back at Jackson.

'Fuck.'

*

Before I make the phone call I step on to the roof terrace for a fag. Afterwards, I have two more. The first and second are to calm my agitation over the terrifying thing I've just been asked to do by the foreign desk. The third, which I really don't need because I'm already buzzing, is a kind of 'fuck you' gesture to the world. 'Lung cancer schmlung cancer. This time tomorrow I could be dead.'

And as you do in these situations, I suddenly start noticing how special and lovely everything is, like the cancer-racked Dennis Potter did with his blossomest blossoms. Below me, through the velvety evening light, the pallid curve of the beach and the dark sea beyond. Behind me, glow the lights of a thousand pastel-coloured villas, with lush, jungly gardens and walls purple with bougainvillea. Directly beneath, is the main strip with its air-conditioned galleries selling crummy New Age art, its elegantly crappy souvenir shops and its bookstores, its open-fronted restaurants where mincing blond waiters with capped teeth serve seared tuna on frisée to young white professionals on rollerblades. It's a warm, clear night. The first stars are beginning to show. Jacaranda scent hangs in the air. Only an hour ago this place was Blandsville USA. Suddenly, it's paradise, California like it is on the postcards and in movies but never in real life, and I want to stay here for ever. With Jackson.

That's another thing. I mean I'm not saying that Jackson isn't a mate. But we have been on the road for two weeks and he does have some very annoying habits and I have been quite looking forward to fucking off home and not seeing him for at least another lifetime. Yet now that I'm on the verge of being dragged away from him towards possible death, he's suddenly become like family. I want to cling on to him so that he can hold me tight and say: 'Don't worry, darling. I won't let them get you. You're safe with me.'

Another part of me, though, feels strangely distant. Like he belongs to a world – fun, leisure, holidays, decadence, frivolity – which I must now renounce.

Everything we do in our last hours together has acquired an unbearable poignancy: the glass of the special Oregon pinot noir Jackson has been saving for our final night (I would drink more but I need to be sober for tomorrow); my condemned man's dinner (a joyless pizza); a listless TV session flicking between comedy (*Are You Being Served?*) and the news channels, so I'm up with latest developments (it's getting worse).

Then it's an early night.

*

The doorbell rings at 4 a.m. and I've had no sleep. Now Jackson's poking his head round the door to say goodbye and I'm giving him a tight hug and a brave smile and then that's it, I'm gone.

My cab driver seems to have learned his lines from some terrible movie.

'You want to go to downtown LA?' he says.

'Yes, please,' I say, a touch worried. Didn't his controller tell him where he was going?

'You're some crazy motherfucker. But that's cool. I'm a crazy motherfucker too. It's why they gave me this job.'

Our journey does not quite live up to our expectations. The freeways are virtually empty. There are no police road blocks. No groups of looters. Not even any burned-out cars. If it weren't for the broken glass and boarded-up windows which become more prevalent the deeper we head into town, you'd scarcely guess there was anything amiss.

I gather later that this is the weird thing about civil disorder. One minute, you can cross a particular street with impunity. The next, you get yourself killed – as nearly happened to a Japanese tourist, badly beaten up just a few hours ago outside the boarded-up but otherwise very safe-looking hotel I'm about to enter.

My cab driver gets a decent tip and a firm shake of the hand.

'Good luck,' he says.

'Thanks.'

The weird thing about this hotel I've been booked into – one of those tall, bland, corporate jobs that you'd never stay in unless your company was paying – is that all the staff are acting like everything is normal. I don't know whether they've been ordered to act this way, or whether it's the ice in the veins of corporate America or whether it's just because it's 5 a.m. and no one's feeling particularly demonstrative. But you would have thought, what with all the ground-floor windows being boarded up and armed security guards on the door and that Japanese tourist and this being pretty close to the epicentre of some of the worst riots in US history, that the mask would crack just slightly.

Take the receptionist. I'd like to very much because, despite or maybe because of her severe, sexless hotel receptionist's power suit, she looks quite ravishingly sexy. She's a trainee, I suppose, which would explain why she has been given the dog shift. The thing that most distracts me about her is her blouse, it's a silken cream and either because the material's too thin or because she has left one button too many undone, you can detect a hint of white bra which – and I really don't know why, unless maybe it's the subdued hysteria in the air, or a case of *morituri salutant* – strikes me as erotic beyond measure.

But it's not as if she's giving off sex vibes, far from it, she's terribly proper about everything, taking my passport and calling me sir and let me just check your reservation.

She gives me the room key, an electronic card-shaped thing. Tells me that at the moment the hotel is offering a fifteen per cent discount. But she doesn't mention why, or ask me what it's like outside or whether I've heard any more news or what the hell are you doing here, you crazy wonderful guy? She just thanks me for choosing whatever hotel it is I haven't of course chosen – and I almost tell her at this point, I almost say, well actually it was chosen by one of the secretaries at the *Daily Telegraph* and she only did because you're close to Riot Central, because I'm a reporter see, I've got to go in there, right now, and risk my life and would you like to wish me luck, I'd feel better if you did, better still if after work you and I had a drink and – and that's it. That is bloody it.

*

'Welcome to the foreign desk,' says a gruff, Australian voice on the other side of the Atlantic. It belongs to the foreign editor, Sidney Blade. His temper is legendary; he does not suffer fools; I'm far more scared of him than of anything he might ask me to do.

What he wants me to do is go to Hollywood Boulevard, have a sniff round, find out what's happening, speak to a few people, then file my story by 11 a.m. LA time. Any later and I needn't bother. The first edition will have gone to bed.

There are so many things I'd love to ask him, from trivial, procedural ones like 'Should I keep the same taxi waiting for me or will I be able to hail another one in the street?' and 'What's the best thing to say if I come across some rioters, is it a good thing or a bad thing admitting I'm a journalist?' to great, imponderables, like 'Um, how safe is this, actually?' But I can't because I don't think the foreign editor wants to be reminded that I'm an unserious twenty-six-year-old who has never done this sort of thing before and besides, it's already 5.30 a.m. and time is slipping by.

*

Deadlines. In features journalism, commissioning editors are giving you deadlines all the time, but they're only pretend.

Even in news journalism, it's not often you come across a story so late-breaking and important that you find yourself writing it right up to deadline.

Now that I'm on one of those stories, though, I begin to realize what those hardened old scribes are on about, the ones who say that you can be the world's greatest prose stylist but if you can't write to length and on time then you'll never be a good journalist.

So it's with growing panic that, towards 6 a.m., I hit Hollywood Boulevard. Like a grunt from a chopper into a battle zone: disorientation, fear and an urgent instinct to do something very quickly, though what I'm not quite sure.

My second biggest fear is that something might happen. My biggest fear is that something bad might *not* happen, because then I won't have anything to write about.

And it looks like my biggest fear has come true. OK so there's a bit of smoke and a cinder-y smell in the air and you can see the occasional burnt-out building, but that's – what? – one atmospheric paragraph. Then what? Where's the story? Who are you going to quote? I mean for, fuck's sake, there's nothing happening and there's nobody around. Why should there be? Anyone with any sense is still in bed . . .

'Riots. What Riots?' writes Josh Devereux in Los Angeles.

Nope. Don't think the foreign desk will buy that one. If I don't find a story in the next hour I'll— Look, God. I'm prepared to strike a deal with you here. If you make sure I get a good story, you can let something bad happen to me in exchange. Not too bad, obviously. No knives. Nothing in the face or groin area. Nothing that involves any form of permanent damage or great pain. But if you can arrange for something simultaneously dramatic and harmless, then I think that would be a fair deal. A bullet through some fleshy part of the arm, say. Or the leg. Or even the head, providing it's only a crease, preferably somewhere where the scar will appear to fetching effect. Or—

Coffee shop! Open! With people inside. People with riot stories.

*

One coffee, one fag and several pages of scrawl later, I'm feeling much better. The ulcerous stomach pangs have subsided and I've at least enough material to spare myself from total ignominy. What I need, though, ideally, is something with a bit more oomph. The quotes I've got so far are just basic vox pop stuff on the lines of 'Gee I was so scared last night, all the noise in the street outside' and 'You wanna know why I'm working in this café in the middle of the riots? Funny. I wanna know the same thing.' None of them carries the story any further. None of them is going to get me on to the front page.

But what did I expect? It's only in books that the young novice journalist stumbles across the tanks hidden under the trees at the Czech border. In real life, he carries on walking a bit further down Hollywood Boulevard, realizes that those miserable quotes are all he's going to get, and that – Christ, is that the time? – he'd better be getting back to the hotel to write this all up.

On the other hand, the streets are starting to look fuller now. There's even a sign of impending action – a long row of cops in full riot gear, their backs to the shop frontages, facing grimly out towards the street, like a scene from *Judge Dredd* (the comic version rather than the crap Sylvester Stallone movie). Perhaps I should stay a bit longer. See if anyone will speak to me.

'Hello. Excuse me,' I say to one of the cops.

He looks sightlessly ahead, like a guardsman at Buckingham Palace.

I move further down the line.

'Excuse me, I'm from London, from the *Daily Telegraph* newspaper. I wonder, could I ask you a few questions?'

'You'll have to speak to the captain,' says the riot cop, jerking his head towards the end of the line.

I'll try just one more and if this doesn't work, fuck it, I'm off.

'Excuse me, but can you tell me what you're doing here?'

'Sure I can. We've been told that this is the place they're going to hit next,' says the cop.

'Who?'

'The rioters.'

'What? Here? Really?'

'Yes.'

'Wow! Cool!'

Once I've left him I realize just how crap I've been. I've got an unnamed, ageless cop somewhere in Hollywood Boulevard saying: 'This is the place that they're going to hit next'. Great.

Now, it's definitely taxi-hailing time because if I don't get back now I'm going to miss— Hang on. What's that? A fire engine? Police cars? Cameras? Microphones?

I cross the street and eavesdrop on the conversation. We're outside this store called Frederick's which I gather by hissing questions to my fellow eavesdroppers is quite a famous lingerie store that I should have heard of. The windows have been smashed. Looting has occurred. The manager is telling the news crew what has happened. Many valuable things have been stolen, including important items from the store's museum. Among them is Madonna's bustier.

Hallelujah! Hallelujah! All around the city of Los Angeles, there have been beatings, lootings, burnings and killings. But if I know my readership and my editors, none of this can even begin to compete with the biggest story of the hour. Madonna's bustier. Stolen. In the LA Riots.

Having ascertained from the store's manager that I heard him aright and that the bustier in question is that legendary pointy-breasted version designed by Jean Paul Gaultier, I trip off gaily in the direction of my hotel, almost not caring whether I get a cab, because in this state I could fly.

I double back past the line of riot cops towards the café I visited earlier, thinking maybe I can call a cab from there. I've wandered several blocks away from the cops, and the streets have started to look very empty again – not in a threatening way, just looking like a normal, broad LA boulevard with no one on it – when I look up and see these five kids ahea of me, in their teens or early twenties I'd guess. Two black guys. Three Latinos. Dressed in the usual, LA young person's kit. Baggy trousers, Raiders caps, baseball shirts, etc.

Oh good, I haven't got any young-people quotes. These guys will do nicely.

*

'Hi.'

'Hi,' they say back. Swaggeringly chilled. Banding round me.

'Um, you couldn't do me a favour, could you? I'm a journalist from England and I'm here to write about the riots and stuff. And I was wondering whether I could ask you some questions?'

They are quite taken with the idea and there's a bit of

jostling for precedence, the younger ones slipping back defer-
entially, the older ones competing to give the first quote.

'So, I'd better get your names and ages.'

They give me their names and ages.

'Great. Thanks. And er, can I ask what you're doing here?'

They look at one another, suddenly a touch shifty.

'I mean aren't you a bit scared to be out on the streets at
the moment?'

'Oh, we ain't scared,' says the burliest Latino. 'We're here
to get ourselves some of these.' He gestures towards the shop
behind him. It's a shoe store.

'You mean—' I think I know exactly what they mean,
'—you're waiting for it to open?'

There is much laughter all round.

'We waitin' for the brothers to arrive,' says one of them.

'Then we gonna open it ourselves,' explains their
spokesman.

'Yeah, so if there's anything you want, just you let us
know,' says another.

'That's terribly kind of you. But I'm not really into training
shoes. In England we wear these things called DMs. Doc
Martens,' I say.

'Sure we got Doc Martens. Look.'

I look in the window. Indeed there are several pairs of
DMs, coloured ones and all.

'Even so, I've got to get back to my hotel so I can write
my story.'

'You're gonna write about us?'

'Yes. I should think so,' I say.

'You tell them you met the Four-tray Crips.'

'Four-tray?' I say.

'Yo. Four-tray.' The big Latino motions for me to give him my pen. When I do, he writes down '43 Crips' in my notebook.

'Ah. Forty-three.'

'We say it, four-tray.'

'Cool,' I say.

'So you gonna put us in your newspaper?'

'Oh, definitely,' I say, trying not to show him just how thrilled I am.

I really need to go. But I make a point of lingering casually and asking a few more questions.

'Well,' I say eventually. 'It's been nice meeting you guys.'

'You too, bro,' says their leader.

'Now you take care of yourself,' says another.

'Yeah, you be careful,' chips in a third Crip. 'Last night, there was a guy here just like you, asking questions. He got himself stuck with an axe.'

As he says it I feel a tingle go right down my spine.

What a fucking *brilliant* quote!

*

By the time I get back to my hotel, I have no more than fifty minutes left in which to write and file a 1000-word story. Correction, forty-five minutes. I wasted five minutes ringing the foreign desk to find out how many words they wanted and whether there really wasn't any way they could extend my deadline. (No.)

If you're not a journalist, you probably won't have much idea how desperate this situation is. So let me tell you that forty-five minutes is normally the time you allocate for just dreaming up your opening paragraph, prior to scrubbing it in disgust and spending another forty-five minutes thinking up a replacement, before realizing, actually, no, the first one was better.

As for the 1000 words bit, usually you'd allow a whole day for that. Half a day minimum. Forty-five minutes? Not in your worst nightmare. And, of course, it's not even forty-five minutes we're talking about here. It's more like twenty minutes because you're going to need at least another twenty-five – this being 1992, remember, before the wide-spread use of modems – just to dictate it all over the phone to the copy-taker back in London.

So I roll up a fag (another minute gone); call up room service for a coffee (another minute gone); drum my fingers on the table, thinking, 'This is awful, this is awful, I'll never do it, I'll never do it' (another minute gone); start panicking that I'm panicking, that my brain has seized and that Jesus, have I really just wasted four whole minutes? (another minute gone); answer the door, tell the busboy where to put my coffee, fish in my pocket for a tip, pour out the coffee, wish I hadn't ordered it now because it has wasted so much time (another minute and a half gone); realize that much as I'd love to I can't piss about any longer, this is serious, I've got to get my intro sorted: something arresting, something atmospheric, some clever connection between Hollywood and the riots. Any famous riot movies? No. How about *Towering Inferno*, then? No, too contrived. Some filmic metaphor, then, yeah, could be good, something to do with the way that the smoke makes Hollywood look as if it has been shot in soft focus, yeah, that'll do, don't dither, whack it down, you've just gone and used up another two minutes.

By the end of my third painstakingly constructed para-graph, it occurs to me that this writing-down is a luxury I can't afford. I'm just going to have to do something I've never done before, something which many journalists never have to do in their whole careers, i.e., dictate the story from the top of my head. My final five minutes' writing time goes in rifling through my notebook for the best quotes, deciphering the bits that aren't legible and drawing little arrows and numbers all over the place so that I can read it all out in the right order.

Then, having rolled another cigarette and drained and refilled my coffee, I dial the freephone number to the *Daily Telegraph* switchboard.

It's answered not by one of the familiar female receptionists because they've all gone home, but by someone male and stilted – night security, perhaps.

When he transfers me to the copy-takers, the phone rings and rings and rings and I start to panic, thinking, 'What if there's nobody there?' and, worse still, 'What if there is someone there but they're busy taking copy from one of those lonely and pathetic old stringers that like to phone in of an evening because they're lonely and pathetic? And what if that bastard stringer's decision to phone the copy-takers just before me is all that stops my story getting in the paper? And what if the foreign editor doesn't realize this? What if he just thinks I'm a crap reporter? What—'

The phone is picked up.

The person I'm hoping will answer is Vera. At least I think her name's Vera, though we never really know the copy-takers by name, only by their voices. Vera has a weathered, warm, mumsy voice that makes you feel strangely reassured, as if the stuff you're dictating to her isn't total garbage, as if – and occasionally she'll egg you on with approving murmurs and clucking noises – she might actually be interested in what you've written. Pathetically, this matters. Reading out your own articles, especially at halting, hyper-enunciated, punctu-ation-inclusive dictation pace, can make you feel terribly awkward. Without your copy-taker's appreciative grunts your fragile ego might collapse completely.

Like most copy-takers, Vera is far too intelligent for a job which entails sitting at a desk for eight hours transcribing the drivel dictated to you by journalists. She's quick on the uptake; you never need to waste time spelling out complicated words; and her guess of how you spell proper names of which you're mildly uncertain is invariably better than yours. If this were a Le Carré novel, she'd be the trusty secretary from the old days whose brain Smiley goes to pick over a genteel cuppa in a cat-infested house on his quest to unearth the mole.

The reason I most want it to be Vera is so I can dictate my copy all matter of fact until she goes: 'Bit off your patch, Los Angeles, isn't it, dearie?' and later 'Madonna's bustier, eh? What a turn up,' and later still 'Now, you're a naughty boy, that sounds very dangerous, you should be taking more care of yourself.'

But Vera doesn't answer the phone. Instead it's some male voice I've never heard before, someone who I can tell is not remotely impressed by my heroic coverage of the LA riots – I suppose because, being a late-night copy-taker, he's heard this sort of dramatic foreign despatch stuff too many times before. Or maybe he's just a miserable git. He's also a lot more pernickity than Vera: you can't miss out the occasional 'comma', 'open quotes' or 'point new par' and hope he'll do it for you. Even when it's obvious, he'll chip in with an 'Is this still in quotes?' or an 'Is this a new paragraph?' Even more annoyingly he's a bit of a smarty pants. When I mention 'Mann's Chinese Theatre – that's initial caps and Mann with two Ns' he says:

'Isn't it called Graumann's Chinese Theatre?'

'Is it?'

'I'm asking you.'

'Erm, well as far as I remember it's Manns and if it isn't, the subs can check it, can't they?'

'I'll put a query next to it.'

'Whatever.' I mean, for fuck's sake. I can almost see it already: the whole of the foreign desk gathered round the Atex screen, gasping at the beauty and immediacy of my prose, chuckling at the Madonna's bustier theft, shaking their heads in disbelieving awe over my encounter with a real gang and that juicy quote at the end. And then going: 'What a shame. If only it had arrived five minutes earlier, we could have run it.'

Approximately five hundred years later, I get to say my favourite copy dictation word 'Ends.' Then I ask to be transferred to the foreign desk.

'Hi, it's me, Josh Devereux,' I say, trying to sound matter-of-fact but not really succeeding. 'You should be getting my copy any minute.'

'Yes, thanks we've got it.'

And? AND?

'Oh,' I say. 'Any queries?'

In the background, I can hear a muffled voice asking whether there are any queries. The even more muffled reply says no, tell him he can have his breakfast.

'No. It's fine,' says the voice. 'You can go and have some breakfast.'

*

Afterwards the *Telegraph*'s New York bureau chief Ryder Flynn takes me out for a 'bit of fun' in his red open-topped Ford Mustang. My instinct is to say, 'No way, I've done my bit.

Don't you realize there's a riot on?' But Ryder is not the sort of person you say no to.

He looks like foreign correspondents ought to look: hair worn quite long in the manner of middle-aged groovers who've never quite got over the passing of the Seventies, semi-permanent tan, lupine grin exposing nicotine-blackened teeth, lean, wiry body forged by a continual diet of fags, coffee and adrenalin, general demeanour of a man who's shagged more birds and ingested more drugs than most of us would manage in several lifetimes. He talks in that gravelly, languid drawl that used to be called public school until public school started to mean fake London glottal stops. He has covered loads and loads of wars including Afghanistan, the Falklands and, most recently, that one in Liberia where drug-crazed factions dress in women's clothes and make-up, mutilate mothers, smash babies against trees, and devour the still-beating hearts of their enemies. To many young *Telegraph* hacks, me among them, he is God.

And to make things even cooler, it's the most perfect LA driving day ever. There's just no one around. You can drive as fast as you like because the cops are hardly going to stop you, they've got scarier things to worry about than speeding tourists. Tom Petty's 'Free Fallin'' on the stereo, wind in our hair, a cigarette holder clenched, Hunter S-style, beween Ryder's teeth. In no time at all we've reached Koreatown.

Koreatown looks just like it does on the news, only slightly less interesting. You can see the barricades and the sandbag emplacements outside the stores, but no serious weaponry like the M60 machine gun I saw a Korean shopkeeper with on TV.

'Seems to be quietening down,' says Ryder, with a touch of disappointment.

We drive on.

The general aim is to find somewhere open for lunch. But before we do, there's a spot of stuff Ryder needs to sort out, if I don't mind. He's got to file an overview story for tomorrow's paper, shouldn't take long, just thought we might head up and see this pastor, Rev Somebodyorother, should find his address in the glove compartment, church somewhere down in South Central.

Until he gets to the last bit of the sentence, I'm feeling quite relaxed. And still I carry on pretending to be relaxed but he must have noticed me twitch, or turn white with terror or something because he looks across at me, with one of his death's head grins and says: 'You can't say you've done the LA Riots till you've been to South Central.'

'Oh. Yeah. Right. No. Sure,' I say, like my mind was elsewhere. 'I was just thinking—'

What, of course, I was thinking was: FUCK! I'm trapped in a red open-topped convertible with a madman. He said he was taking me for lunch. But where he's actually taking me is South Central Los Angeles. Home of the Uzi and the drive-by. At what is undoubtedly the worst time to do so ever in the city's history. When merely to be seen wearing the wrong colours is considered a capital crime. Where actually to be caught in possession of a white face . . .

'—It's all very *Bonfire of the Vanities*, isn't it, this Reverend character, like thingy Jesse Jackson, Louis Farrakhan, what's his name, I forget, no forget it, let's go, let's go and talk to him, should be interesting,' I babble.

Phew. Now he'll definitely know I'm not scared.

Except that Ryder can't be totally fear-free either because as we draw closer to South Central he suddenly declares: 'Might be an idea to lower our profile.' He presses the button which automatically raises the car's roof. It clicks back into place with a satisfying 'thock'. For one sweet delusional milli-second I almost feel safe. A glance through the windshield reminds me why I'm not.

We're stuck in heavy, slow-moving traffic: three lanes, bumper to bumper, and we're in the middle one – boxed in by cars with sinister blacked-out windows and pick-ups full of muscular black dudes in sunglasses and sawn-off vests, jigging to hip hop pumped from ghetto blasters switched to distortion volume. Like most things in America, it looks like a scene from a movie – a gang movie, perhaps. A gang movie that makes *Assault on Precinct 13* look like *Lassie Come Home*. So I don't think I'm being unduly dramatic here when I find myself reflecting on just how easy it would be for them to whip out their machine pistols and turn our Mustang into a colander. Perhaps they're thinking the same thing.

I stare fixedly ahead, buttocks clenched, neck stiff, palms sweating. The important thing is not to catch any one's eye, which is hard when you're being looked at. They're staring at us, everyone's staring at us, you can feel it, like those laser sights which mark you with the evil red dot just before the bullet plumps home. We must be the only white people for miles. Unless you count the occasional ambulance, fire-engine, or cop-car crew, which I don't because no sooner have you been reassured by their presence alongside you than with a whoop of their siren, they carve through the traffic and vanish.

And the National Guard, I don't count them either. You see them in huddles, on the forecourts of burned-out gas stations, at the entrance of semi-looted supermarkets. They remind me of soldiers in the streets of Belfast, only less professional. 'Don't look to us for help,' their bewildered aimlessness seems to be saying. 'We don't know what we're doing here either.' Yeah, I know, *Southern Comfort*'s one of my favourite movies. Anyway, their guns, we later learn, are useless. Someone forgot to supply live ammo.

Ryder spots a gap in the left-hand lane. He pulls into it quickly, before we get boxed in again.

After a few more blocks, he turns into a side road and stops to study a map.

You'd think, with its reputation, South Central would be an urban hell-hole: boarded-up tenements, prowling pushers, piles of trash, burned-out cars. But it's not like that. The sideroads are wide and tranquil, with broad grass verges leading to attractive bungalow houses with shady verandahs where folk loll contentedly in rocking chairs, almost like in an old-fashioned scene from the Deep South. And being as it's California, the grass is well watered and green, the sky is blue and the sun is almost always shining. Most people would give their eye-teeth to live somewhere like this. Except—

Well, perhaps it's my imagination or perhaps I'm just imposing my prejudices but there's something that troubles me about this suburban idyll. While Ryder studies the map, my eyes flit from verandah to verandah, trying to assess the friendliness or otherwise of the people sheltering there, watching as someone strides towards us, a black man in his thirties, one hand in his pocket, maybe clutching something, what's he got, what's that he's got?

'Ryder?'

'Mmm.'

'Someone coming.'

'Eh?'

It's too late now to do anything except wind down the window.

'Hi,' we both say to the man, smiling hugely.

He looks back very gravely.

'You people lost?'

'Slightly. We were just looking—' says Ryder.

'Couldn't think of any other reason why white folks would want to come here on a day like this.'

'Ah yes. Well, we're reporters for an English newspaper. The *Telegraph*. And we're trying to find . . .'

After that the man is more helpful. He gives us directions and wishes us luck, which we will need very much, as it turns out, approximately forty-five seconds later.

We've only travelled a couple more blocks, moving very slowly so we can read the names of the turnings, when ahead of us we see a tall black man loping slowly across the road. The first thing I notice about him is his height: he's incredibly tall, like a basket ball player with gigantism, maybe seven feet or more. The second thing is whatever it is he has got hanging down from his right hand.

The way he's holding it, it doesn't look like anything dangerous. It just dangles casually from his palm, almost like he has forgotten it's there. Black, straight, rod-shaped. Too short to be an automatic rifle, too long to be a handgun. Too narrow to be a baseball bat. Some sort of tool maybe? Something harmless.

We drive closer. Very, very slowly. The man stops half way across the road. He watches us approach, the long black rod still dangling idly from his hand.

Now I can see what it is that he's holding.

I don't say anything to Ryder.

Ryder says nothing to me.

The thing that the man is holding. It isn't harmless.

Ryder slows the car still further.

Why are we slowing down? Does Ryder know what he's doing? I hope to God he knows what he's doing.

The thing that the man is holding is – no. I'd rather not think about it. And I'd rather not look again to confirm that what the man holding really is what I thought it was last time I looked. Because if I do, I'll have to start asking awkward questions like: 'Why is he carrying it?' and 'Who does he intend to use it on?' And frankly, I'd rather spend the next few seconds – which might, quite easily, also be my last few seconds – pretending that what's happening couldn't possibly be really happening because that would just be too awful to take on board. So I'm not going to take it on board. And I'm not going to look. Except just a tiny, out-of-the-corner of the eye look to check what he's doing now which is—

Standing. Just standing there. The thing still dangling from his side. Watching us draw closer.

What so truly appals me is the suddenness of it all. You're driving along feeling, well, not safe exactly, but sufficiently far removed from imminent danger for you to be able to allow your thoughts to drift pretty much where they will: 'Blimey it's not so bad this South Central, quite glad Ryder forced me to come here actually because I would never have come on my own and even though it's been pretty scary, specially that stuck-in-the-middle-of-three-lanes-of-traffic bit, fuck that was horrible, it's going to make a great story when I get home, almost as good as my encounter with the four-tray Crips, "I went to South Central in the LA Riots" definitely some cred points there, so all we need to do now is find this frigging Reverend then get ourselves lunch, wonder where Ryder's going to take me, somewhere cool I hope, not that anywhere will be open, not round here anyway, which will mean a long drive which will be a pain because I'm quite hungry now, very hungry in fact, maybe I should have a fag to stave it off, wonder if Ryder will . . . tall guy that, very tall . . . what's that he's holding, some kind of . . '

When: 'Whup!' You're trapped in this claustrophobic cell of rampaging fear. 'This can't be happening. I don't believe it's happening. It is happening. It fucking is happening. Why is it happening? How do I stop it happening. Please stop this happening! Please!'

It happens when planes go down. It happens in the millisecond before cars collide. It happens when the dark-visored motorcyclist and his dark-visored pillion pulls alongside you at the red traffic light. It's happening to someone somewhere now: this shockingly instantaneous transition from the quotidian world of aching legs and insipid airline tea and dodgy inflight movies and destination expectation and crawling caravans and narrow lanes and planned business meetings and dinners and thoughts of sex and friends and jealousy and ambition and desire and frustration and boredom. To the feral, urgent, vital world of adrenalin, instantaneousness and atavistic animal terror of imminent, inescapable death.

And I don't know whether the thought occurs to me at this moment but it certainly occurs later that this is the Real Point. The one we all work so hard to ignore. We're all going to die, and when it happens, it's going to come like this, without warning. So let's try not to get too worked up about newsroom politics and casual insults and petty arguments and minor slights; about failed trysts and parking tickets and rude waiters and final demands and tax returns. Because in the final analysis they don't matter. They really do not fucking matter.

We're alongside him now. He's so close he could touch the car. Touch me, even, if I had the window open. With his hand. With the thing he's holding in his hand. Which of course I'm not going to look at. Of course I'm not going to look at it. If it comes, frankly, I'd rather not know until I feel the sledgehammer blow – is that how it feels? I think that's what someone told me once, like someone whacking a sledgehammer as hard as they can into your arm, your leg, your shoulder, your stomach, oh, God, not the stomach please not a stomach wound.

Now he's behind us but I daren't look. If I look back it might provoke him.

But this is horrible. The waiting. Not knowing what he's doing. When can I look? When is it safe to look?

I give it one – two – three – four – five seconds. The car crawls forward, so painfully slowly I want to scream, I want to go: 'Floor it, Ryder, now!'

Very slowly, I turn my head.

He's standing there, legs apart, arms still by his side.

Everything is wrong

Lunch eventually happens towards 8 p.m., by which time my arse muscles have contorted into a Gordian knot and my lungs are kippered blacker than a peat-bog corpse.

But I quite like it. I could get used to this sort of thing.

Obviously the terrifying bits were terrifying and the boring bits quite hideously boring, but neither the terror nor the boredom was anywhere near as bad as the elation I'm feeling now is good. We did it. We survived.

And we're hanging out like real men, Ryder and me, smoking fags and drinking beer in probably the only restaurant in the whole of LA where they don't mind you smoking; probably the only restaurant in the whole of LA that's open. There's nothing chic or starry or Wolfgang Puck about it. It's just this place Ryder knows near Long Beach called Captain Ahab's, got up to look like a fisherman's shack, with draping nets and buoys and anchors and tables made from polished driftwood, and mostly seafood served mostly with fries on the menu and a proprietor who looks like Hemingway. A crappy theme restaurant, in fact. But tonight it's cool. It's the place to which all LA's desperadoes have gravitated: the serial drinkers, the incorrigible nicoheads, the rampant socializers and the footloose foreign corrs; the sort of people who aren't going to let a spot of civil disturbance come between them and their Friday night.

Ryder does most of the talking – about chicks, drugs, and hair's breadth scapes in the imminent deadly breach during his career as a fireman (which is what you call those roving foreign corrs who specialize in trouble spots, war zones, disaster areas etc.); I do most of the listening, except when, after a clammy surge of beer-induced sentimentality, I start telling him about how wonderful Simone is and how much I'm missing her and how it's a bummer but I've just got to accept it I could never get away with doing what Ryder does for a living because Simone would never allow it, she loves me too much.

'You don't think that's crap of me, do you?'

'How old are you?' he says.

'Twenty-six.'

'It's hard to say when I don't know the girl. But twenty-six is prettty young to be ruling out your options.'

'So you reckon, if I wanted, I could hack it as a fireman?'

'Sure,' he says. And – like you do when you're a teenager and you've latched on to some geezer who's persuaded you that he's served with the Regiment in Hereford – well, you think, anyone who knows their HQ is in Hereford must know what he's talking about – and you let on that you wouldn't mind having a go at that yourself and he looks at you with the same steely-blue eyes which you know have squinted through a sniper sight in the Dhofar prior to blowing the head off some Arab terrorist and watching it explode like a watermelon hitting concrete and says: 'Nothing stopping you, bright boy like you. It's brains we want in this outfit, not brawn' – I feel a warm, delicious glow of achievement all the more piquant for being wholly unearned.

'But, er – this is probably going to sound stupid – but how scary is it?'

'Sometimes it is. Mostly it isn't.'

'OK, but today for example. The giant with the silenced Magnum. How does that rate on the scare scale?'

Ryder scrunches up his mouth, like he's weighing up the question, and already I'm regretting having asked. 'What giant?' he's going to say. Or: 'Christ, if a trivial thing like that bothered you . . .'

He says: 'Oh, pretty high, I'd say. Definitely pretty high.'

'So er—' this is asking for trouble, but I'm sloshed, 'would it be among the scariest things that has have ever happened to you?'

'Well, you have to remember there's been quite a bit of competition. Landing in San Carlos Water was a bit hairy. The time that Hind gunship came over the crest in Afghanistan – that's another thing I won't forget. And then there was Liberia. Everything is scary in Liberia.'

'Oh,' I say, secretly furious with Liberia being such an insuperably fucked up place.

'The thing about this morning, though,' he adds. 'You never knew. It could have happened the way it did. Or it could have turned nasty. That's the thing about civil conflict. In some ways it's a lot more dangerous than a conventional war, where at least you usually know who the good guys are, who are the bad, where the front line is. So yeah. We did OK this morning, I thought.'

I roll another fag. Drink more beer. 'More dangerous than a conventional war,' I'm thinking. 'More dangerous than a conventional war!' And, no, I'm not going to dwell on the nasty little rival thought that has popped into my head, the one that says perhaps Ryder only said it because he knows it's what I wanted to hear.

'Good God,' says Ryder. 'Just spotted someone I know.'

'Where?'

He nods towards a shady alcove where a man and a woman are sitting.

'Bloody hell,' I say. 'Me too.'

'You know Charlie?'

'Not Charlie, no. The girl with him.'

Ryder cranes his neck for a view. 'She looks all right.'

'Oh she is.'

'Very all right,' he decides. 'What's her name?'

*

Charlie has been covering the riots for the *Sunday Times*, is terribly urbane and charming and generous with Mr Murdoch's money, some of which he uses to celebrate our appearance by purchasing two bottles of champagne. He went to Eton, inevitably. Quite how I find this out I'm not exactly sure, because Etonians never tell you straight out, they just intimate it. When they talk about school, for example, they pronounce it so that you can hear the capital S, so whereas you and I (assuming you're not a fucking Etonian, that is) might say: 'Oh yeah, I think he might have been at school with us,' an Etonian will say: 'Mm. Wasn't he at School with us?' and instantly everyone listening who counts will know and everyone listening who doesn't count won't know but since they don't count who cares? Another thing they some-times do is to drop arcane references – like 'Queen's Eyot' (which, you should know, means a little island in the Thames and is pronounced 'Eight') or Fourth of June or Pop – casually into the conversation. Or, they simply exude that boundless and by-no-means-always-justified self-confidence that only Etonians have. But the most obvious giveaway of all is: they're forever hanging out with Molly Etherege.

Molly is, of course, quite fantastically overjoyed to see me, as I am to see her. She is, after all, quite my bestest most wonderful girlie friend and now that I am away from Simone's malign clutches, I suddenly realize how comfortable and happy I feel in her company. And how utterly absurd it is that, just because of Simone's misplaced jealousy, I don't get to see her more often. We greet each other with huge hugs and there is much mwah mwahing, some of it on the lips. But I'm not sure how much of a deterrent effect this is going to have on Ryder's or Charlie's ambitions. When two lions chance upon a fresh carcass, they don't get put off by the mangy jackal already feeding there, do they?

'Known this boy long?' Ryder asks Molly.

'Not as well as I'd like to know him. You see we've been trying on and off for years to get it together and I wouldn't want to push my luck here, but I've a feeling that tonight might be the night we finally succeed,' is what Molly doesn't reply. She says: 'Since Oxford.'

Which gives Charlie the cue to ascertain which college we were at, before dropping in a few smart names of people Molly might know which of course Molly does.

Which gives Ryder the cue to counter Charlie's name-drop credibility by declaring that he never did get round to picking up his own Oxford degree, having been sent down at the end of the second year after a hushed-up incident in which he supplied the speed-ball that very nearly finished off the earl's daughter he was shagging at the time.

Which enables Charlie to counter that he remembers the incident well, having grown up on the Scottish estate which his father owned bang next to the earl's and having heard the crofters and ghillies talk of little else all summer.

Which enables Ryder to recall how it all turned out terribly well, actually, because she got to meet her future husband in NA and he got to flee to Saigon which is where he got his first scoop because it fell just a day or two after his arrival.

Which forces me to sit there, bored, aggrieved and frustrated, head going back and forth like a Wimbledon spectator's, wondering if I'm ever going to get a game in myself. Unlike Ryder and Charlie there's nothing I can try to impress Molly with that she doesn't know already.

Well, there is one thing: the amazing story of how I covered myself in glory and narrowly escaped death at least twice while covering the LA riots. But I can't tell that one because Ryder's already heard it; and, besides, if I tell it the way I'd like to tell it Ryder will think I'm showing off and exaggerating and that just isn't done when you're a foreign corr.

Then, some time later, through a fuzz of champagne-on-beer, I hear Ryder regaling Molly and Charlie with the extraordinary story about the seven-foot Bloods assassin, gun still smoking from a recent hit, that he very nearly ran over while driving through South Central, and how in the rear-view mirror he could see the guy drawing a bead on him through the sights of his silenced .44 magnum.

'Christ knows why he didn't shoot,' says Ryder.

I seize my moment. 'Yeah, we were both absolutely shitting ourselves.'

'You were there too, darling?' says Molly.

'Yeah well,' I say. 'After hanging out with the Four-tray Crips this morning, I thought it would be nice to get the other side's point of view.'

Molly looks at Ryder. 'He is joking, isn't he?'

'Nope. He's been a clever boy. Made the foreign editor a very happy bunny, which if you know our foreign editor . . .' Suddenly I don't hate Ryder nearly so much.

'But sweetheart. How terribly impressive of you.' Molly gives my arm a squeeze and even kisses me on the side of my cheek. Clearly she's as drunk as I am.

'Just obeying orders,' I say, a bit embarrassed now. 'But how about you? You haven't told us what happened after your Tom Cruise sesh.'

'Oh God, this is going to make you weep,' says Charlie.

'Do oversell it, why don't you?' says Molly.

'I'm serious. You've landed your rag the biggest scoop of its lifetime,' says Charlie.

'Go on,' says Ryder.

Molly does. I can't give you the exact details because it's the sort of story so puke-inducingly jealous-making that you try to blank it all out even as you hear it. But basically, Molly's interview at Tom's home happens to have taken place on the morning before he's due to host an afternoon party for a few hundred of his closest Hollywood friends. By lunchtime, the interview is all wrapped up, Tom and Molly have got on pretty well and in a fit of generosity or possibly lust he decides to give her a lift back to this dive she's staying in on the other side of town because her cheapskate newspaper can't afford anything closer. But they've barely left the gates of Beverly Hills when they come across a burned-out car, an ambulance and a police roadblock, and Tom's advised by a cop that this really isn't a day for driving, the situation's very fluid right now, and the best thing to do is go back home and wait till it blows over.

And so Molly gets to spend the day sunning herself by

the pool at Tom Cruise's house, watching the riots unfold on a giant TV screen that one of Tom's people has thoughtfully positioned in the shade on the verandah so that the swarm of celebrity guests who are now starting to arrive can keep a vague check on reality.

Who's there? Everyone you can imagine. Julia Roberts, Brad Pitt, Mel Gibson, Sean Connery, Meg Ryan, Uma Thurman, Jack Nicholson, Meryl Streep, Mickey Rourke, Stephen Spielberg, Martin Scorsese, Tom Hanks, Arnold Schwarzenegger, Tim Robbins, Susan Sarandon, Michelle Pfeiffer and Madonna would be among my personal guesses, though I might be way off the mark, perhaps none of them was there, perhaps I've even got Tom Cruise mixed up with someone similarly famous, I don't know, as I say I tried to blank it out as soon as I heard it and besides my memory's fucked. But the basic point of the story remains unchanged: Molly Etherege gets to spend the LA Riots enjoying exclusive access to two or three hundred of the world's vastest mega-celebs. And then she gets loaned her very own office, computer, fax machine and personal secretary so she can file the whole thing to her newspaper with minimum inconvenience. And then, as if that wasn't already quite grotesquely disgusting enough for any rival hack to bear, she gets invited to stay the night in one of the guest suites.

'Bloody hell. So what are you doing here?'

'Oh, God, you know what these Hollywood types are like.'

'No.'

'Wandering hands. Not used to hearing "No". So, I've got Jack pawing one side and Mel stroking the other and Clint saying "Make my day."'

'Now you're teasing us.'

'Yes, but you get the general idea. I had to get away. And here I am,' she says.

'Which calls for another bottle,' says Charlie.

'I was thinking of calling for a cab,' says Molly.

'You'll never get one now. Let us give you a lift,' says Ryder.

'Or better still you can crash at my place. I've got bags of extra space,' says Charlie.

'Or mine, if it's easier. They've thrown me in an adjoining suite,' says Ryder.

'Er thanks, boys, that's terribly kind,' says Molly.

'My bedroom's really crap and tiny and it stinks of fags,' I say. 'But if you like I'll have the floor and you can have the bed. And I promise I won't try to shag you.'

*

Which is my rashest promise ever. The moment I try making the tiniest smidgen of a pass at her – and I'm not saying I will – she's bound to say, 'I hope you're not trying to shag me or anything' and whether she means it or not that'll be me finished.

It could be worse. I do at least manage to coax the hotel's night staff into providing a toothbrush and a put-you-up-bed, so I don't have to spend the night on the floor. But not much worse. Though I'm as exhausted as I've ever been, and loaded with alcohol, I still find it impossible to sleep.

Next day's hangover is a bastard. And I can't even compensate myself with the thought that I had a bloody good time getting it. This is a day when everything should be going right. I should be basking in the warmth of the foreign editor's praise, relishing the fact that it's Saturday and I don't have to file any more pieces till Sunday, punishing my foreign corr's expense account. But all I can think of is the snuffling female form in the bed just a few feet from mine. And more specifically, the fact that for reasons I am far too nauseous and headachy and riddled with paranoia and self-hatred to fathom, I did not spend the whole of last night having wild, too-drunk-to-care sex with her in any number of ingenious and disgraceful positions.

'Urrrgggh,' groans Molly.

'It's OK, you didn't.'

'I'm relieved to hear it.'

'Are you?' I say, slightly hurt.

'Depends what it is I didn't do.'

'Have sex with me.'

Molly sits up in bed and plumps the pillow behind her back. Her face is grey as death, her hair lank, her lips are dry and crusty. Given that, it's quite impressive how fanciable she is. She looks at me curiously.

'But I knew I was safe. You promised.'

'Ah but I was drunk. What if I'd forced myself upon you?'

'I'm not sure much forcing would have been necessary'.

'What?'

'Don't think I'm proud of it. I never get that drunk. If you hadn't been there to rescue me, God knows what might have happened.'

She slips out of bed, dressed in the pyjamas I lent her. Christ, do girls look sexy in pyjamas.

She stands by the basin and begins cleaning her teeth.

'You're saying if I'd tried, you would probably have been up for it?'

'Maybe, yes.'

She rinses her mouth and spits into the sink. 'But it wouldn't have been good sex. It would have been raw, drunken, insane, strange-hotel-in-a-strange-country, weirdo sex.'

'And your problem with that would be—?'

'Hmm. Yes. We would have regretted it, though.'

'You reckon?'

'There's Simone, for a start.'

'Couldn't we pretend we're still drunk?'

'I can always tell when a man's faking it.'

'Oh, God, Molly, that is so unfair. You're telling me if I'd have been more of a cad, I would have scored?'

'Isn't that always the way?'

'Would it work maybe if I brutally forced myself on you now?'

'No.'

'Please.'

'No.'

'So what do I have to do?'

She shrugs and smiles prettily. 'Try asking me when you're single.'

'You're asking me to chuck Simone?'

'I'm not asking you to do anything, darling. I'm just not in the habit of sleeping with other girls' boyfriends, that's all. Now, are we going to have our coffee and fags up here *à deux*, or are we going to make it downstairs with Ryder?'

'Up here, it had better be,' I say, sullenly. 'I wouldn't want him to get the right impression.'

Flashback

Norton watches me knit together the Rizlas using this new trick I've learned. It's easier to do than explain, but basically you make it with two papers instead of three, only borrowing the stickiness of the third to make the others airtight.

'Not given up, then?' he says in his flat, non-committal, couldn't-think-of-anything-better-to-say way.

I look up, mildly appalled.

'Why would I want to do that?'

He shrugs. 'Some of my college friends have. They seem to think it's incompatible with being a grown up.'

'We're not grown ups yet, surely?'

'I hope not.' He laughs awkwardly.

'God, is that what you meant?'

'What?'

'That I'd become one too.'

He glances round the room.

And I do kind of see what he's getting at: the walnut dining table is George III, the corner cupboard is Queen Anne, the rugs are all God-knows-how-many-knot Persian, the lamps are mostly Tiffany. The location's pretty good too: mews flat just off Montagu Square in London W1. It's nice, very nice, but I hardly notice it any more. You don't after you've been renting somewhere for nearly three years. As my flatmate Warthog keeps saying, for the amount we're wasting in rent, we could get ourselves a mortgage and step on to the first rung of the property ladder. The problem is that would involve a degree of maturity and effort.

'You should see the bedrooms, the bedrooms are shit,' I say, retrieving an embossed stiffie from the marble fireplace for use as roach material.

'You should see my squat,' says Norton.

'Oh and I suppose living in a squat makes you immune to being bourgeois.'

'Did I say that?'

'Living in a squat is about the most bourgeois activity known to man. Every second fucker went to public school.'

I pass him the joint, not out of good manners, but because I hate inhaling the twist of burning paper at the beginning.

'Anyway,' I go on, 'you could live somewhere just like this if you wanted.'

'What's the rent?'

'Seven fifty? Eight hundred?'

'Do you know what I make in a month?'

'You could make more if you chose.'

'Only if I gave up my painting.'

I take a long drag on the joint. Then another. It's good weed. Rock star quality weed almost. I wouldn't be smoking it normally but I haven't seen Norton in ages. Plus, obviously, I want to rub his nose in what a dope connoisseur I've become and how connected I am to be able to score such quality gear.

And suddenly I'm there, on another plane, with a light, smiling brain. I spring to my feet, newly aware that there's something I absolutely have to do right this second.

I flick through my pile of CDs, until I find the one with the roses and gargoyle-tongued heads.

'What you putting on?'

'Something absolutely and totally fucking ace,' I say, slotting in the CD and flicking forward to track three.

'I think I might know this one,' says Norton, nearly ruining the acoustic guitar intro.

'Shh!'

We sit and listen. I keep wanting to draw his attention to all the brilliant bits, like the way Anthony Kiedis's vocals sound so much better for being slightly out of tune, the way he mangles those vowels so that 'dad' sounds like 'dayd', the magnificent incomprehensibility of the lyrics, the moment where the hippie flutes float in to transport you to a lost Eden. But it seems a bit hypocritical having just told him to shh, so I settle back and let it all seep through me. It's a beautiful song, the sort that makes you tight in your throat; that makes you yearn for a golden time you probably never experienced but would sell your soul to regain.

When the track's over I hop up quickly and put on the Stone Roses instead.

'Can't we have any more?' says Norton.

' "Under the Bridge" is ace but there's too much tedious funk shit you have to wade through to get there.'

'Is this what happens when you become a rock critic?'

'I like to think I was like this already,' I say, taking another long hit of the joint. I hold it in the lungs, for maximum brain-fuckage.

For some time I am rendered speechless.

'Mm,' I say, searching the ether for loose strands of unfinished conversation. 'Mm. That is such a fucker!'

Norton nods, though he doesn't look too sure what in particular I am accusing of being a fucker.

It takes me a while to remember.

'That choice you have to make between art and commerce. I mean why can't we ever have both?'

'You've come pretty close,' says Norton.

'Journalism's not art.'

'At least you're writing.'

'Ah, but that's exactly why journalism's so dangerous. It feels like real writing and it's better paid than real writing. The problem is, it's not real writing. So Cyril Connolly says.'

'Does he?'

'In this book called *Enemies of Promise*. It's about all the things that can stop you becoming a decent writer. One of them is early success, like, yeah, I've really found that a problem. Another one's journalism. And then there's the one I'm least worried about right now, which is "the pram in the hallway".'

'Mm hmm?'

'Yeah, it's like those cigarette packs that say "Warning: smoking while pregnant can damage your unborn child". Much safer than the cigarettes that give you cancer.'

'It's gonna happen, though. A couple of my friends are already there. Kids, I mean,' says Norton.

'Yeah, one of mine too. Fucking scary. Since when was anyone supposed to start having kids at twenty-seven. Twenty-seven is for – well, I don't know what it's for. But it's definitely way too young to be ruining your life.'

'You might enjoy it.'

'I'm sure I will. Just not yet, is all I ask.'

'But if you got Simone up the duff, would you—?'

'I'd be extremely surprised. Especially with our contraception method.'

'Yeah?'

'Yeah. It's called No fucking sex at all.'

'What? Simone? Nympho Simone?'

'Not recently. Not since I got back from LA, almost.'

'When were you in LA?'

'Two, three months ago? Whenever the riots were.'

'That must have been interesting.'

'Yeah, it was quite. Did I never tell you?'

'No.'

'You serious? I've never ever told you my LA Riots story?'

'It's not like we ever see each other.'

So I tell him my LA Riots story. But only in very abbreviated form. I've begun to wonder how interesting it is anyway. It's not like I got shot.

'Wow!' says Norton.

'Do you think so?'

'Don't you?'

I pull a face.

'Shall I tell you the stupid thing? Suppose six months ago I'd been able to choose something brilliant that could happen to me, anything I liked, I don't think I could have come up with anything more amazing than what happened to me in LA. I mean, everything went so right. Like, being there on holiday. Being in the right spot to hear about Madonna's stolen bustier. Bumping into the Crips. And the bloke with the magnum: just scary enough to make a good story, but not so scary you end up hurt. It's like God looked down and said: "This young man deserves a break. Let me see how many implausibly cool things I can make happen to him".'

'Yeah, right.'

'Yeah, and it was almost even better when I got back. Like for one the sex with Simone was better than ever, my conquering hero, you almost died, never leave me again, etc. Until I mentioned France.'

'What's wrong with France?'

'I'll tell you in a second. So, yeah, the sex was great and when I get back to the office there's this long herogram from the editor, saying how creditably I have acquitted myself, or some such understated bollocks. And all these hardened hacks in the newsroom who've previously thought I'm just another Oxbridge ponce who can only write fluff are suddenly coming up to me and saying: "Yeah, well done, mate. Did all right there, didn't you?" and even the newsdesk are being nice to me, and sending me on all these cushy colour assignments, like going to Donegal with this chick photographer to find the village where Brian Friel set *Dancing At Lughnasa*, no, don't worry, it's just this play that's really popular at the moment, that's all you need to know. So my stock has never been higher, I can do no wrong and the sun shines out of my bottom and at some point it occurs to me – it must have done – that maybe this is it. This is the thing I've spent my whole career waiting for. My big break.'

The last bit of my speech is ruined, slightly, by the ringing of the phone.

It's an annoying ring tone and it goes on for ages. Norton looks at me askance.

'It'll only be Simone,' I say.

Once satisfied that I have been sufficiently irritated, the answer machine clicks on.

'Fat lot of use you are,' says the voice and I'm already half way to the phone, 'I'm knackered, I'm jet-lagged, I'm gagging for—'

'Me too.'

'For a drink and some half-civilized company, I was going to say,' says Molly.

'Where are you?'

'My flat and I hate it. The builders were supposed to be finished by now and I've no bathroom, no kitchen—'

'Why not come here?'

'You on your own?'

'Only Norton. Warthog's away on business, so there's a spare bed if you need.'

'ONLY NORTON!' Norton mouths. I blow him a kiss.

'You're sure I'm not interrupting anything?' says Molly.

'No.'

'It sounds like you're snogging.'

'God, we never do tongues. Strictly anal.'

'Anything you want me to bring?'

'Um—' I'm tempted to say 'toothbrush' – 'chocolate would be useful if you see any on the way. Raisin'n'nut, Bounty, but only milk not dark, and er . . .'

'You won't be smoking drugs, then?'

'Molly. Back from America,' I explain to Norton. Before he can quiz me further I escape to the kitchen. From the enormous American refrigerator I retrieve two bottles of Budvar. I love this fridge. I'm going to miss it enormously. It's going to feature in this novel that I haven't told Norton about yet, not properly.

'So?' prompts Norton.

'All I was going to say is that big breaks aren't all they're cracked up to be.'

'I meant about Molly.'

'Oh, you know. She was there in LA with me, then her paper asked her to stay out there for a couple of months and now she's back. And her flat's in a mess and she needs a drink.'

'And?'

'And what? You were at Oxford with her too, for God's sake.'

'Fine.'

'Look, I'm not being cagy. There's nothing going on between us. If there were I'd tell you.'

Norton allows himself a long smirk.

I say: 'Remember all those conversations we used to have at Oxford about all the amazing things we were going to do with our lives because we were so fucking talented and we weren't going to compromise and second best wasn't good enough?'

'Did I say that?'

'Er, no, that was probably me. I should think you were just going with the flow in your Nortonish way. But you remember the conversations?'

'Vaguely.'

'Well, I was just thinking, if I'd been able then to fast-forward through my life, and see what I've become now, I would probably have been quite impressed. You know, the flat, the rock columns, the picture byline, the money, the famous people I've met, the LA Riots. But from where I'm standing now, it doesn't feel at all impressive. I kind of think: "Well, if I did it, it can't be that special." '

'A sort of Groucho Marx thing? Like, not wanting to join any club that will have you as a member?'

'Yeah, exactly. You think true achievement is only ever what other people do. And the thing that's bothering me is: what if I never stop thinking that way?'

Norton laughs.

'What?'

'Never, if I know you.'

'Cunt. Do you really think not?'

'Why would you want to? You'd have no incentive to do better.'

'Shit.'

'It's true, isn't it?'

'I was thinking, this novel I'm about to do—'.

'Are you?'

'That was the thing I was going to tell you. I'm giving everything up – flat, job, Simone very probably because I don't want any distractions – and I'm fucking off to the Languedoc for as long as it takes to write my novel.'

'Bloody hell!'

'Don't be like that. You'll make me nervous.'

'Well, it is quite a big step.'

'Yes, it seems that way now. But you know what? In six months I'll be going, "Yeah, well, anyone can write a novel. It's getting it published that's the real test." Then I'll get it published and I'll be going: "Well, of course, any damned fool can publish one novel. The real test, is whether you can manage fifteen." And so it will go on until I die of exhaustion, never having had any fun in my life because I'll have been too busy trying to achieve.'

'I'll say one thing for you.'

'What's that?'

'You do have the gift of self-knowledge.'

'Oh, God, I know. I know. Let's have another joint before I get depressed. Do you want to roll this time?'

'Sure.'

I pass him the drugs box. It came from Morocco and it's made of amber and I still can't work out whether it's fake plastic tourist amber or genuine fossilized resin. In fact, it's a stupid thing to have as a stash box because every time I get stoned and I'm looking for something to get paranoid about, I find my thoughts drifting inexorably to the plausible rogue who sold it to me in a remote café near the mountain pass of Tizi-n-Test, and wondering whether or not the bastard ripped me off.

I watch Norton nursing the Rizlas into shape.

'My hash or your grass?' he says.

'Your hash?'

Norton unfurls the foil to reveal a pea-sized red-brown lump.

'Any good?'

'It's my usual,' he says with a shrug.

He singes the lump. Oily smoke and the sickly chipolatas.

'Oooer.'

Norton looks up.

'God, I had a real moment, then,' I say.

'Déjà vu?'

'Except déjà vus aren't real, are they? I read that somewhere. They're just your brain remembering something that happened a split-second ago and thinking it happened in another life.'

'You were going to tell me about your novel,' says Norton, firing up the joint.

'Oh God, was I? Do I have to?'

'I thought you wanted to.'

'Yeah, but I've heard from people who know about these things that novels are like sex – the more you talk about it, the less you get done.'

Norton passes me the joint.

It tastes strangely familiar. I take a few more puffs, in search of that elusive memory.

'God, do you know what this reminds me of?'

'What?'

I open my mouth and close it again, like an oxygen-starved goldfish in an undersized bowl. My mind's gone blank again and that's how I like it. A blank mind is a mind free of worries about how and when to ditch your unsuitable girlfriend, about whether you've still time to get things going with the girl you really want, about how to plot your first novel and how to survive writing it on no money, about how deep down you've failed as a journalist, about all the girls you could have shagged and all the good times you could have had but didn't, about the destruction you've wreaked with drink and drugs and fags on your twenty-seven-going-on-thirty-five-year-old body, about the money you didn't save and the property ladder you never got on, about that little subcutaneous lump just to the left of your belly button that might be cancer but you daren't go to the doctor about in case it is, about the friendships you neglected, about the potential you failed to fulfil, about the sweet clever boy you were so long ago only you never knew it, and because you thought you were shit you never gave yourself a chance, you just poured hatred on yourself and squandered every opportunity and now you're old and bitter and fucked. So those are just a few of things that my mind is not thinking about at this moment as I grope hopelessly through the swirling fog of meaningless clues, of sausages and Supertramp, trying to recall whatever it was I was trying to remember just a few seconds ago.

'No, sorry, mate. It's gone.'